Other Books by Michael Ventura

Shadow Dancing in the U.S.A. (nonfiction)

MICHAEL VENTURA

Simon and Schuster
New York   London   Toronto   Sydney   Tokyo

Night Time

Losing Time

Simon and Schuster
Simon & Schuster Building
Rockefeller Center
1230 Avenue of the Americas
New York, New York 10020

1   3   5   7   9   10   8   6   4   2

Library of Congress Cataloging in Publication Data
Ventura, Michael.
Night time losing time/Michael Ventura.
p.   cm.
I. Title.
PS3572.E5N54   1989   88-38697
813'.54—dc19   CIP

ISBN 0-671-62373-7

Grateful appreciation is due the following publishers for permission to reprint excerpts of songs.

ACT NATURALLY by Johnny Russell, Voni Morrison. Copyright © 1963 Tree Publishing Co., Inc. All rights reserved. International copyright secured. Used by permission of the publisher.

AIN'T GOT NO HOME by Clarence "Frogman" Henry. Copyright © 1956 (renewed) by ARC Music Corp. Reprinted by permission. All rights reserved. Territory: United States only.

(continued at back of book)

For Jeff Nightbyrd

*For it is necessary for the troubles to come,
but woe to him through whom the trouble comes.*
—The Gospel According to St. Matthew

*I got t'get t'rockin'
Get my hat off the rack.
I got the boogie woogie
Like a knife in the back.*
—Huey "Piano" Smith

PRELUDE

Quartzsite

ONE   *Being Dead*

Being dead is the best high I've ever seen. Except that even being dead doesn't settle anything.

TWO   *No Big Deal*

Okay. It's no big deal. I don't *miss* blinking, exactly. It's kind of educational, to find out *why* the human blinks. One thing is, if you don't blink, your eyeballs dry. They feel in their sockets like a couple of peeled nuts gathering dust. The dust burns. Not bad pain, just slow burn. You feel little fissures cracking the membranes. They're going to turn to crumbs in your head, your eyes. They go first. Why they close the eyes of the dead. Now you know.

The other thing, if you can't blink, is that you stop seeing shapes and distances. Everything's all line and color, everything's flat and dirty-shiny, like faded patterns on old linoleum. The TV, the bed, the wall, the door fuzz into each other on the same flat plane. Or sometimes something stands out, for no reason, as though a few optic nerves are trying to struggle against the death of the rest; and the bureau, say, becomes perfectly clear, but flat, like a cutout from an advertisement pasted on thick white paper, surrounded with vague designs. And the whole flat papery sight can flare up, bright, as though a spotlight were shining through it into your eyes. Or go gray. Or get soaked, slowly, by a violet wash.

In the far corner of my field of vision there's the window, I know, its curtain pulled back some. If I could see regular, I could say what goes on in this motel courtyard in Quartzsite, but all I see are sky-glare and ground-glare pulsing at each other in the desert

13

heat. Shapes on the other side of the glares. Mountains? RVs? And shadows passing through the glares. People, probably. Except that we don't know. Do we? Anymore? I mean, I've gotten a little suspicious lately about what may or may not be a "person."

For instance, if you don't blink or move for some immeasurable wad of time, you get to feeling things the way maybe a rock or wall would. The way maybe a TV sees the room it's broadcasting into. You get to feeling you have more in common, maybe, with a bare lightbulb than with people. You remember names but they don't seem the names of people, more the names of storms: Hurricane Elaine, Tropical Depression Danny, Typhoon Nadine, West Wind Kathy—moving moods made of air, changing with the sea and land they drift upon, flashing lightning, pouring rain, and lulling into sudden and not to be explained calms. You don't ask something like that for love. You either get in out of the rain or you don't.

Like, what is an Elaine? A cavern, maybe, with water shining on the rocks, sound of an underground stream not far off. I think you got cave paintings inside you, girl, and the bones of things sacrificed long ago, bones with prayers still clinging to them.

I think we all do. When we're not busy being storms or bare lightbulbs.

People? The only place you got people is on TV. They're about seven inches tall and they smile too much and they think they make the world go round. They only say what they're allowed to say, so they cannot say anything to *you*.

The dead can.

Which is a comforting thought if you happen to be sort of dead.

My soul's been riding me all my life. Pretty soon I'm gonna get to ride it.

There must be a Gideon in this room. Damn. In a drawer by the bed, no doubt. They hide those things in rooms wherever I play. Almost never right out in the open, like the phone book. Almost always hidden by the bed, like it's listening in on you. Peek-a-booing. Taking notes and taking names. A greedy white thing with a dark shell, wet like a turtle's, soaking up everybody's business. Open that drawer and it smells of swamp mud.

I hate the thought of dying in the same room with such a thing.

"I'm gonna read around you," my mother used to say. I got sick a lot as a kid. Was famous for my fevers. A hundred and five point two—even point nine, once. And Missy, my mother, would put me on a rubber sheet stark-naked and pack me in ice like a fish. And she'd rub me down with alcohol. We didn't have rubbing alcohol in the house one time and it was late, the stores all closed, so she rubbed me down with Daddy's gin. Can't stand the smell of gin to this day. When she'd get tired of doing me, Daddy would rub. They'd rub everywhere. Daddy'd joke about how little my balls got with the ice near them.

They'd call the doctor sometimes, when they could afford it, and he'd come with his long shiny needles and shoot me up. But they only did that when they thought I was dying sure. Otherwise it was ice and rubs. And between rubs Missy would take her Bible and start to reading, walking around my bed, reading about Lazarus and the woman who touched Jesus' hem and the devils that leapt out of the man's throat into swine. Then she'd put fresh ice on me, rub my thighs, rub my balls, rub my belly. Floor would be wet all around, from the melted ice dripping off the rubber sheet. My head swam and every drop sounded like thunder. That sheet smelled like a diaphragm with that jell the women put on it. The least sexy smell on the planet.

So I'd lie there, Missy'd read and rub by turns, and when she got tired she'd call in Daddy, but he'd just rub, never read.

It's good I'm not dying back there. Here, I'm just another hit-and-run. Neither Missy nor Nadine has the money to ship me back, and only a mother or wife's got the right, I hope. This way I'll end up in the hot dry boneyard of this little desert town, and not in one of them New Orleans tombs everybody likes so much except *me*, I hate them and always have. As kids we'd play hooky and hang out in the graveyards 'cause it's easy to hide there. You've got to bury people aboveground in New Orleans, it's like a city of tombs. The older tombs are cracked, so we'd look in. Sometimes the coffins would be rotted and falling apart too, and you could see the bones.

On some tombs—especially tombs of real crazy people, or tombs of witches like Marie Laveau—there'd be lots of Xs and chalk marks and shit, people making signs over the dead, calling out to them for help. It was strange, later, to go to graveyards in other places and see the stones so bare, like nobody took the dead seriously anyplace else. But like I say, I hated those graveyards back home. There wasn't any feel that the dead ever got any rest.

One time I was packed in ice under Missy's hands and she started talking soft, fast, like she never quite had, and like I never heard again. She must have thought I was so fevered I wouldn't know or remember. With one hand she held the Bible and with the other she kind of idly rubbed on me, up from my belly to my chest, down to my dick, real light rubbing. I was burned and frozen both, the world smelled of alcohol, the rubber sheet dripped on all ends, slow and steady, the drops falling with sharp *pings* into the pots and with dull thuds on the towels on the floor all around the bed, a ping-and-thud syncopation that was real steady but that you couldn't predict.

And Missy saying, "It's okay if you die, Precious, you don't have to fight it, 'cause you'll never be sweeter; your skin so silky cool, you'll never be purer, Precious, and every little thing on you so rightly formed, you'd just lift straight up, still dripping from my cleansing, float straight up, baby, you *have* to be a baby to go to Heaven, I ain't ever gonna see you there, Daddy ain't ever gonna see you there, but you go there and something of us'll be there, so *go* there, this fever's like a hot hand tryin' t'pull you on up, and I fight it, I do, 'cause they say that's my job, but I never *had* a job I liked on this earth, I fight it but why, 'cause they say I should and 'cause Daddy'd kill me did I not, but if I *really* loved you all the way and I really wasn't so afraid I'd wash you clean like this and gently send you off, and cry for happy, cry for happy, it's such a crime you got to get older, hairy, dirty, let it go, Precious, now, now's the time, let it go. . . ."

Daddy called in from the other room, "Missy, will you stop reading from that thing for five minutes, it's making my fillings itch!"

Missy's nails dug into my belly, she was so startled.

I couldn't help but say, "*Ouch*, Missy!" She was shocked at *that*. Her face so strange. I remember thinking real clear, "Who *is* that woman? Where's my mom?" Her face was wiped clean of any particular look. But then it snapped back to the face Missy always wore in those days, a little stern, a little amused, and she said, "How you doin', Precious? You back amongst us?"

Daddy stepped up, stood behind her, his born-broken nose and his gap teeth just like me now. He was smiling.

"He's gonna be just fine," Daddy said. "That's one tough little bugger."

THREE *Something Moving*

Quartzsite, Arizona. A tiny spot in a huge place. A squat of mobile homes and old-timey house trailers atop the desert mountains. It clings to I-10 as the highway begins its steep drop down to the Colorado River, the California border, and Blythe. Blythe gets all the motel and service traffic, has all the dippy little food joints, and is the last of anything for another hundred desert miles. Quartzsite hasn't got but one motel, a couple of gas stations, a café, a donut shop, and a dark little bar. The jagged desert ridges jut around the town at weird angles, raw rocky ground—the stones feel like they're staring. Waiting. And whatever they're waiting for, it ain't you, not *you*, with your squishy little needs.

There's a strangeness in these hills that tells you not to pray to Jesus, he's not lord of this ground; drive on down to Blythe if that's how you pray, Jesus and McDonald's have some franchises down there. Up here, in the day, the ground glares back at the glaring sun and the two glares make a kind of white darkness, a daylight hard to see in. Then in the night the great sparkly sky rolls over the blank thick black of the hills, the heat throbs in the cinder-block walls of the motel, and you know that what lives in the desert is foraging in the town now, critters, snakes, coyotes, nibbling at the town's edges. The quiet is the quiet of something moving that you can't quite hear.

Which may be why nobody ever fixed the air conditioner in

this motel room. It clatters like an engine that needs a ring job and blots out the not-quite-quiet of Quartzsite's dark.

Obviously nobody *means* to end up in Quartzsite. I was heading to LA. Which is my way of saying nowhere. "Nowhere" seemed the only place that was far enough away. But for the first time in my life I couldn't do the drive.

See, in my trade you drive as much as you do anything else. My pride's been I can drive as long as I have to—from playing a gig at The Dawg's in Austin to a gig at Tipitina's in New Orleans—and drive it straight. No pills, no powders. It's not that I have a take against the pills and powders, necessarily. It's just that I like to get where I'm going all on my own.

I know the tricks. Little things, but they're real important, like chewing gum (stuff I don't even like to *smell* when I'm not driving). See, one reason you get groggy, long-distance driving, is that you don't move your face. Your face is used to moving all the time you're awake, talking, smiling, moving up and down. Long-distance driving, your face just sets—like it does when you're asleep. You might not talk for hours, even to yourself. And at night, with just headlights and taillights, white lines and yellow lines, even your eyes stay fixed, instead of glancing around like they like to. The blood doesn't flow in your facial muscles, so you get groggy. Gum makes you move your face. For me the taste of the road is truck-stop coffee and a five-stick wad of gum that's been chewed for hours with hard chomps. Tastes like a cross between burnt rubber and cold grits.

When my stomach was younger—and I've found that every part of you has its own age, your stomach can be fifty-five and your legs twenty-seven, while your "real" age is somewhere around forty—when my stomach was younger I drove the hard drives with a can of Mexican jalapeño peppers on the seat. I'd start to fade, put two jalapeños in my mouth, make myself chew them slow. Your scalp sweats, the roots of your hair shiver, the burn in your mouth seeps through and heats your cheeks. Those juices burn all the way down. You wake from the inside out.

Except that if your stomach's on the high side of forty, then what with the Denny's coffee, the Dairy Queen burgers, the pull of where you've been and the draw of where you're headed, you can get some attack of jalapeño diarrhea, hot shit and then some, pouring out your ass in spurts or dribbling through the crack as you try to hold it back. You can't. You pull off as far as you can onto the shoulder so the passing cars won't see your poor bare rump. A couple of bouts of that, after you've been up twenty hours anyway, and you're wrung. All you want is sleep—but not in the car, because you've wiped your ass with the wax wrapper of your last burger, you itch like hell, you need a shower before you can rest clean. Except that on that long stretch of I-10 in the Arizona desert between Phoenix and Quartzsite there's nothing, not at three in the morning, not an open gas pump, not a motel, not a small-town light for nearly two hours.

LA's five hours past Quartzsite, so I gave up making LA and just kept wondering where the hell was Quartzsite, when would it be coming around the bend—it's too small a place for mileage signs till you're right on top of it. I was wasted, sick, and suddenly so tired—a fatigue like a message from the future. The first feeling of "old" I ever admitted to.

The arts of being wasted are part of my trade, but this was different. The wheel felt thick in my hands. Swollen. And it was like my eyes couldn't see as far into the dark as they should, though there was nothing in that dark to see. And the dark itself felt thicker, sticky, like it was touching my face—like I could wipe it off me with a rag. Sometimes I'd sweat and just as suddenly I'd be dry, and my chest ached, dully, and I felt—littler. Just—littler. And there was nothing out there, nothing but the white lines passing under me like they were *far* under me, as I got smaller and smaller inside. I was scared. And my fear wasn't useful, didn't let any adrenaline go, was just something else to pull my head down.

I woke skidding on a soft shoulder.

I went with the skid and the wheels held. A smaller car might have bounced down the arroyo going this fast, but not my old Chevy, a '69 Malibu, just a 307 engine, nothing fancy, but good graceful lines and stable, just heavy enough to be heavy and just big enough not to be little. I keep her cherry under the hood, but I don't paint her, she's still the original brown, dented on all sides because I let every dent stay, cracked paint, rust, and all—I believe in scars. If your alignment's decent and your tires are good, it's hard to snap a '69 Chevy out of control.

I woke less with the skid than with the racket of small rocks clanging against my underside as the wheels spun upon the desert itself. How many people have woken like that, hovering in life for one last instant before they go smash, go shooting off into the next world right then, their souls swollen with panic, no time even to scream. And I saw such a soul, a gray bag of a thing, welted with boils and cysts, tumbling end over end in the sky, its pimples bursting with fear.

But it wasn't *my* soul.

My hands and feet were all the way awake now, easing with the brake, steering with the skid, and we stopped—"we," I mean me and the car. The only light on this earth was the crescent lit by my brights in front and the dull red glow of my brake lights behind. I got out, sat on my front fender, listened to my heart. No other sound but a light wind, and the little chinks and rustlings of the engine as it cooled. I felt each little metallic palpitation in my thighs and in the itching seat of my pants as waves of fear washed from my solar plexus down through my stomach, into my crotch, down my legs. And knew this for a fear I could use. It would keep me awake at least the forty-five minutes it might take to make Quartzsite. I might even need a drink to get to sleep.

And sitting on that fender I felt how, from where I was, the dark Mojave stretched for all the rest of Arizona north, then all Nevada too; and how, west and east, the desert went under other names for hundreds of miles, surrounding the mountains; and due south into Mexico the names changed again but the desert didn't.

It's not a place very concerned with a highway wreck. If I'd died there, the coyotes would have had me before dawn, eaten me while I was still warm. Jumped in my open window, torn me up right in the front seat. And some rattlesnakes might have sidled next to the warm engine in the cool of the night, then stayed in its shade after sunrise. Any desertman grappling a tow to the Chevy the next day would have known to watch for the snakes.

Above me the stars were clear, thousands of sharp points, no glittery fuzz on them. I was cold, suddenly, and it felt clean to be cold.

Then from way behind me I heard the piston-moan of a semi as it pulled up the long slow grade to Quartzsite. I turned and saw its brilliant double brights, the cab aglow with ambers, the trailer strung with reds. Odds were he was hauling something completely useless to sell somewhere completely ugly, but that was okay, I had a love for that truck, just to see it so strong and alive in the dark. I heard him shift down. He'd seen I wasn't moving, might be in trouble, could tell by the angle of my taillights on the grade. When his brights hit me I gave a thumbs-up sign and waved—weakly, my arm just kind of dangling off my shoulder—and he geared up again. I got back in my car and started her up. She pulled off the hard ground just fine. A few feet more to the right, we'd have been down the arroyo where the truck couldn't have seen.

The jalapeño can had spilled all over the front seat. The fumes made my eyes tear. The juice had spilled down my right leg, the skin burned and that sting helped my wakefulness. That was for sure the last time I'd use the jalapeño trick. I'd always thought of myself as pushing toward the boundaries, but there'd been a change —now the boundaries were pushing toward me. Which is what they call "getting older," among other things.

And I started shaking, a vibrating shiver down and up my arms and legs, like when your teeth chatter, and it was partly fear-shakes and partly that my body had *stopped*, it couldn't do anymore, but it had to, for another half hour anyway, so what it was doing was shaking.

Amid the jalapeño fumes and the shit-laced stink of my own sweat, all I could do was concentrate on how hard my hands could grip, fingers curled around the wheel in two fists, fingernails digging into my palms—a pain that felt good. Women like my hands. They're the only part of me that's not beat up, except for a couple of knuckle scars. Long fingers, tapered, like a lady's. An octave-and-then-some reach. Sure touch. Good hands for my trade. Probably why Missy made me take piano in the first place. ("I was tryin' to get you cultured," she once said to me, "an' look what I got you instead.") I looked at my hands on the wheel and I thanked them. They knew how to handle a skid. Driving and rock 'n' roll are about the only things I'm any good at, so it's all in the hands.

I hung in behind that truck till Quartzsite, glad to watch its lights, and it was like having a friend.

FOUR *Tears and Spit*

One more motel room. Cinder-block walls painted the green of canned peas. Rickety furniture—pieces you could pick up at a garage sale for three bucks. A tinted photograph of John Kennedy in a frame over the bed. In less than three hours it would be day all over again. I was still shaky. If you go out into tiredness farther than most people can bear, you hit a place where you can't see farther than a few feet in front of you unless you really try. It's not that things get blurry—your eye sees all it normally sees, but *you* don't. Things farther than a few feet might just as well be invisible because they don't enter your head. There's a kind of wall beyond which your vision won't go unless you force it. It gets hard to do anything with your body, and at the same time your mind bounces from one thing to another, images and memories and fantasies and dreams crowding in on one another, like they're all trying to force their way through the same door at once. And then if you're like me you *can't* go to sleep, lying down makes you dizzy, as though you'd drunk too much, so you sit and you shake and it's as though your mind is holding you down and bouncing on you, and you can't do anything but watch what it does.

Beer is very good for this state, will ease you up and dull you out, but there wasn't anywhere in Quartzsite at that hour to get the two—more like four—beers I would have needed to reach sleep. Tequila is very bad for this state, but tequila was all I had in the car, and I wasn't about to sit like that without the friend a drink can be, even old tricky tequila, which tastes to me like a mix of tears and spit.

So I turned on the TV real low, low enough so that I would have to kind of squint with my ears to hear it. Some little black-and-white people were pursuing some of their kind. Sat down with the tequila. Just let come what I'd been holding back for fourteen hundred miles, the onslaught of:

22

PART ONE

Ooh Poo Pah Doo
—1974

You go to be hot or cold, 'cause if you're lukewarm the Lord will spew you out of his mouth.

—Jerry Lee Lewis

O N E The Smoke Above the Drums

I played hard, I played down, I played up, *I'm goin' up*
I'm goin' down
I'm goin' up down
Down up
Any way you wanna
Let it roll I hit that piano like a truck, down in the deep notes first, forehead pouring sweat so I couldn't see, dripping on the keys till they felt greasy wet. Little Lee'd hit a note on his Fender, hold it, bend it, screech it with feedback, while I'd run all over it, up and down it, try to crash through it as he'd hold it there, and then he'd blast me down with a run of loud chords, and then . . . real sudden, we'd get soft, so soft, and the whole joint would just kind of hang there, and I'd get delicate, sprinkling high notes that would hang, suspended, while Lee's guitar would trickle like a stream, so tenderly, both of us, and it was like we were painting a picture in the hanging smoke of the club, a picture of some impossible woman who seemed to live behind the veils of sound. And just when it seemed you could reach out and touch her, one of us would *crash* a chord—once I just banged my head and elbows down on the keys at the same time, not a chord but a piano-scream, and the people went crazy and the beat took over, *You got me peepin'*
You got me hidin'
You got me peep hide
Hide peep
Any way you wanna
Let it roll
The piano at Dawg's was a bit out of tune, but I kind of liked that. A piano isn't like a guitar, you can't carry one around from club to club. An acoustic piano I'm talking about, a *real* piano, I don't prefer electrics—the action's weird for me on electrics; don't matter how you hit a key, the sound comes out just as loud. Where on an acoustic you can hit one note real hard and the very next

25

note real soft. But pianos like at Dawg's, they're often a little off. In straight music that would throw your playing, but *this* music . . . sometimes that out-of-tune quality is real special, it's like the piano is trying to tell you something, and if you catch on, you can *play* the out-of-tuness, and if you play it and use it, then it's *not* out of tune, it's just on its own, and you can play things you never played before and will never play again. Because no piano will sound quite like that again. Tuned pianos are pretty much alike, but no pianos are out of tune the same.

Anyway, this music comes from places where they ain't got scales.

We hit the end of that tune like we were skidding to a stop, brakes squealing, rubber burning, and Nadine shimmying her tambourine.

At six-three in heels she was a head taller than me, and compared to my faded jeans, my any-old-shirt, and my snakeskin boots, Nadine looked dressed for church—if you could church it up in a gypsy green skirt and billowy yellow blouse, gold earrings shaped like stars, and white bone combs holding down her halfway-down-her-back black hair. No paint but some lipstick, eyes bright and fluttery, harsh circles under them. Her whole long body kind of rippled to the beat as she stood there with her hand raised above her head, like those Cajun ladies do, palm up, like it was an antenna, as she soared into one of her favorites, *I wanna tell you about*

Ooh Poo Pah Doo . . .
An' I won't stop tryin'
Till I create a disturbance

In your mind Nadine wailed around and over and through it, like someone calling through a bad wind, shaking her head so her hair swung, her voice dark as her hair, tones full in the middle and frayed around the edges, with that swamp-call in it that no Cajun singer can suppress, how it threatened to take over any particular note, which is just what made you listen. And when I'd come in on harmony, my rough screech with her honeyed wail, something got married in the air, something that was never married at any other time for us, something that could be joined only in the smoke above the drums.

Dawg's had a low ceiling, the bandstand spots were close to our heads and bright in our eyes. They felt like desert sun. But the music acted like a kind of radar, you could feel the crowd by how it bounced off them and came back at us, even crazier than how we sent it out. Past the spots' glare I could just make out the vague shaking shapes of bodies dancing, like looking at fish darting under dark water. And what with the cigarette smoke, the air *was* like water in that you could see it move as people moved through it, people making all the quick connections of glances that are the web of a honky-tonk, eyes ricocheting off eyes, each body moving through another's heat. How even on the best nights so many faces are solemn, even blank, weighted with the knowledge of what hasn't happened and what's not going to, watching the dancers, the lovers soon-to-be, used-to-be, been-too-long and never-to-be—and most all of them lit from the bloodstream on out with the inner glare of every sort of booze, pill, powder, and leaf. Eyes looking back at you like neon signs.

Cre
Ate
Dis
Tur
Bance
In your mind
Cre
Ate
Dis
Tur

Bance and they screamed, clapped and whistled when the set was over. I bent to the mike and said, "Thank-you-and-all-that, and now we're gonna take a pause for a worthy cause. That's Little Lee Brammer on lead, Peck Peckinpah on bass, Mr. 'Lady' Fuentes on drums, and a real lady, Nadine Wales, magic vocals. I'm Jesse Wales, and we're Long Distance Call. Thanks again, and we'll be back in a drink or two. Don't go home, you already know what *that's* like."

Dawg's was our home bar in Austin, and this was a crowd of regulars, so once off the bandstand we were just folks, no fuss. Nade and I weren't speaking except on the bandstand, but we hit the bar right next to each other on the same beat. Our habits were married better than we were.

Dawg poured me a Bushmills and a beer, poured Nade a rosé wine, without saying a word. He still tended bar himself every night back then. He had thick shaggy hair to his shoulders, a graying beard, and his big hard belly made him look pregnant. He could never quite get a shirt to button over it. He looked like a biker's version of Santa Claus, patient twinkly eyes and all.

"When you gonna get that instrument tuned?" I said.

"Thought you didn't mind it."

"I don't but it's getting tougher. You oughta give it a chance to start all over, get outta tune in some new fashion."

"Pray for rain, then. Weather tunes *that* piano. *Anyway*— don't be talkin' 'bout *tuning* when you're banging your body parts on my keyboard. Look at his forehead!"

"I've seen it," Nade said. "Looks right manly. Would look a damn sight better with a six-inch nail through his third eye."

"Hey, she's right, man. You've blackened your third eye. Too bad you'll never be famous, it'd make a helluva album cover."

I took a bar napkin and dabbed at the bruise—I'd forgotten all about it. A very small, light smear of blood came off on the napkin.

"Big deal," I said.

It was a small club, two hundred people could pack it, and it was more than packed. Nadine and I, our barstools were jammed next to each other. A couple of girls in their mid-twenties—about ten years younger than us—were having a heated talk next to Nadine. One was pretty and one wasn't. The one who wasn't raised her voice, very indignant, said, "It sounds like she uses her soul's dreams to entertain her personality!"

"Ex-CUSE *me!*" Nadine said, and the girls and Dawg and us all laughed, and Nadine met my eyes just for a moment.

"Well, she *does*," the not-pretty girl said with an East Texas drawl, then turned to her friend, lowered her voice, and went on.

Nadine said to Dawg, "The moon is in hoo-hah and I will do whatever I can get my hands on and you may quote me."

"*I* quote you all the time," I said.

"You steal from me; that's different."

I asked Dawg for a pencil and wrote on a bar napkin: "The

moon is in hoo-hah . . . Watch out f'ya yaya." I put the napkin near Nadine's glass but she wouldn't look at it.

"Jesse?"

"What?"

"How come it's my job to forgive *you* all the time. When's it gonna be your job to forgive *me?*"

"Guess you're just too goddamn good at being good."

"I don't see why you do it anyway. You know you always come too fast with strangers."

"Excuse *me!*" the not-pretty girl said.

I studied my beer real hard. Dawg, pouring beer from the tap, pretended like he hadn't heard.

Nadine said, "If you're thinking I'm jealous of ten-second lays, you oughta know better. Why do you do it, is what I wanna know? Is it premature middle age, or what?"

"I'm looking for God."

"Who ain't?"

"Someone told me I'd find God in pussy."

"Try mine."

Nothing I could say to that.

"Anyway," Nadine said, "you don't look for God, God looks for you."

"Where's it say *that?*"

"On the ladies'-room wall."

"It doesn't either," I said. "What am I looking for then?"

"I wish I knew."

"What are you looking for, Nade?"

"You."

I didn't believe it, but I said, "That's very old-fashioned of you, isn't it?"

"I don't know, I think it's kinda poignant, don't you?"

We *almost* laughed, but we did smile.

"If Danny were here he'd know what we're looking for."

"Danny don't know shit," she said, "but he'd make up something pretty all right. That's *almost* knowing, I suppose."

And I was thinking, but could not say: I *have* tried your pussy, and your mouth, and your ass, and I've come on your tits and in your hair, and once when you weren't home I came in your shoes, and mostly it was better than good, and sometimes it was better than if I were James Dean and you were Natalie Wood, but lately . . . I have been afraid of your dreams and I have not wanted to fuck you out of fear that your dreams would stick to my cock and burrow in like ticks. I don't know which of us is crazy, Nade. And I play music as crazy as I know how and I don't know if it's crazy enough to be real.

Maybe I don't want to know, either.

I avoided looking into the bar mirror—I *know* what I look like, and I'm tired of it. Long brown hair pulled back in a ponytail, thinner up on top than it once was. Thick purplish bags under my eyes; a big hook nose that was crooked even before it got broken. Gap teeth, thick lips, wide mouth. The scars of two wrecks and one beer bottle crisscross at the end of my chin. Danny says I always look like I'm about to ask myself a question.

Well—I'm not.

When we'd stepped down from the bandstand the jukebox had kicked in, loud and tinny above the din of two hundred drunks. It was the best juke in Austin, had everything, old and new, black, white and brown, urban and country—"It's The Great American Novel of Jukeboxes," Danny had said. Someone had played Jimmy Reed's original version of "Baby What You Want Me to Do," recorded I can't remember when, 1960, give or take a couple of years, and the way he did it was relaxed and sweet, an easy loping rhythm, a happy tune with just enough edge to make you wonder. Here it was about fifteen years later and the way we'd done it was like the world was coming to an end, not a love song anymore but something spooky shouted at the sky.

Nadine's hand went between my legs and gently, but strongly, squeezed. I almost fell off the barstool.

"Such a handful," she said.

"Don't stop now."

"I'm not in the mood to do you any favors. It's just that my hand's been lonely for you."

She pulled away.

She said, "I need you, Jesse. And I got a right to. I don't just mean—"

"I know what you don't just mean."

Nadine, Nadine—I'm scared of your dreams.
And, baby, I can't remember mine.
She said, "Time to go back to work?"
I looked up at the bandstand—that little crowded platform where we were allowed and expected to do *anything*.
We went back to work, and the first tune Nadine called out wasn't on our tune list, it was a Big Joe Turner blues, twenty years older than that Jimmy Reed tune:
You're so beautiful but you're gonna die someday
All I want's a little lovin', thank ya,
'Fore you pass away. And the heat of the spots poured down from above us and the heat off the dancers came up in waves, the heat of our bodies soaked our clothes through and the heat of our music made the dark club throb.

T W O *White Darkness*

White darkness. The snow glowed under a moon near to full. You could see a long way through the flat hard light, a light without shimmer or pulse. Even the space between snow and moon seemed whitened. And nothing was moving in that white dark but the rising moon and us.

Danny said, "Cut the lights," and I did.

Danny was right—under this moon we could see fine without the lights. It became more like floating than driving. The road rose and dipped. On the rises you saw miles of white snow-light. In the dips it was like sliding into shadow-ponds—I'd ease off the gas and feel my engine cut just enough so my Chevy seemed to be finding its own way down, while I steered dead in the center of the road—there were no shoulders, and with the snow you couldn't be sure what was and wasn't road around the edges. It was three in the morning, as usual, and there was nothing on the road, no tracks but what we left behind us.

The dash lights on my '69 had already gone by then, so inside the car was pitch. I looked over at Danny. His head was black against the white outside. It was like someone had cut a silhouette and taped it on the side window: almost a bird's head disguised as a man's—the pointed chin, the long straight nose, high cheekbones and thin black feathery hair. What you couldn't see in the dark was how white Danny was, and the sky-blue of his eyes.

November in Texas—it had been hot in Austin the other night, and now, four hundred miles northwest in the Panhandle, it was twenty. We'd been driving the two-lanes from Lubbock, where we'd picked Danny up, through Idalou and Floydada, past miles of prairie spotted with farms, past those grain elevators that call themselves towns, through Silverton, down the Caprock, headed north to Pampa for a gig. The rest of the band would meet us there with the gear. Danny had been working out of Lubbock lately, gigging mostly in New Mexico, so we three hadn't gotten together for a while. We'd looked forward to this gig with him, but then his van had broken down and we had to pick him up. A swing through Lubbock was more than two hundred miles out of our way, but we never thought anything about time or distance in those days.

Any musician can tell you sounds change in different lights. In that snow-light, even under the drone of the engine, I could hear Nadine's breathing in the back seat soft and clear as a drummer's brushes on the cymbals. She'd been curled asleep back there since Idalou.

The road rose and dipped in the silvery dark. There were cottonwoods in the dips now, so I knew the Red River was close. An old woman once told me it really ran with water when she was a girl, not just sometimes in the spring like it does now. These days there's generally just a stream-size trickle down its east shore, the river just a long smooth ditch spanned by a narrow bridge.

We saw it on the next rise. The snow in the riverbed glared back at the moon. I slowed to almost nothing because there'd be ice on the bridge.

"Apocalypse ain't so bad," Danny said, out of nowhere, as was his way.

"It's bad enough."

"Naw, Apocalypse is *fun*. Everybody's havin' such a good time skidding toward it."

"Yeah, I've noticed what a good time everybody in this old world's been having lately."

"Naw, misery's just the only way the poor devils can handle *intensity*. Underneath all that, they're deliriously happy. Anyway, after Apocalypse, there'll just be this—and what's so bad about this?"

Nothing at all. I stopped the car in the middle of the bridge. It was like you could *hear* the light, a note held forever, so low and so high at the same time, so black and so white. It was like the moon and the earth had traded places.

"Should we wake Nadine?" I said.

"That's an interesting dilemma. I was just weighing it myself. 'Cause, like, is she better off seeing this, or letting it pour into her sleep?"

We sat still while the car got colder and the light got louder.

"Oh, Lord!" Nadine whispered. She'd woken soundlessly. She leaned her head over the front seat and shook her hair out. Straight and fine, it swayed near me, and I could smell how clean it was.

"Let's just stay right here," she said. "I mean, let's *settle*."

"The heater fan's busted," I said. "We only stay warm while we're moving."

Our breaths were fogging the windows, so I rolled my window down. The cold stung my face. My jeans chilled against my legs.

"Danny," Nadine said, "stop *grinning*."

"How do you know I'm grinning? You got no idea."

"This car is thick with you grinnin' at all this like you made it up yourself. It's distracting me."

"Well, I kind of did—make it up, I mean. And what's so bad about bein' distracted?"

The moon-shadow of a bird sped over the snow across the road just in front of us. An owl, probably, but I couldn't see.

"I dreamed of Jesus," Nadine said softly.

"Same dream?"

"Same dream."

In the dream she's sitting on the porch swing of the old house in Baton Rouge—but the porch swing doesn't creak like it does really. It's morning. Jesus walks out of the house, where he has apparently had his own room for some time. He's in jeans, bare

33

feet, no shirt. Only way you know it's Jesus is, first, you just *know*; and there's his long shiny light-dark hair; and there's the brightness of his eyes. Like, at that moment, standing on that porch is *exactly* what he's supposed to be doing.

It's not like Nadine's living with him. He's just got a room there. So they know each other, but just to say hello to.

Jesus opens his mouth and a big fat fly comes and lands on his tongue. Then another. Then another. Jesus has his tongue stuck out as far as it will go and the three flies are walking around on it. Then one walks over the edge and hangs upside-down on the bottom of Jesus' tongue. The two flies on top are just cleaning their feet like flies do. The one on the bottom sticks his little sucker into the tongue.

Nadine wants to puke and she wants to pray but mostly she wants just to *say* something to Jesus—but she's scared to speak because the flies might go into her mouth. So she keeps her lips clenched tight, presses them together so hard it hurts. She knows how ugly her face must look, scrunched up like that, but she can't help it. Then one of those fat flies lifts off Jesus' tongue and buzzes toward her, and she's so scared she wakes up.

But when awake, the fear would pass, she'd mostly have an afterglow of being real pleased that Jesus had a room in her house. The first time she had the dream and told it, Danny tried to interpret it, like he does everything, but Nade hushed him *fast*. When we asked her about the flies she said, "That's just dream-stuff."

Two dark horses walked from beneath the bridge and went slowly up the riverbed. Their hooves left black holes of shadow in the snow.

Nadine squeezed my shoulder.

"I wish there were three of them," she said.

Very softly, Danny started to sing:
Then come sit by my side if you love me
Do not hasten to bid me adieu
Just remember the Red River Valley—
Danny had a sweet throat-warbly voice that, soft as it was, could still soar. And as much as it soared it quavered, like something was always half-strangling in Danny's throat. And there was some-

thing in that quaver, more than in the prettiness of his tone, that pulled you in and made you listen. It was unbelievable that a man could sound so sweet and still sound like a man, yet he did. But you heard it clear that somewhere in that unbelievable sweetness something was being squeezed, twisted even, and was letting you know.

He let the song just hang after three lines.

We were *so* cold now.

"Who's gonna admit they can't stand it anymore?" Danny said.

"You just did," Nadine said. "Two more minutes; we won't die."

The horses were standing together, side to side, stone-still, their moon-shadows gray right under them. We couldn't see the moon anymore—it must have been staring straight down on the car —so the light seemed to have no source.

Danny was staring at the horses. "I wonder where the other two are. There are supposed to be four, doesn't it say?"

I hit the ignition key, put the Chevy in drive and eased on the gas. The wheels spun on the snow, the car slid toward the bridge rail, brushed it, but gently, no dent, just one more scratch. The wheels caught, and we rolled slowly across the bridge.

"The horses are watching us," Nadine said.

We watched them back.

Across the river the road dipped and rose again for about thirty–forty miles to Clarendon, the next town.

"I could sure use some coffee," I said.

"There's that new AM/PM in Clarendon," Nadine said. "They're open twenty-four hours now."

"Man," Danny said, "even the *tiny* towns need twenty-four-hour joints these days. Nobody can sleep in this damn country anymore."

At the speed we had to go on this road in the snow, Clarendon was almost an hour away. The car's motion forced the engine's hot air through the heater ducts and we warmed, slowly.

"Naw, we're Apocalypse people, there's no other explanation for us. Not for us, and not for twenty-four-hour joints in podunk towns. Rock 'n' roll is pure Apocalypse."

"I hear *that*," I said.

"Apocalypse is what we do for a livin'. Apocalypse *ain't* so bad."

Nade said, "Shut up, Danny. You don't know a thing about it."

T H R E E *Apocalypse People*

I asked my angel if Heaven was near.
She said, "It's closer than it looks,
But you can't get there from here."
Where do you go when you're already gone?
　　　　　—Butch Hancock

On the outskirts of Pampa it was any old motel room. Two more-or-less double beds, a framed poster of all the state flags, and four plastic cups in the john. The largest towel was just enough to wrap around a very skinny man like Danny. Danny always had to hit a hot bath off the road, no matter now tired he was or how stained the bathtub.

Nadine would mommy him. It would be, "Don't you be taking forever in that tub, and I don't wanna hear that water *slosh*, if you catch my meaning." He'd catch it good and blush, remembering that time when he forgot he wasn't alone and got carried away scrubbing his privates.

"What was *her* name?" I'd teased.

"Her name's always the same," Danny had said. And fished his notebook out of the jeans he'd just taken off. "That's the title of a song."

"The Greatest and Most Unrecorded Hits of Danny Craw-ford," I said.

"Actually," Nade said, "her name is always different."

"*Actually* actually—" and he got that far-off look of his—"her name, since I usually forget it, *is* always the same. I mean what I say—"

"—and I'm mean when I say it," I finished. That was one of my songs.

We'd shared so many rooms on so many roads. In our twenties the three of us, plus some drums and guitars, were a band—the first edition of Long Distance Call. Except that really Nadine and me were rockers—rhythm and blues, if you want to get technical—while Danny was rockabilly and country. (What they started to call "cosmic country"—Danny was one of the first.) Where we went over big, he didn't go over too well, while audiences that loved Danny just tolerated us. I think if we'd been gigging in California or someplace we'd have done all right, but our ground was Texas, Louisiana and New Mexico, and in those days those audiences didn't mix their music much. In fact, in those days mixing it at all was considered downright subversive, though a few years later everybody was doing it. Oh, we did the San Francisco thing for a while, and enjoyed it, but we didn't last, we just weren't hippies—Danny was too Lubbock, Nadine was too Cajun, and I was just too rough. We went back to Texas, Danny formed his own band, Nade and I got married, and even lived together for a while more, in her old house in Baton Rouge. Now I worked out of Austin, and we were just together when Nade got lonely or wanted to hit the road, which amounted to the same thing. We stayed married, though. Or rather, we neither of us could face doing a divorce. But it was different for Nadine. I had women when I felt like it, and she kept almost only to me. I was stupid enough once to ask her why, and didn't get spoken to for two months.

We talked on the phone all the time, when we were speaking, that is. We'd call at all hours. Lately it had mostly been Nade, telling me her dreams and talking about the Bible.

In that room in Pampa, Danny went straight to the tub and Nade went straight to the dresser drawer and pulled out the Gideon.

"Here it is," she said. And read: " 'And when he had opened the seventh seal, there was silence in heaven about the space of half an hour.' Revelations, 8:1. You get it? If you don't you better."

"A cold is about all I'm gonna get if I don't get to sleep right quick."

"But Jesse, we just saw that! That just happened to us! We saw the seventh-seal time! Jesse!"

Her eyes were too bright for me.

"Like a coming attraction," she said, "a special preview just for us. Talk about your 'Pocalypse!"

"Nade, Nade, Nade. Does it make you horny?"

A surprised laugh kind of bubbled out of her. "It kinda *does,* yeah."

"But not in front of the children," we said together—an old joke from whenever the three of us could afford only one room on the road.

But for once I was glad of the accommodations. I'd been having these flashes of Nadine's Jesus-flies buzzing around my dick.

She went, Bible in hand, to the window. It looked out on the little motel court, an old place, the kind you've got to go at least thirty miles from an interstate to find anymore. Each room was really a separate bungalow, grouped in a half-circle facing the highway. The motel sign flashed a white neon star, and underneath the star, glowing blue, it said, PANHANDLE STAR MOTEL.

It was near to dawn. Snow and sky were soaked with a purple just the other side of black.

"I think I'm happy, Jesse."

"Could have fooled me."

"I mean this moment. And back down the road. What's it, a sign, you think?"

I pointed to the neon. *"That's* a sign," I said. "Anyway, how would I know? I'm not happy. I love *you,* though."

"Love you, too."

She went back to the bed. She said, "You know, you're allowed to get wild and feel stuff besides in bed and on bandstands, or hadn't you heard?"

"That a fact?"

"Wait a sec." She browsed the book. "Revelations, uh, 3:15–16. 'I know thy works, that thou art neither cold nor hot: I would thou wert cold or hot. So then because thou art lukewarm, and neither cold nor hot, I will spue thee out of my mouth.' "

"I've always been meaning to ask why you spew me out of your mouth. Why don't you ever drink it down?"

"Jesse!!!"

"Made you blush!"

"Damn right."

She put the book back in the drawer, as though the book shouldn't have to hear such trash. Then she took off her boots and socks and stretched all six feet of herself on the bed nearest the window. Her gray eyes made the dark circles under them seem all the darker.

She unzipped her jeans and peeled them off, and it was just a bit like a tease to me, the way she crooked those long legs to get the jeans off. Underneath she was wearing pink panties with little yellow flowers on them, little-girl panties they looked like. Her bush made a bulge and some wiry black hairs stuck out from under the panties. I flashed on how it could be a wad of flies making her panties bulge, just packed there on top on each other sucking up on her sweet pussy.

I broke into a sweat and forced myself to look out the window. The light hadn't changed at all. I cursed myself quietly and got my bottle of Bushmills out of the duffel, gulped three times fast—the shock and burn in my gullet brought tears to my eyes and wiped the images from my head.

Took off my boots, my socks, my jeans, and lay in my boxer shorts leg-to-leg with Nade. Outside our little room it had lightened a little more, purple-black to blue velvet. Sunset and dawn take their time in this wide, flat country.

Water sloshed in the bathtub, and a beat later the bathroom door swung open and Danny stood there dripping, a little towel around his waist and another around his neck. A big toothy grin, and on his chest you could count every rib.

"Watch this!"

In three strides he was at the door. He swung it open and walked out into the blue twilight snow.

"Danny!" Nade yelled, as the icy air whooshed in.

We sprang up and went to the door. Danny of the Towels was doing a hillbilly jig in the snow under the star-sign, laughing.

He stopped his dance and turned to us, stood still with arms spread and legs wide, all his limbs asmoke. Vapors steamed off his bath-hot arms and legs, his chest and forehead. Vapors rose from beneath his towel and from his feet ankle-deep in the snow. Slowly he raised his arms straight out in front of him and his eyes widened watching clouds rise off his hands.

"Bet Jesus just *loved* to do this!" Danny squealed.

39

Nadine looked at him in pure amazement. Danny stretched out his arms to her, and she walked slowly toward him across the snow, in just that shirt and those little-girl panties. Her feet left clear prints of high arches and long toes. I stood in the doorway feeling my nuts scrunch up so small. No part of my body believed this was happening.

Nadine turned to me.

"Come, Jesse."

The first two steps were wonderful. It was so cold it was like my feet were exploding, but painlessly, without damage.

Danny still steamed lightly as the three of us stood in a circle all giddy and cock-eyed, proud of ourselves for standing half-naked in the snow at dawn for no reason. The cold started to burn through the soles of my feet, hurting so bad. A pickup passed and the amazed farmboy at the wheel stared. Across the two-lane there was nothing till the eastern horizon miles off. And on the horizon, between the twilight blue of the sky and the shadow blue of the snow, the thinnest band of bright green glowed like neon.

Our breaths bunched in small, almost instantly gone clouds. The band of green on the horizon got brighter, the purples of snow and sky faded to grays. A small breeze came up with the sun, making it lots colder.

"They ain't got *this* in the Bible," I said.

Nadine didn't seem to hear. Her eyes were round and bright, looking at the horizon.

"Oh, thank you, Danny," she said softly. "I feel so clean. And hey—I know what I want."

We were so cold now, it seemed like: How are we going to move the few yards back into the motelroom? Which we'd better do soon, before we got arrested.

"I *do*," Nadine said, "I know."

Turning around seemed too much for my poor body to manage, so I just took one step backward, then another, and Nade walked sideways, and Danny hobbled frontways, so we kept our little circle till we got to the open door, Danny grinning a big silly grin, Nadine with tears in her eyes, and me, I don't know, kind of happy in a scared sort of way.

FOUR *A First*

Warming up hurt more than getting cold. Our very bones burned as we put our clothes back on and wrapped ourselves in blankets and rubbed each other's feet, Danny speed-rapping non-stop. "Naw, I wanna invent a time frame called Nighttime Losing Time, 'stead of Daylight Savings Time. *That's* the shit I *believe* in: No matter how late at night it gets, it's never *too* late."

And on like that, like he always did when he got real excited. With Danny, it was as though he was all head. You weren't aware of anything but that birdlike face and those big dark eyes. He was tall, but it didn't matter. He was so skinny, his body seemed hardly there unless he dressed flashy. It was all the voice and the eyes, and sometimes in a club, with a tight spotlight on him, it was like there was nothing underneath his head at all, like it just kind of bobbed around. I wouldn't have been surprised to see his whole body go up in smoke out there in the snow. But he'd done it again, on the drive telling me to shut the headlights, and running out onto the snow—he'd opened some doors. I guess that's why we loved each other so much, us because he'd open doors we didn't know were there, him because he couldn't, just couldn't, go through those doors alone, and we were game.

Not that there'd been anything to do with those doors, once we'd walked through them, but to walk back the way we'd come. Still, we'd been somewhere, though just *where* we couldn't say.

The sun came up bright, glaring off the snow, and we drew the curtains, "like the living dead," Danny was rapping now, "which *is* what *we* know about, being this tired and this awake at the same time, it's *like* being *between*, 'tween the lands of the living and the dead, how we work all night, night after night, how we zap it up with drugs and sweeten it with booze and haze it all with smoke, while all the while what's tired has been tired so long it's dead, but what's awake is *so* awake inside the deadness, like . . ." And on that way, till suddenly, all wrapped in his clothes in his bed, he was asleep like he'd just passed out.

Then a light easy snore.

"The children are asleep," Nadine said softly.

We were dressed in two layers of clothes and clinging to each other under the covers and still not warm. Sometimes, even now, when I get cold, it's as though it's *that* cold coming back, like we never warmed up all the way again. We were lying face-to-face, our stockinged feet wedged together, our clothes bulky and uncomfortable yet comforting under the covers. Nade started gently to kiss my face, with her eyes open, and with my eyes open I watched as she did, not yet understanding, not yet kissing back.

"Don't you wonder," she whispered between kisses, "what I know I want? Just the juice, Jesse. There'll be a baby in that juice, I know it."

My dumb prick got hard. I didn't want it to. It was all bunched up in my pants and painful. Nadine felt of it. I just lay there feeling her hands fumble with my zipper, reach in my underwear, pull out the thing, her hand rough and cold.

Then her hands were at her own pants, and as she worked them down to her ankles she said, "Pretend I'm one of them chippies, then it'll just last about ten seconds and you can go to sleep. You almost always just knock off afterwards, you'll sleep good."

She rubbed herself against me. She was dry and bristly. She licked her fingers and wet herself down there. And lying on our sides like that, awkward and bulky feeling, my face pressed against her scratchy wool sweater now, I pushed into her, she was all but juiceless, it was like sticking my cock into an old crusty sponge, and we lay there moving just enough, no more, eyes open, and it feeling almost airy inside her without the diaphragm, and then I did close my eyes, which was a mistake, because the flies came, lifted off Jesus' tongue, which was down there too and wet now and lapping me from inside her, and those flies settled on my dick, not just three but many, thick as flies on shit, like they say, and the worst was that it felt good, all those tiny feet, all those fluttery wings, all the vibration of that buzzing, and I came in hard jerks, and it seared burning as it spurted, so hot.

She moaned from low and far away in great surprise—she hadn't expected to come.

I was in such a sweat. I thought I'd suffocate now in all those clothes, under all those covers, the wool of her sweater in my mouth, and I pushed off her—her sharp disappointed sigh as I pulled out—and grabbed at my clothing, wrestling out of it like I'd die if I didn't, and heard, as I did, a loud panting that I realized, with real surprise, was my own. And finally lay under those covers in a sweat, naked except for my socks.

And sat up suddenly.

Danny was awake, propped up on his elbow, watching us with a smile.

Nade turned to him, smiled weakly at him.

"Well," he said, "that's a first."

And lay down, turned over, and soon was snoring lightly once more.

Nade and I lay side by side, she in her clothes still. She took my hand. We must have fallen asleep like that. But I woke again, not long after, and drank most of the Bushmills and watched the "Today Show" before I dropped off again, wondering as I did if those people in that box had any idea that anybody like me was watching their silly bright-eyed world.

F I V E   *Happily Ever After*

I slept until the evening news. Slept right through Nade and Danny getting up earlier, connecting with the rest of the band, going out to do the sound check, coming back with a bucket of Colonel Sanders, my breakfast and dinner in one. Except for an empty whole bottle of whiskey—which was rare, even for me—it was as though yesterday hadn't happened, they were so goddamned cheerful.

We ate chicken and watched some sit-coms and then they got

dressed for the gig. Danny's white Stetson was probably the most expensive thing he owned besides his van, his guitar, and his good boots. He wore a blue Western shirt with pearllike snaps, slick black pants with a crease, and orangy ostrich boots—his best outfit.

"You always look like Hank Williams in that getup," Nade said.

"*I'm just in time to be too late*," Danny sang in perfect imitation.

Nade wore that same wide gypsylike green skirt she'd worn the other night in Austin, and a tight white Western shirt, and, with her big tits, looked like a rodeo stripper except for the bone combs in her hair and that she hardly wore any paint.

"We gotta be there in half an hour, Jesse," Nadine said, "ain't you ever gettin' out of bed? You ought at least to shave."

Danny was laying a handful of different-colored pills on the bureau and studying them. He picked up a couple of whites and held them in his palm, then placed a couple of reds next to them, and looked at them closely, like he was examining how they were made.

I slipped my underwear on under the sheets and got out of bed. Danny and I were modest that way around one another.

Nadine kind of glided over to Danny, stood behind him, hugged him around his waist and looked over his shoulder.

"What pretty little pills," she said.

"This'll make you run fast and jump high," he said. He took a couple and she took one.

"None for you, right, tough guy?" Danny said.

"Not that tired," I said, sitting back down on the bed. "Just can't move, is all."

"We gotta dress this boy, Nadine," Danny said.

Danny fished in my duffel bag.

"Man, this stuff is all *wrinkled!*"

Danny got out the little portable iron I always teased him about and commenced to iron my red Western shirt and put a crease in my jeans.

"Please shave, Jesse," Nade said, "they expect it in Pampa."

"Ask not what Pampa can do for you, ask what you can do for Pampa," Danny said as he ironed.

I moaned and groaned and got up and shaved. Didn't like my

face in the mirror. There were blood blotches in the dark bags under my eyes, from drinking that whole fifth myself. But I didn't mind the hangover too much, it was like a gauzy, greasy veil between me and them, their cheerfulness, their playacting like this was our old days and there was nothing to wonder about but who Danny was going to pick up tonight, and would she have the cash for a separate motel room, and how wasted would we all get, and what great thoughts would we all concoct and forget and regret forgetting and try to piece back together on the drive to the next gig, where we would surely become stars and live happily ever after, playing casinos with Elvis, revolutionary casinos, of course, and spending weekends with Dylan, and me and Nade having kids that would play with his kids, back before Danny started occasionally beating up the blondes and before Nade got darker and quieter and before I started taking dreams so seriously, back when Apocalypse was a be-in and you could depend on a Gideon to stay in its drawer.

SIX   *The High Note of Angel Baby*

The gig was in a cowboy-style dance hall, just over the town line, where they like two-steps best, and the couples dance the slower ones in a circle, the guys always stepping forward, the women always stepping backward, with the short sharp steps of cowboy dancing. So it was pretty much Danny's gig the first set. But by the third set it was die-hard rockers in there, people who'd come to hear some dirt. By then the crowd has thinned, if there was a fight to fight, it's been fought, all but the last desperate passes have been made, and the band can play what it likes.

I was into the gig, by then, though playing more straight ahead than normal for me—a minimum of weird chords, and Little Lee on guitar went easy on the feedback, just playing hard and clean to the crowd, and not, like in our favorite joints, trying to drive them out of their hungry heads. You make a Pampa-type crowd crazy, first thing they'll think to do with all that craziness is lynch some-one, probably you.

Things stayed simple until Nadine lost it on the high note of "Angel Baby." Which was a weird call anyway. We were seven or eight hundred miles from any club where you could do a do-wop number with confidence. But if Nadine wanted to take the chance, we'd back her, and do-wop can be a sweet groove on the last set.

She counted out the tune, snapping her fingers in perfect—and I mean *perfect*—time, and we fell in behind her, real slow, like the music is moving toward you on its belly, *It's just like Heaven*

> *Being here with you*
> *You're like an angel*
> *Too good to be true*
> *But after all I love you I do*
> *Angel baby, my angel baby*, pushing her husky voice higher

than it ought to go, but pulling it off, the simple lyrics free of any burden of mystery, floating off into the smoke of the dance hall,

> *When you are near me*
> *My heart skips a beat*
> *I can hardly stand on*
> *My own two feet*, and as I'm playing I'm thinking how shaky

the original really was, that girl's voice paper-thin, the guitar flub-bing the intro a little, and you can almost see that piano player concentrating real hard on those simple chords, while the sax barely manages to hold his tone, the sax dragging worse than the drummer, who drags enough, and yet how sweetly that record worked, people have been playing it on the radio for years and years, it's how that girl sings the word "angel," *my angel baby*

> *Wooooooooo-hoooooooooo I love you*
> *Oooooooooo-hoooooooooo I do*
> *Ooooooooooooooooooooooo*

But Nadine just held that note, she sang it and sang it on and on, and we didn't know what to do. We tried to go with it as long as we could but Nadine just wouldn't let go that note, singing with her lips pursed like a kiss.

Then, still without taking a breath, she bent the note and left it, but still sang, mouth wide now, as her face reddened and her neck bulged—another, fuller *ooooooooo* in another key.

At first the audience thought it was a joke, but as the band ground to a halt and we looked at each other for a clue, Nade held her "Angel Baby" *oooo* till I thought she'd pass out.

My stomach did a quick twist and the Colonel Sanders and the booze started up my gullet. I clamped my mouth shut just before the whole mess spurted out, and swallowed it back down. It stung both ways. My stomach had known before I had, but I knew now: Nadine was holding her mouth open so the black flies of Jesus could fly in. I could just about see them, hovering buzzing at her lips, then darting in, and never coming out, ever.

By that time her voice had stopped, but her mouth was still wide open for the flies. Danny and I looked at each other. I mouthed the word "flies" to him. He got the meaning and gave this high nervous giggle I could have hit him for. None of us in the band could move. Times like that, it's always the women who move first, and two waitresses friendly with the band bounded up on stage, cooing and clucking "It's all right, honey," and taking Nadine to the ladies' room. They seemed to think it was nothing too unusual, just drugs.

Danny followed them, with this kind of bemused expression, like if Nadine was going to do such stuff, well, fine, he'd try to get into the spirit—which was better than me, sick and frozen.

But seeing Danny move unfroze me and I moved faster, getting to the ladies' room before him. There were a half dozen women in there. One of the waitresses stood in my way, said, "Jesse Wales, you can't come in here," but I shoved her aside and went to Nade. She was standing docile while the other waitress splashed water on her face, patted her dry, examined her eyes and took her pulse—checking if it was some kind of OD.

"She's okay," the waitress said, "just on a little voyage all her own, is all. Some people just can't *do* a gig on acid."

Nadine said, "I'm home, Jesse."

"Sure you are, Nade," I said. "Come on, now."

"*You* know."

"Sure I know."

"Well—you'd *have* to. Know. I mean—that's us, right? *Us.* I'd know, if it was you. I will know."

"Hi, Nade," Danny said.

47

"Bless *you,* Danny." Then, to me: "Not you, baby. *You* know why."

"Sure."

"Take my hand, Danny?"

He took her hand. The other women just gawked.

"Jesus. Jesus, Jesus, Jesus. That is the sweetest name. 'It's just like Hea-ven . . . ,' " she sang softly. "I wish this had happened to you, Danny. Then you'd be telling me about Jesus and I'd *love* to listen. I would. But I don't know what to say to you."

"No need," Danny said, smiling.

"Well," she said, "pretend. Pretend you're me right now. I really wanna *hear* something."

I said, "Don't, Danny."

"Hush," Nade said to me.

"Don't," I said to him. "It could pass, you know."

"This is *Nadine,* man."

They stood in the bright white neon of that ladies' room smiling at each other with an understanding I couldn't approach, couldn't even intrude on. Danny didn't have the words she wanted, didn't even try, and that was some small satisfaction; but it didn't matter because Danny, who didn't care about Jesus at all, approved. He just beamed with approval. And his approval looked invulnerable. And it was.

"*I* would really appreciate it" came a voice from inside one of the stalls, "if everybody with a *thing* 'tween his legs would get the *hell* out of here. I cannot number-two in close proximity of a *thing.*"

S E V E N *Fourteen Hours in the Rain*

It warmed up and rained, like it does that time of year, and rained and rained the whole long drive: back due south to Clarendon, then south and east through Childress, Wichita Falls, Fort

Worth, Dallas, then south to Houston, and east again through Beaumont, Baton Rouge, and on into New Orleans. It was like driving through one long low gray tunnel, then a narrower, shiny-black tunnel, while the windshield wipers beat slow soft time.

Little Lee, Peck and Lady went ahead in the van with the equipment, and we followed behind because Danny was driving. I hate for anybody to drive my car, especially Danny, who doesn't take driving very seriously. But I trusted the guys in the band not to hit anything or go faster than the weather could handle, and if he followed them, we'd be all right.

Me, I was in the back seat holding Nade. She had fallen asleep on the way back from the gig to the motel, and had stayed asleep, not even waking up when I walked her from the car to the room. When I let go of her she collapsed on the bed and didn't stir when I took her boots off.

Danny had started grinning in that ladies' room and hadn't stopped. In the motel I said, "I don't see what you're so fucking happy about."

"You ever see somebody cross over? I never did."

"I never wanted to."

"Maybe you didn't, maybe you did."

He looked at me like he knew which. I didn't argue.

"She stepped through that old door," Danny said, "and *stayed* there."

"Yeah, but what door, and where?"

"There's probably but one door. She's calling it Jesus. That's fine by me."

"It ain't by me."

"Maybe there's more than one, maybe there's doors everywhere, that's what *I* always figured. Gotta ask Henry about that. *He* knows about doors."

"Don't be talking to me about Henry now."

Henry was a sore point. Danny had been playing Waco a few months back, and this guy Henry had walked in. All Danny would tell about him was his name, and that he'd become Danny's "Teacher"—he said the word like it had a capital *T*. They'd talked for two days, Danny had given Henry his whole cosmos rap, and it was like old news to Henry. *Real* old. When we'd wanted to meet

this Henry, Danny had said, "Henry says, 'When the time comes,' "
and Danny made it sound like "when the time comes" was a phrase
Henry had invented on his own. Naturally that irritated us, and we
told Danny we didn't want to hear about Henry anymore, we
doubted he even existed, he was probably some imaginary person
Danny had made up so his pronouncements would sound more
authoritative. Which was a trick he should save for his girlfriends,
not waste on us.

"What are you looking at me like that for?" I said.

He had this dreamy gleam in his eye, gentle and sweet, and it
was lovely and aggravating.

He shrugged lightly, his blue eyes sparkling, then bent over
Nadine and stroked her hair.

"We ain't ever gonna be in a room like this again, the three of
us," Danny said softly. Then went and took his bath.

I sat up the hour or so till dawn, which came slow and gray
with rain. I watched Nadine sleep. Slept myself, now and again, on
the chair. Woke Danny, and called the rest of the band, around
noon. Nadine still wouldn't open her eyes, and I took off her singing
clothes and put on her driving clothes like you would do for a little
kid.

And held her all through the day, in the back seat, glad for the
rain. Danny would talk now and again, mostly just to hear himself.
I'd drift in and out of a floating dreamlessness that wasn't quite
sleep, while Nade slept deep, rarely moving, lying with her legs
curled and her head in my lap. The density, the weight of her sleep,
felt sometimes like it was pinning me to the seat. When darkness
came, it was like it was coming out of her. I held her, wishing that
when she woke I'd have something to say to her that would really
matter—and knowing I wouldn't.

After dark I took over the driving and led the van. It was hard
to let Nadine go, but Danny was road-groggy, and we had a gig to
get to in New Orleans. He didn't get in the back seat, which I was
glad of, I really hadn't wanted him to but I would have felt more a
fool than usual telling him not.

He wrapped a blanket around himself and bunched up another
as a pillow against the passenger door.

"You okay, Jesse?" he said.

"I'm always okay."

"I don't mean to drive, I know that. I mean *okay*."

When I didn't say anything, Danny reached his hand to the back of my neck and gave me a long slow rub. The callouses of his fret-fingers felt rough and good on my skin. My eyes teared up, and I was so surprised they did.

E I G H T   *The Ceiling Fan*

We stayed at The Columns on St. Charles, an antebellum mansion run now as a genteel-poor hotel. Thick shiny banisters, worn wood floors and stairs, high ceilings, ceiling fans, and old brass beds way past their prime. We took two rooms, now that Danny had some pocket money from the Pampa gig.

Before we checked in I had to slap Nadine hard to get her eyes open—they wouldn't let us check in if they thought she was sick. But I admit I was glad for the excuse. Her sleep had spooked me good. I liked the sting of the slap on my hand.

Her eyes snapped open, wide awake.

"New Orleans?" she said dreamily.

"Same latitude and longitude as the capital of Tibet—only opposite," Danny volunteered.

"Time to go to work?" Nade said.

"Time to go back to sleep," I said. "After we check in."

"That's sweet." Nadine smiled.

In the room, still more asleep than awake, she took off her clothes, went to the window, just stood there, looking down at the side street, lost and still. I turned off the light and stood almost as still, looking at her long legs, her round heavy breasts, her dark hair hanging halfway down her back. In the dimness the streetlight's glow gave her pale skin a marble shine. I felt a terrible urgency, and didn't know what to do with it.

"Nade?"

She didn't seem to be aware of me.

I went to her, stood by her. The side street below wasn't paved and we were in the middle of the city, a neighborhood that went back more than a hundred years. I felt like somebody was watching us from the street, but saw no one. It felt like some old man with gray hair and ashen black skin.

I took her hand and led her to the bed. She followed like a zombie. Got under the covers, closed her eyes, and her sleep again felt so heavy, made the air in the room so thick.

I went to the window again. No old man.

Then heard my name—"Jesse?"—in that old man's voice. I heard it again. I said, "What?" And there was nothing, only—a receding presence, till my sense of the old man was gone.

And then I *really* felt lost, wanted him to come back, wanted him to ask me what I was doing with my life, just so I could tell him I didn't know. Somehow it would have made me feel better to tell him that.

I lay down in my clothes and stared up at the ceiling fan. The tips of three blades reflected the street light.

N I N E *Ever Sucked on a Crab Leg?*

A small brown New York–style cockroach skitted near my beer and I snapped it, the way you shoot a marble, into the sink behind the bar. The bartender noticed and, with no change of expression, turned on the tap. The roach swirled down the drain. Nobody had a right to be surprised at the roaches in Tipitina's, what with that huge plastic cockroach, an armspread long, hanging over the front door eyeing the bar.

Beside it was a sign: EVERYTHING I LOVE IS IMMORAL, ILLEGAL, OR CAJUN.

"Somebody oughta put that in a song," Danny said.

"Somebody sure put it in all *my* songs," I said, just to say anything. All I could think of was Nadine still asleep in the hotel room—so that was what we didn't talk about. "You got a better shot at a song with that line you're trying to steal."

"I heard it right there"—Danny pointed to a corner of the bar—"and I heard that man say it"—he pointed to the bartender. The line was: "Ever sucked on a crab leg? That's what Cajun music is all about."

The bartender, who had long, dirty dark hair wrapped in a blue bandanna, managed to find a way to say it often. He'd no doubt stolen it from someone, and Danny was going to steal it from him.

"You'll never get that into a song, Danny-O, it doesn't scan."

We turned in amazement to see Nadine standing under the plastic cockroach. She wore one of those crinkly flowery things, light blue, that went from her neck to her ankles and rippled sweetly with any move she made. She looked about five years younger, happy, and more rested than I'd ever seen her.

"My music don't have to scan," Danny said without missing a beat. "It barely has to rhyme."

"It doesn't have to rhyme, but it pretty much has to scan," she says. "Throws the drummer off if it don't."

"Nade," Danny said, "I'm pleased as punch that you finished high school, or I might never have heard the word 'scan.' "

"I know. I take my responsibilities with you dropouts seriously." Then, to me: "Scoot over one."

I moved down one barstool and she sat between us.

"We're waitin' for redfish," Danny said.

"Make it three," she said to the bartender. "And a Dixie."

He brought her the beer. She took a sip.

"You back?" I said.

"For a time."

We told her the sound-check had gone all right, and that we'd made her excuses to the club, but Nade said no, she wanted to work tonight, it wouldn't be a sin.

"Think Missy'll show?" Nadine asked.

"Since I'm hoping not, she probably will."

"I *like* my mother-in-law," Nade said. "More and more."

"Weirds me out, you two liking each other lately."

"Before we got married she thought I was a whore. I didn't like that but I understood it."

"Who the hell knows *what* that woman thinks? Or even if."

"She thinks."

"Everybody thinks," Danny said.

"I think," the bartender said.

"They think they think," I said.

"They think that they hope that a wish is a thought," Danny beamed.

"E-*nough!*" Nadine laughed. But like someone on TV, not like Nadine.

"She better not call me Giuseppe, is all," I said.

I let go my Sicilian name (there are almost as many Sicilians here as there are Cajun French) and took Jesse Wales for a name when I formed my first band before I quit high school, which I did in my junior year, right around the time Danny quit his up in Lubbock. He migrated south and I migrated west to Austin, where we met up as street singers. Every time I play New Orleans I get two kinds of nervous. Musically nervous, because this is a town where a piano player has a lot to live up to—it's the town of the great Professor Longhair, who helped start all this, and Allen Touissant, Mac Rebennack, James Booker, piano-demons every one. And I get Missy-nervous, because you never knew anymore what Missy was going to do—preach, or call us all a bunch of nigger lovers, or try to convince us to have grandchildren, or just get up and dance. Ever since she'd started drinking, you couldn't tell. But at least she'd gotten tender toward Nadine—finally realized that Nadine was going to have her grandchildren one day. Usually I wouldn't call her when we were in town—she'd either see one of the club's posters, or she wouldn't. Usually, she did. So what with the piano competititon, Missy, and Nade's new condition, I wondered whether I'd be able to play worth a shit.

The bartender brought three plates of blackened redfish. Roaches or no, they made awfully good redfish at Tipitina's in those days.

After a few bites, Danny said, "You guys haven't noticed, and I'm real disappointed in you."

"Oh, we noticed," Nade shot back, "but we just didn't say."

"No, I noticed how you didn't notice. I take note of all such non-happenings." Nade and I just kept eating, let him sweat. Finally he said, "I've been keeping a secret."

Nadine pretended to choke on her food.

Danny said, "It's such a new sensation, I've been savoring every minute of it, having a great time."

"Well, now you have to tell us," Nadine said.

"Or we'll get *real* aggravated," I added.

"I know you will. You'll get harsh, and say cutting, accurate things to wound my fragile psyche. Still and all, I'm gonna keep it. But it was no fun keeping it unless you knew I was keeping it."

"Eat your redfish," Nadine said.

TEN — *Anything Can Start Anything*

Nobody loves me but my mother—and she may be jivin' too.
                                                —B.B. King

It wasn't that Nade was pretending that nothing had happened; it was like she was pretending that *this* was happening. Pretending to kid Danny, pretending to eat redfish, to dress pretty, to talk to old friends who visited with us as the club filled up. Pretending to get up on the bandstand, sing her songs, move her moves, that sweet ripply dress showing off the body she was pretending to have.

Me, I just go from place to place, play piano and sing for a hundred people here, two–three hundred there. My job is to make them crazy for a little while, and they appear to need that mightily. But for the rest of my life—stuff happens, yet not because I make it happen. It kind of happens *around* me, though also it doesn't feel like it could be happening if I wasn't there. Nadine wouldn't be going through this stuff in this way if she couldn't depend on me

55

watching her this hard. Like: If it didn't register on me, she couldn't keep it for herself. She knew I was hurting and fearful—I know she knew. But it wasn't that she was trying to hurt me; it was that how *much* I hurt, how much I was baffled proved to her how real her feelings were, and *that* gave her a queer kind of courage. There don't seem to be any love songs about this sort of thing.

In the movies, everybody is always *doing* stuff. In my life, people seem to be *being* stuff, and the doing just sort of collects around that. Even Danny, opening all those little doors—it was less like he was "doing" it than that he was pushed by something inside him that was as strange to him as it was to us.

And Missy that night—did she come to the gig "of her own free will," as they say, or because she'd put on that silly purple Mardi Gras dress, with its outsize collar, its wide sleeves and stiff folds; and that thick-chained necklace with its heavy black cross; had the outfit kind of walked *her* into the club? She'd dressed like that to be something, not to do something—but there was no one she could be it with but me, so that involved going through certain motions which, especially after a few drinks, she had no idea about.

She came in before the first set, sober or thereabouts. In that getup and that blue beehive hairdo she looked like some country-western torch singer the Grand Ole Opry had long forgotten.

We stood about an arm's length apart. No hugs. Stubborn, tough Missy. On her own now, since Daddy "drove himself to Heaven"—which was how she put his car wreck. She'd come to see her son in Hell.

"I can't ever get used to how this is what you *do*" was the first thing she said. "When you gonna grow up?"

She often said that, and I never knew what to say back. I never could quite get it together to tell her that what I do ain't so different in one way, one rule is the same, night-life or day-life: That, whether you pay the cover or you're on the guest list, there's a bouncer at the door. Whether you came to play, came to drink, came to dance, whether you're on the make or on the run or on your night off, there's a bouncer at the door, and if you go over a certain line he'll be all over you, and he won't ask why you came, where you came from, or whether you ever grew up.

"Can I get you a drink, Missy?"

"Already done!"

Nadine had come up behind me with a daiquiri, Missy's steady bar drink. The theory was that if we bought the drinks we could more or less control how far she'd go. Sometimes it worked and sometimes not. The women looked each other up and down in their head-to-toe dresses, Nadine's a genteel hippie, Missy's a Scarlett O'Hara reject.

"Well, don't you look a lady!" Missy said.

"We've added impersonations to the act," said Nade. "You look real sweet, Missy."

"I look old and sinful, like I am."

We sat down at a table by the bandstand.

"*Well*—least you two're well suited," Missy said. We rolled our eyes. We'd heard this rap before. It was designed to start a riot. "Ain't nobody gonna marry white trash *but* white trash, 'cause ain't nothin' lower than white trash. Niggers ain't even lower. 'Cause at least a nigger's a nigger. White trash gotta pretend to *be* a nigger to be anything a-tall. *That's* what ya'll do for a *livin'*, and here you got a room half-full a niggers to watch you pretend to be them. It's the damnedest thing."

I hated for her to use that word, and I knew the best thing was just to let it pass, but I couldn't help myself, had to say, "I been listening to that music from the cradle, same as they have; it's as much a part of me as of anyone."

"I happened to be present at that cradle, and you were listening to *hymns*, I'll testify. And the Arthur Godfrey radio program. Now he had an occasional, well-*behaved* nigger—"

"Dammit, Missy"—she got me—"will you stop using that word around here. Might get us all killed."

"That," Nade said, "is the general idea."

"Well, *I'd* go to Heaven!" Missy said.

"*So—would—I*," said Nadine.

Their eyes locked and Missy got it.

"Why, *child!*"

Missy's eyes teared up. Nadine beamed at her.

"I'm so glad for you, baby."

Tenderly Nadine said, "But I *don't* think Jesus would use that word, Missy."

"*He* can do what-all He wants—He's God, ain't He?"

We couldn't help but laugh. That was pure Missy.

She nodded in my direction and said to Nadine, "The question is—any hope for this one?"

"You tell me," Nade said, "he's more yours than mine."

I said, "He's more mine than anybody's—"

"—so you *say*—" Nade cut in.

"—and there are certain kinds of hope—"

"—you belong to Jesus *too*, Jesus or—"

"—he ain't interested in."

"—Satan, one or the other, and—"

"Nade—"

"—*you've always known it,* just like me! I know—"

"—believe what you want, all you want, but—"

"—you KNOW!"

"—DON'T fucking PREACH at me, EVER!"

Missy's hand whipped out, but she was slowing with age, I caught it by the wrist mid-swing, and held it there over the table as both women looked at me in alarm and surprise. My face must have been some study. I said very slowly, "If that was meant to be any more than a love-tap, Mama, let's all be glad it didn't happen."

"I—won't hear such language," Missy said into her daiquiri.

"Then go home while you can still drive."

"You don't want me here?"

"I didn't say that."

"You're all I got."

I was still clutching her wrist. I brought it slowly toward me and kissed her on the palm of her hand. Then gave the spot where I'd kissed a little flick of my tongue and let go her wrist.

She gave me a brief brush with her fingertips on my chin.

"Love-tap," she said.

"Time to go to work," I said to Nade.

ELEVEN *Ain't Got* *No Home*

I got up there and plucked a couple of chords as a call to the band and a signal to the sound man to turn down the juke. Cigarette smoke had already thickened the air, the tables were full, the bar was shoulder-to-shoulder with people committed to being crazy at least one night a week. Werewolves, Little Lee called them.

They weren't children, either. Average age was probably late twenties, but there were plenty in their mid-thirties, some older still. A gritty bunch, dressed in all colors and several styles, they had a heavy air, as though a night in a joint like this wasn't just supposed to be something on its own but was supposed to make up for something else, something promised but not delivered, something lost without ever having been found or given or earned, some spooky unspoken yearning. That made some people push the night further and further into the morning.

They were *not* out for a good time—though they wouldn't admit that. But the musicians know, the musicians get high on the weirdness that fumes up from their need. I always knew, when I sat down at the piano stool, even before I hit the first key, how strong or weak was the purpose calling to me from the crowd. And in New Orleans, when the house was full, it could be so strong you shook.

It made me miss Nade so much, though she was right there— miss how we used to feel this together and meet it together.

She tapped the mikes to make sure they were still on. Little Lee and Peck strapped on their guitars, and Lady Fuentes situated himself behind his drum kit. Then Nade sidled up to me on the piano stool and whispered, "You were probably right to bust me about the preaching. You'll come over or you won't, I know that. But I'm missing you bad from this side."

I didn't know what to say, just nodded. She squeezed my shoulder and went to her mike. Danny had disappeared—messing around with this "secret," if he really had one, we supposed; but that was all right, he was just going to sit in on some harmonies tonight, this crowd wouldn't have patience with much that was country-ish.

I didn't count off, didn't look around or signal, I just hit the keys and let the band fall in. Sometimes you play piano from your fingers and sometimes you play from your shoulders; sometimes you play from your chest, sometimes from your knees. It was knees and elbows and shoulders that night, not like I was playing the piano but like I was *moving* the piano, pushing it up a hill toward a music that wasn't mine, wasn't anybody's. That classic Professor Longhair left-hand bottom line, which you practically had to do at Tipitina's your first number of the night, but crashing some weird Monk-ish chords on top of it that woke that crowd up and made them turn their heads, while I bent the melody of an old New Orleans rock hit,

I got a voice
I love to sing
I sing like a girl
And I sing like a frog
I'm a lonely boy
I ain't got no home, quoting every kind of style to show I knew what I was doing, a Jerry Lee Lewis sweep up into the high notes, but ending the run on a chord that wasn't supposed to be there, except it *fit,* sweet shit, it fit, like you can throw a square block of wood into a pond but you can't tell from the splash that it's square, the ripples from the splash come out round no matter the shape of what went down. That's how I wanted those chords to fit into those blues. And Little Lee crashing his runs into mine like two stock cars racing side to side so close they bounce off each other with the sparks flying. You can't do this in Pampa. And Nade wailing wordless above it all, and I thought I heard Jesus in her wail, and He seemed to fit fine too, walking on stormy water, why not. And for just a while I thought things might be all right after all —which may be what Nade means when she says "happy."

I didn't have to look down, I could feel the people dancing through my ass, the floor vibrating up into the piano bench. And some yelled as they danced.

I had a mother down there, and a best friend with a secret, and those things felt good, too, while I was inside the music.

Finally, on a slow tune, Nadine singing, I had time to look around again, and there were Danny and Missy dancing in a little circle, she holding him at arm's length so she could look down at her feet. She danced like a little wind-up doll, stiff and bouncy. They looked a couple, of sorts, he with that charming smile and she in that ridiculous party dress, like she'd bought him for the night. (Danny had it in him to make a pretty decent living that way, now that I think of it.)

Later, on the drive back to Texas, he told me how while they were dancing Missy had said to him, "You ever notice that big shiny kitchen knife I got at home?"

"I said, 'No, Missy, not really, why you ask?'

"She said, 'I've always liked you, Danny, but I'll cut your heart out if you stand between my boy and Jesus. He's got a shot now, with that Nadine.' Then in a beat or two she said, 'I always found it hard to dislike that girl.'

"I said, 'Could have fooled me,' but she ignored that, and the tune finished and we sat down. And *Lydia* came over. Good ol' 'I-know-she's-sweet-'cause-we-fuck-all-the-same-people' famous-sentence Lydia. Lydia obviously thinks me an' Missy are, as Lydia would put it, an *item*. Which kind of titillated me some, and *certainly* titillated ol' Lydia. So Lydia sticks her tongue in my ear by way of greeting and plops down next to Missy, saying, 'I like your cross.'

"Then Lydia delicately, with the tips of her fingernails, like she was picking up a dead bird, lifts the cross from where it's resting on top of one of Missy's ample bosoms, and examines it as she's getting Missy's name, rank, and serial number. 'Jesse's *mother*! Why, Mrs. Wales! Mrs. *Andriozzi?!* Missy?' And Lydia gives me such a look. What fails to go through that woman's mind?

"Lydia meanwhile is commenting on the little green stones in Missy's cross and waxing nostalgic about something called a first communion, which I presume is a papist ritual, and which I kind of liked as a phrase 'cause it sort of assumes a whole *life* of *communing*, which is an elevated vision if I ever heard one. But suddenly Lydia says 'My *bag!*' and *runs* away.

"Before Missy can get a chance to gossip with me 'bout ol' Lydia, the woman is back with something like a sequin-covered duffel bag. 'Quite a purse,' Missy says, to say something. Lydia says,

'It's more like my portable pharmacy.' You know Lydia don't exactly *deal,* she likes to say she *shares,* and then you're expected to reimburse her. 'Out-and-out transactions are unseemly,' I seem to remember her saying once.

" 'Can I fix you up with something, honey?' Lydia is saying to Missy. I intercept this with I forget what, but Missy starts acting finicky, exactly as though Lydia is horning in on her *date.* Lydia picks this up and rolls her eyes at me. I am getting *real* uncomfortable, sitting there thinking 'Why me?' and 'The *I Ching* does not cover this.'

"Then Missy says, 'I got a nugget.'

"Lydia says, 'Can I see it?'

" 'Ain't that kind,' Missy says, 'but I sure got it. It gets golder and golder.'

" 'Well, I'd *love* to see it,' Lydia says.

" 'Danny's wantin' a nugget,' Missy says. 'He ain't got one, though, an' he can't have mine.'

"Then she looks awhile at me, and awhile at Lydia, and says, 'Know what I miss?' and Lydia obliges, 'No, Missy, what?' and Missy says, 'That . . . I never taught anybody anything. But now I got a nugget.' Saying which, Missy puts her hand on the back of my neck, digs her fingernails in, in a somewhat provocative manner, and says, 'Get me another frozen daiquiri, sugar.' Lydia is watching Missy bug-eyed by now—bless her heart, being polite is not one of that girl's problems. You and Nade up there start playing a fast song, Lydia says to *Missy,* 'Wanna dance?' Which makes me think maybe we've underestimated that girl."

A couple of beats after that was when I looked down through the sweat pouring off my forehead and saw Lydia and Missy dancing to what was coming out of my hands. Lydia in a clingy dress that was practically underwear, a cheap ring on every finger, catching a lot of light—a good dancer, has the moves; and Missy standing about three feet in front of her, watching with eyes drunk-wide like in a trance. And where Lydia shimmied her shoulders just a little and just right, Missy shook like convulsions. And where Lydia pumped her pelvis just enough, Missy grinded, pumping hip-thrusts on the upbeat, like she was trying to take a shit with her cunt. And I felt sick, sick in my hands as they hit the keys, like my hands were getting nauseous and dizzy.

But the dance floor was crowded, and where they'd been dancing on the edge of the crowd at first, they soon were in the middle and I was spared the details but just kept track of Missy's blue beehive, just one more crazy on a sweaty night. I got to playing harder. The people jumped and swayed and hollered. The smoke was thick —seemed to be rising out of everybody's hair. Bop till you drop. And they got no closing time in New Orleans.

There were two disturbances at the same time. Take it from a honky-tonk man, the first punch almost always lands on the downbeat. In perfect time. I just happened to be looking that way and saw a big fist hit a face, square on, and I couldn't hear but I felt the crunch of the nose breaking and saw blood and nose-stuff spurt while the club's two tank-sized black bouncers materialized— bouncers always seem to materialize, you never really see them coming—and pounced the guy who'd done the hitting. And I was off my bench and jumping onto the dance floor, and felt more than saw Nadine jump with me, pretty dress and all, trying to get to Missy in case the thing turned into a brawl. But Missy had already gone down.

Nadine hadn't even seen the fight, it turned out; she was jumping because she saw Missy's beehive just disappear, and then a bunch of people tripping and falling over her.

The rest of the band just kept on playing. Peck always figured that as long as firearms weren't involved, a band had no reason to quit.

By the time we got to her, Missy's head was in Danny's lap while Lydia fanned her with her hands. Missy's eyes were glazed and crossed.

"Let's get her outside," I said.

Danny and I carried her while Nadine and Lydia cleared the people away in front of us. We took her out the side door and sat her on the sidewalk, back propped against the wall. That purple dress got all bunched up around her waist, and it was weird to see her girdle—I hadn't seen a girdle in years. And how lumpy her legs were, and how thick the veins stood out. I straightened the dress, careful not to actually brush my hands against what was underneath it.

It must have been about one-thirty. The air was humid, gentle, and so sweet after the smoke inside. Missy looked at me with those crossed eyes—it would have been funny if I hadn't been scared—and she half smiled. Her eyes unglazed, uncrossed, and she said, "I'm not used to being up so late."

Then it was like Missy's face had been slapped from the inside, it bulged out, and she wrenched her head to the side and puked, spurts of the stinking stuff, and after each heave she'd gasp, "Jesus . . . *Jesus* . . . Jesus, Jesus, Jesus . . ."

And each time she said the name Nadine flinched.

T W E L V E *Missy's Nugget*

Nadine stood slowly, turned slowly, took three deliberate steps to the curb, and one more into the street. The glare of the streetlight shone through her light, crinkly dress, and her body seemed a shadow within it. She stared off away from us.

Missy spit once more, smiled weakly, said, "Jesus."

I sat beside Missy, holding her. It had been a long time since I'd touched her, much less held her. She felt so small and soft, like I could crush her hardly trying.

Danny looked from her to me with a childlike expression that asked, Is everything gonna be all right? Lydia went inside and came back with two wet washcloths. She cleaned off Missy as best she could. Nadine paid no attention. Inside the club Little Lee, with what he thought was a sense of humor, sang an old New Orleans rocker in his scratchy voice,

The worst person I know—Mother-in-law!
She worries me so—Mother-in-law!
Sent from down below—Mother-in-law! while Danny whispered to me, "Lydia must have some coke. Why don't we just rub a bit on Missy's gums, it'll be like giving her a few cups of coffee real quick—to revive her, is all."

"Just don't let on what it is."

Lydia donated it and I applied it, saying, "This'll help." And it did, it woke her up.

I helped her to her feet. She put her face close to mine—her breath smelled of vomit, it was an effort not to turn away. She whispered, so the others wouldn't hear, "You got a nugget? I got a nugget; I think if we really got unafraid—everything would be obvious to us."

"*What?*"

"I've learned something, haven't I? I have."

"I guess."

"I don't."

"Let's go back inside, Ma. Missy."

We started to go in, but Nadine still stood in the street ignoring us. I asked Danny to see to Missy and stayed with Nadine. Slowly she took off her high heels—it was like a dance step, how she raised her knee, bent her leg, reached down and slipped off each shoe, and the white lace pantyhose that made her feet look ghostly. She sat on the curb, her legs straight out in front of her, and stared at her feet.

"When I was little, they just about had to beat me to wear shoes." Then: "All I knew about Jesus, when I was little, is that He wanted me to do stuff—wear shoes and such. That's what my mother would say. And that He had long hair and wore robes—I thought he was an Indian! 'Cept He was white. And that He'd walked on water, and that He'd died awfully. And Christmas, that He'd been a little baby, and I got presents because He had, which I thought was what we were all thanking Him for. But it was a big puzzle to me, how every Sunday we'd go to church and sing songs about Him, and the preacher would tell us to be good or He'd send us down to Hell. And in Sunday school, where I never paid attention anyway. And how whenever something would go wrong, Father hitting his thumb with the hammer or stubbing his toe, or Mother exasperated with Father beyond all endurance, the venom in their voices when they's say *'Jesus!'* And every now and again I'd hear Mother gasping His name at night in their bedroom for a few moments, like she was delirious. I mean, that name just sort of burst out in all the strangest places. And how it was such a *special* name, nobody was named it that we knew—there weren't any Mexicans in Baton Rouge. And now . . . it's all come together inside me, Jesse. Like all the little separate parts inside me, that have always gone every which way, have finally run headlong into each other and joined, and wouldn't you know the name for that would be 'Jesus'?!

"I just want to go back to Baton Rouge, that old house where we never could manage to stay married, and read and read my Bible, and sing those old gospel tunes, and live forever with Jesus. I wish I could just pour the mystery of how He lives now in me, pour that into you—but I know I can't. I'm finally gonna leave you, Jesse—I'm runnin' off with *another man!*"

And she let loose a peal of sweet laughter that just stopped my heart, it was such a pretty sound.

"Runnin' off with another man, that's what I'm doin'! And He's much older than me, to boot. You jealous?"

"You bet."

Missy's nugget was sort of floating loose in my head. I was trying not to be afraid, but nothing was obvious to me.

"Yeah, well—we're still married!" She laughed. "So you can visit me and it ain't a sin. But no birth control. Talk about lookin' for God in pussy, boy, you're gonna have to take your chances from now on if you mess with me." Then it was like I wasn't there, and she said, like to herself, "The great thing is I'm just starting. I've got so much to learn about my Jesus."

She walked slowly toward me, the light behind her again, her body again a shadow within the dress.

"Take care of our Danny," she said. "I think he sort of trained me for this, opening all those weird doors of his all the time. *He* don't even know what they're for, poor thing."

She took my hand, squeezed it.

"I'll be waiting for you, this side, Jesse."

It was after two. Little Lee had called a break. Tipitina's was emptying out some, about half the people that were there before the fight. Nade and I went in. Missy was sitting with Lydia at our table. Nadine joined them. I went to the bar where Danny was standing.

As I walked toward him I looked at him hard for the first time since Pampa. Lanky, in clean, faded, sharp-pressed jeans, a white shirt, with a string tie that had a clasp in the shape of an armadillo. The shot glass looked tiny in his long bony fingers.

"The womenfolk are sure giving us a run these days," he said.

"They're due, I guess."

"As Nade would say, who ain't?"

I got a beer, just a calm cold beer, and stood by him, wondering whether to tell him what Nadine had said about him, deciding against it.

"Naw," Danny said, "the time of experimentin' is *over* and the time of livin' it out has come. If you ain't got nothin' t'live out, you'll live *that* out."

"That the theory of the evening?"

"It'll do."

"Think we're gonna end up with Jesus?"

"He's been runnin' after us all our lives, and He ain't caught us yet, has He?"

"I don't know," I said. I nodded toward Nadine. "I think maybe He's got ahead of us, and left us behind."

"Then I'd just as soon stay left."

"Me, too. But Nade—"

"Judge not, that ye be not judged," Danny said, lifting his glass.

"Hell, she judges *us* all the time!"

"Well—she's a woman."

We laughed a quiet laugh at that, and he clicked his whiskey glass against my beer mug. And then said a thing he'd said often:

"Ye shall know the truth, and it shall upset ye."

T H I R T E E N *A Walking Secret*

I can't see, it's hard to feel—
I think his magic
Might be real.
    —Robbie Robertson

The last set Nadine and I ever played was mostly slow, intent, old blues, spiked with my freaky chords and Little Lee doing bottle-neck slides on his guitar that sounded like babies crying.

Nade went deep into some old, old stuff—"Oh I wish/That I was a headlight/Shinin' on the east-bound train," sang it like a prayer.

Nadine said she noticed Danny's secret as soon as he walked in. I didn't notice him till she pointed him out. I don't know what I expected Henry Reed to look like, but I didn't expect a fat man.

A fat man of about my height in a very expensive white suit, an absolutely blue tie, and boots that might as well have been made of money—yellow-golden boots of first-class ostrich. He had thick red hair with no gray, which Nadine, with her beauty-parlor exper-tise, said was dyed. He was probably in his mid-fifties, but it was hard to tell. He smiled like a used-car salesman, and the flash and ease of his smile distracted you from his eyes—glittery, hard blue eyes that were the most direct, the hardest to meet, that I have ever seen. And the biggest hands. If he wore mittens they'd be the size of tennis rackets. Enormous, pudgy, white, manicured; and if he touched you, if he put his hand on your shoulder or your arm or your knee to make a point, it was like being touched by living steel. The sense of strength in even his slightest touch was shocking. The *roundest* man, roundest body, roundest face, roundest hands, I'd ever seen—fat, big, but without the sense of anything added or wasted somehow.

We were dying to hear what-all everybody was saying at that

table as we finished the set. On the drive back to Texas, Danny told me: "Lydia takes care of the amenities, oozing on about how great Henry's suit was and how great it was that he's so *big* and what a tie—like that. She loves that huge gold ring of his, and he really surprises me, he keeps this big hi-y'all grin on his face and asks about her jewelry, and then the moment comes I'm waiting for, she asks if he 'needs anything.' He says, 'Coke—a-Cola,' and laughs and she joins in, for want of something better to do. Meanwhile Missy sort of wakes up. She's been sitting there half-asleep with her eyes open. And she smiles real pretty and says, 'I know who you are.' 'I expect you might,' Henry says. 'You're the Sandman,' Missy says. And she sings 'Mr. Sandman . . . bring me a dream.' And he reaches over and gives her a big hug—of course, Henry can't give any hug *but* a big hug—and I'm sitting there sure that I missed something. Which is how I usually feel around Henry. 'Here, turn around,' Henry tells her, 'I'll work your back.' 'Goody,' Missy says. I swear. And Lydia says, 'I'm next.' And it's the laying on of hands at Tipitina's. Henry always gives the vibe like he's doing just what he ought to. So it seems like he was a masseur or something and they'd made appointments in advance to meet him in this honky-tonk at three in the morning. You should have seen the expression on Missy's face."

But I had. I was just going through the motions now up there on the bandstand, my attention was on the table—and Missy looked like she'd died and gone to Heaven.

"And," Danny said, "Henry's just chattering while he massages, about having 'a group' to tend to in New Orleans, and glad his business segued with our being here so he could meet 'Danny's famous friends—famous to Danny, anyway,' and saying all of this with a lot of thick Texas good-'ol-boy chuckles. 'And what group is that?' Lydia chirps—thought it was a band, I guess, and he was a manager of some sort. But Henry says, 'Oh, just a little ol' research group.' 'Business?' 'The business of lifting the veil. The business of breaking the seal.' 'Don't do *that!*' Missy laughs. Which is when you guys said your thank-you-very-muches to the club and sat down."

Henry was working on Lydia's back by then. And she had the same expression Missy'd had. "When this man touches you, you stay touched," she said.

"You next?" Henry said to Nadine. First thing he ever spoke to her.

"No, thank you," Nadine said. He made no such offer to me or Danny, or any man I ever heard of.

"Are you a chiropractor?" Lydia said.

"No," Henry said, "chiropractors work with the muscles, I work with the cells." And left it at that.

It was hitting on three-thirty; most everybody had gone home. The jukebox was on. The band packed their gear and loaded it in Little Lee's van. He and the guys went back to the hotel. Various hangers-on stopped at the table saying they liked the set or whatever. I was wet through with sweat, so was Nadine. It was time to get some food, take a shower, calm down, beer down, pot down, and be asleep around dawn.

Henry bided his time till the small talk had played itself out. Fourish, we all walked out into the sweet air.

"May I make y'all some breakfast?" Henry said, courtly as hell.

"You *cook?!*" Danny said.

"A man should be able to do one complex thing very well, and one humble thing. With these two keys, anything is possible, though I confess I am greedy for skills." He started off, walking as though we were supposed to follow him, and we just naturally did, while he said sort of to himself, "Greed in anything is a flaw. I am flawed, I am flawed."

"Well, I'm starvin' " is what Lydia had to add.

A huge—I mean huge—white camper was parked down the block. None of us were prepared for Henry unlocking the camper door and stepping inside. The camper dipped low on its springs as he barely squeezed through its narrow door. We followed him inside. It was one luxurious camper. Nicer than any hotel room we'd ever been able to afford, with chairs that seemed to hug you when you sat in them. Henry took his jacket off and started working with the ingredients that were already all laid out in the camper's fridge. Eggs, vegetables, cheese, spices—omelet stuff. He turned on the coffee maker and the smell was so rich it revived you all by itself.

"Can I help?" Nadine said.

"But you're my guest. Please simply let it be done."

Sometimes it sounded like Henry was translating in his head from another language.

"I guess it's time to talk about the peregrination of what-nots," Danny chirped, just to fill the silence.

"You're *not* my guest. Pour the coffee." Like Henry was talking to a busboy. And Danny hopped to it. I'd never seen the like. Nadine's face darkened at the sight.

Missy was over by the stereo going through the albums. They were those compilation albums they sell at K-Marts, thinly pressed reissues with some over- or underdressed girl smiling on the cover. She put one on by 101 Strings or something, and they led off with the theme from *Gone With the Wind.*

Danny served up the coffee nervously, filling the cups too high so they dripped as he handed them around. Then he tried to rub the spots out of the rug with paper towels.

"There's a rug cleaner in that cabinet," Henry said.

Danny went at those spots like there'd be hell to pay if he didn't, grinning up at us as he scrubbed.

The silence was weird. It wasn't *technically* silence. Lydia talked through it all, and *101 Strings Play the Academy Awards* went on and on, but it was like that was happening on the surface somewhere and the rest of us were underwater. Lydia chattered commentary on the record. "Oh, I just love that movie, the part where . . ." and Henry was attentive to her as he cooked. "Oh yes, that was lovely, and I liked the part when . . ." But he never looked at her. When he'd look up from his preparations it would be to me, hard in the eyes, or to Danny or Nadine, and it was like we were passing something around with our eyes. He'd pass it to me and I'd hit it over to Nadine and she'd get rid of it fast back to me or to Danny and then it would return to Henry, and it was like the air was webbed with our attentions. That big camper got small fast, thickened with the aromas of Henry's cooking, egg-heavy, with a garlic haze, and lots of little herb scents that came and went in the air, riding cheese smells and bell peppers and asparagus and salsas. While Missy, half-asleep but standing, gently and obliviously conducted 101 Strings.

"You getting any exercise, boy?" Henry said to Danny.

"Henry thinks I'm too fat," skinny Danny said.

"Henry thinks you're too frail," Henry said. Sharp to Nade: "If you *really* want to take care of him, see he stops eating junk." Back to Danny: "But I've mentioned it twice to you now. That's it. It can be unhealthy, bad for the blood, to say some things more than twice. Every truth—or rather, since on our level truth isn't possible, every insight—has its numbers. It can be zero—some things should never be said. It can be a thousand. Some things have to be repeated over and over. Varies with each speaker. Say a thing even once too often, it affects the body badly. Way too often, could be fatal. On the other hand," he laughed, "say it not enough and it's not really *said* a-tall. *Number* is really *somethin'*, ain't it? These here omelets are just about done."

"How do you know the number?" Danny asked, with a hint of awe in his voice that Nadine just beamed disapproval of.

"Your body knows," Henry said. "But don't ask me how to listen to your body till you've dispensed with those entertaining substances of y'all's—nor till you've been exercising steady for about a year. Which brings us back to the body. Aren't circles lovely? Everything turns into one, you follow it far enough."

Henry eyed me, then Nade, smiling with every tooth.

"Of course, too," he said, "if you exercise only to shape your body to your will—and this is what is done with muscle building and aerobics—then your body's only able to speak through and of your will, which means it won't tell you the truth."

He smiled at our total incomprehension.

"What the hell," he laughed. "If it was easy, anyone could do it."

101 Strings went from "Moon River" to "Lara's Theme," with Lydia and Missy ignoring us and giving each other a running commentary on the movies, talking Audrey Hepburn, talking Julie Christie.

Henry passed out the omelets himself. Lydia bit into hers first and declared it "dreamy," and for once "dreamy" was the right word for something. You took some in your mouth and you couldn't quite believe how good it was: I'd never felt so many tastes come together in one bite.

"You're an artist, sir," Nade said, mocking his formality.

"Ah, you're the artists. I'm a—salesman," he said.

"I noticed the dealer's plates," she said.

I hadn't. I looked over at Danny and he smiled sheepish. An RV dealer!

From Lubbock, no less, with outlets in Amarillo, Waco, and Wichita Falls, soon fixing to appear in his own TV spots. Lubbock was a good twenty hours from New Orleans in an RV. That must have been some "little ol' research group."

We ate mostly in silence, except for Missy humming "Chim Chim Cheree" along with the strings. And then she just curled up in that chair and fell instantly asleep, like a cat. And Lydia took one look at her and did the same. She had started to roll a joint, but set it down beside her without finishing.

"That is good," Henry said, as he put blankets over them, "this is fine. Now there's not a Western mind in the room."

"Did you—did you put something—" Rage rose in me. He was big, all right, but Nade and I between us could have handled him.

"Their pulses, you'll find, are in perfect time, perfect sleep."

"I'm asking you—"

"Jesse!" Danny said. "He wouldn't do that."

"Who the fuck knows what he'll do?"

"I promise you," Henry said, "they ate exactly what you ate. I admit I—hypnotized them, but just a little; they didn't need much, they were very tired."

"I didn't see you hypnotize anybody," I said.

"With the proper skills, you can hypnotize certain types silently, or from other rooms, other countries even."

"Then why don't you rule the world?"

"Because I'm not a fool, first off. Second off, nobody has *that* much skill. And a little power over one's immediate surroundings is all that is needed for the Work."

"*What* work?!" Nade hissed. "I smell Satan in here."

"Fee, fi, fo, fum, I smell the blood of a Christ-i-an."

"Damn right," she said.

"Why haven't you hypnotized us?" I said.

"Doubt very much I could. Y'all are stronger than you know. See, most people are hypnotized already—"

"I hear *that*," Danny said.

"—they walk around hypnotized all the time. Not much work to hypnotize 'em a little more. You-all have *intent*—of a kind. Anyway"—he smiled—"equals don't behave that way with each other."

We all sat there eyeing one another. I believed him. I could feel that Nadine did, too, though she didn't want to. Still, she got up and arranged Missy's black cross over her sleeping heart.

"Feel better?" Henry said to her.

"Not much," she said.

It got light out. I could smell my own dried sweat. From a couple of yards away I could smell Nadine's. After a gig she always smelled like a smoldering piñon log that's been soaked in cheap perfume. It used to make me crazy for her. But our smells mixed with the now-stale cooking smells, the smells of the RV's rugs and plastics, and Henry's thick aftershave. It made a soup just this side of sick. Henry started brewing some more coffee, and all those smells sank beneath the coffee smell.

"Now what?" Nade said.

It was like we were here for a meeting and we all felt it. Official business.

"Danny has got to decide," Henry said. "He's—"

"*Who* made *that* rule?" Nade blurted.

"—how, though not why, we're here."

Poor Danny looked confused and worse.

Henry, facing Nadine: "The rules aren't made or interpreted. They *are*, and either they're known or sensed or not. Known or sensed, either they're observed or not. And whether or not you observe the rules, they observe you."

This last with quite a smile.

"How come it's okay to ask questions *now?*" Danny asked. Then, to us: "It's not usually okay."

"One of you couldn't properly remember an answer. Between the three of you there's just enough real memory capability to make it worthwhile answering."

"Say *what?!*" Nade said. "I remember everything."

"I even remember most things," I volunteered.

"Memory is a map. A map's no good without coordinates. And it's worse than useless with only one thing marked on it. At your stage you just remember how you felt about something. Big deal, if you'll excuse the expression."

Nade said, "It's a big deal to *me*—"

"I'm glad."

"—and none of *your* damn business."

Danny sat on the floor with his lanky legs all bunched up, his arms around his knees.

"Well," he said, "what did you mean about Western minds?"

"You've been changed," Henry said. "We don't—"

"Who's we?" Nade grouched.

"—know why. Perhaps it's your music. Without having consciously participated in the Work, you have done part of the Work. An important part. But the difficulty is—you haven't done the first part. You've done a part somewhere in the middle. Now you've got to go backward and forward at the same time. Might not be possible. Might be you're stuck all your lives at this stage of the Work—'cause you haven't done it consciously—which would be a damn shame. Still, if anyone can pull if off, y'all can.

"Your minds—are at a point both before and after the West. Both more primitive and more advanced." He laughed. "If *half* what this skinny fool tells me is true, y'all have been opening doors right and left, at will, and more or less straight. Hallucinogens don't count in this sort of Work—though they may count in other sorts."

"That's just Danny's crazy way, *he* does that, it's—a game," I said.

"He does? It is? Number again. Very important. *That* sort of power comes in threes, most usually. Twos, very rarely—both need what I call 'direct access.' In ones, rarer still. My own most powerful numbers are fours and sevens—though"—he twinkled—"I can do the ones when I must."

The weird thing was it made a kind of sense. It was like we understood it without knowing how, or even what.

"Your pain," he said, "is to be caught in the West without a Western mind. Now, there ain't no *where* else to go, but there's another *how* to go. The doors y'all have been opening—the problem is, they've been shut, in the West, for a long time, and *forcibly*. Intentionally. The Church—*not* Jesus, that ol' door-opener—started it, the nations and the *ist* people, the capitalists, the Marxists, took it up. One task of the Work is to open as many of the doors as possible—once a door is open it tends to stay slightly ajar; sort of ventilate this world with the Other World. *Otherwise*—this old world ain't gonna make it. Politics don't matter a shit, if *this* isn't done."

"I don't understand a word, thank God," Nade said.

"You do, or you wouldn't be angry. *This* man"—he nodded toward me—"has direct access. In spades. I suspected as much, but had to see for myself." To Nade: "So do you—which I didn't suspect."

"I am gettin' *real* aggravated," Nade said. "Access to *what?*"

"What about me?" Danny said.

"You don't want it."

"I *do*. I don't."

We all laughed quietly at that. But Nade got right back on Henry.

"Direct access to *what?* Be fucking specific. All these fucking things could mean fucking anything. You don't sell RVs this way, I'll bet."

"The man who knows won't make a precise statement. He will make general statements, so as to allow for individual interpretation."

"But shouldn't it be just the opposite?" Danny asked.

"Not if you wish to survive," Henry said darkly.

"What about . . . Jesus?" Nade said.

"I've said all I *ever* say 'bout that ol' boy!"

"Really?" Nade said, her gray eyes sparkling with something darker now. The eyes of a woman who'd eat flies for her god.

And I felt the cloud of flies within her. Felt if she opened her mouth and screamed, the room would fill with them. We'd all be driven mad by them, even Henry. Who felt the moment too—tensed, he waited to see would she go over the line, that line that somewhere in her long sleep she had decided to cross back over so she could be with me just one more time.

But Henry suddenly looked at me, eyes cutting through me—and I saw myself seeing Nadine's flies. And that I had, and that I could, finally *got* to me, and frightened me good.

What had I seen them *with?* I asked myself—and it was like a hole had opened inside me.

The moment passed. Henry turned to Nadine.

"Have we lost you, then?" he said.

"How can you lose what you never had?"

He sighed, and for the first time looked quite tired.

"Then we won't be four. And these men and I can't be three. But we will be friends."

"But . . ." Danny stuttered, utterly disappointed.

"For this work, in this time, no group can be all one sex or the other. That's a change. No one knows why, nor from where the change came, but the Work is falling to pieces in many places because many Workers have not realized this. Ahhhhhh . . . so . . . Well, you're on your own."

Outside the light was bright, and the city had started its round, that workaday world that did not care about any of this, and maybe was right not to. We drank some more of that thick, scented coffee. Nadine went to the john down the narrow hall. I heard her urine whisper with the water. But she stayed awhile after that, mumbling. Prayer? I expect so.

She came back and Danny was next.

"Don't look for no doors in there," Henry chuckled.

We didn't meet each other's eyes as we listened to his strong bubbly sound. By the time he got back I was dying to go, but there was something too public about it, with the sound so clear, I just clamped down and wouldn't. Sat real still.

"Well," Henry said. "It was worth the try. Nothing like this is ever wasted."

"You're just gamin' with our heads," Nadine said.

"Some call *that* teaching." He nodded toward Danny. "*This* cripple here certainly does."

"You son of a BITCH."

"Nadeeeeeeeeeen!"

Danny, who was always pale, was now so pale he looked dead. Nadine was pale too, anger-pale. I don't know what I was. I had to pee.

Danny's lips trembled as he said, "This—is only—a test. For the next sixty seconds your station will be testing the emergency broadcast system. We repeat. This is only a test."

"I meant no offense," Henry said.

"Not much," said Nade. "My Danny's worth ten of you."

"That's even true," Henry said. "Any one of you is. Not being humble, it's just a fact."

"Shit," I said.

"And Danny's better at being a cripple than just about anybody I've ever seen. And he's got a couple of first-class crutches."

I thought Nadine was gonna swing on him—and, of course, I'd have had to back her play.

"You're way out of line, man," I said.

"Intentions don't matter anymore," he said. "It's where the energy is coming from that matters. That—and the connections."

As though *that* had anything to do with anything.

"You don't know anything about us," Nade said.

"I know where your energy is coming from. That's more than you know.

I had to pee worse and worse.

"I love Danny," Henry said. "You think I should respect his personality, but I respect his *function*. It's through the weakest ones that the connections are most often made. The raw, other-worldly energy reaches them first. They have less structure to resist it with."

Danny stood slowly, and shook out his long feathery black hair with a gesture oddly womanlike. He went over to Nadine and pulled her to her feet. They looked hard into each other. Then he hugged her, hard. At first she didn't hug back, but then she did, and fiercely, a long, slow hug, the two of them rocking back and forth slowly, as though they were saying good-bye at an airport, like they were a brother and a sister who'd shared the same room many nights and now were going off in different directions, for keeps. And watching them holding each other, I saw how much brother and sister they were, more than friends even—the way brothers and sisters, no matter how different, seem sometimes to be carrying the same message.

They let go of each other and smiled into one another's eyes, the smile of people who don't have to explain *anything* to each other.

"Well!" Henry said. "You've gotten *enough* outta me! You think *I've* been doin' all this?! You think *I'm* in control here? Y'all sucked it right outta me, you're such a powerful three. This had to be"—he faced Nadine—" 'fore you went all the way with Jesus. Now we'll never forget each other."

"The way you talk," Nade said, but without anger now, "it's like we're part of some big conspiracy, and that you know it and we don't. I'll tell you straight out, Henry, I think that's *got* to be crap."

"Nothing so coherent as a conspiracy," Henry chuckled. "Just —a Way. Somebody once called it The Fourth Way. But, man, my body has been telling me for ten minutes to stop speaking. *You!*"

I almost did in my pants. His eyes were two blue fires cutting through me.

"This has all happened—because of you."

" 'Scuse me," I said, and half-stumbled out the door. Danny followed me. I peed out there in the broad daylight, not caring who saw, on the RV's left back wheel.

It was a long hard piss, and it shined that big hubcap good.

F O U R T E E N   *Stop Don't Go Any Further*

"You okay?" Danny said.

"*You* okay?"

"Hell, no."

We walked slowly down the street. Stopped in front of a liquor store's plate-glass window. In its transparent reflection, in which so many details disappeared, I looked so much younger—just a stocky, long-haired dude in jeans and a white shirt, my face lost in a display ad for cheap champagne: a fancy black woman holding up a long-stemmed glass and inviting me to step through the window.

What the *hell* had that man meant, "because of you"? And why did I believe every last fucking word he'd said, without really understanding a one?

I said, "Let's get us a couple of beat-up guitars and go down to Vieux Carré and street-sing all day for spare change."

That's how we'd met, in Austin, two runaways (except that no one was running after us).

"That's almost a good idea," Danny said. "We'd be local color."

"Is that what we were back then?"

"We were disturbing the peace back then, as I remember."

"*Somebody's* been disturbin' it, that's for sure."

Meanwhile, as Nade told us later, she and Henry just stared at each other. Suddenly Henry threw his head back and laughed a deep, reckless laugh.

"It's so wonderful," he said to her, "to be with people with whom I don't have to be afraid of going too far."

"You're a damn fool, Henry Reed."

"Ain't that a fact?! Now that we're friends—"

"Now that we're *what?*" Nade laughed.

"Oh, we're friends, all right. *You* know that. We can say *anything* to each other. That's about as good a definition of friendship as I know."

"Wouldn't it help if this 'anything' included some stuff that made some sense?"

But Henry was right, he was a friend to each of us, from then on—though we'd rarely meet, and the four of us together never would again. But Henry would visit Nadine in Baton Rouge sometimes on one of his New Orleans runs, and she'd welcome him, and they'd argue and enjoy it. And Danny or me would use one of his RVs for a motel room whenever we gigged in Lubbock, which he'd chosen as his base because there's more UFO sightings up around there than just about anywhere.

Danny and I were sitting on the curb at the end of the block when the huge white RV pulled slowly up to us, Henry beaming at the wheel. Lydia was in the shotgun seat, daintily snorting some coke from her pinky nail. Nade stood behind Henry, almost smiling.

The RV stopped a few feet from us. Henry was grinning ear to ear. Danny grinned back. I didn't know what all that grinning was about, but it felt all right. I thought to myself, Where does it say that *I've* got to understand anything.

Nadine got out of the trailer, and Missy followed, rubbing her eyes. Nadine's long crinkly light-blue dress looked too bright and slight in daylight. While Missy's purple monstrosity shone in all the wrong places, so much more frayed than it had seemed in the half-light of the club.

"You gonna be okay to drive, Mama? Missy."

"Boy, I feel like I've slept for a week. I was plannin' on callin' in sick this morning, but I guess I can still make it to work if I hustle my bustle."

"You turning into night people?"

"Beats *me* with a stick. 'Member how I used to always say that? And your daddy never got the hint." She laughed.

Not understanding was sort of becoming my forte that morning.

"I'm fine, don't worry," she said. Then she recited a little rhyme she used to sing to me when I was small: "Love ya once, love ya twice, love ya more'n beans 'n' rice."

She kissed me on the cheek and walked off jaunty down the street toward her old green Dodge.

Henry opened his side window.

"We're born to lose, y'all."

"Speak for yourself!" Nade said.

"Just let's don't lose by omission, let's lose by excess." Then: "I'm gonna drive your pharmaceutical friend home. I'll be thinkin' of you!"

A big smile and away they went. We watched till the RV slowly, very slowly, turned the corner.

"Think he's gonna boff her?" Nadine said.

"Boff?" I said.

"Boff," she said. Then to Danny: "Don't look so panicky."

"Know what *I* want to do?" Danny said. "Just walk. All day. Till we can't walk no more."

"Walkin' the dog," I said.

The weird thing is, we did. Not only weren't we tired but we were electric. Lying down wouldn't have done a bit of good. So we walked and chewed over everything that had and hadn't happened, walking over to St. Charles, taking a trolley up past Tulane, then taking the trolley down again to Canal, with all its shoppers and workers and traffic, the day people who think they own the world.

And then walking into and around Vieux Carré, the oldest part of the city, drinking coffee in plastic cups as we walked, over to the Mississippi, away from the Mississippi, past the tourist-ridden streets of the Quarter down to Esplanade. Weathered wood-frame houses that have been there a hundred years, old black people sitting on the porches, looking like they've been there even longer. Nade walked in the middle, usually, and sometimes I walked with my arm around her waist and sometimes Danny did. Three only children.

We were following Danny's lead, it was Danny's walk, and Danny went just any old way. When we were gallivanting on Poland Avenue I got a little nervous because of this weird thing near there on St. Claude. In the middle of the block, embedded in the old cracked sidewalk, are tiles that spell out: STOP DON-T GO ANY FURTHER. It's real old, maybe a hundred years, maybe more. Half the tiles of the "STOP" are gone, and most of the *U* in the "FURTHER," but the rest is clear there at your feet as you decide whether or not to step over it and wonder what it could possibly have meant, and when. Nobody knows that I ever heard of. I used to love it when I was a kid, wander all the way there just to see it and dare myself to step over it, and dare my friends.

Of course, everybody steps over it every time.

Later, back in the Quarter, we sat on a bench eating oyster po'boys. Danny said, "I want to know what he knows."

"You don't even know *that* he knows," Nade said, "much less what."

"All you know," I said, "is that he's weird even by our standards—and we don't have any."

"Well, who *else* you ever met that's older than us *and* weirder than us."

"Bo Diddley."

We were tired, sure, but with a light, almost weightless fatigue that instead of dragging you down made you feel like if a strong-enough breeze gusted up you'd just float off on it, loving every second. My legs were stretched out straight in front of me, and in my thighs and in my calves my muscles spasmed in little spurts all on their own, as though in each leg these tiny snakes would suddenly come alive and wriggle a lick and die all over each other.

Like if I stood up and shook, a whole mess of them would fall from my pant legs.

I took Nadine's hand and put it on my right thigh so she could feel my spasm-snakes. She said "Oh!" and took her hand off fast.

"Feel of mine," she said.

Her muscles were crawling too. She put her hand on Danny's leg then, and he on hers, and she put her other hand on mine, and it was like I could feel Danny's trembling through her, and we all started laughing and couldn't stop, not for tears, not for shortness of breath, and I thought of that Woody Guthrie line *Everybody might be just one big soul . . .*

And the word "soul" made me vaguely uneasy.

Meandering around the Quarter, Nadine finally asked Danny why he took that "cripple" shit off Henry. I remember how Danny stopped in his tracks, dug his hands into his pockets, hunched his bony shoulders—and how, hunched like that, with his long straight blue-black hair, I thought for the first time how much Danny looked like some bright-eyed human crow.

His eyes shone with a deep, troubled excitement. But he said nothing, just looked back and forth from Nade to me, for the longest time. His eyes fluttered a little, his mouth twitched just a bit—I thought he was talking loudly to himself the whole time, while we shifted our weight from foot to foot, looked at each other, at him, not knowing if this was about to be a joke or a speed rap.

But it wasn't about to be anything at all. That nervous silence was his whole answer. When he seemed satisfied that it had gone on long enough, he turned and walked on ahead of us back where we'd just come from.

FIFTEEN *After Last Call*

Late that night, in bed with Nade, she and I naked, staring up at the ceiling fan—daylight just kind of soaked into that room's bright woods like a syrup.

"You asleep yet?" I said without looking at her.

"You know I'm not."

"I'm a little scared," I said.

"You too?"

"I'm not even real sure why."

"Henry?"

"Everybody."

"Yeah," she said. "That man—not him or even what he said, so much as just that he showed up at all."

We watched the ceiling fan. I thought of—was it yesterday? the day before? You lose track of the days in this road life. I thought of how I'd felt the presence of that old man underneath our window, and how he'd said my name.

"What are you gonna do, Nade?"

"Go back to Baton Rouge and pray my ass off."

A little later I asked her, "You really think you conceived back in Pampa?"

"We'll know soon enough, won't we."

And a little later she said,

"Honey, I can't sleep." It was one of the things she said sometimes that meant she wanted to make love. It wasn't the thought of having a kid that turned me off—I figured if she wanted to take that chance, I had to back her play. It was just that, even though my eyes wouldn't close, I didn't think I could move.

"I'm dead to it," I said, "but if you get me going, I'm willin'."

"Just real easy," she whispered, "real easy, baby," and said that over and over softly as slowly she lifted herself up, bent her head down, and put me, little limp me, into her mouth, gently, ever so. Like a mama will put her tiny infant's hand into her mouth, right up to the elbow. And slowly I got bigger in her loving mouth, and finally, just as slowly, I laid her on her back, long Nadine, and then, inside her, we hardly moved at all, like dancers after last call, the way they hold each other on the very last dance of all, kind of leaning on one another, not dancing but swaying. So we swayed lying down, and I came in a slow sweet spill, and felt her feeling every ripple of it, and she came back, shuddering just there and nowhere else, and I could feel it all, and she made only the merest moan deep down, it never left her throat.

"That's how it'll be when we're old," Nadine whispered. "Oh, I loved that."

S I X T E E N   *The Hall of Some Luxurious French King*

My mind is like a row boat
On the stormy sea—
It's with me right now,
In the morning where will it be?
          —Bessie Smith

I don't remember much of the dream I woke from, all I remember is a youngish-looking old woman I found in the bushes in a shallow ditch, dead-stiff; and sometime in that dream I heard a man somewhere nearby, he was yelling, "Not my eyes! Not my eyes!"

So it was *real* weird when Nadine, feeling me awake, wakes herself, says, shaky, "I was just in this extravagant, pretty, pretty room. A real big room with high ceilings, a castle room, like the hall of some luxurious French king. And the light is the most perfect and beautiful thing, but it's not from flames or electricity—it's eyes. A chandelier with thousands of eyes—instead of candle flames, eyes. And smaller lights along the walls throughout the room, and they had candles with eyes for flames too, and the eyes flickered and changed shape as fire would. And a huge fireplace with eyes. The mirror above the mantel was lined with eyes imitating jewels, as were all the other mirrors in the room, in the whole castle. The curtains were kind of lacelike, gauzy eyes. And I was touring this place with a group, I didn't live there. And I lost the group and wandered around a few less showy rooms trying to find the entrance. Then in this small room near the kitchen I overheard how the eyes were obtained. They were removed from live humans. But apparently the donation involved some kind of religious awe and was done more or less voluntarily. Still, I was frightened, and I ran away."

That wasn't the first time we'd seemed to listen in on each other's dreams, but it was the first time it hadn't made us happy.

PART TWO

The Way She Spreads Her Wings—1975

Nevertheless I have somewhat against thee, because thou hast left thy first love.
—Revelation, 2:4

O N E *Nine Months Later*

I hadn't seen Nadine in nine months, and ever since I'd mentioned the word "abortion" she hadn't taken my calls. So I wasn't prepared for the Nadine that sat on that creaky porch swing of that little frame house on that old tree-lined street in Baton Rouge. The woman was enormous. It wasn't just that her belly was huge—her face seemed thicker, her neck, even her hair, hanging Cajun-black over her shoulders down to her breasts. She was so huge it seemed like I could bite into her, take whole mouthfuls of her, chew, slurp and swallow, and she wouldn't even notice. All that hadn't changed was how here eyes could shine.

How they did shine, as I got out of the car, walked across the lawn, up the five porch steps, to stand before her, where she sat like a queen on the same porch swing she'd sat on in her dream of Jesus and the flies. As though she'd been waiting for me there the whole time.

"I can always count on you, Jesse."

"First time you ever said *that*."

"I didn't *mean* depend on you, I meant *count* on you."

I looked her up and down. I couldn't get over her size.

"Big Mama, eh?" she said. "But I knew you'd come for it. At least, I *hoped* I knew."

"You look great, actually."

Her hair so shiny, her skin so rosy, she looked like she could have stood on her head if she wanted to, monster belly and all.

"He's comin' soon," she said. "Any minute now."

"Jesus or the kid?"

"*Both.*"

"How do you know it's a 'he'?"

"I'm his mama. Knowing about Little Jesse is my job. That's right, I'm namin' him after you, so that you can't forget him. So that whenever you say your name you're saying his."

("Naw, ain't it a trip," Danny would say later, "how namin'

89

him after you she named him a name *you made up*, not Giuseppe like your mama named you?")

"I'm glad that's his name," I said.

"Good for you."

We just looked at each other a few beats. Her eyes glinted. Finally I couldn't meet them, and looked out back at my Chevy.

"You want me to leave, Nadine?"

"Shit, no. I'm just pissed at myself for being so glad to see you."

I eased myself down on the porch swing beside her, afraid any sudden move would break the old contraption and we'd have Little Jesse right there. We sat quietly, wordlessly. The swing moved ever so slightly, creaking. We breathed that scented Louisiana summer air, so humid it's just this side of water. Feels like a colorless jelly that slowly ripples when you move against it. Car engines revved on other streets. Flies buzzed.

"I'm trying to get it real to me. It's hard," I said.

"You know, you'd think it'd be real to *me* by now, what with all you go through, but it's hard to feel real when I look in the mirror and it don't *look* like me. I try to put my hands in my lap and I don't *have* one! That kind of thing. So lots of the time it's like I'm watching it happen to somebody else. But not today so much, with its being so close. It's happening to me, all right. And I knew you'd know—the way you do; and I knew you'd show. Seeing you pull in the driveway in that ever-same car made me feel like I never did before. Made me scared, kind of."

"What do the doctors say?"

"They say I'm the kind of a gal could pick cotton all morning, squat, dump the kid, pick cotton all afternoon."

"You probably could."

"You been worried, right?"

"Sure."

"That's why you sent me all that money, to make sure I was all right?"

" '*The life I live—*' "

" '*—is all I got to give.*' I've heard *that* song before, the Thunderbirds do it real good, and you can sing it out your asshole if you're gonna sing it around here."

She stood up faster than I thought she could, rocking me on the porch swing.

"The mistake you made is marrying me once," Nadine said. "You're my husband and the law says you gotta send me money. Shit, we ain't even divorced."

"I'll give it when I get it, but I ain't gonna work in no goddamn factory for it."

"I didn't ask that!"

"I do what I do, and whenever that brings me more money than I absolutely need, you'll get that money, *and you know that*. I work hard at what I do, and you know *that*. And I don't piss too much money away on bullshit, and you know *that*. And—"

"I know this: Once this baby is born you better send me money regular. You'd better, or so help me, Jesse, I'll put you in jail. I *will*. You'll get butt-fucked by tattoo-people, an' I'll be glad."

She stomped into the house and let the screen door slam behind her. I stomped right after her, smoking mad but . . . I saw the Devil, and in his mightiness he stopped me cold.

His thousand hands. There were hands with pricks instead of fingers, hands with snakes for fingers, and hands tipped not by fingernails but eyes. There were his many bulging pricks, and some had eyes, not holes, at their ends, and not testicles beneath but little tits. And his many tits, which have pricks for nipples, and fingers for nipples, and beetles for nipples, and dog snouts. His many cunts, some with teeth, and with tongues sticking out, and flies on the tongues. His many faces, with cunts for mouths, assholes for mouths, bloody wounds for mouths, so that where a true mouth smiled with true lips and teeth, it looked all the stranger, like there was no such thing as a mouth anymore. And all the Devil's hairs around his pricks, cunts, and heads were of the brightest yellows, the brightest reds, the brightest blacks. And one of all his faces was truly his, a huge black featureless swirl, unspeakable.

I really saw this. It wasn't a vision. It was a drawing.

Nadine had got this big roll of brown paper—butcher's paper, they call it?—and had drawn her personal rendition of the Devil. That's what she'd been doing in that house alone, with nothing else to do but work a day job and grow a baby. Not that Nade was an artist or anything. It was like some kid's drawing, awkward and wild, and it went on forever, as she'd drawn it over the weeks, draping it all over the living room and into the hall, over furniture, on the walls; some of it in charcoal, some in pencil, but most of it in crayon, and in some spots the crayon had been pressed so hard that the Devil was all flaked and smudged wax.

I gave it a good long look. Followed its coils draped every which way through the house. There was an awful silence about this Devil, except that when a breeze came up, the whole thing would kind of rustle, and I could imagine waking in a bedroom upstairs and hearing all that draped and hanging paper rustling with the night breezes, and it would be like the thing was whispering to itself or to you.

Nadine sat halfway up the hallway stairs, one step above what was left of the roll of paper. No longer angry, she looked forlorn, like a little girl. The box of crayons was beside her, and there were crayon stubs here and there, everywhere—which wasn't like Nade, she usually liked to be neat.

"Watch your step," she said.

"Don't worry."

I picked my way to her among the coiled drawing draped across the hall and on the stairs. Sat beside her, thigh-to-thigh. We were quiet a while. For want of anything else to do, I crayoned the nails of my left hand black.

"Think I'm crazy?" Nade finally said.

"I wish I really did, but I don't."

"Thank you."

"I don't even think you're much outta control."

"I only been outta control one day in my life, that time in Pampa. I've been wild, but that's different. I've been full of sin, too."

"You're wild for Jesus now."

"Oh, I am."

I imagined how the place would look when she took that Devil down. Like a new house. A house she hadn't grown up in, a house we hadn't had any married life in, a house that was finally hers by virtue of what was gone.

"Oh!" she said. Then: "Feel of us."

She pulled my hand to her belly.

92

There was movement inside her. I pulled up her thin cotton dress, rubbed my hand over her bright belly, up to her heavy breasts, back down to her belly, lightly, lightly.

"I'll always come back," I said.

She smiled. "That's just your way of saying you'll always leave."

"What *are* you gonna do for money? You ever gonna sing again?"

"I'll sing for Jesus. I'll sing to Little Jesse. For money, it's been back to the beauty parlor."

"How is that?"

"It is how it is. But it's *people,* I'll say that. The shop has a nice feel, and you hear how everybody's talkin'. I like that. Got a good new friend there, she'll be over soon, take me to the hospital. I'd rather you didn't go. I don't want to get used to that."

"How do you know it's time?"

"The pain. The rhythm. Same way you know anything."

"You gonna let that beauty-parlor lady see *this?*"

"She *has.* And she loves it. Jesse, you find crazy people *all* over, that's America's secret weapon."

"Sounds like something Danny would say."

"Danny did. How's he doing?"

"The way he does."

"I almost love this hideous thing," she said of her Devil. "Hate to finish it. I learned a *lot* about my religion, doing this."

"Like what?" I asked, before thinking better of it.

"We live inside the Devil. It's called 'the body.' "

"That's bullshit, Nade."

"That's *life,* Jesse."

"Doesn't it say somewhere about being made in the Lord's image?"

"Just Adam. Only him."

I hadn't heard *that* before, even from TV preachers. But I'd promised not to argue with her about this stuff.

"I'm not asking you to understand. Say *that* for me, I've *never* asked you to understand, not this, not me, not anything." She turned her face from me. "I lie in bed at night, I ask questions; not to get answers, just to get rid of the questions, get them *out* of me,

I'm *tired* of them. What I got in my belly, that must be how the Lord answered me. Answered me somethin' I hadn't even *asked*. But that's all right."

She wiped her brimming eyes. "Man, I see you, I just spill my guts, don't I? Jesse, Jesse, Jesse."

She stood slowly. I looked up at her as she looked down at me, and it was like some weird camera angle in a movie; she looked like a building that was about to fall on me, like a mountain that was about to walk on me. But in her fattened face her eyes hadn't changed at all, and they were more full of love than I knew what to do with.

And I wish I knew what I looked like to her. A man who loved her with a love that was absolutely useless for anything she needed.

Then the mountain moved, walked heavily down the stairs, bare feet tearing the Devil, the paper bunching around her ankles. She dragged it after her, the brown roll jerked with each step, then rolled down the stairs, and as the paper tore and crumpled and rustled, it was like her Devil was cackling and sighing and whining.

Slowly, almost stately, like she was doing some dance, Nadine picked the coiled drawing from the floor, from where it was draped over the furniture, from where it was nailed—not tacked, nailed, with thick four-inch nails—on the wall. And she moved faster as she went, eyes wide and bright, moved jerkier, with little convulsion-y moves; she grunted, she tore at the thing, knocked over stuff, chairs and lamps, a light bulb exploded like a pistol shot, as she tried to force that serpentine drawing into a wad she could somehow hold in her arms.

I just gawked, full of a kind of inside-out admiration, and didn't even notice the little skinny blonde at the door till she yelled, "Whoopee! I'm in time!"

The blonde looked at me like she'd known me all her life.

"Wouldn'ta missed this," she said, and *winked*. Rock 'n' roll is here to stay, I thought.

Trailing her Devil, Nadine moved toward her.

"Connie! He came!"

"Praise the Lord!" this Connie said.

"*Praise* the Lord!"

And Nade went back to having her own party with her own Devil, and this Connie joined in, this tiny woman in a skimpy white dress, and I wanted to join in too, why the fuck not, but when I made my move Nade said, "Not *you,* Jesse, 'less you're ready to praise, which you ain't!"

She twirled and the Devil flew after and around her, but then she stumbled and I was up and to her. But even as she winced and clutched at herself, victory was wild in her eyes. Sweat broke out on her face as suddenly as though someone had thrown a glass of water on her.

As I helped her to a chair, feeling the great bulk of her in my arms, I knew a wrenching panic that maybe our baby had been hurt, and from that panic I knew how much I wanted that baby. And my wanting it must have gone straight through my arms into her body, because when I sat her down she looked up at me and into me, and me into her, and we just held that, married.

"I'm all right now," she said.

Nadine stood up slowly and with Connie's help scrunched all that paper into a big loose ball that Connie and she could barely manage between them. Not that it was heavy, but it was hard to keep organized.

All the while Connie chattered. "Well, I didn't think Nade would stretch a truth; still, when she'd tell me how you'd just show up at things just right, without knowin', like you was some kinda Indian, well, I took it with a grain. But here you be, useless as any man, but *here.* So, like she says, you'll probably come to Jesus just one song before the Rapture."

"You say that?"

"I say lots of things. Why shouldn't I?" Nadine said.

They went to the driveway, me following. Connie ran to her car and came back with a lighter, handed it to Nadine. They set the Devil on fire.

It burned faster than I expected it to, the crayon wax sizzling and blistering as the paper flared. The burning wax smelled like candles. Little sparkling flakes of ash rose on the smoke.

We watched the shrinking wad until the last ash sputtered out. Then Nadine said calmly, "You better take me, Connie. The pains are regular." To me: "Connie an' me have been in Lamaze. Every once in a while, in the classes, I'd crack up laughing, imagining you doing it. Disrupt the whole class."

"A real disciplinary problem, this one," Connie said.

"Yeah. I know," I said.

"I'm proud to have our baby, Jesse."

I just looked at her, thankful for that. Proud of her.

"And, Jesse—I'll kill you if you fail this baby."

"Not a long, lingering death, okay?"

"Right between the eyes."

"That's my girl. I love you, Nadine."

"Oh, I know that. 'Night." And she turned on her heel and they left.

It wasn't even close to night.

T W O   *The Old Rich Chords*

There was twilight, then mosquito time, then night. I sat on the porch swing, listened to it creak. Jesus did not appear. I thought maybe I should tidy the house, pick up the overturned chairs, sweep up the broken crockery and crayon stubs. But all I did was every now and again peck the black crayon off the fingernails of my left hand.

Finally, when dark had set in, I went back in Nadine's house with every good intention, but couldn't even bring myself to turn on a light. Her Devil didn't feel like a Devil to me, and her Jesus felt like a conjurer, but both were hers, all right, waiting on her in that house, the Devil downstairs and Jesus upstairs, their presences like two invisible balloons that had been inflated to fill the rooms and press against the walls till the house was about to burst.

I made my way over the mess in the dark to the piano bench in the living room. Ran my hands over the smooth keys of her old upright, hitting a note here and there—the action was perfect, the keys so responsive. Someone had played that piano nearly every day for almost fifty years. I layered a few chords one on the other, the rich old chords of the spirituals, till one started to play itself, kind of, and I followed it along softly with my voice,

Amazing grace, how sweet the sound
To save a wretch, and let one tune drift into another, the way I'd bet Nadine had been doing, for hour on hour and day on day, now that she could not only sing the songs but sing her belief. That *must* be something, since even just to sing them could get you going,

Precious memories how they linger
How they ever fill my soul—
In the silence of the midnight
Sacred secrets he'll unfold—

I've been known to do this on my own now and again, alone on some quiet afternoon or real late at night. You have to love gospel music if you love rhythm-and-blues, musically there's hardly a difference. Gospel you talk to God, blues you talk to women. Half the tunes have almost the same lines, you just turn "Jesus" to "baby."

That night I sang them like I meant them. It seemed the only way I could be there for Nadine—a way to cover her flank, kind of, and send her some juice, and to wish her well.

I did slip once into
I got a sweet little angel
I love the way she spreads her wings, but it was all to keep her company.

What else could I do?

INTERLUDE:

Quartzsite

O N E   *Too Far*

... turned on the TV real low, low enough so that I would
have to kind of squint my ears to hear. Some little black-and-white
people were pursuing some of their kind. Sat down with the tequila.
And let come what I'd been holding back for fourteen hundred
miles, the onslaught of all those moments that pushed, dragged,
coaxed, and ran me to this Quartzsite motel, on this old wood chair,
my body so still but my brain like a bowl of red-eyed snakes crawling over and under each other.

Everything's gone too far, even my face. Blotchy color, scares
me to see it. The cheeks too fleshy, hanging loose. The heavy bags
under my eyes almost dead-black. It would take six months of
taking it easy to make this face even passably acceptable at, say,
your average mid-price restaurant.

Got to pee so bad suddenly. Been dribbling it for hours. Hurts
when I pee. Hurts when I come, most times now. I'm about five
steps from a bathroom right this minute, but more of my kind have
died in bathrooms than any other profession, seems like. I'd rather
pee right here. And I just might. Who's to say peeing in my pants
won't open a door I've only knocked on, into what some people
might call degradation, but let's don't be hasty, let's not assume that
sitting in your own piss at my age will teach you nothing.

But no. I don't quite have the courage.

So I propped me up, I dragged me over, I limped but did not
crawl into the bathroom, where I sat me down on the pot and peed
like a girl.

T W O   *Fat Chance*

My body's very still, the tequila's gotten me past the shaky stuff, now there's just twitches here and there, a twitch at the corner of my left eye, a twitch in the flesh between my right thumb and palm. My little toes are numb on both feet. But my eyes are open as though they'd been pinned open. Ain't no sleep in *this* room. Guess when I went to sleep at the wheel I should have stayed that way, if I wanted to sleep. It might be that I'll never sleep again. I'll *awake* myself to death.

All that's moving on me right now is my sweat. It just started oozing through the pores, down my forehead, into my eyes, stinging. Rivulets down my chest, soaking the back of my shirt through. And the smell of it—there's tequila in that smell, and meat grease, and jalapeño, and something I never smelled before, not from a body, something like when you can smell that's it's going to rain.

Hey, there's Nadine's Devil, wriggling its infinite parts in infinite space. Oh, Nadine, Nadine. It's not so bad, Nadine. Just looks like life to me, Nadine.

I believe to my soul you're the Devil in nylon hose, I started to sing in a whisper, that Big Joe Turner tune—

Well, the harder I work the faster my money goes
I said shake rattle and roll

—but the tune didn't want to stay at the tip of my tongue, which is where you whisper, the song wanted my throat—

I been over the hill, way down underneath
I been over the hill, my way down underneath
You make me roll my eyes, and then you make me grit my teeth

—till it jumped from my gullet, loud and raw—

I said shake rattle and roll
I said shake rattle and roll
Well, you won't do right
To save your doggone soul

102

I expect to hear some banging on the walls, but it seems the good people of Quartzsite don't give a damn. It's coming on to dawn and I'm just another coyote.

A little-bitty woman on the TV screen sashays through piles and piles of rolled carpets singing a little-bitty jingle by someone who mainlines Sweet 'n' Low. I'm supposed to buy a carpet. Good. Then a thin sly-looking guy in a cowboy hat goes dragging a lion— I'm talking about a *lion*—by a leash through a used-car lot, smiling while talking a mile a minute about giving me any deal, standing on his head to give me any deal; and sometimes the lion jerks him back and without missing a beat the guy laughs at it, tugs its leash, and keeps on a-rapping. I know I could get Jesus on another channel, but would he have a lion on a leash, Nadine, and would he make me a deal? Nadine says to me, with her gentle severity, "Do you know how to spell 'fat chance'?"

PART THREE

White Ants
in a
Sack—1980

She's got the answer to the answer.
—Captain Beefheart

O N E   *Elaine*

You sure look fine tonight
In the beer-sign light—
        —Joe Ely

Nothing else counted until about five years later, when I met Elaine. Even Little Jesse didn't count much, because every time I saw him—even if I'd just seen him a couple of months ago—he'd grown and changed and seemed like a completely new person to me. And each of all those people were purely Nadine's. But Elaine . . .

Even now something squeezes my voice just a little when I say her name, I can't help it. Danny told me it was healthy, for some reason, falling so hard for two women that looked so different. Where Nade was all of a piece, Elaine was pieces. Elaine was ages. Elaine had skin at the nape of her neck down to her breasts that was all creased and gullied like a woman past fifty, while the skin at the small of her back and half the way up was a child's. She was my age, about forty, but her hair was eighteen, a thick flaming dirt-red bush of it, not to be managed. Her face was set in it and sur-rounded by it, like it was on fire. A roundish and thickly featured face, wide mouth and big lips, fleshy cheeks, high cheekbones, eyes that changed color with her mood. Never saw that face look pretty in a photograph, the camera just caught its thickness, but in life it could grin with every muscle and beam a feeling across a crowded club in the half-light. The skin of her butt and of her thighs was still baby-perfect, while her tits and her belly had gone to flabby folds, so that her stomach was the softest of things, not fat quite, but like another, bigger breast. Dry skin bunched on her knuckles like an old lady's, on her long fingers and around their thick brightly col-ored nails, hands strong as a washerwoman's. Her feet were older, too, the toenails had started to thicken, the veins to bulge, and on her calves thin blue lines of blood vessels lay just beneath the pale, transparent surface. But her moves were girlish, light. Everything about her was a layering, a weird clashing mix, yet somehow it was all Elaine, standing defiant with her feet wide apart and a hand on her hip and her grin like a kid's and her laughter like a woman's. Wearing all her ages like colors in a shawl.

I had it *bad*, right?

Well, those are just my lover's eyes. I'm not such an idiot to think you can *know* somebody you love like that.

T W O   *Forty-Seven Miles of Barbed Wire*

Danny sang slow and soft, his lips brushing the mike. There was a single spotlight on him, and from the bar it looked like his head was floating in the smoky beam. Dawg's dance floor was packed with people grinding their hips on each other. Danny hovered above them all, haloed by the light, a voice pouring its sweetness through the strainer of some bitterness in his throat, an all-but-forgotten Willie Nelson song, *You're gonna dream a dream or two*
But be careful what you're dreamin'
Soon your dreams'll be dreamin' you, singing like he was telling you in particular a special secret that he knew *all* about, which of course he was, and which of course he did.

The bandstand spots came up on the last note, people clapped and hollered. Danny smiled that apologetic, sly smile, like he'd been found out, the way he always smiled down into applause. He bobbed his head once or twice by way of bowing. In the usual faded but precisely pressed jeans, sweated-through Western shirt, and shiny lizard-skin boots, he counted his one-two-three-four of the next tune, a blues he sang up-tempo rockabilly,
If you see a bad-lookin' girl in Austin
She's either rich or from another town, and that Austin crowd yelled and yodeled at his eager lie.

I'd just walked in at the end of the last number, and my eyes hadn't adjusted to how low Dawg keeps his lights. I sidled up to the bar. Elaine walked at me out of the dark.

"Hi, Jesse Wales."

I nodded hello. She could still fill a pair of tight jeans pretty well—the slight bulge of the abdomen just looked like something good to rub against. And that shiny black blouse, and that thick red hair. Still, I'd always avoided her, because she was a writer. You can't trust a writer.

She ordered a drink beside me at the bar, some girl-drink like a Black Russian. I think she did it just to aggravate Dawg, who didn't believe in any mix more complex than soda.

"Your liver won't love you for this, sugar," Dawg said.

"I *got* a husband, that's like having two livers."

I'd seen her husband around, which also encouraged me to keep my distance from her. He was quiet, weird, and tough. Had a strange name: Johns. He didn't run through the clubs with Elaine, but you never knew when he'd show up. Word was she was loyal to him, but you couldn't guess how a woman like Elaine would define a word like "loyalty."

"Could I talk to you, Jesse Wales?"

"Officially or unofficially?"

"Well, officially, sort of."

I didn't mean Elaine was a *real* writer, I mean she wrote about what she called "pop" and what I still call "rock 'n' roll." She had a gig on the *Austin Sun,* one of those free weeklies that cater to the night people, and she was a stringer for *Rolling Stone.* When you're still a kid and ambitious, you let those people court you and you court them back; later, when you know that this is just what you do for a living, you ain't ever gonna be a star, then you tend to stay clear of them. If it's a slow week, they might take a little thing you said, or a little thing you didn't say, and jack it up to some juicy bit in a bad-mouth column. Or they'll make a big deal of how maybe you popped some guy when they were there and know he had it coming, or they weren't there and they don't know anything. Or they'll say you gave a rotten performance when actually the sound system was rotten—but they won't say *that,* because then the club owner will pull his ad or stop letting them in free. And here's something else while I'm at it, which makes me very suspicious of them: It is rare to see one of these so-called critics dance. What do they think this music is for? Taking notes? How can they know about it if they won't dance to it?

I was on my third whiskey on an empty stomach, so blamed it on that when I surprised myself by saying, "You can talk to me officially if you'll dance."

"I dance all the time."

"I never seen it."

"I dance in my living room for hours on end, with the volume turned up *all* the way."

"Doesn't count."

"It *does* count—more than *you'll* ever know."

She had green, green eyes—that night.

"Anyway," she said, "nobody's asked me to dance tonight."

"That's true. Nobody has."

"You wanna dance?"

"I guess I brought this on myself," I said.

"I guess you have."

Dancing is one of my things, but I held back, just kind of shuffled, watching her. She didn't rock, she danced like a little kid —it really surprised me. Whatever I'd expected, it wasn't how she'd kind of skip and do these cute little kicks, swinging her arms and smiling a lot, to a jingle-type rhythm that was all in her head and had nothing to do with Danny's band. But how free and easy she did it, like she didn't care who thought what about it, like she was all by herself in her own world, an impish little girl. But the little-kid air stopped with the tune, and there Elaine was again, pushing forty with a glide in her walk and liquor on her breath.

We went back to the bar.

"I want to do an article on you for the *Sun*—a cover story."

"*That's* ridiculous."

" 'The Living Legend of Jesse Wales.' "

"You're out of your fucking mind, girl."

"You're a legend, you don't even know it. They talk about you in New York."

"*That* makes me a legend?"

"Well, how come, whenever the big names play the stadium

or something—and I'm not talking about the bubble-gum acts, I mean the *good* ones—if I wanna run into them at one in the morning I'm likely to find 'em right here catching the last set at your Saturday-night gig."

"They're just slumming. I mean, it's fun and all, but they're just reminding themselves of how far they've come and how good it feels."

"That's not what they tell me. They tell me, '*That's* rock 'n' roll.' "

She knew how to push my buttons all right. But I'd stopped daydreaming about cover stories such a long time ago, and I didn't want to start in again. It's like meeting up with your high-school sweetheart, who you never slept with (not when *we* were in high school!), and she's just gotten a divorce and she's ready for a one-night stand. Even if it happens now, it ain't gonna matter.

"*Elvis* is a legend. I'm a working stiff. I work the night shift. Give the day shift something to do."

"I wish I had that on tape."

Dawg was leaning on his side of the bar, listening and grinning. He looked from Elaine to me and grinned some more.

"What are you grinning at?" I said.

"What Wittgenstein called 'the stream of life.' "

"You know, you owe the Army a debt for getting you out of college."

"At gunpoint, no less. Guess I owe them gooks a debt too."

Dawg had been a piano-man, and a pretty good one, before Nam tore up his hand. He could still use it, but not for anything detailed.

"Otherwise," he said, "I'd be like you guys, edging into middle age in rented rooms and old cars. I got me a new foreign car, I got my own club, can hear all the good music I can buy, got *two* houses, a large and pleasant stomach; and soon's I find a waitress who enjoys belly-lovin' *and* can keep the books, maybe I'll get married. Shouldn't take too long, I got a lot to offer. Full security *and* nasty habits. Most women have to choose between the two, and they're sorry either way."

He stuck that last sentence right into Elaine. They knew each other some.

"*I'm* not sorry," she said.

"I'm pleased as punch," Dawg said.

"What's bothering *you* tonight?" I said.

"Danny's singing too pretty." We'd been talking under the steady flow of Danny's voice. "I swear, sometimes the prettier he sings the meaner I get. Makes me wanna break the glasses—and I *own* the glasses. You sing nasty, puts me in a great mood."

The bar was packed. Elaine and I were standing shoulder to shoulder, hip to hip. And something passed, both ways, through my denim shirt and through her shiny black blouse, some signal, sweet and sharp, something we'd felt a thousand times for a thousand people, and most of those times just let it pass.

It's hard to explain what happened next. The strangled sweetness of Danny's voice pierced the club with another ballad, Dawg was off down the bar paying attention to other people, Elaine and I were watching Danny, and a door opened, all of itself. A kind of slippage. Like the whole room suddenly slid a few inches to the left, and nobody had felt it but us. I *knew* she had, without looking at her. I had never felt one of *those* doors open but with Danny or Nade or both—though not for some time with them. Somehow, without Nade around, it was a big strain for Danny to make those leaps, so it was as though that part of our lives was over except for the talk, and except for how every now and then on the bandstand the music would force an opening for the length of a song. But here it was, beside this woman at this bar, almost by mistake, with no strain at all, a feeling a little like déjà vu but more like sticking your head out over a high cliff. If "dizzy" could be a feeling that wasn't physical at all, you could say it made me dizzy.

I shifted just a little, so that my elbow wasn't brushing Elaine's, and the door closed, the feeling all but gone. But not quite all. Like Henry had said, when one of *those* doors opens, it tends to remain ajar, just a bit, for who knows how long? Maybe later a waitress, picking up empties after closing, would walk through this spot and sniff some weirdness and not really notice—though I'm just guessing, and for all I know Henry was just guessing too.

I didn't look at Elaine, but her breathy voice was so welcome to me when she spoke next, though it was just to say, "I'm interviewing Danny Crawford tomorrow. What's a good question to ask him?"

"Ask him about the money he owes me. He's my best friend, so I can't."

Then Danny told the audience that a good friend of his was in the room, and if they hollered loud enough, this friend might get up there and beat that piano till it begged for mercy. And he called my name, and led the holler, and as I went up to the bandstand I knew Elaine's green eyes never left me.

"This is a man," Danny said, "makes music with the stuff of dead elephants. Hit them ivories, Jesse Wales!"

I'd sat in with his guys time and again, so they just fell in with me as Bo Diddley's shuffley beat kind of jumped out of my hands, the beat that goes like: bo-diddley bo-diddley bo BOP BOP, bo-diddley bo-diddley bo BOP BOP, my right hand riffing on the top BOP BOP:

I walk 47 miles of barbed wire
Use a cobra snake for a necktie
Got a brand new house by the roadside
Made from rattlesnake hide
Got a brand new chimney made on top
Made from a human skull
Come on, baby, let's take a little walk
Tell me
Who do you love, —Danny coming in on the chorus which does nothing but repeat *Who do you love who do you love who do you love,* and then just me—
Got a tombstone head and a graveyard mind
I've lived long an' hard an' I don't mind dying —and me and Danny on *Who do you love,* and me—
I ride a lion to town
Use a rattlesnake whip
Take it easy, baby,
Don't give me no lip
Who do you love who do you love who do you love
Night was dark and the sky was blue
Down the alley an ice-wagon flew
Hit a bump and somebody screamed
You shoulda heard just what I seen
Who do you love who do you love who do you love
Arlene took me by the hand

Said ooooooooo-eeeeeeee Jesse I understand—and pounding the keys, and ripping my voice, *Who do you love who do you GODDAMN love . . .*

By the time I got back to the bar, Elaine had gone.

T H R E E   *Open That Sack*

It was about two in the afternoon and I'd just gotten up, put on my jeans, a T-shirt, and one boot. Hadn't yet brushed my hair or teeth, and it wasn't a day that I had to shave. I looked up—and now I don't remember, was Elaine walking a little in front or was Danny? I saw them out my window walking across the lawn. They rippled a little in the glass.

I had a room off the hall on the first floor of an old house I shared with some Austin musicians, which means it was a pigsty. My room was just big enough to cram all my stuff into—a stereo, boxes of records one atop the other, my old upright, a mattress on the floor, magazines, my dirty clothes bulging out of the closet.

I heard Elaine's and Danny's steps on the front stairs, heard them open the front door and walk down the hall. Still in one boot, I opened my door to them.

"You're fixin' to be interviewed!" Danny said. "This is Elaine Thompson!"

He said her name as though he'd invented her himself and I'd never seen her before. And Elaine, for her part, held out her hand for me to shake, kind of mock formality, and I took and shook it, that long-fingered, bony-knuckled, red-nailed hand. And was surprised at her grip. I think now how hard that hand grabbed my cock the first time she ever touched it, just grabbed and held on and squeezed, not sexy—desperate. There was something she *wanted* out of that thing, and she'd damn well *pull* it out if she had to. "Nobody knows what sex is," she used to say.

"Danny told me," she said, "not to bring my tape recorder in right off—"

"—I told her how ornery you can be."

"—'cause we'd never get in the door."

"Danny was right," I said.

It was one of those times when I couldn't meet Danny's eyes. That had been happening lately. It was as though some hard, hungry question had been eating at him, and he'd beam it right at me, but it was never spoken and maybe he wasn't even aware of it. Or maybe it was just that he was getting older and the same old questions got more desperate the longer he asked them. Most people sort of turn them off at about our age and figure that they were a part of being young. But with Danny, those old questions just got hotter.

Nothing fastidious about Elaine. She flopped right down on that unmade mattress like it was hers. Danny chattered good-mornings and I pulled on my other boot.

"I feel right about this, man," Danny was saying, "it's time for you to fess up," while Elaine scanned the walls, the photos I'd tacked up: Little Jesse as an infant, Little Jesse now, pushing five years old, sitting in his mama's lap; Nade, me, and Danny sitting on the hood of my Chevy in front of the Baton Rouge house; Nade at twenty-four or so, looking up laughing as she brushed her hair from her face. Some old Long Distance Call posters from various clubs in various places. And a recent Jesse Wales Band poster, from a Soap Creek Saloon gig: my face drawn as the grille of my '69 Chevy, my eyes the headlights, my hair blown back like a mane over the hood.

"Fess up," Danny was saying, "exorcise, proselytize, extemporize, but watch 'er eyes."

"Did you know," Elaine said, slipping out of her shoes as easy as you please, the nails of her big toes bright red, "that the great great-grandson of Crazy Horse has a Jewish mother? And that the great-grandson of Pancho Villa is a United States Marine who makes recruitment commercials that are broadcast out of El Paso? Those are true facts. Are you gonna let me interview you?"

"Shit."

"Don't be *mad*."

"I'm not mad, I just *got up*, man."

She just stood up and walked out. Which taught me how much I didn't want her to. I didn't ask what she was up to, just watched her hips move under that country-girl dress as she walked out the door.

Danny laughed quietly. He sat perched on the piano stool, looking down at me where I sat on the edge of the mattress.

"Naw," he said, "the messages are still comin' at us, the messages are still comin'."

"That so?"

"Indubitably, inevitably, and unaccountably."

"*That* is a song title."

"*That* is the story of my life. Here I am tryin' to evolve spiritually, an' I can't get no further than a song title. *That's* rock 'n' roll."

"It's too early in the morning, Danny."

Out the window I saw her walking back this way across the lawn. It shocked me: Her face was grim, bitter, her mouth turned down at the corner like a sick old lady's. So it got me dizzy again to see her walk into the room ten seconds later with a wide-mouthed victory grin that you couldn't doubt. Even then I had the sense to know that this was something more ornate than a contradiction.

She had a little Japanese tape recorder. She squatted down where she'd been before and turned it on.

"So, Jesse Wales—tell me the story of your life."

"I don't believe in life stories. I never knew anybody to tell a life story that wasn't just a lot of good reasons for them being whoever they happened to be on the day they were telling that particular edition of their life story."

"That so? Well—make up stuff."

So I said the first thing that came into my head, told her about that great black radio station New Orleans had in the fifties, used to play Muddy Waters and Howlin' Wolf all night. I'd listen in my bedroom in the dark, hauling that old wood radio right under the covers with me. It seemed almost as big as a suitcase. The tubes glowed through the casing and made my under-the-covers world glow orange. But that radio got so hot, and most of the time in New Orleans it was horribly humid-hot anyway, that with the covers pulled up I'd be drenched. Didn't care. The deejay would do the commercials in rhymes, Little Walter would wail on his harmonica,

I'd listen to those wild bent notes and those guys moaning lines like "If I don't go crazy I will surely lose my mind," and something in me just *turned around*, because nothing—not in school, not in the street, not in our living room felt more right and real to me than those sounds I heard under my covers.

Well, when I said all that, that was the first time I saw Elaine's eyes change color. They went from mostly green to something just green-ish and flecked with red and shining, as she got all excited telling me how she'd been in Lubbock that same time, seven–eight hundred miles northwest of me, under *her* covers, listening to the same station, which you could hear up in Lubbock at night if there weren't any thunderstorms in the way—the same Magic Sam, the same Guitar Slim.

"At first I listened to them because I loved their names," she said.

Danny had been under *his* covers, too, in the same town—but they'd gone to different high schools, so they'd never met. But he'd been listening to the Grand Ole Opry, country stuff. Which was the same as his parents were listening to in the living room, so he was just staying up too late, he wasn't sinning against the Holy Ghost. Our parents had no truck with our music. Missy called it "that nigger-preacher noise." *She'd* rather I beat off under the covers. When she caught me playing with myself she just made me pray. When she caught me up late with the blues she'd beat me with a stirring spoon.

"Then," Elaine said, "I was sixteen with phony ID in a club in Dallas, standing by the bandstand, when B.B. King pointed his guitar straight at me and grinned as he hit a note and *whoooa!* Flash flood!"

Everything in my laugh said I wanna fuck you, girl, right now.

"Naw," Danny said, "the good and the bad thing about my music is I got all my ancestors there when I play it, but you got somebody *else's* ancestors with yours."

"No, man," I said, "what about what just comes up from the ground? This music's in the *ground* in this country. And, what about that past-lives stuff you and Henry are always talking about? I mean, there's ancestors and there's ancestors."

"I *feel* past lives," Elaine said, right on the downbeat. "But it's like all of mine were my family-type ancestors anyway, and like everybody in my family's been dragging these genes like a sack of coal across time, you know? One day one of us in one generation or another is finally going to *open* that sack, and it'll be a sack o'diamonds."

"It already *is*," Danny said, all excited. "It's diamonds, and birds that got human heads, and white ants. Open that sack, you'll see."

"Ain't no white ants in *my* sack," she said.

"Oh yeah, there are." Danny said.

"Oh yeah?"

"Oh yeah."

This is how me and Danny talked when we were drunk or drugged or it was just real late at night. Now it was the presence of this woman, as though wherever she was it was nighttime.

And it flashed on me that whatever was in her sack, there were sure enough white ants in Danny's. Why hadn't I ever known that before? And of *course* birds with human heads, 'cause that's what Danny *was*. And whatever she had in her sack, it wasn't just coal. Flame-ants, maybe. Or those little white scorpions that if you stick a pin through them and hold them up to the light, you can see through them. And little very old dolls that don't close their eyes when you lay them down. And something else, something I couldn't see to, that scared me deep. And what was in mine? A mangy coyote pup with its paw smashed, whimpering. And broken branches, barkless, very dry. Kindling. And, oh yeah, a couple of Nadine's flies had got in. And a lot of small water-smoothed stones. And a lizard barely breathing. And stuff I don't know about, can't think about. And there were holes in my sack, and that scared me. And I saw Danny's white ants in the fur of my coyote pup, which wore a lump of coal on a string around its neck, and all of Elaine's little dolls in patchwork dresses stood 'round us in a circle unblinking.

That was gonna be *my* album cover.

"Ask him," Danny said softly, "if he wants to become a star."

"You fucker."

"Do you?" Elaine said.

I got real down suddenly.

"Not really."

Nobody said anything. All the sacks had suddenly closed tight.

"I wanted it once," I said. "Who didn't? I can get sad about that now and then, but I don't get sorry. I mean—Texas, Louisiana, Mississippi, Tennessee—that's where this music comes from. And it doesn't have to *go* anywhere, it's always *been* home. It comes out of the way people here live and it goes back into their lives, back and forth, in the clubs every night. It changes because they change, and they change because it changes. And what stays the same in the music is what stays the same in them. It doesn't have to be explained or excused. But you take it to New York or LA, and you make a beggar out of it. They like it or they don't, but what they're mostly wondering is how does this fit into their 'mainstream,' or their 'new wave,' or whatever. Which is what *they* always do, right? Well, who gives a dry heave about their mainstream? I don't. I don't mean that they don't make good music, but why does my music have to be judged by theirs? *No* reason I can see.

"What I get sad about is the memory of how we had a *great* band, we played so good, but when we played for them we played like beggars. I'll never forgive myself for that."

Her eyes were gleaming at me. I'd wanted to say this stuff out in public for a long, long time, and hadn't known just how much I wanted to.

"I mean," I kept going, "you make it big and it means records and album covers and stadiums, and everything is a big production. But what we do is a *life*. Not a production. That ambition, it was like we were dreaming of something else for somebody else's reasons. And you don't think Dylan would just like to be able to play the clubs without a lot of hoopla? He got famous, he made money, and all his money's good for is to protect him from his fame. Is that what I'm supposed to be so bitter about not getting?

"Anyway, it's too late now. The people who buy most records are about sixteen. They think they're gonna be twenty-five in about six months. You gotta be young enough so when they look in the mirror they can pretend they see you. I'm gettin' a belly and I've got a bald spot under this long hair. I look like I been in three wrecks, two fights, and one flood in the last week. There's no kid out there wants to grow up and be me."

119

"Mothers of the world, rejoice!" Danny said.

"You're not so dumb about this stuff, are you?" Elaine said.

"Hey, lady—it's what I *do*." Then: "You gotta become a Yankee to be a star, and it ain't worth it."

"What?" Elaine said.

"You gotta start thinking like a Yankee, and before you know it, there ain't no difference. See, Yankees are smarter than we are. Or their smarts are different. We got the *spirit*, we got what they don't even know exists, but they are sure as shit smarter. Rock 'n' roll, it started in the South. Black rhythm 'n' blues, then white rock 'n' roll. New Orleans, Memphis, *Lubbock*, for Christ's sake. Elvis recorded in Memphis in fifty-four. By fifty-six, he's working for Yankee RCA in New York. Buddy Holly recorded in Clovis fucking New Mexico in fifty-what? Hit records out of *Clovis*. A few months later, Nueva York. We couldn't hold on to the business for *two years*. By fifty-nine Elvis was in the fucking Yankee army. Muddy Waters and them had to record in Chicago. We lost the shot. We're so flat-out scratch-ass beer-belly dumb that even now, as soon as anybody here gets any popularity, if he wants to sign a contract that's worth a shit, he's gotta sign with a Yankee. And that Yankee ain't gonna sign you unless he sees you're prepared to think like him or let him do your thinking for you."

"What about Colonel Parker? He was Southern," Elaine said.

"A Southern sheriff working for the FBI."

"You don't mean that, really?"

"Don't I? The FBI sent that motherfucker to put a hex on Elvis and get him in his power. Probably hoodooed him. They were scared Elvis could become President or something. Kids'll read about it in the history books one day."

"But you can't do music indefinitely," she said.

"Why the hell not?"

"They call it 'age.' "

"Muddy Waters, Willie Dixon, they're old men. Them and their kind, they do it till the day they die. And hey, here's my vision of old age. Me and Danny own us a little club, a little bar, on the outskirts of town—any old town, so long as it's got outskirts. And this bar serves gumbo at all hours, and has a little bandstand and some room to dance. And it's a place where old-timers can get up and play if they feel like it, and kids starting new bands can get up and have their rehearsals in front of real people and, no offense, no critics. And it would have a Paradise jukebox, Muddy Waters's 'Mad Love' right next to Hank Williams's 'Lovesick Blues' right next to Dylan's 'Like a Rolling Stone' right next to Ray Charles's 'Tell the Truth' right next to Aretha, Hendrix, Patsy Cline, The Doors, Elvis, Smokey, Janis, Lou Reed, Beefheart, Robert Johnson, Patti Smith . . . "

"*Three* jukeboxes!" Danny said. "Wired together to work like one. Infinite numbers on them. Numbers with decimal points. Inverted numbers. Magic numbers. The jukebox as Möbius strip."

"And I'll sweep the place up every night myself—that's what I see clearly, me, after everybody's gone home, sweeping out the place, and I hear the straw of the broom scratching the wood floor like drum brushes on the cymbal, real slow."

"What does Danny do while you sweep up?"

"There'll be two brooms."

" 'Cept you'll be sweeping with yours," Danny said, " 'an I'll be dancing with mine."

"I already know that. I *know* who's gonna do the sweeping, didn't I say?"

"I make better gumbo than your mother," Elaine said.

"Then you can cook the gumbo," I said.

"We'll all have white hair," Danny said, "and we'll all have to wear loose shoes 'cause our feet have swelled up."

"I want a broom, too," said Elaine.

"And do what with it?" I said.

"Why, ride it, of course."

"See you in forty years."

Happy, the three of us. But happy in some way that made each of our sacks heavier.

Then we just sat for a few beats, so quiet we could hear the soft click of the tape machine's counter as the reels turned. I looked her up and down, and she didn't seem to mind. She looked back as I watched the way she wet her lips with a tongue coated sickly pale. She had a ring on the third finger of her right hand, and it had a shiny green stone. I thought of that Dylan song: *An Egyptian ring sparkles before she speaks.*

I wanted to rub my cheeks against her knees.

While Danny, perched on his piano stool, looked like a crow with a human head, a crow with his wings folded in, and as I watched, Danny's crow feathers went from blue-black to black-black.

"But maybe," Elaine said, "you don't have the kind of sound that plays well in a studio."

"Yeah, my sound is down and dirty. They tend to purify sounds in studios these days. If you cleaned the dirt out of my stuff you wouldn't have anything."

"Does that mean it's not good music?"

"I wouldn't know about music. I play rock 'n' roll."

"You don't mean that."

Did I care about what I was saying? Not hardly. I cared about how she'd curl her legs under herself one way, then another, and how she'd flex her toes, and how she'd put her cigarette between her lips, and how the smoke would leave her mouth so slowly.

It was late afternoon, pushing into early evening. I knew Danny had to leave soon for a sound-check, and I didn't know if Elaine would leave then too. And I knew that Danny didn't want to leave Elaine and me together.

"You wanna come to sound-check with me, Jesse?" he asked. "We're playing the Broken Spoke, and their piano's in lots worse shape than Dawg's. You can try it; if it's no good, my slide player's got an electric you can use."

"Man, I dunno if I'm psyched up to work tonight. Maybe."

"You could come," Danny said to Elaine.

"When would we have to?" I said.

"Ten minutes ago."

"Shit, it's that late? Guess I'm enjoying being interviewed after all."

"Surprise, surprise," Elaine said.

"Well, she's got enough stuff," Danny said. Then to Elaine: "Don't you?"

"I don't have all I want."

"There it is," I said.

"Well—she could come."

Danny looked from me to Elaine and back, bobbing his head a little, looking like he was trying to swallow something down that wouldn't quite go. It didn't occur to me till right then to wonder why they'd come together.

"*You* started this, man," I said.

"*She* started it!" He laughed. So did Elaine. "Insofar, I mean, as anyone can start anything. I mean, who *knows* who started it. Naw, see, *you* started it, man, you musta had this need that, like, *constellated* us into startin' it—'cause Elaine did this interview with me where I talked a lot about you, and now she's got *you* talkin' a lot about you, so that makes *two*."

"Well, what'd you *say*?"

"He said you were like this real smart animal that lives in little tunnels underground and can tell what's goin' on in the world by the thuds of the footsteps that walk over his burrow."

"That so?"

"And I said you're a firebug, your music's out to burn down the house, you want people to dance in the flame light. While me, I want to sing people to sleep, so they'll have good dreams. I'm for the lullaby."

"What's so bad about dancing in the flame light?"

"Nothin'. What's so bad about good dreams?"

"Nothin'." Looking up at him I could see on the wall a photo of Nade holding Little Jesse in her arms. "Nothin' at all."

" 'I'll let you be in my dream if I can be in yours,' " Elaine quoted Dylan in a good imitation of his raspy croon. Then: "There's no such thing as a good dream."

" 'My ancient empty streets too dead for dreamin',' " I quoted back.

" 'And if my thought-dreams could be seen,' " Elaine sang, 'they'd probably put my head in a guillotine.' "

" 'But it's all right, Ma,' " I finished out the verse, " 'I'm only bleeding.' "

Danny came in with that full round sound Dylan had when he sang country-like, " 'And there are no truths outside the Gates of Eden!' "

"Man," I said, "it's been a *while*."

Danny turned on the stool, faced the piano, and heavily hit a

couple of chords. Then, not imitating at all, but singing as pretty as
he could, kind of like Joan Baez might sing it if she were a man,

> I dreamed I saw St. Augustine,
> Alive as you or me,
> Tearing through these quarters
> In the utmost misery,
> With a blanket underneath his arm
> And a coat of solid gold,
> Searching for the very souls
> Whom already have been sold,

and his slow sweetness made the words shine again, new, while
Elaine and I looked at each other hard, and it was like Danny could
go on singing this song over and over and we could make love if
only he didn't turn around, because the way he sang it made it
perfect for touching in some utterly unexpected, haunted way:

> "Arise, arise," he cried so loud,
> In a voice without restraint,
> "Come out, ye gifted kings and queens
> And hear my sad complaint.
> No martyr is among ye now
> Whom you can call your own,
> So go on your way accordingly
> But know you're not alone."

Elaine's dress had ridden up high on her legs as she'd curled
and uncurled, and she'd seen no reason to pull it down, and I could
see down the tunnel of her thighs, but I couldn't see her panties, if
she was wearing any, I could just see dark, and I knew she'd let her
dress ride up as a kind of test of whether I'd have the gumption to
stare, so yeah, I stared, and the song was like a sickly sweet smell
in the room, the thick smell of a body rotting:

> I dreamed I saw St. Augustine,
> Alive with fiery breath,
> And I dreamed I was amongst the ones
> That put him out to death.
> Oh, I awoke in anger,
> So alone and terrifed,
> I put my fingers against the glass
> And bowed my head and cried.

And Danny leaned heavily on the chords, playing awkwardly, while I felt strangely released by this song of the death of a saint, and I saw the fingers pressed against the glass, and the glass dissolve, and the hand dart back in surprise but then tentatively reach through, where the pane had been, into the cool air outside.

And said, "I love where he presses his fingers against the windowpane."

"It's not a window, it's a mirror," Danny said.

"It's a window at night, where you can see through your reflection," I said.

And didn't say how it had just hit me that Danny had been singing about dreaming when Elaine walked up to me in the bar, hadn't he? And then this. And I remembered Nadine looking out that motel window in Pampa saying, "You think it's a sign?" But this wasn't like a sign, this was like a coaxing. Coaxed to what, from where? Asking does no good, it's just a stall. Go the distance or go home.

Elaine scrunched my loose sheet between her bony toes. Her eyes said, It's your move.

Danny looked down from the piano stool with his eyes full of plea.

I had a flash of a huge room with a thousand doors, all of them open.

I said, "I ain't goin' to no sound-check, Danny. The sound, as far as I'm concerned, has been checked and double-checked, and checked again, and do you know what? The sound—is fine."

Elaine giggled. And out of that giggle, with a coughed rasp, came a laugh, a forced laugh, and she didn't care that we knew she was forcing it. She laughed up at Danny, her eyes blank as pennies. And there was a smell in the room just then, pennies again. You never sucked on a penny? It smelled like that taste. It was coming off Elaine. And now it was less like Elaine was laughing than she was barking; there was "laughing" over it but it was this woman sitting on my mattress on her knees barking up at that man, not like a dog would bark but like a woman would if barking were a thing that women did.

He tried to look at her as she barked but his eyes would bounce off her to me, and I felt her bark-laugh start in me, too, but

I didn't want to make that sound, not ever, and swallowed it back, but had to look away from both of them and down at my knees to do it, so my last picture of that moment is Danny perched on the stool like a spooked crow kind of jerking his shoulders and forcing a kind of caw-laugh back at her. She barked, he cawed, but he was like a crow flapping its wings afraid, and I was like a kid who's run out into the yard to see a woman on her knees barking up at a crow.

It dwindled. It stopped. Doors slamming open and shut.

Then this wave came off Danny, out of Danny, as awful as an oily fart that even your eyes can smell. The bottom went out of the room. It was like when engines suddenly gear down on a jet, you're sitting there and nothing seems to have changed but you *know* you're falling.

Without making a sound or moving a muscle, Danny had the floor. His eyes were sparkly with panic. Elaine's too, but her panic excited her. Me—I felt like I was a hole that something dark was falling through. Danny stood up.

"So it's you two!" he half-laughed. *"You* two? It's you. You two! Yeah. Well. I gotta go meet myself somewhere. I'M GETTIN' OUTTA HERE!"

FOUR   *Tape Hiss*

Danny bolted out of that room, that house, and Elaine and I didn't move a muscle till we heard him rev his pickup and roar off. Suddenly I was so tired. Wanted to stretch out and lay my head in her lap. To sleep and nothing more. I would wake and she'd be gone; her scent would be on the sheet.

I smelled last night's tequila in my sweat, tasted it. Tequila will do that, the taste suddenly sits at the back of your mouth like a little lizard poking up from your throat. That lizard stared at her through my slightly open mouth. Something in her throat, a snake's head, stared back.

126

Stares that met. Drifted. Met. Locked.

—I will give you no quarter.

—Good. Mercy is for captives.

—I will eat your heart out.

—Good. That's what it's there for.

Each of us were at both ends of the transmission, staring through a silence that shimmered, faded, thickened, then fell apart.

She sat now with her back against the wall, her legs stretched straight out. Her bare feet, with their dusty soles, were just a couple of inches from my knees.

She lit a cigarette and, since there was no ashtray, flicked the ashes into her cupped palm.

I picked up her recorder, pressed "rewind," let it run a bit, then pressed "play." Those barking laughs, Danny's choked caws, then tape hiss, then what Danny said—but like it all had been squeezed and shrunk, and was being said by little people in an aluminum can. The voices weren't *too* distorted, but the silence was —you couldn't hear it swell or thin. You'd think that with all the listening I'd done, I'd have realized sooner that no mike can pick up the quality of a silence.

Elaine's palm filled with ashes. She dumped them on the floor and rubbed them slowly into the wood grain.

I hit "rewind" once more, looked at her, asked her with my eyes could she stand to hear it again? She answered out loud, "Only if you have to."

"Presto-chango," I said, hit "record" instead of "play," erased those moments, and let it record this different silence, which would show up on the tape only as a hiss. But that would be more accurate now, because a hiss had come between us, a static that fizzed between the sole of her foot and my knee.

She stood up, had one foot sunk in my pillow and the other on the floor where she'd rubbed the ashes. Said, "You're going to be the first new man I've kissed in four years."

Then walked over the mattress and out of the room. Left a footprint of ash on my sheet.

The screen door slammed. She walked away across the lawn without looking back. I heard her engine rev, it sounded little and foreign.

She hadn't even taken her shoes.

INTERLUDE *Quartzsite*

It ain't a hard-on, it's a dream-on. In Quartzsite. For no reason. The kind of hammerhead hard-on a man has when he wakes out of a dream—any dream, not just sexy dreams. It was flat up against my abdomen, and the way I was slouched in the chair, it pressed up against my belt and hurt. I undid the belt and unzipped my fly. The hard-on lifted my underwear up like a tent. I popped it out of the slit and there it stood, rosy and pale, with what the doctor said were varicose veins sticking out, curling around the trunk of my dick like roots.

I laughed, and it sounded like a needle sliding on a record. My eyes felt as though they were covered with crinkly cellophane. I touched the hard-on's swollen tip lightly with my fingertips, then just rubbed my right palm slow on its head, and that felt sweet, sweet.

Just a few touches. Nothing serious.

On the TV somebody was speaking *very* serious to somebody else about somebody *else*—an actor and actress, both young, every feature so perfect they'd be great candidates for human sacrifices. My hard-on kind of bobbed "hello" at them.

Then it eased back on down.

FIVE *A King Bee Rap*

I needed to talk to Danny, so I waited till about three in the morning and drove out to where he usually went to eat after a gig, the King Bee Diner up on Airport. The place always smelled of weeks-old, years-old grease. The hash-browns were little potato filings stuck together with griddle-goo. After two, when the clubs closed, the all-night grills would fill with musicians and club people coming down off the night. But at the King Bee the food was so bad that the regulars were just airport and hospital people getting off their swing-shifts. We could talk till dawn without running into anybody we knew. Around dawn the cops would come in for breakfast as we were leaving.

I sat at a window booth with a coffee in front of me and a can of beer in a bag on the seat beside me. The only others in the place were the cook in the kitchen and Marie, the waitress. She was about sixty-five, had dyed bright-orange hair, and no flesh on her. Pure bone, and always had been. At the far end of the counter she'd poured some sugar on the Formica and was making drawings in it with a toothpick.

"Marie, can I get a refill?"

"I wish nobody knew my name."

"No, you don't."

"Yeah, I do."

She came and poured the refill reluctantly, the way she did most everything, pouring without seeming to pay attention, staring out onto Airport Boulevard.

"Here comes your boyfriend," Marie said.

Danny's blue Ford pickup pulled up right in front of my booth. He had a girl with him I hadn't seen before. She couldn't have been a day over seventeen. Blond hair, good lines, sly eyes. Danny pointed at me and they both laughed and waved. I didn't wave back.

Danny introduced her as Lil, and she grabbed my hand and shook it like a man.

"The jailbait that's known as Lil," she announced.

"Just call me Uncle Jesse," I said. "Marie! Banana splits all 'round!"

Lil pealed out the kind of laughter you only have at seventeen. Marie rolled her eyes.

"He's not serious," Danny said to Marie. "Two servin's of two-over-easy and hash browns, whole-wheat toast—"

"—white for me," Lil said.

"—and coffees."

"Ya said banana splits first," Marie said.

"I said, he wasn't serious," Danny told her.

"I'll bet," Lil said, "he's *always* serious."

"You ain't so scared of him now," Danny said to her. Then to me: "She was nervous about meeting you. She's seen you play, said you look too rough."

"Me? Naw. Just worn."

I tried to smile at her. Why not? But it probably looked like I was about to be sick.

Lil was perfect. Perfect blond hair hanging perfectly down her perfectly straight back. Her denim jacket and denim skirt fit perfect. I didn't see why she wasn't in a store window somewhere. If she hung around Danny long enough he'd sooner or later beat her up and she wouldn't look so perfect anymore. I always thought I should warn them but I never did.

I said, "Well, what the *fuck* was that about, Danny-O?"

He whisper-sang, *"Could be a spoonful of diamonds,/Could be a spoonful of gold—"*

"No singin'!" Marie yelled from the kitchen.

"Just a little spoon of your precious love."

"Makes it sound like medicine," I said.

"Ain't it? She wants to give you a spoonful," said Danny.

"You're not talking about me?" Lil said.

"Shut up," I told her.

She didn't quite believe I'd said that. She looked to Danny to say something on her behalf, but of course he didn't.

"I'm sorry," I said to her, "sort of."

"I said no singin' in here!" Marie came out of the kitchen. "An' I've said it to you boys before. We don't got nor want no license for that. I've heard my last damn song, far's I'm concerned."

"I like your hair, Marie," I said.

"No, you don't."

"Yeah, I do."

Elaine's hair would look like that in twenty-odd years, short, dyed, coarse. In fact, if I fucked Marie, the wrinkled skinny age of her, I'd learn a thing or two about Elaine, a thing Elaine couldn't teach because she wouldn't know it yet; I'd have an edge on her. God knows I needed one. And fucking Marie looked like a better and better idea as I watched her sassy-girl walk, which proved something had stayed fresh in that old woman even if she didn't know it had, as she went around mumbling with those false teeth slipping. I got the makings of a hard-on thinking of her toothless gums.

Danny burst out laughing. He'd read my eyes. I think I blushed.

The jailbait had no idea what Danny was laughing at.

"Are you guys brothers? You don't look like—"

"Shadows," Danny said. "I'm his and he's mine."

"Is *that* so?" Lil said. "Well, I think it's time for me to go tinkle." And she darted off to the ladies' room.

"I feel like that woman gave me some sort of injection," I said to Danny.

"Give her one back."

"I intend to." Then: "*You* were weird enough!"

"I had, like, this big shock, like . . . " He trailed off, then found it again, "Like I realized I can't get there alone. And I don't even know what *there* means! But I just *know* there's a *there* there.

"Yeah, I can't prove it, but I can feel it now and again."

"Exactly right. I'm just not prepared for the idea that you can't get *there* alone. 'Cause like—none of the writings, and nothing Henry ever told me, said diddly squat about that. Most said just the opposite. Even Henry. Well—wrong. Maybe once that was right, but now it's wrong. 'Alone' don't work at this point in the time-space. Zap. *That's* why all the songs are love songs."

"You lost me. Way back."

"Naw, love's all anybody wants to sing or hear sung 'cause 'alone' doesn't cut it on the *path*. The path to *there*. Something's changed in the spirit world, at least in the way it connects to this one hereabouts, so that you need at least two people to even get the *information*. Like, the *path* now is for *couples*. *That's* the scariest flash I *ever* had. And the couples are basically man-woman, no matter what you carry twixt your legs, and even if y'all are 'just good friends.' And even friends, there's a heavy and a light, manly/womanly. Or maybe the womanly is the heavier, how would *I* fucking know? But I mean that's the craziness right now, that relationship craziness that's so deadly to everyone: that feeling of being *so* lost if a relationship isn't going, because what they're *for* now is *holy,* is of the *path.* Every single person looking, unknowingly, to get spirit-world stuff outta relationships, outta love songs. *They* think they're just cruising for pussy and listenin' to the AM *radio.*

"Naw, this couples-on-the-path—*that's* why Jesus doesn't work anymore, why now He only makes folks more crazy. Nade an' them think they can couple off with Jesus, men as well as women think so, but you can't couple off with the Son of *God;* that's a *last* step, not a *first.*"

"Slowwwwwwwwww it dowwwwwwnnnnnn, Danny-O."

"Naw, you'll get it. I think stuff, but you *get* stuff. But see—I guess I always thought it was you and I on the path. You, me, and Nade, till she coupled off with Jesus. You and me, after. Till today. Elaine, man. I *know* you guys are *goin'* somewhere, some *path,* some Way, but *that* means, like, that you and me are going different paths, and—I always felt a little like your guide. But I always thought that you were like my protector. But suddenly today I felt cut loose, you know? Like I wasn't your guide anymore, so I didn't have a protector. And—I got scared of dying."

"If I knew what you were talking about, I'd probably agree with you." It was something I often said when he'd take a breath on one of his raps.

"Hey. I'm gonna need reports," Danny said. "And, well, I'll send you some from wherever it is I'm . . ." And his voice trailed off. But his eyes didn't. Danny's blue, blue eyes just bore into me. His long thin black hair was matted with sweat from the gig, his yellow Western shirt stuck to him where it had soaked through. He needed something bad, and even if I had known what it was I doubted I could give it to him.

For this rap was garbled even for Danny's King Bee "caffeine metaphysics," as he called it. Like all he could do was garble the message, because if he didn't he couldn't stand it.

Now he was looking nervously toward the ladies' room.

"I'm always afraid when someone takes so long in a bathroom that they're committin' suicide."

"I think ol' Lil just wasn't telling the whole truth when she said she was goin' to tinkle. So let's you and me get outta here, ditch her. You know that type don't exactly bring out the best in you." Weird thing was, he never beat up on any other type. "If it's not tonight, it'll be next time you see her, so let's go."

"People change, you know."

"I know. They get worse."

"You ain't only slow," Danny said, "you're *gloomy*."

Too late. The ladies'-room door opened and Lil walked toward us. There *is* a way that jailbait just shines.

"What's she doin'?" Lil whispered, nodding toward Marie, who was back to drawing with her toothpick on the spilled sugar, like she often did to pass the time.

"Repressed artistic natures," Danny said. "It's a national crisis."

"Don't be thinking I don't understand what you mean just because I'm a freshman."

"What's your major?" I said.

"Television. I'm gonna be a broadcast communicator."

Watching Marie, Danny whispered, "You oughta try it, man. Neither one of you would ever forget it. You know, in China they don't suck on an egg till it's real real old."

"Oh, *gross!*" Lil had caught our drift. "You *guys!*"

"I keep telling you, Danny-O, people like us gotta be careful, not mess with people who live by Daylight Savings Time, they can't handle it. Just because they go to a club every couple of weekends or so don't make them night people."

"Ain't nothin' Daylight Savings Time about Marie."

"I wasn't talking about Marie."

Lil said to Danny, "Is he talking about me?"

"Just a touch of human sacrifice, sugar," I said. I reached for my coffee, and to my surprise my fingers were trembling. She saw that and pretended not to. Good manners. I almost liked her a little for that.

Danny said to me, "I—got to. After today I—do."

"Is it gonna be bad?"

"Not too."

"How do you know?"

"I can feel it in my hands."

"*What* are you two *talking* about?!" Something in Lil had gotten scared, and she wasn't quite sure what, but she wasn't a pushover either. "You two are very rude; anybody ever tell you that?"

"Not lately, but you're right," I said. "I'm sure you were right about something else once, too."

She said to Danny, "I wanna go."

"What's stoppin' ya?" I said. "Only kidding."

Danny said to her, "Naw, we're just ruminatin' on the ol' cosmic hairball, is all. It's just like playing music, only different."

"I'm—I'm gonna make a call," Lil said.

"Want a dime?" I said.

"I *got* a damn dime."

The pay phone was by the door. As she dialed, two Mexican hospital orderlies came in. They'd probably spent the night collecting linen stained with cancer-pus. They eyed Lil up and down. They sat at the booth near the door, the better to watch her.

We could hear Lil going through the years-old phone book for cabs. Maybe she'd find one and maybe she wouldn't.

The black folk got a saying back in New Orleans and I said it: "Well, it ain't nuthin' but a wheel."

I stood up.

"Leavin' so early?" Danny said. It was after four.

"Leavin' early and alone."

"Good song title."

"Maybe so."

His long guitar player's fingernails drummed the tabletop.

Marie looked up at the sound.

"You want sumpin?"

SIX   *A Piano Lesson*

I slept naked in the Austin heat. Maybe that's why I was naked in the dream. It was one of my piano-lesson dreams. My teacher in this one is a fat man, old, with a muscular face and with that deep black skin that seems highlighted with blues. He was naked too, with thick thighs, and a belly that folded over itself time after time, huge forearms, massive hands. But this nakedness isn't strange to me in the dream. He's trying to teach me a very slow, pretty Scott Joplin rag I've never heard before. So pretty you're afraid of it. Touch any note wrong and it might fall apart. But so strong, if it's played right, that you know the melody will never leave you. (The worst thing is to wake from these dreams and just to be able to remember a phrase, never the whole piece.) I get it wrong, and my teacher patiently goes through it, his fatty black fingers so light on the keys that the music seems just to float out of that shining baby grand. Then I play, he listens; but I can't hear what I'm playing, though he can. Then he shows me what I'm doing wrong, and I hear his playing just fine. But when I try to do what he showed me, I still can't hear my playing, can only watch my hands and try to get it with my eyes, mimic what his hands did. The more I'm scared of not playing it right, the more I sweat. Sweat streams down my body in many rivulets. A puddle forms beneath me on the piano bench. We're close together on the bench; it's a long bench but because he's so big our thighs are almost touching. The puddle of sweat works its way into the crease between his butt and the bench and I'm very embarrassed. But apparently I'm playing all right because he's pleased, and he's a very stern teacher. I ask him what the name of the piece is—I can hear our voices, just not what I play—and he tells me the piece is so beautiful a name would disturb it. That's why it's never been published or recorded, because you can't even call it "Unnamed," it shouldn't be called anything. You can only learn it this way, and it's a great honor to be taught it. I'm more and more frustrated that I can't hear the way I play it. But I don't tell him that I can't hear. I'm playing it again when a dancer appears in the room. I don't know where she came from, there are no doors, no windows. She's petite and sharp-featured, with deep brown eyes and long blond hair. From head to toe she wears a bright white leotard, satiny, little bands of color seem to flit across it, but if you try to look hard at them they disappear. It's not that she's beautiful but her intensity makes her beautiful. Now I'm self-conscious that my teacher and I are naked. She waits for me to play again. She dances to the music, but I have to watch my hands or I won't get it right, and all I know of her dancing is that I hear her feet brush across the highly polished floor.

I woke to a knock on the door. I was soaked in sweat, my cock huge from the dream. I had this horrible sense of loss as the melody vanished from me. I knew I wouldn't be able to remember even one phrase. The knocking continued. I wrapped a towel around me and, half asleep, with a throbbing hard-on held down by the towel, my long hair all sweat-matted and knotty, I opened the door a crack.

Elaine stood there with a great grin. She wore tight little shorts, blue, with some yellow flower pattern on them, and her legs were thin and well-curved still, though the muscles had gone to mush. An orangy kind of blouse, very thin. Her grin surrounded by that bright dirt-red thick hair.

She held a rough bunch of flowers, little yellow things with some blue and some red, picked with roots and all, the soil still clinging to them. But she dropped the flowers as she took a quick step inside and threw her arms around me and held so tight. I wasn't really awake yet, couldn't be sure this wasn't part of the dream. She dug her nails into my back and my hands went under her thin blouse, sliding on the slight film of sweat she always had in this heat, like she'd have when she made love. And she felt my hard-on against her through the towel, and just reached down and pulled the towel off and *grabbed* that thing, hard, all the pressure it could stand.

I said, into her neck, "You think that's for you, don't you? You think I just open the door and *pop*, I just can't help it, don't you?"

All she said was my name, "*Jesse,* oh, *Jesse,*" like it was half a curse and half an incantation.

"Well, it ain't for you," I said as she rubbed it up and down now and I rubbed my cheeks against her sweaty neck and shoulders. "It came ready-made out of a dream."

"Oh!" A sweet surprised gasp of an "oh."

And she just sank down and I was in her mouth and could hardly stand while she reached behind me and clutched the cheeks of my ass with those long red nails. It felt like she was drawing blood, and it turned out she was, but that just made me crazier. And when I burst in her mouth it was like somebody was holding an electric cattleprod to the small of my back. The blackness inside my closed eyes flashed white. I felt the tip of my cock against the back of her mouth, and I was scared of her teeth, and scared of falling, I felt so weak suddenly as she gulped it down. (Oh, Nadine, why'd you spit it out? I felt such *gratitude* when Elaine chugged it down.)

She let me out of her mouth and I crumpled to my knees, we were both kneeling in front of each other, and she kissed my own stuff into my mouth, both our tongues slippery with it. Our first kiss.

Then she stood and pulled off her clothes and lay down next to where I'd stretched out. Lay against me. I was exhausted. Like she'd sucked the dream right out of me. Like the tune I couldn't remember was playing itself inside her now.

Then the cavity inside my mouth felt huge and empty like my tongue was flapping around in a cavern in my head, which is how I feel *that* desire. And I slid down her, easy, and pressed my face hard between her legs, and she was soaking down there. And when she finally stiffened and called out low, "Oh," just "Oh," I held her awhile, my cheek to her bush, my face wet with her.

Finally I stood, went to my whiskey, and gulped it down, loving the blend of the tastes. Passed the bottle to her. Then we lay together on the crumpled, soiled sheet, her skin so soft and satiny against mine. And it was like—not the dream, not the particular dream, but the song of it, the sense of it, the dreaming itself—had been passed back and forth, and like I hadn't really gotten it till I'd got it back from her, from her come-slippery mouth and her spongy pussy. So that the song I couldn't hear was almost, almost, on the edge of my hearing now. I still couldn't hear it, but could feel it out there, its shape and movement and lilt.

I must have passed out, because the next thing I remember is hearing that god-awful babyish "Chopsticks" being bashed into, more than out of, my upright. Elaine sat naked on the piano stool, her hands stiff and clawlike as they pounced on the keys.

"Stop, *please*."

She stopped.

"I thought I was playing it kind of punk," she said.

"You sure were."

I sat up, and, finally, rubbed my cheeks against her knees. Thinking it was a strange thing to want, and knowing I would go right on wanting it, for years and years, no matter what else I wanted, and whether or not I ever got to do it again. In some weird way it felt like the purest wanting I'd ever done.

She leaned over and kissed my hair. On my knees, I held her as she sat there, pressing my face into the luscious softness that was the slackness of her belly.

"You and me ought to go to Mexico," Elaine whispered. "It would be easier in Mexico."

I guess I'm not very bright. I didn't ask just *what* would be easier.

S E V E N *Long-Distance Calls*

I couldn't get Danny on the phone, so I called Henry.

"Danny headed your way?"

"Seems so."

"Danny there?"

"Seems so."

"In other words, Danny's not *all* there."

"Seems so."

"But he's also *right* there, and you don't want him to know you're talking to me."

"Seems so."

"He's in that bad a shape with this shit, huh?"

"Seems so."

My heart half-stopped: "He didn't *kill* that chick, did he?"

"Not even close."

"Henry, this kind of conversation with you drives me crazy."

"Seems so."

"Driving me crazy wouldn't be such a bad idea, huh?"

"Seems so." A beat, then: "Keepin' any secrets?"

"Seems so," I said. "But only from a husband."

"That's what you think."

"He *knows* it's me on the phone by now."

"Seems so."

I could hear Danny laughing now in the background.

Then Henry must have handed him the phone.

"Feed my cats, hey, Jesse?"

"Just tonight. We're goin' to Mexico."

"Don't get lost, man."

"You can only get lost when you know where you're goin' in the first place."

"Ain't *that* the truth."

"How's Henry doin'?"

"Not bad. Just dyin'."

Nothing for a beat. Henry had been dying for a little while now.

"Later, man," I said, and hung up.

And had a drink and just stared a little before I called Nadine.

"Hi, baby," I said.

"What are you doing calling at a decent hour? Something wrong?"

"Just about to take a trip. Wanted to check in."

"Hold on, I want you to hear something."

A few beats later I heard a painfully slow and heavy chord progression, gospel-type chords, no foot pedals—Little Jesse couldn't reach them.

"Tell him he sounds good, I'm proud of him."

Little Jesse was scared of phones, refused to talk or even listen with one.

"What's the matter, Jesse?"

"Nothing."

"You sure?"

"Yeah."

"How's Danny?"

"He's up with Henry."

"How's Henry?"

"The same."

"Is that what's wrong?"

"Nothing's *wrong*," I said.

"None of my business, right?"

"Just wanted to hear your voice."

"But don't get my hopes up, right?" She laughed with that bitter edge.

"I gotta go."

"That's the story of your life. Imagine the shock one-a these days when you hear yourself say, 'I gotta *stay*.' "

"Take it easy—"

"—but take it."

"Right," I said.

"Take good care, okay?"

"What, and change my whole life?"

She laughed well this time.

"Jesse, Jesse, Jesse."

"Nadine, Nadine." Then: "Kiss him for me."

"I always do. Once for me, once for you, and once for Jesus."

"Can he tell which is which?"

"Don't start."

"I gotta go."

"Sure you do. Well. Bye." A long beat. "Jesse?"

"Bye."

"Bye."

EIGHT *The Morning of the Magicians*

The plan had been to pick Elaine up at her girlfriend's at twoish in the morning, and head out, like I like to, driving off in the dark, two hundred miles down the road by sunrise. She'd lied to her husband Johns, up, down, and sideways to make the time— that she was taking this trip to do an article, and going with her friend Marge, and to see the ruins. Having to stop at Danny's before we hit the road kind of dulled the edge for me.

He had a little place up over a garage in back of a nice house in a nice part of town. Just a living room—bedroom in one, with a little kitchen and bath. You walked up this narrow stairway on the side of the garage.

I had a key. Inside, except for smell of cat, it was clean and neat; bed made, floor swept, everything in place, the dishes done in the little kitchen, the glasses upside down in the drainer. A detail that impressed Elaine.

The place looked even smaller than it was because of all the books. The shelves were just planks across cinder blocks, but there were shelves almost to the ceiling against all the walls and even covering one side window. Starting at the kitchen door with the Zs, the books worked their way counterclockwise in backward alphabetical order to the As. Another detail that impressed Elaine.

Mojo, Media, and Whofell (short for the The Cat Who Fell to Earth) met us whining at the door.

I hate cats.

Prissy, simpery little fuckers.

I put their smelly food into their buggy plates. Because it doesn't matter how hard you try or how neat you are, if you've got liver chunks and cream in the open air every day in Austin's heat, you get those Texas three-inch-long cockroaches, you get ants, you get fat flies. They were all over those cat bowls.

As per Danny's routine I put the cats' glop into the three bowls and cracked an egg over each, and poured cream—cream, mind you—in the three little cream bowls *without*, as per the routine, washing the bowls first. Who could touch the things, what with the kitchen light glinting on the backs of the cockroaches?

As I tended the cats, Elaine talked to me from the other room.

"I can't get over that he's *read* all these books?"

"He's a reader, Danny is. Always has been. In our hitchhiking days his guitar case would weigh a ton with books. If we had to do any serious walking, I'd end up carrying it or we'd never get anywhere."

"*You* a reader?"

I was a little offended at her tone of voice.

"I read album covers. Though I did read a book, once. *The Yearling*, in high school. I fucking hated that book. What were they supposed to be teaching me with such a book? I quit the damn school the next week."

As I fed the cats she read titles out loud, at random: "*The Morning of the Magicians . . . In Search of the Miraculous . . . The Fourth Way . . . The Late Great Planet Earth . . . The Dance of Shiva . . . The Tao of Physics . . . The Kabyllion . . .* a whole *shelf* of Edgar Cayce . . . *The Secrets of the Great Pyramid . . .*"

I finished with the cats and went to her.

"Let's go."

"Do you love me, Jesse?"

"Suddenly and stupidly."

She laughed.

"Well," she said, "do I love *you?*"

"Who cares?"

"Who *cares?* Well, *I* just might." A beat. "Who cares. Then this is *really* a strange relationship."

"You're not gonna start using *that* word, are you?"

"What's wrong with it? People use it all the time."

"Yeah, but have you ever heard it in a love song?"

She ran her hands over the backs of some books on a shelf, as though they were cats and she was scratching their necks.

"Jesse—let's stay here tonight."

"No way. Let's go."

"If that's an order—ordering me around is a *real* bad idea."

"I've never ordered anybody around in my life—but I *have* made some forceful suggestions."

"Jesse, I'm tired. *You're* tired."

"Don't tell me what I am."

"I want to stay here tonight."

There was something stiff in Elaine's voice, and for some damned reason, something in my pants got stiff in response. Which annoyed me no end.

"We only got so much time, Elaine. I don't want to spend it here, if that's all right with you."

"It's just that—I got this feeling we would smash up on the road if we go now."

"Don't hustle me, lady. Lie to me, mess with me, but don't you try to hustle me."

"You won't think I'm hustling in about an hour when we hit that last skid of all."

"Shit."

But I was hard now in my pants, aching hard, like what was happening in my underwear had nothing to do with what *I* wanted to do. It made me madder.

"We're goin'," I said.

"Why?"

The cats had gorged themselves and had come in to check us out. They rubbed against Elaine's shins, big white Mojo, fat gray Media, and skinny nervous orange-fire Whofell. She kneeled and ran her hands roughly through their furs.

"All right—*I'm* goin'," I said.

"You do that. I'll just spend the next three–four days holed up here reading."

"Well, you *got* ten fingers. Two to turn the pages, two to play with yourself, and six left over."

"I use all ten, mister. You oughta watch sometime, it would make you *crazy*."

"Well, have yourself a *real* good time."

And I headed for the door. I stopped with my hand on the doorknob, looked back at her. She'd picked up the big white cat.

"You'll crash and die," she said.

"And as I do I'll call your name, and you better hope I say it nice."

And out I went, down the stairs, down the gravel driveway, under the tall trees in the dark.

And then heard my name like I'd never heard it before.

"JESSSSSSSSSSSS-EEEEEEEEEEEEEE!"

She threw my name with such a screech, threw it like it was a long thin knife with a curved shiny blade that sank right into the back of my neck. I felt it go down deep but kept walking. She threw it again.

"JESSSSSSSSSSSSS-EEEEEEEEEEEEEE!"

I turned and looked up at the lit window. Elaine was standing naked, clutching the white cat to her cunt. It squirmed wildly, bright white fur against pale white flesh. She was standing on a chair, her breasts and head were cut off by the frame, and she rubbed her cunt up and down the cat's back as the cat got crazier trying to claw her. Elaine was yelling my name again, and windows lit up in the houses one either side of the driveway.

I took the stairs two at a time and flicked the light switch off as I ran.

A heavy thud in the half-dark: Elaine jumping off the chair. The phone rang.

I picked it up, but my eyes were on her eyes, which weren't eyes but wide white disks in the half-light.

"Mr. Crawford? Mr. Crawford?" It was the voice of a very old lady, Danny's landlady. She lived alone in the big house.

"Yes, ma'am?" I tried to sound like Danny.

"Is everything quite all right?" She pronounced it "quaht awh raht."

"The stereo, ma'am. I'm real sorry. I've turned it down, it won't happen again."

"We've spoken about this before, Mr. Crawford."

"I couldn't be sorrier, ma'am."

Elaine was bent over double with her hands over her mouth, shaking with laughter. It scared the cats. They hid under the sofa bed.

"Well, *please,*" the old lady said.

"Yes, ma'am. Good night, now." And I hung up.

And I started laughing with my hands over my mouth.

We ended up sitting beside each other on the floor.

"You're wounded," I said.

That cat had scratched deep enough in a couple of places above her knee that the blood had run down her leg, and as she'd laughed she'd tracked it on the wood floor. We were going to let it dry and leave it for Danny, but after we calmed down the cats came out and lapped it up. Then disappeared back under the bed.

"Dress my wound," she said.

I licked her wound. I licked her all over. Me with my clothes on, she with hers off, squirming and rolling, gasping and twitching, with one hand stuck in her mouth as she sucked on her fingers, till finally I unbuckled my pants, pulled them down to my knees, and was going to ease, so sweetly, I thought, into the cunt-mouth, but she flopped over as fast as a fish on a deck, and reached her hands behind her and spread her butt-cheeks. I looked down into the creased brown ass-mouth. My throat clutched itself. And why did I feel such dismay at how easy it was to go into that hole? And she shoved her ass upward, right to the hilt of my cock, and—ten seconds, Nade? More like five.

And all I felt, coming, was the muscles contract, didn't feel my stuff go out of me, didn't feel electricity, didn't feel anything.

Pulled out of her real sudden as she said, "NO."

I sat back on my bare butt, my jeans bunched around my knees, and she turned over and finished herself off, with all ten fingers, like she'd said. And I went crazy, like she'd said, but not the kind of crazy she had in mind. I thought: When she starts to come, I'll beat her face in.

I wasn't feeling any anger, the thought was cool as the floor against my ass.

But instead I got up, my jeans fell to my ankles. I didn't lift them, walked with short steps, like my legs were shackled, into the kitchen. Washed myself off. The running water made me want to pee.

I peed on the roaches in the cat bowl.

"What the hell are you doing?"

She stood naked in the doorway, smiling.

"Relieving myself," I said.

INTERLUDE:

Quartzsite

You can drive all day and never leave
    Texas
You can drive all night and never leave
    home
Everything's real but not everything
    mixes

—Butch Hancock

ONE *Sunup in Quartzsite*

The sun coming up in Quartzsite is like an idea coming up in the mind of a stupid person. First you can barely see the change, it's so dim; then gradually the glow spreads, till in a little while it burns so hot it blots out all else. Almost everybody here lives in mobile homes that are the same brownish-white, whitish-brown as this ground and these hills, as though they'd taken on protective coloring. A few live in RVs that are the same colorless color. A few in pickups fitted out as campers. I'd pulled the curtains open a bit when I'd come in—I hate a room you can't see out of—and watched as those mobile homes took the light. The soft light of dawn. Then the brittle light of morning. I tried to move. I couldn't. I felt as though my body and I were sitting in the same place but we weren't the same creature. And then it came to me that I was dying.

TWO *Speak Now or Forever Hold Your Peace/Piece*

DYING'S NOT SO BAD.
You again. Thought I'd left *you* back in Texas.
YOU'VE BEEN DRIVING STRAIGHT TO ME THE WHOLE TIME, AND YOU KNOW IT.
I don't know shit. Thought when I burned that place down you'd rise on the smoke.
THE FIRE SERVED ITS PURPOSE.
Its purpose, maybe, but not mine.

149

TOO BAD.

And too late.

AFRAID?

Shouldn't I be?

FEAR IS A GOOD DOOR.

Something somebody thought was the news fuzzed onto the TV screen. A lot of people killing each other in some other desert, near where God lives. But in this desert the motel walls seem made of a kind of tequila Jell-O—the light sort of seeps through them from the outside, the unforgiving light of that moment when a Mojave morning turns hot.

If somebody came into this room right now they'd think it was occupied only by the part of me that's thinking, the part of me that stinks, and the part that hangs out in the mirror—which made this joint crowded already, as far as I was concerned. Now—*you* again. This is fucking unreal.

JUDGING WHAT'S REAL NOW? YOU'VE MOVED UP IN THE WORLD.

So Nadine was right about the Devil after all.

I AM NOT THE DEVIL.

Oh yeah?

BUT THEN—PERHAPS I AM. DOES THE DEVIL HAVE TO KNOW WHAT HE IS?

Naw, why should he be any different? Shit. Are you actually *something,* or just a trick in my head?

DOES IT MATTER?

Yeah. It does. It really does, man.

THREE   *There's a There There*

I'm gettin' to the *there* that's there, O Danny-O. I guess I'm even trying. 'Cept it ain't quite how we figured—*if* we figured. Fuck, I can't think about it. I—can't.

THINK ABOUT ELAINE. SHE'LL LEAD YOU THERE. THAT'S HER FUNCTION.

No shit.

DON'T BE BITTER.

PART FOUR

The Snake and the Garden Are One

And then he was interrupted by the slow-motion speeded-up sound that sometimes cut so deep.

—Jimi Hendrix

ONE   *Stories*

People tell stories—about themselves, about each other, about other people they don't really know anything about.

Elaine and I didn't have a story, we had a state of mind.

TWO   *Love*

Love didn't have a thing to do with it.

THREE   *You Can Believe Things*

You can believe things on the road the way you can believe things in the middle of the night. There's no "day" on the road, just road-time. Night can be anything, and on the road, day can be anything because it's just light, always moving, always changing, coming at you, going away.

FOUR *Headed South*

We slept at Danny's, but not much. Three, four hours. Then headed south through the Hill Country toward Brownsville and the border. The Hill Country was miles and miles of rolling wildflower meadows, yellows and oranges and blues against deep damp greens. You could focus on one spot and hold it still with your eyes as you passed, or you could let it swirl by in the easy sixty-five-miles-an-hour glide up and down that rolling sweet road.

Elaine lounged across the seat, leaning against the passenger door, her thick fiery hair whipping in the wind, skirt up to her hips to cool her legs, the skin of her thighs shaking just a little with the engine's vibration. Her bare foot pressed against my hip. Sometimes I'd reach down and rub on it.

In one wildflower meadow we saw the whitest horse, so much brighter in the sun than even the tiny colored flowers that spread around it on all sides. As though that horse was the white, white center of every color in the hills.

And it stood utterly still.

We passed it in an instant, I didn't slow down, I never slow down but for gas once I'm rolling, but that horse and its meadow seemed to travel with us just out of sight, still sharp and bright in our minds. So that I knew exactly what she was talking about when she said, a little while later, "I'd be so happy if I'd dreamed that."

"You saw it. Ain't that better?"

"But—what would you think if you dreamed it?"

I stroked her foot, and she dug her toes into my side.

"I mean," she said, "if it was a dream, you'd ask what did it mean."

"After I'd peed, and while I was having my coffee. Then it'd fade."

"But—if it was a dream you'd ask what does it mean, so why shouldn't you ask that if it's *not* a dream? If it happens in *this* world. It didn't happen by accident in the dream. I don't think it happens by accident in the world, either. If it means something in the dream, maybe it means something just about like that in the world. I always say to myself: What would I think if I dreamed it? Makes things— kind of echo."

A mile or so later, at sixty-five miles an hour, she said, "Was I making sense with you?"

You're making speed, I thought. Speed with me.

"Let's just say," I said, "you got a roundabout way of going about it."

"I *know* you know what I'm talking about."

"What if I might?"

"You don't have to make me feel like I'm crazy here all by myself."

"No, you ain't crazy. You're sweet as a prom queen. There's nothin' *off* about you a-tall. Are you *kidding?*"

"Jesse, I've never said that to anyone. I don't act like this with —anybody but you. Why do you even think I'd be *with* you?"

I thought of how bad I'd felt last night, not being able to satisfy her. And then how pleased she'd been, seeing me pee in Danny's kitchen, as though watching me do *that* with my cock was as good as anything else I'd've done with it inside her.

"You believe me, don't you, Jesse? This is—because of you, *for* you, this Elaine that I'm . . ." And her voice trailed off.

It was no time to lie.

"No, Elaine. I don't believe you."

"Stop the car."

The road had no paved shoulder. I pulled slowly off onto the dirt of a curve on a gentle slope. Texas kind of rolled out in waves on all sides—meadows, fields, a few horses, a few cows, a farm- house with a windmill, and, off past the hills, the water tower of the next town. A sweet place to live, long as you didn't say what was on your mind.

I'd stopped the car but not the engine, it hummed under us.

"Okay, I've stopped the car, now what?"

"That's why I'm with you. Why else would anybody be with *you*, you crazy son of a bitch."

"*I'm* crazy?"

"All the stuff I usually have to swallow down and act like I'm not feeling it—I don't have to do that with you, I don't scare you that way. I know I scare you other ways, but not *that* way, you just go with it. Because it's inside you too. You *must* know that. I feel like I'm on mushrooms when I'm with you. You're a contact high, Jesse Wales."

I didn't say anything.

Elaine said, "The way you look at me—I feel like I can do anything in front of that look. *Anything.* Like, you know when you're a kid alone in the house and you go into your parents' bedroom and play-act in front of the mirror, except that it's not really play-acting, it's *being* stuff you can only be *there,* like that, you know? You better say something or I'm gonna die."

"I don't know what to say. 'Thank you,' maybe. I don't know."

"I'll bet Danny feels the same way, and Nadine, too. I think maybe you're a drug. You're an uncontrolled substance, Jesse Wales."

"I love you, too."

"Love ain't got a thing to do with it."

"Speak for yourself. Can we get moving again?"

She didn't say no, so I pulled off the shoulder and gained speed.

"Do you do rituals?" I heard myself ask. I didn't think of saying it, it just came out. I knew some people who did.

"Sometimes" was all she said.

I didn't press that.

"Do you do much drugs?" Elaine said. "I haven't seen you do any drugs yet, 'cept alcohol."

"I did a little bit of everything, I guess, but never that much. Practically nothing since Little Jesse got born."

Little Jesse's father might phase out, fizz out, wreck out, implode, explode, crazy out and maybe even jail out, but in some deep way I figured I owed it to him not to OD.

"You do much?" I said.

"Just whatever I can get my hands on. You really don't do hallucinogens? That's so strange to me."

"I hardly *ever* did any of those—and it must be ten years since the last time. I always figured I had to get to *that* place on my own or I had no business being there."

"Drugs are as 'on your own' as anything. You just find what's *in* you."

"Yeah, I've heard that. But—what if you find only what's in the drug? And what if that's different from what's in you?"

"You're *weird.*" She laughed. "A girlfriend and I once had a long discussion about what kind of drug you used—"

"*What?* Why?"

"Thinking about your *music.* I'm a *writer,* remember? Wait till you see how our interview looks. It'll be on the stands when we get back. Anyway, we decided you did heroin."

"You *decided?*"

"'Cause you play so crazy. Like you're trying to do Hendrix on the piano while you're singing like a kind of guy Janis, and they were heroin people."

I was pretty damned flattered, except for the heroin part.

"I did it some," Elaine said.

"Did it or do it?"

"Did. A few times. It's like dying, and going to heaven or someplace, someplace sweeter than you ever thought could be, then coming back—all at once! I loved it, and loving it scared me *so* much that, the last time, I had *diarrhea* for two whole days. 'Cause I realized how susceptible I was. See, you're not a human being when you're on heroin. You don't care about anything human. You *go* someplace not human, even though it's inside you. So I made this decision, while I was *glued* to a toilet seat, that I'd forsake that, and stay loyal to being a human woman. That's why I didn't go over. But I loved that drug so much. And people who play real crazy, like you, always love it. You wanna try it, I could get you some."

"Anybody could get me some. No, thanks."

And I had a flash of Elaine stuck all over with needles like a voodoo doll.

FIVE *If We Come Back At All*

I *wanted* to tell her how good it felt to me, to be on the road with her, to feel her raw beauty beside me, to breathe in her wild spirit. I wanted to tell her that I'd never tire of looking at her, never tire of the strangeness in her. I'm so sorry, now, that I never said any of that.

"Will we come back this way?" Elaine asked, further down the road.

"If we come back at all."

"I know what you mean."

We had no plans. Just drive to some Mexican place down the east coast, Tampico maybe, hang out, lose ourselves. Lose ourselves not enough, and it wasn't worth the time; lose ourselves too much, and who knows if we'd ever go back?

She hiked her dress up and took off her panties and played with them with her toes on the car floor.

"I don't know why," she said, "but I'm always *aware* of my panties when I'm with you. You're weird."

"*I'm* weird?"

SIX *The Nameless World*

The hills flattened out into a more desolate, nameless kind of country as we neared the Gulf.

The silences between us stretched out for miles.

SEVEN

What Would You Think If You Dreamed It?

She fell asleep a bit before twilight, curled on the front seat like a kid, her feet pressed against the door and her head against my leg. It was like she was there and not there at the same time, a wonderful feeling. And I thought of the whiteness of that horse in the meadow.

EIGHT

Over the Border

We crossed over into Mexico in the dark.

Elaine was still asleep.

Mexico's dark is different from the dark of Texas, thicker somehow, as though when you stare into it it's staring back at you. And you breathe in that different darkness, and it makes you different. "And how is that different from doing drugs?" Elaine might say. And I might not have an answer, except that there's no drug like the night. And there's nothing, for me, like driving through the changing darks with the smell of sleep coming off a woman I love as she breathes the dark we share, takes it wherever she goes in that measureless darkness within her that can only be called by her name.

NINE ~ *The Horizontal Plummet*

Further on down the road
You'll find out I wasn't lyin'—
    —Bobby Blue Bland

In Mexico at night you can't relax on the road at all because those people don't drive, they plummet, horizontally, on this *major highway* that wasn't anything but a two-lane with no shoulder, no warning signs before the curves, and the curves too tight for the speed. You never know when you'll have to swerve into the other lane or off the road to avoid a pothole you could bury a VW in. My Chevy was running perfect, but nothing is good enough if you suddenly find yourself staring into the headlights of a bus coming straight at you as it passes three cars and two trucks in one swoop —behavior not considered untoward on the Mexican night-way, especially the day before the Day of the Dead.

So I drove with both hands tight on the wheel, wide awake with adrenaline, eyes hurting as I tried to see through the dark, for nobody down there ever thought of putting reflectors on those insane turns. Maybe they figured it would take the fun out of travel. It occurred to me that nobody knew where we were and if we died on this road it would be weeks, maybe months, before our people found out. But I had a thing about making Ciudad Victoria around daybreak. Anyway, between us and Ciudad Victoria there was nothing, not for gringos, at any rate, and this was no place to sleep by the side of the road with Texas plates (if you could find a road that *had* a side).

Driving like that, on that road in the dark, I tried to figure what Elaine had said, that I was like a mirror she could dance in front of. I don't mean I thought about it—how could you *think* about such a thing? I mean I mulled it, sucked on it, chewed it, not like when you chew gum but like when you chew tobacco: If you swallow the juice, it makes you sick.

When she saw herself in my mirror she saw some kind of white gypsy stripper that she'd always wanted to be, head full of spells and a satchel full of gris-gris. All right, I *got* that, that was easy enough. She was dancing to my music. But what do I see when I look at myself in *her* mirror?

I didn't even like to ask the question, but there it was. And I saw myself with long white hair—not gray with age, but white like in a photographic negative, bright, shining white, and my face black, the whites of my eyes black, but each iris a piercing bright point. White darkness. Here we go. I'm afraid to smile in *that* mirror, afraid to see black teeth around a gaping white hole. Dark tongue, like when you die. When *that* mouth sings, silence pours out, a silence so strong that as it fills the room, it presses you back against the wall. You fall to the floor, you're lying on your back, the silence presses down on you. You open your mouth to scream but the silence rushes in, pours down your throat, into your belly; the silence fills your belly till you think you'll burst; your belly swells, your breasts swell; lying on your back now you have the body of a pregnant woman. You can't gasp. You lie there trying not to breathe, afraid you'll burst, you lie there waiting to give birth.

I drove feeling fat in the Mexican night. What was it about this woman? Something fumed off her, and if you breathed it in deep enough, you crossed over.

But that's what *she* said about *me*.

I didn't feel like a man anymore. A man could have gone into her ass last night. I felt like something in between everything. All I *knew* that I knew was how to drive, and I drove. But I'd crossed over. Slid off something like solid ground onto something that shifted in waves all around. And it came to me that this was what Jesus meant by walking on the water.

It would tear Nadine a new asshole to hear me say that.

Driving on the water, it was.

And taking turns at fifty that shouldn't have been taken at thirty-five, because I had this big truck tailgating on me so close that if I so much as slowed down we were history. Why wouldn't he pass? But maybe it was a she. Maybe it was Nadine. Nadine saying, "You got my message, you asked did she do rituals, she left it open for to ask some more, but did you, no, not you." We knew people in Louisiana who had some rituals, and I'd found out the rule was: Best not to ask. But Nade harped, tailgating, "It *is* written, 'Thou shalt not suffer a witch to live.' "

I imagined volcanoes all around. And they *were* on this road, somewhere between us and Tampico. But all I could see were headlights in my eyes, and the truck's brights in my rearview, and shrubs glare-lit by the side of the road; and once, on a curve, two little girls and an old woman carrying baskets. The wind whipped by the cars pressed their thin dresses against them. They stood frozen in my lights as I shot past.

Then I hit a pothole deep enough to slam the frame against the suspension; such a hard slam, my jaw snapped shut as though I'd been punched. God knows why the tires didn't blow. First the front wheel slammed, and the instant that registered in my bones, the back wheel hit, and my stomach lifted in my chest and I swooned a little with nauseous death-fear.

The jolts knocked Elaine clear off the seat.

"Mexico!" I hollered, and gave the Cajun yell: "Aaaaa-EEEEEEE!"

Elaine got back up on the seat and tried to see out into the dark.

"Air smells like tortillas," she said.

"You all right?"

"Bit my tongue, is all."

"I'd like to bite your tongue."

"I'd like for you to."

She slid over to me, stretched her left leg against my right, all the way down to the gas pedal.

"How far are we from where we stop?" she asked.

"No way of knowing for sure. They don't believe in mileage signs on this road. Like they like you never to quite know where you're at."

"If we'd driven the same distance north, where would we be?"

"Nebraska, I guess."

"How about west?"

"Somewhere in Arizona. Almost to Tucson."

"And east?"

"Mississippi. Alabama, maybe. Why?"

"I just like for the man I'm with to know where we are." Elaine laughed.

"Don't worry about it."

"I don't worry about you at *all*."

"You worry about your husband?"

"Hush about Johns. That's none of your business."

"I know that. I need to know just one thing, and it's all I'll ever ask about him. Do you love him?"

"Yes."

A straight simple jab of a yes.

"I need him, too," she said.

"Shit."

"I know."

"I'm glad you love him." She didn't say anything. "I love Nadine, too."

"Why don't we stop at the next damn phone booth and call them up? Why are we having this conversation?" A beat: "Why did you say you were glad?"

"Because then we're not doin' this 'cause we want to, but 'cause we *got* to. *And the NAME of the place is 'I Like It Like That.'* "

"So do I. I don't know about got to and want to. I've never seen much of a difference between the two. All I know is ever since this started I feel like we're under some spell. And I don't want to come out of it. Ever."

"Neither do I."

"Was that a vow we just took?" She laughed.

"If it wasn't, it'll do for one."

She slid her hand up under my shirt and rubbed my belly. I swear I felt pregnant. It was the weirdest damn feeling. Too weird to tell even *her*. But she rubbed on my belly like she didn't need to be told.

"You ever been pregnant?" I said.

"Off and on," she said. "Hey?"

"Yeah?"

"*How* do you drive so long?"

"Same as how I play. I get *into* it."

"Don't you even take speed?"

"Danny says I don't take it 'cause I *are* it."

We were silent a ways. Then she said, "We're probably the only white people for a couple hundred miles."

"So?"

"Makes me feel like I'm glowing. Like we glow in the dark."

TEN *Sunrise in Ciudad Victoria*

Mexico seemed to rise into the dawn like an island coming up out of the sea. You wouldn't mistake it for anywhere in the States. The colors are laid on thicker, even the stems and petals of everything seem more dense—edible, like you could just bite into Mexico. And get high. I don't know if it's the light or the latitude or the Virgin of Guadalupe or what. I don't know how it can be so dusty and so tropical, so down to earth and so up in the air, so peaceful and so ready to explode.

Half-light turned to light, cool and sweet. Elaine had slept and woken again. I felt, suddenly, as tired as I had a right to feel, a leaden wooziness I could afford to feel as we slowed down into the town. Church steeples in the distance, but here on the outskirts there were small adobes, with here and there old women all in black sweeping the dust from the front of their doors—women who'd seen so many dead, their mourning never stopped. TV antennas stuck up above the flat roofs, making the hovels look even smaller. Farther into the town were one- and two-story houses; each had a wall, and the tops of the walls were studded with shards of broken glass stuck in cement. Then into the older, central part of town; narrow streets of block-long walls with shutters painted in pastel pinks, greens, and blues. Occasionally a door opens not into a room but into a dark passage that in turns opens into a courtyard, like there are these little hidden villages within the town. It felt like every place you passed, some secret was being kept.

The hotel was off the central square, old but nice enough, like a hotel in an old movie, except in the old movies there isn't lots of dust and there are no lizards darting across the walls. The guy at the desk wasn't happy about anybody checking in this early. Long-haired gringo men are never very welcome anyway, and with the strain of the drive, I really looked like shit. As for Elaine, she refused to put on her shoes, best hotel in town or no. "This is Mexico!" was all her explanation.

The room was small and clean and had a ceiling fan.

My arm and leg muscles quivered as I let down from the drive. I needed sleep. But Elaine was full of energy, wanted to go exploring, take a walk, attend morning Mass.

"Attend morning *what*? Aren't you some kind a Baptist?"

"I'm not some kinda anything. But I saw that cathedral, and I want to go there while they're doing something."

"Then put something on your head."

"I have to?"

"Absolutely. No big deal. A kerchief, even a handkerchief, will do."

"A napkin?"

"If all else fails."

She came out of the bathroom with toilet paper draped over her hair.

"You're not serious," I said.

"Not very."

She balled up the paper and threw it neatly in the little tin wastebasket by the dresser.

"You gonna put some shoes on for church?"

"You're gettin' awful fussy! We ain't *married*, you know."

"We could *get* married. Big church wedding down here would cost about twenty-five dollars, I imagine. Bigamy is a crime I've never tried."

"I'll consider it, in that case. We don't wanna leave any crime untried."

She suddenly clutched me, dug her face into my neck. I smelled her hair, it smelled of pencil shavings wet with dime-store perfume. She held hard. I held gentle. I was so tired. We swayed back and forth, holding each other. I closed my eyes. And saw us dead on that white bed, faces stretched in death-grins, blood from head to toe.

Hugged her hard, then.

"Jesse? What's wrong?"

"Just real tired. But don't let me sleep past lunch."

Within my closed eyes we were long dead on that bed, yet somehow, even dead, I turned toward her and buried my face in her blood-sticky hair.

Opening my eyes, I stepped back from her, held her at arm's length. She smiled as though we had all the time in the world.

"I'm gonna go," she said.

"Don't get lost."

She left, barefoot.

Elaine, on her knees, before a row of candles, in the shadow of a Virgin, across the aisle from a cross. The Virgin says, "Life is a whore." Elaine says, "Speak for yourself." And the all-but-naked God, hanging from his beam: "You must be Elaine. Don't I have nice legs?"

. . . which was the last stuff to happen in my mind as I lay naked on the white bedspread sliding off into sleep, before I lost it in Ciudad Victoria.

E L E V E N *Hear That Long Snake Moan*

I woke, but wouldn't open my eyes. I was not yet fearful. No; it was that my fear awoke more slowly than the rest of me.

Needn't open my eyes to feel the dark outside. And how I wasn't alone.

A stench unbearably sweet. Like the feces of one who ate only roses. And that smell hovered within another: candles of Catholic incense. And still another, a stink that could stab through anything: mescal. Imagine a syrup of turpentine and manna, spiked with battery acid and spat into, thrice, by the Virgin of Guadalupe herself. Mescal. Somehow the thickness of these smells made for a terrible heavy stillness in the room. A stillness I could not violate.

Across my back I felt light strokes—a brush or a feather. That hadn't been a dream, then. And something in me said: You are in danger of your life.

"Aren't we all?" Nadine! Under my closed eyes I saw her seated naked, yet primly, on an old wooden chair, her hands folded over her privates. And beside her, on identical wood chairs, sat naked Danny and Henry, each with hands folded as in school or church.

They shimmered, became transparent, faded into air.

The brush strokes on my back were forming words. Perhaps the words that made this spell? I felt for the letters, felt an *o*, and an *i* with its tender dot. The stroking stopped, then continued higher, by my shoulder blades.

I lay loosely fetal on my side, hands down over my crotch, knees slightly bent. Soon I must open my eyes. And knew that once they opened I'd be *in* this instead of just kind of under it. My skin was already out there, participating; but I lay far below inside it. Only the smells entered deep down to where I was.

Finally, flutteringly, I opened my eyes slightly. Fuzzily, through the lashes, I saw small dancing flames. Candles. The brush strokes moved down my spine. I opened my eyes all the way, saw two candles in a dish in front of my belly. Past them, shining with their light, the two full moons of my knees.

My toes felt funny. It took hardly any movement to shift where I could see them: wee white flowers stuck out between each toe. How had anybody done that without waking me?

"Don't you see?" Henry said, sitting naked straight and rigid on his chair, fat like he used to be, fold on fold of his belly cascading down to his thick-thighed lap. "Don't you see that human life itself is a drug?"

Then he faded away again.

I wished he wouldn't do that.

Rolling my eyes without moving my head, I scanned the room. Candles everywhere. And white skulls, made of sugar, some small as thumbnails, some big as fists. Customary candy for the Day of the Dead.

My voice didn't know what to do with itself. There was a word I wanted to say, just a name, just *Elaine*. As I thought it, out it came in a hoarse whisper.

"Hush," she hissed. "Don't move. Let me finish."

"But the smell?"

"The seven perfumes. Sloshed all together. And spilled wherever. But hush."

The way she said "the seven" raised some fear to my throat.

Her fingers, wet with something thick and sticky, kneaded my back.

"Thou shalt not suffer a witch to live," toned Nadine, hardly appearing before she faded back away.

Hot breath at my asshole, then the wet warm touch of her tongue there. Then the thrust of two long, long, long fingers, sharp pain deep in my ass, but I couldn't move for fear of her sharp red nails. Pain shot through to my cock. Would I pee blood? I clenched my ass around her fingers as she slowly drew them out. Smelled my smell. Broke into sweat as the pain faded—but wouldn't fade all the way; some pain hovered deep there.

Danny, bony-kneed, bony-hipped, bony-ribbed, appeared in his chair with a very old book in his lap: "Says here that *that* door, once it's opened, never closes."

And away he went!

Elaine said, "Here comes the part I don't know."

It was as though her voice was what smelled.

"Can I move?"

I'd asked permission! When had I become so willing? Many years ago, I knew now, on some bandstand somewhere, in the midst of a riff, without wanting to or knowing I had.

Henry slowly formed in his chair: "Y'all were so busy wondering where the road ends, you never thought to wonder where it comes from."

Oh, shut up.

And away he went!

Then appeared Nadine, her breasts hanging so heavy: "You can kill her if you have to."

Does that mean I *could,* or just that it was fine with Nade?

And she, too, went away again.

"Jesse?" Elaine's smell of a voice. "Move, baby."

But that was hard. There was heat at my butt and at the small of my back and in the crook of my knees. Candles. Had to raise myself, real easy, and I was shaky, that rose-shit stink like to make me puke. The bedspread wet with "the seven perfumes." They'd never get the stench out of this room.

Sitting now, with my feet on the floor, looking down at a candle that flickered between them, looking down at my body in the candlelight. How lovely my skin in such light! When had I seemed lovely to myself before?

Felt no movement from Elaine, heard no breath.

Stood slowly, looked down at myself, my prick not hard but slightly alift. Awake. My prick was awake.

"I—I was watching you sleep," that musk-voice said, "and watched as you got hard in your sleep. It stuck up so thick and strong, so—independent! Of both of us! Just a life all its own. I felt a little left out, you know? A little jealous, even. But it was so pretty to see. And then it went down, slow, while you slept on. That's when these images came on me. So I went out and got all this stuff, to make the images come true, praying, and I *mean* praying, you wouldn't wake up. That's what happens, how I do ritual. I get an *image* and *do* the image. Nobody ever taught me anything. My feel is: If you do the image pure enough, it has power. You're so beautiful, Jesse baby. I wish you could see."

How could she speak so *conversationally?* It offended me.

I said, "Quiet, baby."

I turned slowly. She stood naked across the bed from me. The small flabby breasts. The bulge of her abdomen, how its little wrinkles folded on itself. The sweet trim thighs. The dark-red bush, inside which only my tongue had yet been.

She had painted herself head to toe. Swirls of color. Groups of letters—but not any words *I* knew. Words to make the spell, maybe. And feathers around her breasts, stuck there on gobs of paint. They looked to be all from the same bird. I knew how she must have gotten them, knew the moment when that pigeon learned how strong her fingers really were.

" 'What's a little death here and there?' is a favorite saying of God's." So Henry said, now cancer-skinny on his chair. Then transparent, then gone away.

I giggled a little. *Giggled*—me! Seeing Elaine's body all marked with colors and weird words, it looked like on that old show "Laugh-In," when Goldie Hawn go-go danced in a bikini, how she'd be painted all over with silly day-glow words and the camera'd zoom in on her parts. That was all I'd ever seen like this, except that it was not at all like this.

"Where are you?" asked Elaine.

"On television."

Danny-O, what would you say and do?

Nadine suddenly there, in her chair, behind Elaine: "Stuff the room with his words, or try to, would our Danny-O. No, probably be huddled in a corner by now crying for his mama, don't you know?"

Then Danny there beside her in his chair, writhing at that verdict as his chair burst into fire, and he didn't just disappear, he was *gone*—before he could even scream.

"Where *are* you?" Elaine had to know.

"Here—and—there."

"Stay here."

"Sing to me."

So she hummed something wordless, without tune, without key. A lullaby, but for white ants. And as Elaine hummed, Nade groaned, her chair smoked, burst with flame. Nadine was *gone*.

As Elaine's growl of a lullaby went on.

Closed my eyes. Could see the room better that way. Its candlelight, its skulls. The stink shaded the darkness pink. And, with closed eyes, I saw a ceremonial bowl of mescal, worms at the bottom, worms curling and uncurling to the uneven rhythm of Elaine's humming, and with just a touch of flame that mescal would ignite, those worms dissolve in stinky pink smoke, as Elaine hummed now, *Hold you in his arms, yeah, you can feel his disease!*

And with her song Henry's chair engulfed him in flame, his head shook on his shoulders, *exploded,* pink wads of brain flew past me, he was *gone.*

Opened my eyes. The candled dark seemed so clean after the pink that my closed eyes had seen. A new dark in which Elaine shone. A human candle. Smiling now.

Everything was all right.

We were alone at last.

My eyes went lightly, gently over her, I pronounced to myself the words upon her, words like "iotlecit" and "yaaaaa," "kitahnta" and "sahn." A scribbling in tongues. I liked the big blotches of yellow between her breasts, the swirls of black at her hips, slicks of color all over, how each daub gleamed in the candlelight.

A black line cut across her neck. So I'd know where to cut if the time came.

And she: "Everything—that's on me—in front—is on you—in back."

Oh.

I went, moving very slowly, to the mirror, stood with my back to it, looked over my shoulder. She watched me do it, smiling like a pleased mother. It was as she'd said, the same, but where her breasts were circled in feathers there were two breast-size circles at my shoulder blades, yellow, filled with blood-red, and a gob of white in the center of each, like eyes in a mask.

I went back to her, stood close, looked down. Her feet were painted white to above the ankles. They looked, not dead, but like the ghosts of her real feet.

"There has to be a part you don't know, or it doesn't work," she said. "We're moving into the part I don't know."

"Where are your things, baby?"

Her eyes went wide with happy surprise. Hadn't she expected this? It seemed so obvious.

She pointed to the floor, at the foot of the bed: bowls of finger paints, a kiddie-box of watercolors, a cup of water, a brush.

I turned her around.

"Be still, baby."

I will serve you—is what I thought, but didn't, couldn't, say.

If you do the image pure enough.

I stood, who knows how long, awaiting the image. Hearing the candle flames beat ever so slightly against the air. The image stirred. It rose from where it had always slept curled upon itself, breeding dreams. Not as though I'd thought of it, but as though it had simply awoken and seeped out from under Elaine's soft flesh, to outline itself upon her back. All I needed to do was fill it in.

And with the image rose a song, *I got a great long snake crawlin' round my room,* that blues so old, *ooooooooooooo hear that long snake moan,* sung low in my head as I dipped my fingers in yellow, in black, in white, in blue, in red, a mixed gob slimely on my fingers. I stuck the rainbow wad on the small of her back, just above the crease of her ass.

She tensed. She sighed.

I fingered a thick wavy line up her spine till it disappeared under her red hair. Did the same on my front, from my crotch to my chin, circled my mouth, a streak mixed of reds, blues, yellows, whites, blacks, and their blended shades. All it needed was to follow where the image showed itself so plain to me on the paleness of her back. Drew more snake-line down from her neck in circles and waves, a snake curling around and through itself, stopping at her wide hole for shit.

End of the line.

Lifted my hand from her.

And stuck two paint-wet fingers deep into her practiced ass.

She clenched.

I pushed them deeper still. Forced a third finger in there, hard.

She grunted. She farted. I liked her smell the way, on the bowl, you always like your own.

Pushed in harder.

"Oh, Jesse, baby."

Yanked them out.

And reached my hand, that smelled of her, around to her mouth, right under her nose.

"Spit, baby."

She spat thrice.

I took my hand, which was mine and now not-mine too, and with it painted the snake's head at my groin, crude and ugly, and its eye was white.

Then painted the snake-head at her asshole.

"Stay put, babe," I whispered.

And went to write our names in colored shitty grease backward in the mirror, that our reflections, when they looked back at us, could read their names. For a reflection, I now knew, does not know its name.

Went back to her, stood behind her.

"Turn 'round, baby."

She turned, eyes tearful. She was happy. Somewhere in that world on the other side of mirrors I had made my love happy.

And I said to her, "What's on me—in front—is on you—in back. I'm not the mirror you stand in front of. I'm the mirror—you stand behind."

"I see my reflection—on the black side—of the mirror."

She got it perfect.

And, just like that, as though two people couldn't hold it perfect for any longer than this, I lost it, the spell slipped off me, the very thing that had sucked me in seemed to spit me out, and just like that I felt so—*stupid*. So—*silly*. Like we were stars in some porn show on Times Square where the neon blinked LIVE KINK! TOPLESS BOTTOMLESS MEN AND WOMEN! ZOMBIE LOVE! Like we were being watched by rows of sixty-year-old mama's-boys, eyes agog, jerking off, their shoes sliding on the come-slick floor.

I wanted to throw up. I wanted to take a wire brush and scrub us both till we shone with blood, bled to death scrubbing.

Thou shalt not suffer a bitch to give.

Dear Mama, I have become a pervert. Your loving son, Giusseppe.

Forgive me, Father, for I have rock 'n' rolled.

She knew *something* was happening to me. Said:

"Baby, *what?*"

Her thick lips trembled.

But the dumb cunt didn't get it.

Her eyes met mine and fell. And there she was, a painted woman if there ever was one, *really* all dressed up with nowhere to go—and, finally, for the only time, in my power. For she was waiting for me to make the next move, to take her by the hand through the mirror, so we could roll in orgy with those reflections who had just now learned their names, where she could suck on herself, where I could suck on myself, where she could watch me stick it in every hole of her image, where her image could sit on her face while my image went into her ass while I went into her cunt and we all SCREAMED coming together and would step back out of the mirror as one. And when we looked back into that mirror we'd just left, *there would be no reflections* and we would take that mirror with us back to Texas and keep it hidden and bring it out when we were alone and look into it and nothing would look back at us and that cleansed mirror would emit a happiness that would feed us as the gods were said to be fed. ALL THINGS ARE POSSIBLE. This now I knew. Or had known, wafted to that knowledge as though by the stench in the room. But it wasn't knowledge anymore, now it was just one more jerk-off fantasy. I got no more power, you stupid woman, I have done the image as pure as I was able and *it* had no more power. This room is nothing but the toilet bowl of our cheapest dreams.

Now she got it. Just she said, "*No, Jesse, baby.*"

Giuseppe to you, cunt.

But I couldn't make a sound, was frozen, really *didn't* see how it was possible to *move,* to or fro. And had the sudden flash of Jesus on the cross, with no nails but staples in his hands, fastened between this world and the next.

"I need a drink, *baby.*"

She made no move.

"Don't STAND there, you pitiful cunt, get me a fucking drink. I can *smell* the mescal. GET IT."

"Don't talk to me like—"

"WHAT? NOW! RIGHT FUCKING NOWWWWWW!"

The clit flinched. Yo, Nade! I made the witch flinch. And I'd rather see 'em flinch than burn.

Elaine looked real obedient for a beat.

But when she moved it was like I had the DTs. For the snake moved upon her. I swear to fucking God. She turned in the candlelight and stepped with short steps to the corner of the room, where she bent down to pick up something, stood again, her back to me all the while, yet I saw *she* didn't know what was going on, that on her back the fucking goddamn snake had *moved.* And then I heard its Moan. For the first time in my life I mean I HEARD that long snake MOAN, that song I'd sung a hundred and heard a thousand nights, heard the song but not the snake; now I HEARD the *snake* MOAN—

—snakes are supposed to hiss, not moan—

This snake MOANS.

Jesus, Jesus, Jesus, help me. "Can't, kid. They got me stuck to this wood, can't you see? I can't help shit. I thought YOU knew that." Jesus, I'm sorry, I'm sorry, I'm so fucking sorry, help me. "I can't budge, Giusep. Sorry."

She stood in the corner, shoulders hunched, keeping her back to me, as though to keep the snake between her and me, but I knew she didn't know why because way beneath the Moan I heard her whimper, her shoulders quivered as she whimpered but it wasn't shaking shoulders made the snake on her back move, the SNAKE SLITHERED, MOVING, MOANING—while she whimpered, the cunt, the shitty smelly slutty fucky pissy sweaty CUNT.

"You bring me that mescal"—my voice squeezed out high and scratchy—"you BRING it to me NOW or I—will—kill—you—Eeee —LAINE."

I *meant* it, but I wondered, if I had to *do* it, could I *do* it without the drink *first?*

Elaine turned towards me. She held a porcelain basin, the kind Tijuana hookers swab their pussies over. Full, I knew, of the mescal that had spiked the room's smell. But hadn't I seen that before when my eyes were *closed?* Oh, shit shit shit shit shit. It sloshed as she, oh so slow, stepped toward me.

A bowl full of mescal and worms, that I could light afire with a candle if I did so desire, we could burn with the cactus-worm. How had I taken my flashes for granted all these years? Those quick images that had kind of sat up in my mind and spat at the roof of my skull? I'd just let the spit dry there, hadn't thought about it; now the inside of my skull was caked with snake-spit and the Snake was wanting it BACK.

Moaning it back.

Felt the lapping of that quick tongue on the underside of my cranium.

A flash, itself, that took less than one of Elaine's short steps toward me. Stepping carefully, she was, between the fluttery candles, walking through the Moan as through neck-high muddy water, slowed by the pull of currents that could drag her, too, down, down, down, and I thought maybe what I needed, *all* I needed, all I lacked, all she'd left out of her rented room of a temple, was a bad *bad* drummer and a crazed guitar to wrap the air around the Moan so a weakling like me could bear to hear. Was that neglect Elaine's very last mistake of all? 'Cause it was about to cost her, it just might cost her everything. If all I could do to stop this was to *kill* her ass, well, maybe I could live with that—and maybe I couldn't, maybe I'd have to go too. Or go first; if that's what it took, then that's what it took. You got to be *willing* in this old world.

Oh, then how I hated my dear love who stepped across the Moan with chalk-white feet, each awful step so slow, a slowness full of low Moan, and not *Snake does the Moan* but *Snake IS the Moan*, Snake is the Moan how you see it, Moan is the Snake how you hear it, "Black Snake Moan" Blind Lemon called the song, his song in my mouth, the Snake in my mouth, using me for to moan, oh don't hurt me, I have served You, I have sung You, oh, Mama Eve, Snake curled round you, put Snake-head in your mouth and lick its always-open eye and tell it of its servant, me; ask that Snake if tonight we gotta die, though the Moan's in the music and the music's in me, like Moan is *Snake* in another way oh music's *me* in another way, just as real, how could we not see, we who churn our flesh to song, song's low far echo of the Moan, oh so, so oh, *my* skin ain't flesh at all, from Moan you come, to Moan you go, in the beginning was the Moan, the Word came so much farther down the road, a box they try to stuff Moan in but it won't stay, Elaine steps so slow in white feet on black Snake's back, Snake flex into her ass, go through her out her mouth, Elaine's strung on the Snake like a pearl, and *all* skin's Snake-skin molting of MOAN, so no me, no me, no body here, ain't nobody here but us Moaners. Mama Eve, you knew; the Snake IS the Garden, yeah, I don't like it neither but The Snake And The Garden Are One, *Got to read way back got to read way back*, Papa Muddy Waters sing, snakes live in muddy waters, why he chose that name, *read way back to the days of Adam and Eve*, Muddy Teacher of What Lives In Mud, *Adam said Watch that Snake, Eve, got his EYE on you, know EVERYTHING that you gonna do*, Elaine is mistress of the Snake, but oh, poor Elaine don't know, maybe gotta kill her for to teach her, for she'll know as she goes, goes down slow, under the Moan, know what she IS, that's worth a death, ain't it, Mama Eve, and when she's dead my snake'll snake inside Elaine where snakes like to go to come, okay to come and go in dead Elaine's snake-ready holes, Oh, snake curled in the Drum, *Adam still ain't woke up a thousand years or more*, so I'll wake not up but DOWN, *Every time Eve GET READY Adam he's ready to go*, I'll go cut my snake-thing off for sacrifice and stuff it in lifeless Elaine's darkest darkest hole while I blood-come all over her red hair, make it so much redder, get it blood-sticky so I can bury my face there, die wet with Moan, but

Elaine she steppy slowly to me, slowly, her eyes such wide green snake-holes begging, begging though she don't know what her green eyes say, begging, "Jesse Sweet Pretty, don't *be* like that, baby, don't be 'fraid, see you have Snake for fingers, see you have Snake for toes, see Snake-head of your cock hard for all my pretty holes, see you have Snakes for hair, even thin wee Snakies peer from out your armpits so friendly, Snake coiled in your skull lapping Snake-spit from its bones. Ain't no need to die tonight, cain't you jus' be sweet in the Moan, sweet ALL over me?" Which don't come out of her like words but comes out in come-moans, speaking in tongues be for people of the Word, we of the Moan speak in Moans—in the nighttime which is the right time, when our Moan-music reach way back, way back, wrap the dancers all in Moan, only a drum and a guitar and Elaine could live, only a little Hendrix, how he made guitar sound like THE UNIVERSE 'cause the man could play SNAKE-MOAN like NOBODY, like nothing EXISTS but the SOUND, and how he went from us, now I know, 'cause HE couldn't stand it EITHER without the SMACK, but the SMACK made him STAY TOO LONG in Snake-time till it SUCKED him DOWN down down, like I'm goin' down down down, *I didn't MEAN to take up all a your SWEET time,* Elaine, Nadine, Elaine, Elaine, *I'll give it RIGHT BACK one a these days,* Elaine slowly stepping oh I say *If I don't meet you no more in THIS world,* FROM which you are about to GO, *I'll meet you in THE NEXT ONE,* all our dyin' done, *And don't be late DON'T BE LATE,* no PROBLEM, *I want you to LOVE ME, baby,* I moan with the Mud-man, though "Love ain't got a thing to do with it," says Elaine, *till I DROP DEAD in front of yo' door,* you got to be willin' in this old world, all right, Elaine, I see, I owe you for the Moan, so *you* stay, *I'll* go, I'll get to make you MAKE me go, you'll be glad to kill me 'fore I'm through, I'll DROP DEAD like the man said, right in front of yo' cunt's door, *I want you to LOVE ME, baby, love me and DON'T get me killed,* but THAT's where Little Walter stretched a mouth-ORGAN deep into the Galaxy to return with MOAN raw, *I want you to love me till the hair stands on my head, I want you to LOVE ME, baby, till you know I wished I was dead,* oh, dead in the Garden where NOTHING dies, for Mama Eve lay down on my deadness and she CONCEIVE, say "You fool, you fool, you poor

white fool, ain't your time YET, jus' wait a bit," AND ELAINE
STANDING BEFORE ME NOW HOLDING THE PORCELAIN
BOWL OF SLOSHING MESCAL, the wee worms dead in the bot-
tom of the bowl, she Giver of Snake-moan and don't even know,
can't hear, poor thing, don't know Earth's Strung On The Snake
Like A Pearl, she don't KNOW WHY she loves my music, SHE
LOVES MY MUSIC, *that* got a thing to do with it, Oh, Hear That
Long Snake-Moan, Stars Strung on the Snake Like Pearls, *Every
time Eve gets ready Adam he's ready to go*, Elaine, Servant of Eve,
I—will—not—kill—you—Eee—Laine. And where's Papa Adam, I
NEED Papa Adam, THERE's Papa Adam, who say, "You silly shit,
let these bitches run you ragged, don't you KNOW, ain't ya'll's time
yet, you AIN'T ready to go, ASK YOUR SOUL." Ask my WHAT?
And ELAINE OFFERS ME THE BOWL, and we gonna live after
all. One more night, one more day, one more Moan along the way,
live without mercy, live without pay, live and ask my WHAT? Live
far down, live far away, live far far from what the day-folk say, live
in the trampled Garden NOW, The Snake And The Garden Are
One, ya, ya, ya, ya, and far, far, oh, so far, far back, THAT far what
is tenderer, what is tenderer than Damballah? That word you
painted on your inner thigh. And on mine. My very own Eve. Adam
is what you've made me. Ask my WHAT. I have a WHAT . . . oh, I
feel it move on me, I am so bottomless scared . . . No wonder I
wanted to die. I have a Soul, don't you know. See it shine in Snake-
spittle. It's what hears the Moan. Oh, for knowing this, for knowing
so, I'll be your Adam forever and forever and forever. And I do
pity you. For, you, you do not know. You have given what you do
not know. So right you were, how so you said, how it would be
easier in Mexico. Have given with your Soul, your Soul which you
do not know. Have given with your Soul. Stand you now before
me, eager, frightened, painted, silly, offering mescal. You are not
human. NOBODY is. For we, don't you know, have Souls, AMPLI-
FIERS of the Moan. I have learned this in the Moan. I will never
forget, I will forget. At the same time. I am forgetting, now, what I
will never forget. And oh, Elaine, I love you so . . .

Fuck with the angel, live with the snake. That's a law.

Elaine stands in front of me holding the bowl up to me. I have
no idea how long she's been standing like that. I am in Snake-time.

I look at her thick red hair, red like dirt if dirt could burn. The paleness of her flesh set off by bright paint. Thick lips of the wide mouth. Just one more white woman with a snake painted on her back. Except I knew it wasn't there anymore. Knew the snake I'd drawn on her had crawled right up her ass and *become* her. Looked straight into her eyes. Snake-eyes. Craps. She didn't blink 'cause snakes don't have to.

I'd turned her into snake. Man, what *can't* you do if you do the image pure enough?"

I took the bowl from her and gulped mescal.

It's like drinking electricity.

Doesn't feel like it's going down your gullet, feels like it's going down your spine.

Bitches' brew.

Know what tequila is? Tequila's mescal *after* mescal's been pacified, distilled, numbed, spiffed enough to make it presentable in mixed company. They leave the worm at the bottom of the mescal bottle. Mescal thinks tequila is a joke.

I gulped, slightly amazed I could. I'd never done more than sip it before. Lots of little places on me started to sweat independently of each other.

Still without blinking, Elaine looked down. I followed her eyes. She was staring at something that surprised me: a huge hard-on, coming out of me, stuck out and up, throbbing, its one eye open wide. My prick, yeah, but not *my* hard on. I'd never felt less sexy in my life.

She took the bowl, sipped from it, then bent down slow so as not to spill it. Let the mescal just flow out her mouth, dribble down her chin, drip the length of my cock. I could see down her back, my drawing of the snake, the drawing was still there, but the snake had gone into her, I knew. See down my front, an empty drawing, the snake gone inside. I stood dazed, the Moan a far-off echo now. Would I ever remember? Would I ever forget? Would our skins suddenly, burningly, peel, molt off us, and would we melt down till we were wee lizards, swift and small, darting 'cross the hotel walls, quick tongues to snap flies from the air?

Her lips hovered near the tip of my hard-on. I knew *she* knew that now was not the time to come. Keep it in. Let it cook. Let it simmer. So she just took the eye of my cock between her lips, lushed it with her tongue, licking my groin-snake with her mouth-snake—just to connect them, make the connection. IT WASN'T SEX.

Minutes seem like hours
And hours
Begin to seem like days

She pulled her mouth from my cock. She had not blinked, much less closed her eyes. Nor had I. It wasn't sex, it was homage, connection, benediction. Benediction.

She stood slowly up, not to spill the bowl, and took a longer drink, and offered the bowl to me. I gulped and gulped, and still we had not blinked.

Oh! I'm sinking. To my knees.

I hit the floor hard, I knew by the thud, but felt nothing. Was kneeling in front of her. A candle flame licked against my right thigh.

Felt like the softest, softest tongue.

Burned not at all, and left no mark.

So. I'd heard, somewhere, that that could happen. Wanted to tell her so, as the flame burned sweetly against me, but couldn't. Wanted to tell her *all*. No way. Looked down at her white feet, bright in the candlelight, the grease of the paint aglare with the flame. Slowly looked up, as far as her knees. "Latima," on one knee she'd written. "Sklytilan" on the other. "Damballah" on her inner thigh. Kissed each knee, kissed gently. Kisses of good-bye, good-bye.

Out.

T W E L V E *The Bell*

I woke to the sound of bells.

It was like being about three feet underwater and looking up at the sun. But those three feet that you are underwater is longer than those millions of miles to the sun.

My skull burned. Daylight seeped through my eyelids, which were too heavy to open. Yet the bells felt nice behind my eyes. You wouldn't think they would. You'd think they'd be unbearable. They felt wonderful. Like each deep note rippled through my skull and down my body and carried a kind of health. A huge bell like that is a being all its own—and *on* its own. It can't go but so fast, it can't go but so slow, and its one note doesn't change unless the wind comes round strangely with a harmony that keens the feel of the bell-sound into something farther from men. I like it, how a great bell is hung so high in its own tower. Men make that tower. Hung so high, yet the note so deep. So it belled out there, several bells, but one was close, deep but sweet, and it came to me like sleep, and I went on back down.

THIRTEEN *The Hot Wet Thing*

I was more awake the next time. And there were no bells. And I was nothing but smell. The god-awful stink of the seven perfumes. And mescal-smell, that seemed to be coming out of me. I was breathing it into the room. And vomit. All over, it seemed, by the smell, but I couldn't, didn't want to, open my eyes.

And then A HOT WET ON MY FACE, HOT WET THING, and I *screamed* and the wet hot clutched around my mouth and I punched out and opened my eyes and saw Elaine and blood.

The blood was all around her mouth. I'd split her lip. She was holding it and blood was coming out from between her fingers. I felt sorry, tried to move toward her, but puked as I sat up, puked clear white stuff. I don't think I'd eaten in two days. Elaine was crying. Raspy sobs. I tried to say something and felt a crust thick on my lips and cheeks. I must have been puking in my sleep. She must have been trying to clean it off with a washcloth.

And then something happened to my face. My cheeks worked in little spasm. Tears started squeezing out of my eyes, hot. They almost hurt. My chest hurt, too, and my shoulders, and my back. I think I was saying "I'm sorry," or trying to. Our arms reached out at the same time and we held each other. My face buried in her neck, her face buried in mine. How hot her neck was.

F O U R T E E N *The Crystal*

Babe, you're just a wave, you're not the water.
            —Butch Hancock

What I wanted more than anything was a beer. I'd awakened for the third time. Drowning, you stay down for the third time, they say. Guess I was *un*drowning.

I lay there, weak, but knowing I could move, or move enough. Thinking: I can drive now—let's get out of here.

A pale light through the open window—last light of the day. And lots of noise, music, shouting—the Day of the Dead. A happy day. White candy skulls everywhere. Skeletons that play guitars, skeletons that get married, skeletons dancing; soldier and priest and mama and baby skeletons, Don Quixote skeletons; made of wood, made of plastic, made of plaster, everywhere—all those shining bones. And flowers everywhere. Flowers in the graveyards and in the hair of all the little girls.

Street sounds came from both near and far away as I lay on my back, staring at the ceiling fan. I was still naked, but clean. Elaine had washed me down while I was in between awake and asleep. She'd pulled off the filthy sheets. I lay on the bare mattress. The perfume smell was still strong, but the other smells were gone. She'd dumped all the signs of our—our ceremony? our fiesta?—into the tub with the sheets, except for the candy skulls, which she'd lined up in neat rows along the wall beneath the window.

On the bureau mirror, in lipstick, she'd written, "Hi!"

Hi, yourself.

I supposed she was out enjoying the street, but had no impulse to join her. Lying in bed wasn't such a bad way to celebrate the Day of the Dead. It was as though I was lying in state, yet able to appreciate it. I wasn't thinking about what all had happened. It was enough for now to lie and listen to the din of human voices. And it was wonderful not to understand them. Fragments of Spanish in no particular order—shouts and normal speech and even, through some acoustic twist, the hiss of an occasional whisper (or was that in my head?). The musical voices of men, women, and children rising together in a cloud of sound over the town, accompanying the Dead to wherever it is the Dead go (and all we know about the Dead is that they do go). I felt the churning cloud of gathered voices rise like smoke off the celebration, as though something in Ciudad Victoria was happily burning.

The ceiling was a fine view. Just fine. I even forgot to want the beer. Near the tip of a blade of the ceiling fan, the crystal began. It looked like a broken piece of mirror, just hovering up there, all on its own. And out of that piece of mirror came another, and another, and another, facet after facet, unfolding from each other, till the many-mirrored crystal was so large I couldn't see the ceiling fan. It brightly hovered above me, many-faceted, gleaming, sparkling. It had no color of its own, but all colors passed across it.

Watching the crystal grow, I'd taken it in delight. Nothing had seemed more natural than for that marvelous many-mirrored thing to be shining above me in that room.

But suddenly something in me thought to be surprised. And I heard myself say, straight out loud, "That's not supposed to be there!"

And ZAP—the crystal disappeared.

With no sign that it had ever been, nothing but my ache of loss.

I wanted that crystal back, tried to will it back. I missed it terribly. I think I still miss it. I'm still so grateful I saw it.

I didn't and don't know what it meant, and I wish I did. The eye of the snake maybe? Maybe, maybe. But it was a vision, at least I know that. I don't mean it was imaginary, it was *there,* my whole body knew it was there. But I'd been able to *see* it, *that* was the vision.

Sober, and with no hoodoo.

I didn't know what to *do* with it except to remember it.

FIFTEEN *A New Dress*

It was a little after dark. I was dressed and packed, sitting on the high-backed old wood chair, looking out the window, waiting for Elaine. Pictures of what had happened formed and dissolved in my head, and to keep them at bay I concentrated on the people in the street below, well-lit just in front of the hotel, pitch-dark just down the way. Then Elaine strode out of the dark down there, the only redhead on the block, in high heels and tight jeans, with a brown paper parcel under her arm, walking like a Dallas hooker. From that third-floor window, she looked young and tall. People, mostly men, watched her as she passed.

I made it my business to be looking out the window when she walked in. I wanted so much to see her face, I wouldn't let myself.

"Jesse?"

I kept my eyes fixed on the street, said, "Hi, baby."

"Hi, baby."

Heard her sharp-heeled steps behind me, felt her strong hands knead my shouders.

I turned and looked up at her. She still had a fat lip from where I'd hit her.

I rose slowly, a little shaky, the kind of weakness you feel after a long illness when you're well but not yet strong. We embraced. I couldn't tell whether she was trembling or I was, or whether we both were. In those heels she was a little taller than me.

"Take a little walk before we leave?" I said.

"I'd like that."

She let me go, went to the bed, stepped out of her heels. Took off her blouse and bra, peeled off her jeans. Her body so pale, so soft. Couldn't I just eat her, Lord? Bite into her, and it wouldn't be

186

like meat at all, would be like sinking my teeth into a blood-soaked cheesecake, and it wouldn't hurt her at all, she'd love it as I just kind of chewed her down to the bone, not to kill her but to *keep* her, keep her inside me, couldn't I, Lord?

"You like it?" she said. She was holding the dress that had been in the parcel, draping it over her. A thin light thing of white, with swirls of blues and golds. She slipped into it. It was just right for her, had the sweetest line, she looked graceful in it just standing there still.

"It's real nice," I said.

"Now if somebody asks, 'What did you do in Mexico?' I can say one thing that's true and makes sense. I can say, 'I bought a dress I really like.' "

We walked to the town square, holding hands like children. The square was crowded with every sort of people—every size and age, barefoot and shoed, elegant and dusty—everybody talking, and two or three currents of music blending in shifting combinations everywhere we turned. We walked aimlessly, half-smiling, not speaking. It was a sweet feeling to walk among all these people whose lives were so different from ours and who cared nothing about us. We walked as though invisible, like two of the Dead their day had called back to earth, back for a stroll, and to eat an ice.

Suddenly all the street lamps dimmed at once.

The crowd, with one voice, went, "Ooooooooooooo."

The street lamps flared up again to full strength. It felt to me as though the square had faded a little out of this dimension, then had come back. Then the lights dimmed again, another "Oooooooooo," and laughter and cries. Then the whole square went black, and the crowd let out a cheer, like it was all part of the festival. Elaine and I held hands tightly. We just stood there as people bumped into us, squeezing us together as they rubbed against our backs, stepped on our feet, called into our faces the names of others, "Carlos!" "Esperanza!" "Liliana!" I could hardly see Elaine, it was so dark.

INTERLUDE

QUARTZSITE

ONE *As Little a Thing As a Blink*

The next day was pretty long.

In fact, it's still going on.

Like this room in Quartzsite, Arizona, is just down a narrow, ill-lit hall from that room on the east coast of Mexico.

I mean—I got hoodooed good.

I ain't complaining.

But I ain't blinking, either.

You'd think that wouldn't be a big deal, as little a thing as a blink. But it is, if you haven't done it in what seems like a long, long time. Hours. Or maybe I've slipped into a different time zone where it's *always* hours between blinks. I ought to be able to check this out by looking at the TV—whether it's happening in superslow motion or just regular—except that I can't quite *see* the TV anymore. It's like I'm looking through thin, white, sparkly goo. Just see shapes and light. Can't tell if the fuzz is on the screen or in my eyes. Maybe I'm seeing *between* the 'lectronic dots? Maybe I'm *that* geared down?

A R E N ' T   Y O U   G E T T I N G   A   L I T T L E   T I R E D   O F   A L L   T H I S ?

Funny you should ask. But don't you think I'm dying well? Ain't nuthin' chicken 'bout *this* white boy.

D O N ' T   B R A G .   Y O U ' L L   G E T   P I M P L E S .

PART FIVE

Meet Me in the Middle of the Air

I went to the rock to hide my face,
But the rock cried out
"No hiding place!
There's no hiding place down here!"
—The Carter Family

O N E *Marriage and Divorce*

She drove. I didn't trust myself to. The world just didn't look right yet. Near was far, far was near, slow was fast, and every color shone too much. Even the dark seemed like it was shining.

She drove with that new Ciudad Victoria dress pulled up over her knees, one bare foot (looking fragile without white paint) on the gas, the other tucked up under her. She leaned over the wheel, peering into the night, the way a kid learning to drive tries to see out over the hood.

"Sorry I hit you, before," I said. "That bruise'll be tough to explain when we get home."

"Not so tough. But, like they say: 'God punishes, and cheatin' shows.' "

"One way or another, it sure does. Every time."

"I don't want to think about that now."

"Then don't."

Way off there across the seat of my Chevy she felt so separate from me. It made me lonely. I wondered what it would be like to live every day with this woman. How I'd like just to watch her, in her own place, see how she does the little things, and how she does nothing at all. I really must not know her at *all*, because I couldn't even imagine her boiling water, much less cooking.

"I'm sorry for something else, too," I said.

"I love it when a man is sorry. Tell me."

"Sorry I—fainted. The other night."

"You didn't faint. You passed out."

"There's not much difference."

"Sure there is. Passing out seems to me a worthy activity. But fainting—I just think of the Southern belles in all those old movies who fainted all the time and who were all heavy masturbators. I mean, you *know* Scarlett O'Hara beat off constantly. Continual clit-patting—that woman just reeked of it. But passing out—a person's got to *go* a ways to pass out."

195

"I went a ways, that's for sure. I ain't quite come back yet."

"You never will."

That was far past what I was ready to handle, I just let it go.

"You *can* be sorry for saying you were gonna kill me, though," Elaine said. "I'd accept that apology gladly."

"Can't be sorry for that 'cause I meant it."

"Wouldn'ta solved anything."

I shivered, cold with the memory of how close we'd come to bloodying those sheets. Wasn't sorry 'cause I would have been right there beside her—I loved her too much to let her die alone.

The movement of the car now felt less like driving than like sliding over an oily, gritty darkness. What we were leaving wasn't Mexico—I'd hardly even *seen* Mexico this trip. We were leaving a room where *anything* could happen, a room protected by thousands of miles of strangeness on all sides, thousands of miles of candied skulls, dead volcanoes, and tropical forests guarded by thousands of Virgins of Guadalupe standing aglow inside what's always looked to me like a wide-open pussy. And I knew that that room was more *home* to me now than anywhere else, and that I was headed north to a newly foreign country where all I knew was the language and a mad music that some of us played in the night.

"You scared me, baby," Elaine said. "Even more than I was scaring myself. Your face would change so fast, like quick cuts in a movie. You'd go from looking like a perfect angel to looking like—like Charles Manson! Back and forth, I never saw anything like it. I forgot all about myself, looking at you—*that's* a change!" She laughed. Then: "I always thought Manson and them made a big mistake."

"No shit."

"I'll bet," she said, "they got close to the power. I'll bet they got really *out there*, further than us, maybe lots further. And they sure stayed longer. But they locked on to the *blood*. 'Cause there's blood out there, too, blood with a capital *B!* It's just *one* of the things that's out there, but it's *familiar*. The power out there weirds you out so much, comes at you in so many *overwhelming* forms, you want to focus on what you're used to—so as to avoid the fact that you're *out there* at all. That's what they did. They locked on to the blood and got into violence as a way to avoid the *rest* of what was out there! They got stuck in the blood and in humping 'cause *that* stuff was exciting enough that they could kid themselves, could say, 'We got blood, we got sex, we've brought 'em back from out there, we got the power!' *Big* mistake. Back here, all that sex and violence was *just* sex and violence, nothing new, nothing special, nothing you had to go *out there* to find—no *real* power at all. They went around messing people up in the name of a power they'd run away from."

"You've thought about all this a lot."

"What else I got to think about—'cept *boys*." She laughed.

I thought of Nade and got scared for her. Like maybe Jesus on his cross is stuck in capital *B* Blood too. Like Nadine and them are stuck in the blood just like Manson, and for the same reason.

I admired her rap. It reminded me of Danny. Except that Danny was usually just improvising, while Elaine, like Henry, seemed to be talking of something she knew first hand and had thought through some. It made me feel sorry for Danny—like he did all that frantic improvising so he *wouldn't* have to draw many conclusions. And in that moment of feeling sorry for him I knew that he was right about one thing: I was leaving him behind. Which made me lonelier still.

"I feel kinda like we got married back there, Elaine. *Really* married."

"If that was the marriage, what-all's the *divorce* gonna be like!"

T W O 'Anything' Is the Key

A few miles on, Elaine asked, "How many people you married to?"

"Nadine. Danny. You, now."

"I got Johns. You. I'm not married to any women. I wish I was."

Silence awhile. Then I had to ask the question that had been gnawing on me. It blurted out low and fast:

"You ever do this stuff with Johns?"

"I told you: I never shared it like this before."

I wondered what she thought we'd shared, but I didn't ask. It seemed plain she hadn't any idea what happened inside me in that room, no more than I had of what happened inside her. Couldn't say that, though, because then she'd want me to *tell* her what happened, and—I couldn't even think about it then, much less tell about it. But how could we be so far from each other already? Our connection was so strong, but it was like the connection was a long electric cable that we were on opposite ends of, both of us holding on to it, the same juice shooting through us, both of us trembling with it, but miles apart.

She told me about cleaning the room, washing me down, and being so scared that even when she washed me I didn't wake up. She told me about sitting for hours watching me, looking over me, wondering if I *ever* was going to wake. Finally she couldn't handle it anymore, she went out to walk in the festival, wondering if I'd be dead or alive when she got back. "If you were dead I figured—I'd just disappear. It would be the biggest sign of all. Take the car, head south. Maybe go into a convent. Spend the rest of my life lying to God. Fool Him. Get into Heaven so's I could burn the place down."

She told of her fear to see I'd puked all over myself in my sleep—"Sick would be *worse* than dead. All the *phone calls* I'd have to make, all the ruination they'd cause." Then she wiped the dried vomit off me, which was when I'd hit her in the mouth. Said *that* was a relief. After I punched her she knew I'd be all right. Slept beside me awhile—I wish *I* remembered that!—then went out again. And the whole time her body felt oddly trembly and light.

When I realized she'd had less sleep than me, I took the wheel. The car felt strange under my hands. Like when you first learn to drive and you feel the machine is just waiting for you to slip up so it can go off in a direction of its own.

At first I wanted to ask how she'd come to this stuff, but just thinking of the question made me think of Danny, of all those doors he'd opened with all those weird inspirations of his—how close he'd come to this without quite knowing, without really wanting to

198

know. Never closing the door behind him after he went through, like we'd done.

And I wondered how many, many people skirted the edge of all this in how many, many out-of-the-way ways. Thought of the voices people sometimes hear just as they're nearing sleep. Thought of the sudden sense of falling I used to feel when in bed as a child. And of all the people, drunk and sober, drugged and straight, who'd had a taste of it and thought they were crazy—or how just the taste had *made* them crazy. Or how the taste had been enough for them, and how they'd think of it, wistful, in far-between quiet moments. Thought of how Nade got Jesus. How *Jesus* got Jesus. Thought of the Pentecostals talking in tongues and falling to the floor with the holy shivers. And of all the songs where this stuff shined through the music as the people danced. Thought of all this and didn't feel I had to ask anymore. Elaine had just taken it farther than most people. Out of loneliness or sadness or madness, booze or drugs or rock, or simply the night—one day she hadn't waited for it to come by chance, she'd done a little something to bring it on.

Finally I did ask something: "You're a writer. You ever write about this stuff?"

"And have everybody think I'm silly? No, thank you. Anyhow —wouldn't do anybody any good. You and I could tell exactly what-all we did, and somebody could do the same stuff, but they'd just be copying. I don't think it does any good to try somebody else's image. The whole thing with this stuff is that you do the image pure enough. I guess what I mean is nobody can copy the purity. You come to that, or you don't. A person's gotta be willing to do *anything*. 'Anything' is the key. Any holding back at all, and they'll never cross over."

"Just tell me one thing. How can you go back to Johns now?"

"Don't worry. I'll find a way."

THREE   *Half-Light*

I drove. She slept. The early morning hung in half-light for what seemed a long time.

FOUR   *Healing in His Wings*

Brownsville's awfully quiet for a border town, but it's got that same mean-eyed border town feel. This is no place to fuck up.

It was church-time on Sunday. The wind was wet off the Gulf. The sunlight was like this thin yellow soup that poured over everything. The buildings and streets were sticky with it, the people on the sidewalks were stained with it. Little Mexican kids, girls in white dresses and boys with starched white shirts and black pants, walking a few steps ahead of their mommies and daddies, everybody walking stiff in their Sunday best—they looked like wound-up toys. White families parking big American cars in front of the First Baptist church, they looked even worse, looked official, more like they were going to an actual "meeting" than anything else. Like they were going to call the club to order, read the minutes, ask about old business, new business, and then vote *no*. And the sky looked the kind of yellow that you get in the whites of your eyes with hepatitis.

We were looking for a good motel, the kind with wake-up calls and a restaurant attached. She was going to pay for it with a credit card, which I was amazed she even had. I refrained from asking if Johns might find out about us when the bill came. Everybody who lies like Elaine does, leaves little clues about. It's only fair.

We found the kind of place where they don't trust you if you pay cash. Thick carpet, thick drapes, two huge beds, air-condition-ing, heater, and on the TV you could get Atlanta, Chicago, LA, New York, the HBO and the PTL. The toilet even came with one of those little wraps around the seat to let you know that somebody had personally inspected it before you, yes, you, sat down—*your* ass is that much worth saving. The soap dish had Camay. The plastic glasses were individually wrapped. The ice bucket was like Tupperware. It felt like we could invite those nice First Baptist white people over and they could have their meeting right here.

Day people sure must be afraid of the dark, to pay fifty-sixty dollars for a place like this. But the hot water goes on forever. Day people have hot water *down*.

Elaine went straight to the bathroom. I went straight to the TV.

I heard the bath-tap running hard. I turned up the volume on the tube. Gene Autry. Pudgy little Gene, looking up at the sky, singing thin and high, his voice a perfect match for his watery eyes. A guy in a black hat comes up to Gene and snarls and Gene takes a swing at him with this lame right hook that's *so* hooked it swings way out in a curve before it reaches Mr. Black Hat. The poor guy has to stand there with his chin stuck out, waiting for it. Then he falls down. Gene's lady smiles. Gene smiles. People love this man.

Gene started to sing again and I changed channels. Jimmy Lee Swaggart. Nadine's favorite. I turned the volume off and just watched the man. He runs up and down the stage with his Bible flapping in his hands. He stops, holds his mike up to his face, leans into the crowd, hollers, hollers, hollers. Runs up and down in place a little, throws his arms into the air, shuffles his feet, hollers some more. I loved his act. With the sound off, there didn't seem any difference in the world between his routine and James Brown's, except James Brown is a better dancer. Still, Jimmy Lee does all right for a white boy. The man has the moves.

Nadine would sit with Little Jesse in her lap and watch this stuff for hours. When Swaggart sings, she harmonizes. When he yells, she yells back. When he cries, she weeps. And the poor little fucker—my son, I mean—doesn't know what to do when his mama cries except to cry with her. They were probably watching Swaggart right this minute. Some Sunday mornings I'd watch him just kind of to be with them.

You can't do a lot of time in motel rooms without learning Jimmy Lee's rap. I started saying it for him, syncing with his moves, whispering his holler: "I'm a watcher for your *souls!* That's my *business!* When Got looks at you He sees you as rotten and stinking with corruption and full of SIN! And the only, the *only* thing you can do, what you *got* to do to be a Christian, you here in Hawii-ah, and you there by television, is to *go* to Jesus, GO to him, He's *waiting* for ya, ah, *go* to Jesus-ah, and say-ah, I am rotten-ah, I am no good, I am *filthy*-ah, You are the ONLY one who can help me-ah! I'm talkin' 'bout the One-ah, the One who's comin' for you with HEALING IN HIS WINGS!"

"What, Jesse? I can't hear you with the water running?"

I had yelled without realizing. My mouth still had the word "wings" in it. It felt like the yell had splattered like grease off my burning tongue.

"That wasn't me. It was the television."

No answer.

I watched on as Swaggart mouthed the Lord at me, but I was thinking of that angel at the end of *Barbarella,* that big white blond angel with great feather white wings, how he rose slowly in the air with Jane Fonda under one arm and the black-leathered Queen of the Evil City under the other. The angel is blind. The women wear plastic fuck-suits. He's saving them both, because he's an angel, doesn't care which is good or bad, is just delirious-happy saving them, it's such a high to *save,* to be *saved.*

Now that angel, *he* had healing in his wings. And would he swoop down on this hotel and scoop us up in his arms, Elaine all soapy with bubble bath, me naked wrapped in this bedspread, Elaine rubbing up against him as we rose in the air, *me* rubbing up against him too since no angel can be a "him" 'cause he's an *angel?* And his arms so strong you don't even *think* of falling, and we rise above the city, and we rise above the world, and we become younger as we rise, Elaine's wrinkles smooth out, my belly shrinks back down, my hair is thick and all black again, my nose not broken anymore, no scars on my chin, no scars on my knuckles, no purple bags under my eyes, me rising in the thinning air, sweetness in my mouth, sweetness in my heart. Oh, my chest ached with the feeling of it, and for the first time I understood, understood how and why

Nadine went over. I wanted him so, that angel, wanted for him to pick us up right out of here, right away, wanted to be held by wings, the softest wings; I'd do anything for that. Be anything. Say anything.

Meet me Jesus meet me
Meet me in the middle of the air
And if these wings should fail me
Meet me with another pair
Well well welllllllllll
So I can die easy
Jesus gonna make up
My dyin' bed

My dyin' bed. My bed is dying. That, too.

"I love that one!" Elaine called from the tub.

I hadn't realized I was singing the song with my mouth.

She said, "I didn't know you could sing like that. Pretty. You always sing so rough."

Is it like this, Nade? Do you feel your chest tear open, and something, some kind of horrible glob, lifts out of it, and you're—lighter? Light as a feather on some great wing?

Boy, you can't blame anybody going over for *this* high.

"Sing another one," Elaine called from the tub.

Swaggart's kid is on the show now. It's the commercial. His kid is asking me for money. The guy is in his early twenties and has a wide, weak face, a face that looks like it knows everything there is to know about jerking off. A kid who spends half his time wanting to play with himself and the other half praying he won't do it again. He's asking for my money in particular. He's got this high weedly voice you don't even have to hear, you can see it on his face.

It doesn't seem possible that a face like that ever felt any of what I'd just had an inkling of, but who can tell? I can see him beg to feel such. Kid, why don't you just get on your knees right now and use your voice for what it does best: beg.

Beg, you little fucker.

And the kid gets on his knees, and out of his eyes come big gobs of hamburger grease, the grease runs down his cheeks, makes his face all sticky and shiny, and his prayer smells like a McDonald's but it's a *prayer*. And his chest starts to come apart under his clothes, like in *Alien,* but in slow motion, and this big rancid glob of half-cooked grade-F beef kind of bubbles out, popping his shirt buttons and oozing down his clothes, and he's begging and laughing and crying and singing and gagging and coming, and the meat that was his soul starts to sizzle at his feet and . . . it ain't the kid, it's *me.*

Jesus, it don't have to be You, You can just send me some ragged dog to come and chomp up my hamburger soul and lap up its grease and go back off to You and spit it at Your bright white feet; I don't deserve any better . . .

Now they're running this address across the bottom of the screen over this film of Swaggart hugging on a couple of bewildered African skeleton kids. Swaggart looks none too happy about having to touch them, like he's afraid he'll catch something. Like he's about to throw up. People love this man.

An awful churning twisted my stomach, something burning shot up my throat, I doubled over, spit some milky fluid onto the shag rug. My stomach twisted worse, like the Snake was inside me, biting me, all I could do was grip my gut and shake, begging the angel in my heart not to pass over me, not to; oh, if I didn't hear the beat of those wings I would surely die . . .

Elaine stood over me in nothing but soap suds. Some angel. She took me in her wet arms.

"Jesse? *Jesse?*"

On the floor, cradled in her cool wet arms, I looked back at the TV. The camera was panning over a row of fat weeping faces.

"I'm okay," I said to Elaine.

"Sure you are."

She held me till I could breathe again.

"What would you say if I got religion?" I asked her.

"I'd say you'd gone crazy."

"Coming from you, that is quite a mouthful."

PART SIX

The Living Legend of Jesse Wales

It's not the i-dea, it's the THING *that's real. I just wanna get funky for ya.*
                    —Etta James

A perfect monster has no end.
                    —Roky Erickson

O N E *Somethin' Else*

~~~

"The Living Legend of Jesse Wales" my ass. But my face was all over town on the cover of the *Austin Sun* the day we got back, with that "legend" business in big letters for God and everybody. Me—those Mexican potholes had ruined my alignment so bad that by the time we made Austin my front tires had worn bald. I was shitting mud, my teeth were loose, and my heart was hers.

"Ain't metaphysics somethin' else?" Danny laughed.

T W O *Breakfast at Dawg's*

~~~

"Dawg, I'm in spiritual pain."

"Take two aspirins and watch some television."

"PTL?"

"Game shows. Stick to game shows."

He poured me a beer, broke an egg into it, and stirred the mess. With his shaggy beard and his belly he looked like how a Saint Bernard rescue dog might look if it decided to turn into a man. Which is probably why someone, somewhere, had started to call him Dawg, and why it had stuck.

"How's the living-legend business?" Dawg smiled.

"Lay off. I got enough trouble."

"You must be in love."

"Shit. Almost got religion down in Brownsville."

"Brownsville ain't a good place to get *anything*. Man, don't be getting religion on me. I stop speaking to my men friends who get religion."

"What about your women friends?"

"Gotta give some leeway to the people you fuck."

"That so? I hadn't heard."

Danny came in, and Dawg drew him his beer and stirred in his egg without Danny needing to ask, same as he'd done for me.

"The Living Legend tell you 'bout his adventures?" Danny said.

"Told me all I wanna hear," Dawg said. "I love you guys, as you well know. I will put eggs in your beer till Doomsday, assuming that day's not too many eggs off. But if you're gonna talk your spacy brand of bullshit, go sit at a table. I promise I will not feel neglected."

As we headed for an empty table near the jukebox, Dawg called after us, "Why aren't you guys nonverbal like the majority of your colleagues?"

"Bad luck, I guess!" I called back.

"We may be verbal," Danny laughed, "but we got limited vocabularies."

"Not limited enough, if you ask me," Dawg said.

THREE *Winds Between the Worlds*

I was stuck between not being able to keep Ciudad Victoria to myself and not being able to talk it either. The night before, or early morning, at the King Bee, I *had* tried. Danny sat grinning while I described Elaine walking on the back of the Snake, and tried to give him some idea of the Moan, but all that I told pretty much the way it had happened was about the crystal and a little of that *Barbarella*-angel stuff in Brownsville.

Sitting near the silent juke at Dawg's, I said, "You know, I haven't touched a piano since we got back. It's like I'm afraid to play."

"It's *hard,* bein' a mystic." Danny laughed.

"I am *not* one of *those*. I don't even know what one *is*."

"A mystic—"

"And I don't *wanna* know. I mean it."

"What *do* you want?"

"Somethin' for nothin'—just like everybody else."

One problem was that everybody, now, felt like they were at least ten yards away—like Elaine had seemed the whole trip back. Danny, two feet from me across the small round table—it was like I was looking at him through the wrong end of a telescope. He was the same skinny awkward tallish guy, in the same jeans, in a red Western shirt I'd seen him wear a hundred times, the same feathery dark hair, the same birdlike face with its high bony cheeks, the same glittery blue eyes, just as sharp, just as intense—but way away, somehow.

"Naw," he said, "now there's Nade *and* you somehow crossed over, and here I am all by my lonesome still on *this* side. Apocalypse must be comin' soon, is all *I* can figure, if it's got *you* ruffians already. Maybe my kind's the last to go."

"*Your* kind? There ain't no 'your kind' that I ever heard of."

"I *know* it. An' it's beginnin' to get on my nerves."

I sat there guilty that we weren't the same kind. We never had been, I guess, but we'd thought we were. But that was gone, now.

"Naw, maybe that's how Apocalypse *really* begins. Some doors start slammin' open, others start slammin' shut—and they *stay* slammed. Slammed by winds blowin' between the worlds. *That's* what Apocalypse is. It's a *storm*, a big old thunderstorm full of funnel-clouds blowing in both worlds at the same time. But *Henry* says we gotta open the doors to save *this* old world, says that's all that'll work. Maybe that's like in a house, when a tornado's comin', you open all the windows so the pressure won't suck the house down. *I* don't know. Naw, I do. And when the storm's over, the great clear sharp feel in the air—whole world'll feel like that, in a hundred years, if there's any world left. *I* don't know. But no, I *do*. I got the *big* picture down pretty good, it's the little pictures I'm having trouble with these days. You got more doors slammin' open than you can stand; I feel like all mine have slammed shut. Why do you think that is?"

"Danny-O, Danny-O. *I* don't know *anything*. Maybe you're

just supposed to lay low for a while." Then: "There's nothing to *do* with this stuff, man. What do I *do* with it?"

Danny couldn't say, but he did something he'd never done. He reached across the table and took my hands in his. His were cold.

"Your hands are hot," he said.

He kept ahold of my hands. It made me squirmy. I felt myself blush. Finally I pulled my hands away.

Way at the wrong end of the telescope, Danny was smiling.

F O U R *Bring On the Dogs*

I was supposed to be looking up over the piano at a skylight that wasn't there. They were going to film the skylight some other day, some other place. I was supposed to pretend to see some furry fanged female monster-critter growling down on me, then pretend to act accordingly.

It wasn't hard to pretend. I was scared enough just sitting at the piano. I ran my fingers over the keys, pressing lightly, making no sound. They felt cool and tender on my fingertips. It felt like a long way down my arms to my hands. I knew I could play if I had to—and I'd have to soon enough. But it wasn't like the piano was a part of me anymore—and if it wasn't, then what was?

I'd gotten into this silly movie because of Elaine's "Living Legend" story. These Hollywood low-budget people woke up their first day in Austin and needed a local band for a honky-tonk scene and my face was all over the place, so they called me. I guess Elaine, in her way, had conjured them up.

The director was too young to be bald but he had only a few brown wisps left and they stayed matted to his skull with sweat. His name was Eric Bergman. "No relation to Ingmar" was a joke he expected us to get. It was obvious he'd said the line too often by the time he was twenty, and he was at least twenty-five. This was his first time directing and his first time in Texas, which is why he didn't know that the tea which was supposed to be in my shot glass was actually Old Bushmills, and that most of the pitchers on the tables were full of actual beer instead of whatever they use in movies to look like beer. It was ten in the morning at Dawg's.

Eric Bergman had explained his movie to me earlier when we were trying to figure out what tune I should play: "It's kind of a Manson thing, but with creatures. It's sort of a combination of *The Texas Chainsaw Massacre* and *I Was A Teenage Werewolf.* There are these monsters, who are looking for each other—to mate. And on the way to finding each other they kill everybody they come across, and usually kill them while trying to mate with them, because it's the creatures' rutting season and they'll screw anything. We're gonna do a great scene with the female fuck-killing a pit bull —if we can figure out the effects for the dog. So it's kind of a soft-porn thing, too. Our young hero and heroine want to stop this, but then our hero gets a thing for the female monster."

"Did you think of this?" I asked.

"No, I'm not a writer."

Most of Dawg's regulars were taking off from their day jobs to be extras in one movie before they died, and not incidentally to have an excuse to drink in daylight on a weekday. Lyn Ann, Dawg's honcha waitress, was disappointed that the "set" didn't feel much like "Hollywood," since it was the same old joint in brighter light. "Everything's the same, same people even, 'cept no dogs and kids." But a little later she stepped on a three-year-old and hollered "Bring on the dogs!" in the middle of a take they call an "establishing shot." Eric Ingmar, as we started to call him, yelled "Cut!" and lectured everybody on the importance of what we were doing here today and could we please refrain from yelling "Bring on the dogs!" or anything else that he didn't tell us to yell.

I was for *any* excuse to yell, especially since Elaine had walked in with the monster-lady. The last I'd seen her was when I dropped her off at the all-but-deserted airport, where she intended to sleep in a chair till dawn and call Johns when the Houston plane landed and tell him she'd flown Mexico City–Houston–Austin. Now she made quite an entrance walking beside the monster, whose real name was Deirdre. Some monster. A magazine body. I don't know how they did it, but they'd just sort of molded this beautiful light-brown fur all over her so it looked like that was her real naked body. Naked and not-naked, like an animal, all her features normal. Only her hands, feet, and head weren't covered with fur.

Elaine walked beside her in that Mexican dress. Nice touch. I flushed all over, looking at her. And took my hands away from the keyboard as though it was a hot griddle.

Walking just behind them, like a servant, was a tall old man with bushy white hair, a swollen red nose, and thick eyeglasses. He carried Deirdre's monster heads, hands, and feet, variously awful for various states of monsterness—lots of claws, bulging eyes, and vicious snouts. You noticed him because of how out-front he was about keeping his eyes fixed on Deirdre's and Elaine's asses as they walked in front of him, like those behinds were all that enabled him to keep his bearings in this unfamiliar place.

Eric Ingmar brought Elaine and Deirdre to the bandstand.

"Hi, there, Mrs. Thompson," I said to Elaine.

"Hi, there, Mr. Wales."

"I didn't know Texans were so formal," Eric said.

"Yeah, well—you live longer that way," I said.

Eric seemed to have a way of passing over anything he didn't understand, so he didn't miss a beat saying, "Jesse, this is Deirdre, our star."

"Stars don't die in the end, Eric," Deirdre said.

FIVE *Deliver Us Now*

Elaine and I looked hard into each other's eyes. In some awful way I felt closer to her than to *my own hands* that rested on the faded white keys.

Deliver us now and at the hour of our Snake.

SIX *The Church of the Long Distance Call*

Which is when Nadine walked in with Little Jesse. I saw Dawg give her a big hug by the door.

When I'd told her on the phone that I was going to be in a picture show, she'd packed the kid in the car and driven all night. She'd just got in. On the phone, she hadn't even asked whether it was all right if she came, said only, "You can pay our trip with that check they give you, just sign it over when you get it, can't you?" I hadn't argued.

Without saying a word to Elaine, Eric, or Deirdre, I just got off the bandstand and walked slowly toward Nade and the kid. The movie lights made the old club brighter than it had ever been. Every worn spot, every stain, every cigarette burn on floor and table looked like it was trying to hide. The joint looked stripped naked. I felt Elaine's eyes on my back as I walked toward Nadine.

She didn't *look* saved. Tall and still trim, in tight jeans and white boots, she stood with her hip cocked to one side, thick dark hair hanging way past her shoulders, a bright yellow blouse, a small gold cross on a gold chain glinting in the light, half smiling. Little Jesse came just about up to her hips, and her hand rested easy on his shoulder.

Little Jesse is a real self-contained little guy. Doesn't say much, but he can read already because his Mama reads to him all the time, mostly from the Bible. He has quirks like being afraid of telephones —has to have his mama hold it up to his ear, won't pick it up himself. He's real sturdy in his body, but real delicate in his moves, like he doesn't *know* he's sturdy. Has my nose, was born looking like he'd broken it in a wreck. A dark kid—dark hair, dark eyes, and a dark kind of shine to him.

He asked me once why I wasn't "good," and I asked him what he meant, and he said I was going to Hell because I wasn't "good," and he cried and ran off. I damn near knocked Nadine's teeth out for that. Now he watched me come toward him like he always watched me at first, unsmiling and alert, like he was waiting for one of us, him or me or Nade, to do or say something wrong.

Dawg stood by them grinning.

"When was the last time you saw this lady in a club?" he beamed.

"Pampa, actually. Some time back."

"Hey, Jesse."

"Hey, Nade."

I kneeled in front of the kid, stuck my hand out for a shake.

"Hey, little man," I said.

"Hey," he said soft, with his eyes on the floor. He put his hand to mine, and I pulled him toward me and hugged him hard. He put his arms around me without pressing at all, I could barely feel them.

I stood up with him in my arms. We hadn't seen each other in months.

"Where's Uncle Danny?" the kid wanted to know.

"*There* he is," Dawg said, "surprising no one."

Danny was by the bandstand with Elaine and Deirdre and the old man who carried her heads and claws. Even from here we could see how Danny's eyes were all over the monster-lady.

"Can I go see him?"

"Sure." And I let him down and he scampered off. Danny visited whenever he was anywhere near Baton Rouge, and my kid was lots more comfortable with his "uncle" than with me. Danny never fought with his mama.

"I, uh, gotta go," Dawg said; "make sure these people don't tear up my place."

He left us with a troubled smile.

"You know this place *stinks*," Nade said, "if you're not used to it. Smells like puke."

"Just old beer spills."

"I know."

"Why'd you come?"

"Don't know. Kind of felt you out there. *Almost* like you needed me. Needed us. *That's* a joke, isn't it?"

"I sure need *something*," I said. What I felt like I needed was a drink, it was so weird to see Nadine back in what had been our natural habitat. That all seemed a hundred years ago now.

"Let's get a drink," she said. "Oh, don't look so surprised, I don't believe *everything* the TV preachers say."

"I never figured you did."

"Thanks."

We went to the far side of the bar and leaned up against it shoulder to shoulder like gunfighters in Westerns. In the mirror behind the cash register, we stared back at ourselves.

"I don't know if Little Jesse should be seeing this thing," I said. "It might get pretty raunchy."

"Don't be a doting daddy, Jesse, it don't fit."

"But should he?"

"I had me a dream. Our boy had these eyes painted all over his cheeks. It was a sign that he could see more ways, more things, than me. It was my dream and I got to respect it. He needs to see lots of things, fill up all those eyes. It's worse for them to be hungry. I gotta trust my faith'll protect him."

"How do you know that dream didn't come from Satan?"

"Funny *you* should ask."

"You don't know how funny."

I ordered a whiskey and she ordered a beer and we stared at each other's faces in the bar mirror.

"I used to hate singing here, though I do love Dawg. But the sound in this place—it was like singing into a sock."

"I'm not too fussy."

"I know. I am."

Sometimes now we didn't see each other for six, eight months at a time, but when we got together we didn't need any warm-up time, we were right back where we'd left off as though it was just yesterday. Even though she, too, seemed strangely far from me, still we stood at that bar as naturally as if we'd met there every day.

"I pray for you and Danny every day and every night. I'm like a walking prayer for you guys."

"Sounds like a good Indian name: Walking Prayer. We in that much trouble?"

"Not much. It's just that the world's coming to an end."

In the mirror I watched the movie people moving the lights around, moving the cameras around, arguing. And saw Danny, the kid, Elaine, and Deirdre sitting at a table near the bandstand, talking and laughing. Elaine had placed herself so she could just naturally take in me and Nade.

"You know what my fantasy is?" Nadine said. "The three of us start our own church. We rent a storefront, or a little wood-frame, and we call it The Church of the Long Distance Call. The name of that old band of ours fits real nice, don't it? We'd all preach. Couldn't you see Danny preaching? And we'd sing rock gospel. We'd go for the *real* lost souls, the Out There people, the people who are *never* gonna listen to any TV preacher, people who hardly come out in the day. We'd have our services at night. That would be some church, The Church of the Long Distance Call. And when the end came—and it's comin' soon—we'd lead the motliest, most-saved bunch of ragamuffins through those Gates."

"They'd say, 'There goes the neighborhood.' "

"Not my Jesus." Then: "That's where I go inside myself to pray, that very church, and we're all there."

"I like it."

"I came here," she said, "because our boy's been asking about you lately. This movie thing seemed like a good excuse. I just wanted you to know I didn't come with any—designs."

"What's he been asking?"

"Oh, like, 'What does my daddy do at this time of the day?' or, 'Does my daddy like red better than green?' Like that. He just needed to hang out with you some."

"You could have just asked me to spend a few days."

"Right. As good as I am at asking for things. And as good as you are at giving."

That was fair. She'd've asked and I'd've said, "Sure, soon." And "soon" wouldn't't've happened for months, and the kid would have spent them asking if it's "soon" yet.

"Does *he* like red better, or green?"

"For a while after this," she said, "he'll like whatever he thinks you'd like. It's always like that after he sees you. He starts imitating you in all these small, real accurate ways. He's not even aware of it. Drives me nuts, frankly. But it's natural, I guess."

They were all laughing back at the table, except for Little Jesse, who was just staring gah-gah at furry-naked Deirdre. It didn't surprise me that Danny hadn't rushed over to greet Nade. He had

Deirdre's scent, and when Danny caught the scent he just couldn't help himself, which of course Nade knew.

"I feel like an idiot," she said, "but I have to ask this, and I can't blame you if you don't answer. Just don't lie. You seeing any woman here that I'm going to have to make small talk with?"

"No."

"I don't know why I asked. There's no way I can believe you. Probably that blousy redhead over there."

"I said, no."

"I shouldn't have asked."

"Nade—there's something I need to tell you, but I don't know if I can get it out."

"Uh-oh."

"Just—don't get mad at me till I finish, okay? What I'm trying to say is about Jesus."

She turned her head away, so that what I saw in the mirror now was her profile—her long forehead, strong nose and chin.

"A little while back, a week or so, I realized something about you—and about Jesus. I realized what it must feel like. Or *might* feel like. I felt it." I felt the ache for the healing wings as I said this. It surprised me how close I still was to that ache. "I don't mean—I don't mean—I still don't think I'll ever go that way—" I could feel how still she was beside me. "But—I never could see before, why you did . . . I never could see that, it seemed like such—such a cop-out. Now—I guess I'm saying I get it, now, it's okay with me."

A hoarse harsh laugh coughed out of her.

"You mean God and I finallly have your approval? I'll have to tell God, He'll be *so* pleased."

"I knew it would sound stupid, but it's a big deal for me."

I knew what she knew: If I had come that close, and hadn't gone over, I probably never would. Her five-year hope was sizzling out like a wet cigarette.

"Maybe things'll go a little easier for us now," I said, and as soon as I said it I regretted saying it. Neither of us wanted things to go easier. As long as things stayed edgy between us we knew we hadn't given each other up.

She forced a smile. Poor Nade. It wasn't that she cared about me agreeing with her, and it wasn't even just that she wanted me to be her husband and Little Jesse's father every day. She truly feared for my immortal soul.

"Your WHAT?" Papa Adam laughed somewhere deep inside the mirror where he couldn't be seen.

I gulped down my whiskey and ordered another.

"I have this other fantasy," Nadine said softly. "It's about the Rapture Day. You're gonna be visiting. We'll have gone out, like to a McDonald's, and we'll be driving back, you and me and Little Jesse eating our Big Macs—our boy in the back seat. You'll be telling him tales about how great a car is your '69 Chevy and how far you've driven it and all, but right in the middle of your rap the Rapture will come down, so fast, faster than thought, but so gentle, gentler than anything that's ever been. The Rapture will just suddenly *be.* And everybody truly Christian will just—up and disappear! That's the Rapture, that's what it is."

"I know what it is. What they say it is."

"And you'll be driving that car, and, in the middle of a sentence, you'll be looking at your son in the rearview, and he'll have up and disappeared! And you'll look at me—and I'll be gone, too; there'll just be a pile of my clothes, and my Big Mac, and a large Coke spilled all over the seat. And you just won't believe it— except you *will,* you'll believe it so bad. 'They've gone to Rapture,' you'll whisper, so afraid that you can't even call it fear, 'cause that fear'll be *all* that's left on this old world. And you'll stop your precious car, and get out, and leave it, right there, and you'll start walking. In a daze. Because you'll know, then, that nothing matters for you from then on, because no matter what direction you walk, you'll be walking straight to Hell. And I'll be up in Rapture with you wiped clean from my mind. Oh, Jesse, I won't even remember you. Amazing grace."

She had tears in her eyes and she was smiling. Every word she'd said was absolutely real to her. I loved her for that.

"You *sure* you haven't taken to church-preachin'?"

"I have, actually. A little bit. How'm I doin'?"

"Pretty damn good. 'Cept—I don't mind you passing judgment on me—who's got a better right?—but you may be wrong about my car. You don't know what *it* believes. It may just zip to Rapture right with y'all, and I'll be left ramming into the ground with a Big Mac in my mouth."

"You're crazier than I am."

"I am *not*."

"I think," she said, "I think I have to go to the little girls' room." She wiped her wet eyes. "Get my child off that woman's lap, will you?"

S E V E N *Elaine's Lap*

Mars ain't no kinda place to raise your kids.
                    —Elton John

I envied the kid. To be five and small and sitting on Elaine's hot lap. Though you could see she didn't care a thing about kids, could see she'd just put him on her lap to use him as a kind of transmitter to beam her raw stuff at me and at Nade—and I was even proud of Nade, that on some level she'd dug that, hadn't been fooled, though they hadn't yet been so much as introduced.

But to be on Elaine's lap, all that power shooting up from her crotch and thighs into your little butt and out the top of your head, you wrapped in arms so much stronger than yours, wrapped in purpose so much stronger, and that huge head of red hair looming over you, you pressed against that sweat-wet thin dress. But then I flashed that this was nothing new to *this* kid, who'd spent a lot of his short life on Nadine's lap while she was weeping watching Jimmy Lee Swaggart, shouting her a-mens, crying her prayers, with those black gospel stations on the radio full-blast all the time and his mama howling her wild harmonies, his mother using him as a transmitter too, not consciously like I knew Elaine was, but just as powerfully and maybe more so, the kid a transmitter not just to me but to his mama's awful god. No wonder Little Jesse shined so dark.

"I got a new boyfriend!" Elaine said, giving Little Jesse a squeeze as I pulled a chair up to their table.

Little Jesse couldn't decide whether it was safer to look at the floor or the ceiling. He sure didn't want to look at any of us.

"I'm available, you know," she said in his ear.

"Don't believe her, kid. She's married," I said. "Get on over here."

He looked at me with immense relief at having an excuse to slide off her lap.

"Where's your wife?" Elaine said.

Danny laughed. Deirdre laughed too, just because he had. You could see they'd already decided to crawl all over each other at the first opportunity. If it were me, I wouldn't want her to take that fur suit off. In fact, it would be a little sickening to see her white body kind of worm out of that sleek fur.

We small-talked about why this movie outfit couldn't seem to get anything done. Dawg's regulars-turned-extras just drank on, boredom hanging in their air like thick cigarette smoke. Nade came in a bit and gave Danny a big hug. Then she held him at arm's length and looked him up and down. In the harsh movie-light his cheeks were gaunt, his eyes hollow—much worse than I'd realized in the dimmer lights I was used to seeing him in.

"You look like hell," she said.

"I don't look no worse than Jesse," Danny said.

"He looks beat up, you look wasted. There's a difference."

"But you're nevertheless *real* glad to see me!"

She smiled her mother-smile, couldn't help it.

"Yeah. Real glad. I love you, fool."

"Don't you love Daddy?" Little Jesse said as naturally as you please.

Elaine laughed and Nade shot her a killing look.

"Course she does," I said.

"Course I do," she said.

"Course, course, course," Elaine said.

"Do I know you?" Nade said.

"Course you do," I said, by way of admitting everything.

"I don't believe I've had the pleasure," Nade said.

"That's probably true," Elaine said.

Little Jesse tensed so much at their voices that he seemed to get smaller and stiff in my arms. Felt like a wooden puppet all of a sudden.

"This is Deirdre, the movie actress," Danny said, "and this is

Elaine, who makes living legends out of just plain folk at the stroke of a pen."

"You *really* believe this legend business?" Nade said. " 'Cause *I* think all the legends are in hiding, like the saints."

"Woo!" Danny yelped. "That's my ol' Nadine."

"If this man ain't in hiding," Elaine said, "I don't know who is."

"Just testing," Nade said. "No offense."

And Nadine stuck out her hand and Elaine took it and they shook firm, like men.

"None taken," Elaine said. "I admire professionalism in all things."

"So do I," Nadine agreed.

Danny turned to me. "Do you feel outclassed?"

"Perpetually."

The boy was still tense in my arms. And just then a wave of fatigue washed over me, my guard dropped unexpectedly and totally, not in my head but in my body, which felt its ties to Elaine suddenly taut and painful, and felt its connection to Nade slack and thin. At which my boy slipped off my lap and got his own chair, pulled it up near his mother's.

"Where did you get those earrings?" Elaine asked Nadine.

"Now earrings we can converse civilly about. We can exchange clandestine information on the subject of what we hang from our ears."

Nadine's were silver crescent moons inlaid with jade. I'd got them for her birthday, some birthdays ago. Elaine's were wide round shell-things, aswirl with colors that just looked noisy against her hair. Nadine, ever vigilant, informed Elaine of this fact.

"I know," Elaine said. "I get tired of things matching. Even matching-while-not-matching, you know, like people do now? If things are not going to match, they should *really* not match and not look like they secretly do."

"It's a theory," Nadine said, "isn't it, Danny? And how come *you* don't wear earrings yet?"

"Men," Little Jesse said seriously, "don't wear earrings, Mama."

"Who's talking about men? I was talking about musicians."

"*Pirates* wear earrings," I told my kid.

"That's true, Mama," he informed her.

"So it is," she said, stroking his hair, "so it is."

"It's so *hot* in this friggin' suit," Deirdre said, tired of being ignored, as, with one swift move, she opened her fur costume from the top down to the belly button—a very unattractive belly button, too, the kind that sticks out like a knob of chicken gristle. Her tits didn't quite pop out of the costume, but almost. It happened so fast —the outfit had one of those Velcro zippers, you couldn't tell it was there—and her skin looked sickly pale next to the fur. But her tits were huge and rosy-perfect. Danny like to wet his pants. Elaine laughed and Nadine rolled her eyes, smirking at me—she knew my taste in navels.

"Sugar," Nadine said, "those things look like plastic snow cones."

"They're just props," Deirdre said, "but you're correct, I'm a miracle of modern medicine—*sugar*."

"You're kidding," Nade said.

"Could we, uh, go to the little girls' room?" Elaine said.

"Come again?" Deirdre said.

"Honey, if that's silicone, I wanna really *see* it."

"What's silicone, Mommy?" Little Jesse said.

"Ask your father."

"You really string for the *Stone?*" Deirdre asked Elaine.

"Cross my heart and spit."

"All right, then, let's adjourn to the Tampax dispensers."

Now that Danny knew he would be sucking up on plastic, he was *really* hooked.

"Mind if I join y'all?" he said sweetly.

"Behave yourself," Nade said.

"Why start now?" he said.

"Look who's talkin'," I said.

"You backslidin' today, Miss Nade?" Danny said.

"*Not*—really," Nade said.

"We're off," Elaine said, standing.

"Don't go, Mommy," Little Jesse said.

"It's okay, Daddy's right here. Aren't you, Daddy?"

"I'm right here, kid."

The women up and went. Little Jesse watched them go, desperate in his eyes. And looking at him was like looking into a mirror that looked back at me lots younger but just as anxious as I'd been lately. I suppose if you live with your kid every day, you get used to being mirrored like that; but if you don't, it can be pretty shocking.

"I'd say," Danny said, "that we three guys are pretty lucky with this profusion of women."

"I'd say we're in deep shit."

I felt like Elaine and Nadine both, with their very different eyes, had been looking right through me, and that under their gaze I'd shrunk down, *The Incredible Shrinking Man* for sure, till I was no bigger or older than Little Jesse. As if he and I were two versions of the same helplessness, and that somehow he knew this too. So he was scared to be with me in this strange place, because he didn't think I could protect him, because I was so *like* him.

This stuff came over me in quick wordless waves. The knowing that that dark shine of his was *my* dark shine—that that was how *I* looked to people, like a boy-man; beat-up and raunchy though I was. A boy-man, quiet-like except when I played, always waiting somehow, looking about me darkly; absorbing, shining. That these people who were so important to me, and the people on the dance floors in the honky-tonks—that that was what they liked most about me, the same thing I knew least, something in the darkness of the shine. That you've got to trust a music to dance to it, and that for all the wildness of my sounds this strange darkness in me was what they trusted. That I, somehow, had got to begin to trust it too. Because I'd carried it, but I'd never trusted it. It had come out of me in music and it had weighed on me in life, but I'd sat with it just like Little Jesse had been sitting at this table, wide-eyed, suspicious, and ready to run.

That I wasn't like I thought, wasn't *really* very tough at all; that this darkness was soft, or maybe gentle, or maybe helpless—I didn't know. Maybe it was only nameless, and satisfied to be what it was. A living secret that drew other secrets to it. But I knew that this darkness in me went on forever inside me, the way something in everybody goes on forever inside them to someplace none of us knows a thing about. And that this darkness was my portion. And my boy's.

Hadn't Henry said, ages ago, that I had a thing he called "direct access"? I knew now it had something to do with the dark shine—so maybe my boy had it too. Yet if "direct access" was what had gone on in Ciudad Victoria, hadn't it done me more harm than good? For it felt like the piano-touch had left my hands, and if it had, what the *fuck* was left of my life? And it seemed like lots was coming into me and nothing was going out, and soon enough I'd burst and I just wouldn't be there anymore, there'd be nothing left of me but what Papa Adam, from his place of great concealment, had called my "soul," and *that* didn't feel like *me* at all.

"What's silicone, Daddy?" Little Jesse said.

E I G H T   *The Learning of Words*

Elaine had left a book of matches on the table. I reached for them with a shaky hand. Sitting there, these thoughts hadn't felt like thoughts, had been more a kind of deep-down bass-line reverb, amped in me till my shakes were like the vibrating of a speaker when the volume's been turned up so high the fabric's about to rip. Still, I managed to light a match, and with that act the shaking subsided down to the slightest shiver and didn't show. With the match, I melted a swizzle stick onto the table.

"Silicone's kind of like that stuff, kid, but not hot. Doctors can put it in parts of the body to make them look bigger and smoother."

"Like that lady's knockers?"

A barf of a laugh burst out of me so hard it hurt my lungs, and Danny laughed too, and Little Jesse—he smiled real for the first time that day. A sweet dark little smile, but it was like he'd come to my rescue. In some inside-out way it made me feel like a father just a little.

"Like that lady's *knockers,* right!" I finally said when I could talk again.

"Do you like her?"

"No."

"Do you like the other lady?"

"Yeah. I like her a lot."

"I don't like them."

"How come?"

"They're scary."

"Man, we're all a *little* scary, sometimes."

"Uncle Danny's not."

Danny was like a small spotlight with a dimmer, he got brighter or softer depending on who was around. He'd been real bright when it was just him, Elaine, Deirdre, and the kid at the table, I'd felt it from across the club; then he'd dimmed way down when Nadine and me had come over. Now he was bright again.

"Well, I thank you, boy," he said. "I think."

They smiled like two people who didn't have to explain things to each other. Made me feel left out. I flashed on Little Jesse grown and playing in Danny's band, listening to Danny like I—used to. Him just taking it all in, in a kind of dark awe. And Danny would be just the same, except older—he'd never change. And my kid and I wouldn't be able to talk, and he wouldn't like my music.

Now that the women were away, Little Jesse relaxed some. And hung on Danny's every word.

"Don't you love," Danny said to me, "how this place isn't this place anymore? All these wires and lights and strangers. I guess that's how they do it up in Hollywood; they can't open doors, so they just bring in all this machinery and noise and make stuff *different*, so it's the same and not the same. Then once you see it in a movie, it's never the same for you."

"I like—your way better." I had started to say "our" way, and it had surprised me, and I'd stopped myself.

"Their way's neat, 'cept the door ain't really there. Or like—if you paint a doorway onto a real wall, and then somehow you open *that* door, well . . . *that's* really something. But if you make a fake wall, but put a real door in it, and then you open *that* door—what's *that*?"

The movie people were pulling their lights and wires all around; Eric Ingmar was arguing with somebody, his gofers were

225

trying to keep Dawg's regulars from leaving—all the extras were bored silly with waiting.

"I said to Deirdre, 'What's it like to be somebody else by profession?' and she just kinda blinked. And I said, 'Isn't that a weird job description? Cop says, 'What you doin' here, lady?' And you have to say, 'Officer, I was tryin' to be somebody else.' I loved that she didn't know what I was talking about."

"You're an expert at finding women who don't know what you're talking about," I said.

"That way I can hear myself think." Then: "You know, that even as we speak, that monster-lady and our Nadine and Elaine are bearing their breasts at each other and taking their damn time doin' it? If that don't make you horny, you need help."

"What's 'horny,' Daddy?"

"Ask your mother."

Danny and I laughed.

"He *will,* too, you know." Danny said.

"Serves her right."

"No, *you* tell me, what's 'horny'?"

"Nope, I already told you what 'silicone' is; it's her turn."

"You'll find out in your dreams soon enough," Danny said.

"Cool it, Danny-O," I said.

"How will I find out in my dreams?" the kid wanted to know.

"Shit," I said.

I glared at Danny, and he flinched under my glare. But in that moment I'd ripped a veil that had been hanging in front of my eyes, and I *saw* Danny, saw him in the bright unnatural light: how thin his skin seemed now, thin as tissue paper. His spirit just barely contained under it, like the tissue was ready to rip. I felt a nauseating fear: Are we going to lose Danny?

Little Jesse looked back and forth from Danny to me: the grown-ups. Sure we were.

Little Jesse fixed on me, like he'd caught my fear but didn't know what it was about, and the not knowing made his worse.

Which was when Danny said, like the tagline of a conversation he'd been having with himself: "Bad dreams may be the only way out."

"*What?*"

"Surprised?"

"Only at myself."

Surprised because of how strongly I didn't, I couldn't, believe that. Which meant I believed something else. But *what?*

And felt Papa Adam, deeply hidden, smile slightly.

"Daddy?"

"What, kid?"

"I don't want to have any more bad dreams."

Tough, I thought. But said, "Come on up on Daddy's lap."

He climbed up on me and pressed his face to my chest. He felt so little to me. Like I could crush him in my arms. And again I felt no difference at all between him and me. All *I* wanted to do was crawl into *somebody's* arms and get told something, anything, to hold back the weirdness.

"You have bad dreams, kid?"

"Mama says the Devil brings them."

"You ever seen this Devil personally?"

"No."

"Me neither." Not yet, anyway. "Bad dreams are . . . they're . . ."

"They're . . ."

"*Cool* it, Danny-O."

". . . where you gotta go, where *I* gotta go, Jesse, like you did down in Mey-hee-co, but . . ."

"Goddammit, Danny, lighten up in front of him. Don't you dig?"

"Don't be mean, Daddy."

"I'm not, kid. Am I, Uncle Danny?"

"No, no, no, no. Daddy's right. *Now,* Daddy—you were saying, *Jesse-O* . . ."

Fuck.

"See, dreams, kid—they're like little movies in your head, see? Like these people making this movie here. See, those are the cameras and those are the lights and all. Well, something in your head makes movies and shows them to you while you sleep, and some of them are scary movies and some of them are like cartoons and all. It just depends on what channel you tune into, what movies you get, dig? But since it's a channel you tune into in your sleep, you can't control *which* channel. So sometimes it's a movie, a dream, you don't want to see. But it can't hurt you any. You might not want to tell your mama I said this, you might want to keep this between you and me, but—I don't think the Devil's got shit to do with it."

"Nicely done," Danny said.

"You use so many bad words, Daddy."

"What, 'shit'? That's not so bad."

"Is so."

"Ain't either. You try it."

He raised a blush, and his blush raised a little smile.

"Can't."

"Yeah, ya can. Shit. There's nothin' to it. Shit. Even your mama does it. Says it, I mean."

"But then she tells God she's sorry."

"Well, you tell Him you're sorry, now, in advance, for every time you're gonna say 'shit' in this life. Go on."

He just looked up at me.

"Well?" I said.

"I did. I only talk to God in my head."

Shit.

Then he said, "But—I can't say it still."

"Aw, *shit,*" I said.

He giggled.

I said, "Awwwwwwwwwwwww—"

But he didn't say anything.

"Danny'll help us. Come on, Danny, awwwwwwwwwwwww —" And Danny joined on the "—SHIT! Now you do it with us, kid, Awwwwwwwwwwww—" And Little Jesse came in real quiet on our loud *"Shit!"*

The tables nearest us picked it up on the next one.

"AWWWWWWWWWWWWWW—SHIT!"

And on the *next* one, the whole joint, even some of the movie people.

"AWWWWWWWWWWWWWW—shit!

Eric Ingmar got on a microphone and said, "Uh . . . uh . . . uh . . ."

"AWWWWWWWWWWWW—shit!"

"—look—we have to hold this down, people, now—"

"AWWWWWWWWWWWWW—shit!"

My boy was *into* this now, face getting all red on the "aw" and eyes scrunched tight as he yelled "Shit."

"You people are being paid good money, now, and—"

"AWWWWWWWWWWW—shit!

Our women rushed in a pack out of the bathroom and made their way to the table.

"AWWWWWWWWWWWWW—shit!"

Nade stopped in her tracks about halfway to us. She didn't know *what* to do. She looked straight into my eyes and mouthed "Aw, shit" silently to me.

"AWWWWWWWWWW—"

Our eyes locked and I hated Jesus.

"—shit!"

And Deirdre stood by Elaine, half naked and not caring. And standing there catching the eye of most of the men and loving it, aw-shitting and hollering, she said "Eric, film it! Film it!"

But Elaine just stood in her Mexican dress and stared around her, like it all didn't quite register.

Somebody I couldn't see was yelling in a megaphone for us to shut up, and then: "You get what you pay for, Eric!"

"AWWWWWWWWWWW—shit!"

But you can only yell "Aw shit!" for so long.

We gradually, with coughing and laughter and hoarseness, settled down. And I sat Little Jesse in front of me up on the table and said, "Well, you been in your first riot, kid. How d'ya like it?"

"I hope I don't have to ask who started that," Nade said.

"I'd consider it a serious lack of faith."

"You proud of yourself?"

"Fairly."

The kid looked at his mother, real anxious. But she just mussed his hair.

"I guess this is what I came for," she said, "though I'm damned if I know why."

NINE *The Ladies' Room*

Nadine's nipples are dark, almost blue-black, and as large as the palm of my hand. The tips are as thick as the tip of my little finger. Her breasts hang heavy now, so how full they must have looked beside Elaine's much smaller, sagging, puffy things, which, if I opened my mouth wide enough, I could almost suck up whole. I loved to do that. What a shock to them, "examining" Deirdre, "like playing doctor," Elaine said later, when they dug that Deirdre *liked* it, had thought that that was what this was all about, and was more than willing. So Nadine had talked Jesus at her, to mend her sinful ways, and Deirdre had let her, while Elaine looked on bothered. Real bothered. Bothered enough, Nade told Danny later, to go into one of the two stalls by herself and sit the lecture out mumbling something Nade hadn't been able to make out as she spoke to Deirdre. Nadine had felt good, talking the Word in the ladies' room, and the women who'd gone in and out while they were in their would ask was it a meetin', and comment, and learn about Deirdre's tits, and ask, and some would feel, and Nadine and Deirdre would laugh, and Nadine would talk, all while Elaine hid.

TEN *It Just Won't Work on You*

Up until our little riot the movie crew had treated us homefolk like we were invisible. Just like some people act around their kids —standing right there and talking about us like we couldn't hear.

"You put that light there and his bald spot's gonna shine like the friggin' moon. He's gonna be moonin' the friggin' camera with his *head,* fa-Crissakes."

"You think we could get some women at those tables who don't look like they work cash registers at the goddamn K-Mart."

"Some a dem are pretty, if you ask me."

"A pretty check-out girl is still a check-out girl."

"Fuckin' looks like we got these people in a trailer park. Where are the fuckin' *cowboys?*"

Now that we'd messed their set a little they got stern, like we were schoolkids. We had nothing to do for a while but watch them clean up. They didn't even let us wipe our own spills. They were making a big fuss about filming us, but they sure didn't like us, and we sat there not liking them back.

A young albino guy in a sweat-wet T-shirt came over. The T-shirt said, "He Who Dies With the Most Credits Wins." He carried a megaphone in one hand, had a walkie-talkie on his belt, and a little earphone-mike setup on his head. His red eyes, white eyebrows, and white hair made him look like he'd spent the morning with a wet toe stuck in a wall socket.

"We're ready for you, Mr. Wales," he said.

"Glad to hear *somebody* is," Danny said.

"Could we rehearse the number now, Mr. Wales?"

I had wanted to play one of my own tunes but Eric wanted "something everybody knows," so I'd suggested "Got My Mojo Workin' " and he said, "Right, Creedence, great." I didn't bother telling him that Muddy Waters made the record ten years before the guys in Creedence got their learner's permits, nor that we were all still singing it in order to figure the damn song out, Muddy was that far ahead of everybody.

My guys were pissed at me for disappearing into Mexico and canceling gigs, but it's hard for a band to stay mad when the leader gets on the cover of a magazine, *any* magazine, so they were giving me some slack.

We weren't Eric Ingmar's ideas of musicians—Lady Fuentes with his purple eye makeup, Little Lee with his prison tattoos, and Peckinpah with his rotting teeth. Nor me either, naturally. They wouldn't have put it this way, but we didn't hardly look like white men to these Hollywood folks.

"You guys look like—I don't know *what* you look like, truck drivers or wrestlers or—I don't know."

231

Lady said, "*I* don't look like no truck driver—though I do feel a wreck."

He'd put on that fag-talk with people he didn't like.

The guys were practically standing up in their sleep. It was pushing noon, which was the middle of the night for us, and they were awake by virtue of whatever they could sniff or pop. Me, I didn't need anything to stay awake with Nade and Elaine in the same room.

"Hey, *amigos,*" I said to them. "We play this one straight, *comprende?*"

Little Lee looked at the ceiling and Peck looked at the floor. Lady just sneered. His nickname for me was Chord Chrusher. "It's like hearing the blues during a traffic accident," one critic had written about me, and though he'd meant to put me down, I sort of approved of that description. That's just what I'm hearing, that's just what I'm trying to play. Wakes people up.

Little Lee did a quiet polite run on his Fender Telecaster. "You been always tellin' me to get crazy, boss, an' now I'm tellin' you: It may be too late to behave."

"I don't want to fight with these people all day about something they know nothing about. They just, like, picked us out of a phone book, man. I can't even remember why I said yes to this."

"Does the word 'rent' ring a bell?" Peck said. "You know my motto: Rent is reason enough."

I sat at the piano and rested my fingers lightly on the keys. The albino shouted through the megaphone for everybody to shut up, they were doing a run-through to test sound levels. It got quieter than it ever really gets in a club. They cut all the lights except the spots on us, so that all there was was silence and brightness and me thinking: I need to see Elaine, don't they know that?

Elaine had left the ladies' room quiet and had stayed quiet, her eyes full of a vague hurt. A pushing-forty broad who was suddenly looking like a little girl. And, looking like a girl, she'd receded from me like the rest. But I wanted her back. My hands needed her back. I wanted to see her.

The albino's steely voice blared through the megaphone:

"Is there something wrong, Mr. Wales?"

"Are you kidding?"

That got a little laugh out of the dark.

"Jes?" Peck said.

"Yeah, yeah," I said, and I counted the tune off and we hit it, the guys finding the groove on the first bar, good ol' boys even on automatic pilot, but me—it was like I was Little Jesse's size, like my feet couldn't reach the floor and my hands hadn't a five-note spread, like I'd just learned everything and had to think each chord through though the tune didn't have but three, as I repeated the song's great line:

Got my mojo workin' but it just won't work on you, singing it shaky but thinking, What's so bad about that, who wants somebody your mojo works on? You gotta get out there beyond where your mojo's good anymore. I was surprised at that; I'd never got that before. These songs just keep teaching me and teaching me. But as I thought *that* I realized my left hand had fallen way behind, Peck on bass and Lady on drums had got out of sync with me and then with each other and we all just skidded sloppy to a stop.

"Is anything *wrong*, Mr. Wales?" the megaphone said.

"You okay, Jes?" Peck said.

"One more time."

"Can't get any worse."

"Wanna bet?"

I took the tempo a little slower. It was like the keyboard was a pillow my hands just kind of sank into; I managed to hit the right notes at more or less the right time but I could feel the sounds flatten out and die as soon as they lifted off from the piano. Piano tone is a very tricky thing, it's all in the wrists and the touch, one guy's sound is rich and deep while another's is thin or muddy on the same instrument, and the thing that had always got me by, the rich clear tone I got no matter how crazy I played, that was gone, gone, gone, and my music spilled instead of poured. We got to the end of the tune on pretty much the same beat, but I could feel the unease out there in the dark, knew the number hadn't reached into that darkness at all. My hands felt thick and heavy, like two soggy mittens, as I lifted them off the keys.

The lights came up.

"Good, great, good," Eric Ingmar was saying.

"These guys are easy to please," Peck said low.

"We'll do the scene in about twenty minutes," the albino said through the megaphone.

The guys got off the bandstand but I couldn't move.

Elaine came to me with a drink in her hand. Gave it to me. Even holding the glass my fingers felt thick and clumsy. It was a straight shot and I gulped it down.

"You okay?" she said.

"Do I sound okay?"

Her eyes got teary.

"I'm sorry, Jesse."

"I'm not. Do you understand me?"

"Thank you."

I'd never seen this Elaine. Lips trembling. Eyes so soft. She took my hands in hers. I didn't have to look to know how Nade was staring at us. But Elaine suddenly glanced up at her and dropped my hands.

"*I'd* hold your hand," Nade said, "but somebody already has."

"Nobody asked you here, Nade."

"I *know*."

"Aren't you the one who's always talking about a person can't just walk in and out of another person's life?"

"I sure the fuck am."

"Mommy!"

"I'm sorry, baby."

But the kid just stared sternly at her. She rolled her eyes, looked at the ceiling, said, "Sorry, Lord."

Danny reached over and took one of Nadine's hands in his.

She pulled her hand away.

"Oh *damn*," she said.

Now she reached and took Danny's hand.

"Is this a game I don't know about?" Deirdre said.

"You bet your foam rubber it is," Nade said.

A movie lady with a clipboard came over. She was older than Eric but not as old as us. Dark, fine-featured, and her clothes seemed nothing special but fit absolutely perfect. Made everybody around her look disheveled. That's called class, I think.

But the woman had a voice like a busy signal. It was as though she spoke not with her vocal chords but by complicated contractions somewhere high in her nose. New York to the max. I couldn't imagine an entire city filled with such ugly voices.

She said, "Mr. Wales, I need a word with you."

"Yes, ma'am?"

"Are you serious?"

"Pardon?"

"Ma'am! I look like a ma'am?"

"No offense—"

"—Ma'am, right, I know. Christ. Look, what all the waiting around has been, it's a rewrite. I'm assuming Cecil B. Bergman over there told you the plot? He-monster, she-monster, et cetera and et cetera? Good. So now he thinks what's good is for you to get fucked up, so to speak, meaning killed, by our Deirdre here, who"—she looked into Deirdre's eyes—"has taken such a shine to the locals, et cetera." Back to me. "I personally wish our director wasn't being so creative this morning, but that's life, am I right? I, by the way, am the producer, and you can call me Jackie or Ms. Mayer or anything else except ma'am."

There was something in the awfulness of her voice that made you wonder what noises she'd make in bed, but she had a surprisingly clear, earnest smile.

"In other words, you want me to get killed in your picture?"

"You got it. It means you and the band'll get another day's work out of this. At least. The effects will take hours. We intend for Deirdre, here, to rip you into pieces. It's a lot of detail work, but you won't need to speak. Just scream, move, and look dead."

"Looking dead could be arranged," Nade said. "Just give me a getaway car."

"Excuse me?" Jackie said.

"Daddy's gonna *die?*"

Little Jesse looked from Nade to me, his cheeks twitched, his eyes teared.

"Don't *die,* Daddy."

And he started to cry.

"It's just make-believe, hon," Nadine said.

"What ain't?" Danny said.

"*Please,*" Little Jesse whimpered. "Just—*please.*"

There was an awful hovering moment, when we all knew what

was coming, and then it came. The child cried with nothing held back, cried the way people cry when they've got no hope of being heard, cried the cry that knows it can't change a thing, like the last cry of all. And all us grown-ups were made small again by his wail of weeping.

I knelt beside him where he sat on Nadine's lap, clinging to her. One hand on Nadine's thigh, one hand on his, and looking up into Nadine's sorrow-eyes, I just said over and over, "All right, son, all right. Daddy ain't gonna die. All right, son, all right. It's all right, son, it's all all right."

"I don't blame you," Jackie said, "but I hate it. Am I to understand you're off the picture?"

"Danny could do it," I said. "This guy, Danny Crawford. He's —a better singer than me, anyway. Lots better."

"To me," Jackie said, "who's a better singer means not much. No ear, you see. And we already did the paper work on you."

Danny smiled at her, and let out with *They're gonna take an' put me in the movies*

They're gonna make a big star outta me, singing low and suspended-like, but even Danny singing a cappella soft could cut through a noisy room like a shaft of light through smoke, his voice just as full as it was high, and that waver way back in his throat like a high-tension wire in the wind.

They're gonna take an' put me in the movies
An' all I gotta do is
Act naturally

You didn't need "an ear" to hear Danny. Jackie's attitude changed completely. She said, "How refreshing. People who know their business. What-aya know. See—this friggin' place, no offense, might as well be Mars as far as I know what's what here. At least I admit it, correct?"

I just looked at her. Then at Nade, who, without sound, mouthed, "Thank you."

E L E V E N   *Instant Time Warp*

"He's too pale, Jackie," Eric said as though Danny weren't there. "He'll film dead."

"There's such a thing as a makeup person on this payroll. Or would you rather we call LA and tell them we're falling a day behind on the shooting schedule because we signed a native who's afraid of cameras?"

I was surprised Little Jesse didn't object to Danny being in the picture, but nobody else seemed to notice.

Deirdre went off with Eric and Jackie. A couple of makeup people came over—a fat lady whose own makeup was thick as a mask, and a plain girl, crisp and quiet. Their four hands worked Danny's face at once, which he loved.

Nadine didn't love it much, though. The makeup people didn't know it, but they were making Danny look like he used to: rosy, bright, no shadows under his eyes—ten years younger at least. Do-it-yourself time warp.

Nadine just stared as Danny got younger in front of her. Small smiles half started, then died, on her lips.

Finally the makeup ladies handed Danny a mirror and left.

He looked into it with a sweet smile. "I feel pretty"—he sang the tune country-style—"oh so pret-ty."

Then he *really* looked.

"I *remember* him," he said.

"So do I," said Nade.

The connection between us three geared in again right there. Like when you're rehearsing with guys you haven't played with in a long time and after a few tunes you hit a bar where you're all at the same spot on the beat, right *there,* and everybody looks at everybody else out of the corner of their eyes and bears down and it feels so right.

Elaine looked on with a look vague, slightly hurt, left out.

"Has Jesse really changed?" Nade said to Danny.

"More than he figures."

"Good. He's needed changin'."

We smiled at each other. And it wasn't just that Danny's face was younger. Somehow his eyes seemed younger too. They didn't seem so—scared. When *had* Danny's eyes gotten so scared, all the time, so that you'd stopped noticing it—it was just how Danny looked? Yet hadn't Danny changed the least of the three of us.

"Look at me, Danny," Elaine said.

He did, and she reached and cupped his face in both hands. At first I thought she'd lean across the table and kiss him, and my chest got tight. But instead Elaine clutched Danny's head, dug her nails into his cheeks—not scratching, just pressure. Danny, startled, pulled his face away and—it was like his face came off in her hands; rosy makeup smeared all over her palms and caked under her fingernails, and Danny's face all splotches and streaks now, like he had some kind of science-fiction-movie sickness.

Elaine looked nervously at her hands and wiped them off on her Mexican dress. Danny took the mirror, gave his ruined face a hard look, and chuckled.

"I remember *him*, too!" He laughed.

T W E L V E *The Rock*

The movie people took Danny off to one of their trailers to make him up a second time. They'd caught on that they had to keep an eye on him. Elaine went with them, to get some material for her story, she said.

When they'd left, Nade said, "You gonna show Daddy what you got him?"

The kid tried to sink into his chair, it made him so shy.

"I got it right you-know-where," Nade said.

He slid down onto the floor, dug into her big purse, and came up with a bulky something wrapped in tissue paper. He needed both his five-year-old hands to hold it.

He laid it on the table and I unwrapped it. It was a rock. Or some kind of rough, rocky crystal. I picked it up. Heavily it filled my whole hand. One surface was rough, black and sparkly. The other surfaces were curved, but met at sharp edges, and were veined with blues and reds. On its smoothest side was what might have been a print of what might have been a leaf, or maybe a fish.

I put the rock on the table to look at it, but with an oddly formal air he picked it back up in both his hands and held it out to me again, so I took it from him. I turned it this way and that with great admiration.

"Little Jesse loves that rock," Nadine said. "It's just about his favorite thing."

"And you wanted to show it to me?" I said to him.

"Give it to you."

"Well. I don't know what to say. Thank you. Thank you so much, son."

I made a show of looking at it some more. Then rubbed the rock against my face. He liked that a lot, I could tell. I rubbed it against his face, and he was real pleased. I may not be much of a father but I know how to accept a rock.

I asked him if he'd tasted our rock. He hadn't. I could see he was taken with the idea, though. So I licked the bright sparkly part. You could taste the hardness. Like your mouth's a little afraid of it because you don't often let your tongue touch something harder than your teeth. I told him that. Held the rock out to him and he stuck his tongue out as far as it would reach and lightly licked the rock.

I gave Nade lots of points right then for not saying what I knew she'd be dying to say: "Get that *object* outta y'all's mouths, you don't know where it's *been*."

I placed the rock in the middle of the table and put our empty glasses and bottles in a circle around it. If you do the image pure enough . . . Little Jesse asked me why I'd done that and I said I was just making a special place for our rock for now.

To which he said,

"Is the end of the world gonna hurt, Mommy?"

"Not if you love Jesus, honey."

"Is it gonna hurt Daddy?"

"Daddy can take care of himself," I said.

"Sure he can," said Nade.

THIRTEEN *Something to Think About*

I went to the bar because I needed a breather from Nade, and because I figured Elaine, at the other end of the club now, would see me at the bar and suddenly feel the need of a drink herself.

Dawg was behind the bar again.

"Is this the most boring day of your life, or what?" he said.

"Not really."

"Do you know Elaine's husband?"

"Lay off, Dawg."

"Stop tellin' me that."

"Do I wanna know Elaine's husband?"

"Not for long. I mean, *I* like him fine, we've been in groups together at the VA, he's a stand-up guy. But—on the other hand—he ain't goin' around saying he's gonna kill *me*."

"Where'd you hear that?"

"Word gets around. And around and around."

"I think I know where that word came from, too," I said.

"Wives are like that, yeah."

"Thanks for telling me. It's something to think about."

"I wouldn't worry about it too much."

"Long as you don't get caught in the crossfire."

"I *been* caught in crossfires, and I'm still here. No, something I learned in the Nam. If it's your time, there's nothing you can do. And if it's not—there's nothing *he* can do."

"Now that's *really* something to think about."

"Uh-oh." He nodded toward Elaine, who was heading straight for me. "See ya." He faded to the other end of the bar.

"Hi," Elaine said.

"And then I say 'hi' and then what?"

"I don't know." Her lips trembled. Her hand reached toward mine but pulled back. "I really don't."

"Me neither."

FOURTEEN *A Great Thing*

It must be a great thing, to know what you want.

FIFTEEN *It Sure Wasn't Morning Anymore*

It sure wasn't morning anymore, and those silly-ass movie people were just starting to get their act together. I couldn't get used to Danny being King of the Time Warp. Looking at a guy with a face like he had ten years ago but eyes like he has now. Turn around, see my eyes in my boy's five-year-old face. Look up, see my wife who isn't my wife anymore, then a woman in a cat costume, then a green-eyed woman in a Mexican dress who only seems to come alive for me in small out-of-the-way rooms and who's some out-of-work killer's wife. And all this in a real honky-tonk that's being used as a make-believe honky-tonk, while a TV over the bar with the sound off plays a commercial telling me I should vote for the guy on "Death Valley Days."

In the midst of all, Danny was rehearsing "Matchbox."

He would have preferred something slow but Bergman wanted tempo. They'd agreed on that Carl Perkins version of "Matchbox," which was probably already an old song when Blind Lemon Jeffer-

son first recorded it in '29. Jackie thought it was a Beatles song and
would be too expensive till we explained where they got it.

I'm sittin' here wonderin'
Will a matchbox hold my clothes—
I ain't got no matches
But I sure got a long way to go—

Danny couldn't play piano but he could pound it, and with my
guys behind him he could get away with that on a number like this.

Jackie sat at our table watching. She leaned over to me and
said, "Look, I'm not stupid, but tell me the point of this song."

There wasn't any point in asking if she'd ever lit her last match.
She didn't know there was such a thing as a last match.

I said, "Ain't no point. It's just a song, ma'am."

Well, she gave me such a look. She was sharp, all right, and
she knew she'd been talked down to, and by the likes of me, and
she flat couldn't believe it. So she laughed. I decided I liked her.

They did a run-through of how the camera was going to move
and all, and at the end of it Danny said, into the stage mike, "Hey,
it's probably none of my business, but y'all got it all wrong."

"*Everybody's* a director!" Eric said, running his fingers
through what was left of his hair. "Define, please, 'it' and 'all.' "

"Looks like a church supper from up here, not like any honky-
tonk I ever been in."

"We-haven't-got-time-for-this," Jackie said like one word.
Yankees have this way of saying whole sentences like they were
one big word, which is why we have a hard time understanding
them sometimes.

"Wait-a-minute," Eric one-worded back. Then, to Danny:
"What-the-hell-are-you-talking-about?"

"Everybody's sittin' polite around their tables, smiling, being
all attentive, while really half the people are always talkin', and
going about their business, unless it's real late and crazy, when they
stand up and dance and holler. You mixed all the tables, so there's
none with just guys, none with just girls. People are swaying back
and forth to the beat together, like you told 'em to, which I've seen
in church and nowhere but. Nobody's glum, nobody's mean.
There's not even an angel."

"We're not making a documentary, all right?" Eric said.

242

"What do you mean, 'angel'?" Jackie said.

"I thought we don't have time for this?" Eric said.

"There's always at least one angel. Dancing alone. Or sitting at the bar. All the guys want her and she doesn't know what she wants but she looks like she knows all there is to know about what *you* want. That's who *I* sing to, I don't know about anybody else. Hard to sing right without an angel out there."

A smattering of applause from anyone not too bored to care.

"How do you *know* there's not one?" Jackie said.

"Oh, I'm sure there is. But not where I can see her. And one thing about those angels, they always pick their spots. It's like a light's on 'em. You don't have to guess who *they* are."

A smaller scatter of applause.

Jackie looked like she wanted to kill Danny. Eric looked like he wanted to kill himself. It would obviously take their slowpokes another hour to rearrange this place, probably another day, at the rate they worked, to pick an angel.

Actually, it was a rotten moment to see. Eric was going to choose the lesser thing, and he knew it, and it looked like he knew he was always going to choose the lesser thing and that his relief would be when he finally stopped thinking of it as a choice and did it automatically.

"Let's go with what we have," he said, and Jackie said, "Thank God," but she didn't look happy saying it.

Danny proceeded to kick the shit out of "Matchbox." There was this tension between him and my band that pushed out a new sound altogether, neither his nor mine. My guys were trying to hold back to accommodate Danny, but Lady Fuentes hated the one-two country rhythms Danny was used to, so Lady jacked those drums, accenting all around, so you had like a calypso "Matchbox." And Danny's voice, which always wanted to go sweet, pulled away from where my guys wanted to go, which was always too far, the way I wanted it. Little Lee was all over the guitar, playing against Danny too. The only one on Danny's side was Peck. Peck's bass tried to follow Lady's lead and hold Lady back at the same time, while Danny, who always sang from his throat like a bird, was singing from somewhere around his knees. I could feel his voice probing, searching, trying to get in their snug between Little Lee's harsh prods and Peck's go-ahead-boy bass. I could feel Danny's voice opening wider, wider than I'd ever heard it, to try to kind of throw a vocal tent over the band's full-ahead sound.

Let me be your little dog till your big dog come—
When your big dog gets here,
Show 'im what this little puppy done—

What he started to do was to sing slow over the fast beat, holding the notes long and tense and slow over the changes the guys were running on him, the words bent almost to the breaking point above the music. It was like the song had gotten hurt and swelled up and was moaning, but the rhythm stayed fast. I've never heard anything quite like it before or since.

The best thing was that Nadine and I looked at each other as the guys got into the tune, and just laughed out loud, just a couple of musicians again, hearing something too good to be true and too strange to repeat. Nobody's ever recorded this kind of moment because you got to get the moment before you even think to record, so when you finally do get it down it's not quite the same, not as raw, you're just a little used to it. (Well, maybe Robert Johnson . . . maybe he *was* that moment made into a man.)

They finished the number and Little Lee said, "Why're we playin' so good for *these* queers!" And he didn't have time to duck before one of Lady's drumsticks popped between his shoulder blades and ricocheted onto the dance floor.

"And *you* go pick it up, sweet," Lady laughed, and Little Lee was in such a good mood suddenly that he was even about to, but the albino picked it up instead, and asked could they do it again, just the way, and just the length, they were going to do it for the shot?

Peck said, "This is a pussy gig."

Danny didn't say a word.

S I X T E E N   *The Eye of the Beat*

A couple of run-throughs later, the albino asked everybody who wanted to get on the dance floor, to see what dancers they wanted to use. Danny and the band had gotten into their groove, and it was good, but it wasn't *as* good. Like one of those big-time recording studios where everybody plays their part over and over till there's no surprises left. And when that's been officially decided, no possibility for ambush, every instrument taped separate, some businessman comes out of the booth and says, "Y'all can go home now, we'll mix the tape ourselves." And they wonder why music isn't changing the world like it used to.

"You like to dance?"

Deirdre—or something passing for Deirdre, some garage-built custom racer, part fur, part sweat-caked makeup, part somebody else's idea of tits, part somebody else's idea of a smile, part more booze than she was used to, part coke; and somewhere, under all that, a girl once, still in there, I bet, wondering, What am I doing here?—like I said, Deirdre, was giving me her best I'll-fuck-you-if-you're-the-only-one-left smile and asking me to dance.

I wanted to sweat some whiskey off, but not with her.

"Thanks, but this dance is taken," I said.

"Let's do it!" Elaine said to Deirdre, which wasn't what Deirdre had in mind, but she and Elaine started dancing anyway, Elaine hop-scotching around in her kid-dance way, Deirdre pumping a New Jersey grind.

I looked at Nadine.

"Now," I said, "I know good Baptists don't dance. They think it's a sin."

"I'm not a Baptist."

"And the Pentecostals—they don't dance."

"I'm—not *really* a Pentecostal."

"Now—the Sanctifieds, *they* dance."

"In church only. But there ain't many white folks in the Sanctifieds."

"Church of Christers, now—they do not dance."

"I'm not one a those either."

"Well, what *is* the doctrine, toward dancing, of the Church of the Long Distance Call?"

"Stay in the eye of the beat."

She stood up. It was the first time all day I'd looked at her as a woman. In her calf-skin cowboy boots she must have stood six-one to my five-nine, her jeans weren't exactly tight but they were certainly trim, and at fortyish she still had an ass. She wore a billowy yellow blouse and a cross on a chain around her neck, and her black Cajun hair hung straight down her back. Her gray eyes, as always, looked right through me, knew what I was thinking—and she was flattered, I hope.

Little Jesse, he was *all* eyes as we stepped in rhythm out to the edge of the dance floor and started, tentatively, our old moves.

Nadine sure knew what the soul-songs meant by "let your backbone slip," and she could pump her hips *while* she did her slides, not just one or the other, like most white girls. And her every step was smack down in the eye of the beat. For the beat's a big place. If you're on the beat's edge instead of in its eye, you can move every flashy way and you won't be seen; while next to you someone's doing nothing fancy, but if they step right on and into the eye—they hypnotize. And so we graced each other, two good dancers dancing on the eye, two old flames flickering at each other, while our son watched all amazed, and Danny smiled down at us as he sang over us, a voice that sweetened the beat with a menacing prettiness. And Nade and me we pumped and slid, never touching, never needing to with the air so thick between us as we moved that the space itself became a body part we shared. And me knowing the beat not in my hips or in my feet but in my knees, something my knees knew about that I didn't have to worry over at all, it was right there in my knees whenever I needed it, the beat I live by.

The Beat Giveth and the Beat Taketh Away. And the Beat Goes on. So saith the music as Nade shimmied so pretty, hip-swiveler, rippling her parts, hair in the air afloat as she swayed. And past Nadine was Elaine, staying in my sight on purpose now, Elaine

—moving like she was playing jump rope, but not her green eyes, they were stone-still, green stones looking only at me.

And when I'd swirl a turn I'd see Little Jesse looking so surprised—*Remember, kid, remember* was the prayer I danced in the beat's eye in the Church of the Long Distance Call. And turning I'd see Danny, grinning now through his song. And Nadine gliding, eyes hid by the whirl of her hair. And Elaine's eyes glued on me. And Nade and I thigh to thigh, so rapt in the beat's eye that she didn't need to look at me to match and play off my moves, nor I at her.

But Elaine, Elaine—somewhere in the dance I remembered what it was to sleep beside Elaine, how, asleep, our skins would weld onto each other, how perfectly we'd breathe together, in no matter what position. How, a restless sleeper even with Nade, I hadn't slept restless with Elaine, but would wake two or six hours later to find we had not moved; we, who could never relax around each other, we slept in impossible harmony, perfectly. And what would it be like to spend a lifetime sleeping like that every night, no matter how crazed the days? Would our sleep bend our waking toward its perfection? It took the rock-calypso of Lady's drums as they spoke inside my knees, it took this move-moment, to understand that stillness. As Nadine and I danced, so Elaine and I slept, our very sleep itself like a tenor sax that held one bending note so long it isn't music anymore, it's a muscle of sound that wraps our bodies around.

A snake of sound.

Oh, no.

Oh, the Moan.

Down there all along, the Snake had wrapped us round, and I found in my dancing what it was we slept in, so absolute and easeful, throbbing yet still: Snake-skin.

Danny sang one Blind Lemon tune while I heard another, that one that goes:

Black snake is all I see—
I woke up this morning, black snake was movin' in on me—
Ummmmm—Ummmmm—
Black snake was hanging around—
He occupied my living room,
Broke my furniture down.

His song ends on that line, as though he can't get past it.

I've broken out in a cold sweat—please please please—please please please—

And the last thing I saw was Nade alarmed in mid-move as I slid out of the beat's eye, toppling, suddenly so hollow, hollow in my knees—

SEVENTEEN *Could He Feel the Snake in My Arms?*

The next thing I remember is my kid crying.

I heard it in my cheekbones, they pulsed to his sobs.

Smell of Nadine's soap. Smell of Elaine's scent, like treebark crushed with roses. Both smells soaked in the stink of beer and cut with cigarette smoke. Trace of hash. Then something overpowering them all, sickly sweet and sharp as paint remover—Deirdre's deodorant.

I opened my eyes. Nadine's face big, Elaine's over her shoulder, Deirdre kneeling on the other side of me. Nade held my wrist, was taking my pulse. No, baby, it's not a heart attack. Not yet.

The hard wood floor felt good under me, except that one of my legs had curled under the other and hurt. I straightened the leg real slow and the pain began to fade.

Danny's face. Jackie and Eric behind him. Little Jesse's crying was lots softer.

"He's okay, baby," Nadine was telling him. Then to me: "You okay, baby?"

248

She started to pull me up, but stronger hands took me from under the armpits and lifted me like I was nothing: Peck.

"You okay, boss?"

They had me in a chair. Nade held my hands hard. The rasp in my voice surprised me when I said to her, "You still sure are one great dancer."

"You would be too if you didn't fall down so much."

"Hey—kid?"

I didn't need to get Little Jesse's attention. He couldn't take his eyes off me.

"Daddy?"

"Daddy's cool. Come'ere."

He climbed into my lap and held on. I held right back. He pressed his head under my chin. But I got distracted from him by Elaine staring at me from across the table. Slide out of your skin, baby, drape it over my shoulders, nothin' else can keep me warm. (When I finally wrote *that* song, I played it *so* slow, nobody danced.)

"Well, little guy—you've seen your first riot and seen your first man pass out. Nothin' to it."

It scared me to hold him. Could he feel the Snake in my arms? I could.

But I wanted to be held so much, and the only way I could get some of that was by holding him.

"Somebody get me some straight whiskey, hey? Irish."

Nade went to get it. Everybody started telling me I should go home and I wouldn't. When that was settled, they went about their business.

And as they did, blood seeped slowly from Little Jesse's rock.

Tiny blisters of blood. Then the blisters broke, dripped, soaked out of sight into the table.

It didn't scare me or make me feel crazy. Until I realized it didn't. Then it did. And as soon as I felt crazy enough I couldn't see the blood anymore.

Nade plunked a fat shot glass in front of me.

"Don't rocks bleed in the Bible?" I said.

"Now and again," she said.

"They don't really," Little Jesse said hopefully.

249

"Everything in *my* Bible is a fact," Nadine said to him, "but everything in my Bible happened long ago. I don't think rocks bleed anymore. *I* never seen it."

I had.

No whiskey ever tasted cleaner.

E I G H T E E N   *Screams Call to Screams*

They do things back-assward in the movies. First they were going to film everybody screaming and being terrified, running from the monster. *Then* they'd film ol' Deirdre wasting Danny.

It didn't take much to get *this* crowd running for the exits. But it took a lot to get them to stop. Poor Eric and Jackie and the albino were all over the place, trying to corral the folks here and there, set up cameras, tell everybody what's what. But each time they yelled "Action!" they got more than they bargained for, people knocking over chairs and tables and each other, falling all over the place drunk. The ones that were supposed to scream were trying not to laugh. The ones that were supposed to fall, they fell just fine, but the ones that were supposed to run fell right on top of them. Then everybody'd crack up. Then somebody'd yell "Cut!" Then Eric Ingmar Bergman would scream. Then everybody would laugh some more. You should have seen that albino get red. I mean, even his hands got red, he was that furious.

Finally Eric started to cry. He just stood in the middle of everything looking straight down at his shoes, blubbering.

So Jackie took over. As soon as she did, you could see she should have been doing Eric's job all along. She threw out everybody who didn't really want to stay, saying they had enough crowd footage. "We'll do the rest in close-ups," she said, and then she started the weirdest—well, it was like a ceremony. She set the camera up with a lot of harsh light right in front of it. Then she put people real close to the camera, and told them to scream bloody murder right into the lens. She explained to everybody—something Eric hadn't stooped to—that once the monster showed, they'd show some shots of the audience running, then lots of cuts of faces screaming, "intercut with the monster mauling the piano player." Then Jackie lined people up one by one to stand in front of the camera and scream.

At first it was a joke. Dawg said he'd be happy to scream if his scream was needed, it was a good day for it. His first try he did a hog call. Second, a Cajun hoot. But finally he let out a deep-throated curdler. He seemed a little surprised at himself. He looked over at Jackie, to see was it okay, and Jackie said, "Fine. Cut. Next." And Dawg walked back to his office looking kind of distracted, like he was still tasting the scream in his mouth.

Screams call to screams. Dawg's scream called out the scream in the next person, a girl I didn't know. Her very first scream was fine, too fine. It leapt out to find Dawg's. By then it was clear that the place you hear a scream is the back of your neck, just below the skull, a place that tightens and stays tight till your body's convinced it's not going to hear another scream.

NINETEEN *The Telling*

I didn't get within thirty feet of one of the more important conversations of my life. I sat with Little Jesse at the table while Nade and Danny talked at the bar, the only time they were one-on-one all day. I glanced over there now and again, but I didn't even wonder what they were talking about.

But I knew by how Nadine walked toward me that something had changed.

Danny followed a little behind her, sheepish. He wouldn't meet my eyes. Somebody screamed.

"Hon, go with Uncle Danny for a bit, I gotta talk to dear old Dad."

Little Jesse didn't want to go but he went. Somebody screamed.

"I'm gonna get Danny for Jesus. Get Jesus for Danny. I'm gonna get him away from you and that red-haired witch. You hear? I'm gonna call him every day, I'm gonna pray and pray, I'm gonna *move* the Heavens and I'm gonna *get* him. And if you try and stop me—I'll kill you, Jesse."

I didn't say a word, but somebody screamed.

" 'Cause Danny's—precious cargo. Danny's *my* Danny, and always has been, my little boy, almost like Little Jesse. *Lord,* I'm sorry now I named that boy after you. Have you got any *real* memory left, you bastard? 'Member how Danny used to be? Not these harsh bright eyes he has now, but that gentle playful way he had, before he started hittin' on blondes and studyin' with Henry and getting deeper and deeper into something he couldn't get himself out of, something *you* kept him in—"

"Me!"

"—you all along, the Devil in you, you crazy, fucked-up son of a BITCH."

"*What?*"

"Danny told me. The short version. He's gonna tell me the long version later. He told me stuff you don't even guess yet, you poor fool. You knew he'd tell me, didn't you? 'Bout Mexico? I'm so mad I'm *weak,* I'm shaky weak. Do you know that you're a *Satanist?* DO YOU KNOW THAT YOU'RE AN AGENT OF THE DEVIL OF THE WORLD? Do you even know?"

At least I knew now what he told her. And somebody screamed.

"Of course I'm not. This is *me,* Nade."

"You and that grabby witch did Devil-work, DID THE DEVIL'S OWN WORK, let Satan possess and work through your flesh, and you are so lost, so deep in Hell, you are too piss-ant dumb to feel it, you craven lying FUCK."

"Keep it down, you guys!" the albino called.

"In a way it's good," Nade said, breathing hard, "I think I can work up some hate for you now. Touching my BOY. TOUCHING him with your DEVIL's hands."

I heard the next scream with my stomach. It echoed around down there.

"He's my boy, too, Nade. Nade, you got it wrong."

"The hell, you say."

"You wanna listen to my side?"

"I will hear none of your corruption. You shit with your mouth, Jesse Wales. But you listen up, now. You stay away from us. You stay away from my boy. I know some crazy Christers, mean-ass bastards, wouldn't know Jesus if he delivered their mail, but if I was to present this to them rightly, they'd come for you. They do that sort of thing. You savvy? Stay a-fucking-way."

"DON'T poison my boy about me. Don't say ONE WORD of this to him. If I find he's heard any of what you're thinking now, I'll fuck you up so bad they'll take him away from both of us."

"I wouldn't put it past you."

"That's wise."

We stood there, while somebody screamed, and I was glad of every scar on my knuckles, for my hands remembered their violence, they got hot with it, they were mine again, though I couldn't say for how long, a gift from my boy. And if they could do violence, they could play music, hotter now, suddenly more alive than any of the rest of me.

"I wouldn't tell him anyway," Nade said. "He's gonna be loving you too much after this day, it'd kill him to tell him. But you stay 'way, Jesse. For a while. A good long while."

"I'll call."

"You can call till you run out of dimes, but stay the fuck away." Then: "I curse our love, Jesse. You hear?"

TWENTY *The Screaming Line*

Elaine was on the screaming line. Third from the last. But first there was Eric Ingmar himself, shame-faced, quiet, walking kind of carefully. He must have had a few drinks since he'd cried. He let out a shaky, weak howl.

Nadine was hugging Danny good-bye at the bar. Little Jesse was sitting on a barstool. Then Nade went to the ladies' room. Deirdre went and sat with Danny and the kid.

I sat a little dazed, watching Elaine build her scream. I could see it kind of coiling up inside her. I knew she'd be feeling like me, that all the other screams hung in the air now, waiting for the last one, to see what kind of stain they were going to leave in the room. So I was watching Elaine, regretting everything and wanting it all over again, when the fat guy screamed.

He was just a fat guy with a plain face. One of the crew, somebody said later. I don't know what he did, I hadn't noticed him before. He had baggy gray pants and his T-shirt was soaked through. His blond hair was cut close to his skull in a buzz. You'd never notice the guy.

If cancer could scream. Cancer itself, not someone *with* cancer. Or if, when you're a kid and you get an old newspaper and pour syrup on it and wait for it to be all over with ants and you set it on fire—if burning ants could scream. The scream that came out of that fat guy seemed like it couldn't possibly have anything to *do* with him. Elaine's eyes went wide and shut tight. And that fat guy didn't stop.

TWENTY-ONE *The Craziest Person*

You never know who the craziest person in the room *really* is.

TWENTY-TWO *The Crack of Bone*

Jackie called "Cut!" then yelled "Cut!" then tried to take hold of the fat guy, but he was jerking like a Holy Roller, flapping his hands like they do, and his eyes had rolled back so you could see only the whites, and his screams kept coming, short, impossibly high yelps now, like the ants screaming one at a time.

Little Jesse leapt right off that barstool at the sound, running till Danny caught him and swept him up in his arms, and as I went toward them Danny held the kid over his shoulder like he was burping him, and I saw pure crazed-nothing in my boy's face. And Deirdre started making funny faces at the kid, laughing at him, like it was all a joke, and the kid was white and Danny said, "Hey, he's *peeing!*"

Deirdre shrieked with excitement, but Nade was suddenly there, and she spun Deirdre by the shoulders out of the kid's face, then took him from Danny, both of them saying, "It's all right, boy, it's all right," under the fat guy's screams as some people held the poor bastard down. And Nadine held Little Jesse but Deirdre was too giddy-crazy from the screams to stop and she hung in Little Jesse's face laughing. I grabbed her from behind and spun her around like Nadine had but I didn't let go of her shoulders, kept shaking her, crazy too, I guess, 'cause when she saw my face she stopped her mouth. But I couldn't help it, I shook her, and Nadine yelled, "Jesse! Behind you!" And I felt more than saw that albino coming at me with a chair raised and I whipped Deirdre around to take the blow and his chair hit her shoulder and a bone cracked.

That was the last sound, really. The rest was just whimperings. Deirdre was whimpering as I sat her easy in a chair. Her pain hadn't really started yet. The fat guy was whimpering. Jackie and a couple of people were holding him down, clucking at him. The fucking albino was whimpering, sort of, gasping, seeing what he'd done to

Deirdre. I was waiting for him to move on me, in which case I knew in my hands that he'd die.

With my hands back *I* was the craziest person in the room now, and I was just aching to prove it all over his face.

But he just stood there holding what was left of the chair and staring helpless at Deirdre. Dawg was shouting into the pay phone, "*Two* ambulances!"

And Elaine—Elaine stood where the fat guy had stood, in those harsh lights before the camera, and one light in back of her, that made it so you could see the line of her body through that Mexican dress. She was staring dreamy at the ceiling, where the screams hung. The one she'd been building would have to stay inside her now. That was okay, she had plenty of room for it.

Whereas that fat guy hadn't had any room left at all.

The club seemed empty, though there were about thirty people still there. The only thing moving was the TV screen over the bar, soundless, fuzzy, pale colors, some perky lady holding a microphone in the face of somebody terribly important who thought he governed us. Me, I didn't feel very governed just then. I just kind of stared around as people got the fat guy water and such, and then Jackie and Eric found out about Deirdre and *that* fuss started. But nobody ended up pressing charges on me because they were afraid that the albino might get in trouble too.

When they started fussing at me I didn't pay any attention, had my mind instead on Nadine, to see how our kid was doing and to thank her for warning me, which of course she had to do, because Satanist or not, I was her man still. But Nadine and Little Jesse were gone.

When I realized it, I ran out after them. After spending all day in Dawg's smoky half-dark, the daylight was vicious. It tore into my head. For moments I thought it would drive me back in. I tried to stand against it. I stood against it. I walked against it, to my Chevy. And it was as though the light made the alcohol I'd drunk all day rise into my brain. I sat behind the wheel suddenly so drunk I could hardly hold up my head. That's why I didn't think to go back for Little Jesse's rock. And the next day, when I finally did think of it, it was gone. I even looked through Dawg's trash, but never found it. I still think of it sometimes, how it must have swollen with all those screams, and how somebody would feel even if they just stood next to it now, never guessing where the feeling was coming from.

When my eyes could take the light, I saw that Nade's car was gone.

Nothing to do but go back to my place. But I was in no shape to take the main roads. I could barely look up at the traffic lights. I took the side streets. From stop sign to stop sign I drove a route of pauses home.

PART SEVEN

Blind Love

I was in my bed sleepin'—
Oh boy what a dream—
I was dreamin' 'bout my TV Mama—
The one with the big wide screen—
                    —Big Joe Turner

O N E *A Call*

The voice on the phone was low. No hello, just:

"I know what's goin' on."

"Good. Where do I sign up for lessons?"

"You don't know her at all." I liked his voice. There was no faking in it. It was desperate and true.

My hands were behaving funny. They hung up on him. That surprised me.

T W O *A Mess*

The mess of my room bothered me—my unmade mattress on the floor, my records scattered all over, magazines, empty Colonel Sanders boxes, dirty clothes. The thought was new for me: I'd hate for my kid to see this.

I called the motel where they were staying, but Nade had checked out. She couldn't have been on the road more than an hour, but I called the Baton Rouge house—just to make the phone ring there, I guess. To listen to the ringing in those empty rooms.

Which kind of made me sick when I realized what I was doing. It was like the worst sort of country song.

I was hungry and thirsty but felt too shaky to go anywhere. Then that call came from Johns. I lay down, but that didn't work. Too sick to sleep. So—shivery and dizzy every time I had to bend down—I commenced to clean the room. Each piece of the mess, even records I'd loved for years, even my old upright piano—who could remember how they'd gotten there, or what they were doing there, or why they should stay? Because everybody knew Nade was right, Danny had been right, it's the end of the world, every-body was crazy with it, fat guys and witches, we were all greasy pieces of trash, balled up scraps in week-old Colonel Sanders boxes, to be swept away, everybody knows. Henry had said lots of doors had to open, and fast, to save this old world—had to let air in from some other plane. But doors had been opening around me left and right, and if it was doing anybody any good, that had yet to be proved.

I cleaned the room slowly and nauseously. At least the place wouldn't weird my kid out now, in case Nade hadn't really gone, in case she'd popped into a movie and was waiting to come and tell me off again as soon as she got her second wind.

Which I was hoping for, I guess, as I lay on the bare mattress —I'd taken off the soiled sheets, and had no others—staring at the walls as the light faded. The walls stared back. Photos of all of us. Posters of old gigs. We'd made a lot of music. None of it recorded. It had disappeared into a lot of nights, just kind of soaked up by the dark.

THREE *A Visitation*

I woke to the sound of my name. Thought I'd heard it in my sleep. But no, it was soft at the door. Elaine.

"It's open."

I didn't open my eyes as I heard her turn the knob and walk in.

That would be a solution. Just keep my eyes closed. Or blind myself. Give me a whole new set of stuff to deal with. Keep me busy. I loved the breathy sweet tone of her voice, its West Texas lilt. I didn't have to see her or anybody ever again.

"You got a lot of faith," she said.

"In what?"

"In people not opening your door and blowing your head off."

"Oh, hell, he could just as easy get me through the windows. Small room, it would be hard to miss. He told you he called."

"Told me he was going to. You gonna open your eyes?"

"Maybe not. No, I don't think I will."

"Guess what I'm wearing, then."

"A long, long gown. Bright white. Threaded with golds and greens, with a great green collar that looks so rich behind your red, red hair."

"You have high hopes. Yet, in fact, you're exactly right."

"Your gown flows behind you, oh, maybe ten feet, but it's all soiled and dirty 'cause you left your minions back in the castle when you decided to visit my cave. Yeah, there's a tire track across the end of it where a pickup ran over your train as you walked, without looking, as always, against the light."

"I'll have to take it off then."

I heard some cloth fall lightly to the floor. Then one clear ringing note on my piano: high C. She kept her finger on the key till the note faded.

Stillness for a time.

Then the soft brush of her bare feet on the wood floor.

A tugging at my boots. She took them off. Unbuckled my jeans, slipped them off, with my no doubt soiled underwear. Then she pulled me up—I gave her no help—and unbuttoned my shirt and peeled off my T-shirt, which nobody had done for me since I was a kid, at least not when I was sober enough to remember. Then she eased me back down.

Stillness again. She was looking at me. I felt my cock rise into the dark.

Then she lay beside me, thigh to thigh, on her back, one foot hooked with mine, and she took my hand.

"Okay," she said, "I'm closing my eyes too."

"How's it feel?"

"Great."

"How about this? We'll put each other's eyes out. Get married. Your old man wouldn't shoot blind people. We go on welfare. Don't ever have to do nothing again. Play records. I'll play the piano for you. Sweetly. We'll roll around on each other when we feel like it. Grow old in the dark."

"We'd feel each other's bodies get old, but we'd never know what we looked like. We'd always see each other as we are right now. Which may not be any great shakes, but it can only get worse."

"End of the world comes, we'd hardly notice."

"End of the world coming?"

"So they say."

My cock subsided as we listened to each other breathe.

We fell to sleep awhile. Woke without having moved, still hand in hand. No way of knowing which of us woke first, but I was first to speak.

"Elaine?"

"Yeah."

"Talk to me."

"Talk to you?"

"Yeah."

"I feel like I'm talking to you all the time."

"Maybe, but it's no fun for me when it's just in your head."

"It's fun for me."

"Talk to me," I said.

"Your eyes still closed?"

"Sure. You?"

"Sure. See, it's hard to talk to you because with you I don't have any past, don't have any life, and I can make myself up for you as I go along. I'd hate to give that up. With you, I'm anything that comes into my head. Or anything that comes into *your* head. 'Cause you *believe*. Not so much you believe in me, but just—you believe. You have this quality of being right there in that very moment that's going on, and nowhere else. So it's like a person comes to you fresh—all grown up, but fresh, like a child. It's a sweet, high kind of feeling, like I've never had with anybody. I think that's why we seem to relate best in small, enclosed spaces. There's nothing to intrude on that way you make me feel. I'm just free. For the first and only time. So it's not *me* you're with, not who Johns and my friends and my family and me myself think or *suppose* is me, it's—it's like you let me just fly in the window and fly out again, how I please and when I please. Or not like you *let* me— 'cause you can't help it, which is sort of the strong part of your weakness, you know? Or the softest part of your strongness, I don't know. So I feel like I have all these *powers*, and I *do,* that's the weird thing, and—didn't I say something like this to you before?"

"A little," I said. "But I'm slow."

"So, I don't know, maybe I'll get tired of it or even resent it, but these days I just think about being with you again so I can feel it. It's like all this energy just pours into me when I'm around you, or when I'm conscious of carrying you around inside me. You're who I do my magic with. Isn't that enough?"

"You know, it's not a bad idea, putting out our eyes. It's really not."

"Don't scare me, Jesse. Being scared is awful."

"I thought you liked the idea."

"I like it as long as it stays an *idea.*"

"Well, I wouldn't put out our eyes unless you approved, okay? But think about it."

"You're serious?"

"Half. Or maybe an eighth. But I *might* could be serious with a little encouragement. 'If you do the image pure enough' and all that."

"I like things this way just fine for now."

All the conflicts of Dawg's seemed far, far from where we were when we were alone. Whatever happens, I thought. Whatever.

"Hey?" said Elaine.

"Yeah?"

"What do we do about going to the bathroom?"

"I've been trying not to think of that for the last few minutes. It's down the hall."

"Well, I *have* to think about it, right now. I know. I'll find your door with my eyes closed, go to the bathroom, and close them again when I get back to your door."

"I hate compromises. But I guess that's what we'll have to do."

F O U R   *A Visitation Continued*

We slept a little. We woke. It was still dark out, but you could feel morning close in the air.

"Jesse?"

"Yeah?"

"How long you been awake?"

"I'm not sure."

"Me neither. Jesse?"

"What?"

"Do you ever eat? I've almost never seen you eat."

"I'm almost never hungry around you. Yeah, I eat, sure. I follow the Duke Ellington diet. He used to have a huge steak for breakfast, with all the fixin's, because, being a musician, he could never be sure when or what he'd eat again that day. He lived to be an old man that way. Why, you hungry?"

"A little. But I don't think I want to have breakfast with you."

"Don't you like steaks?"

"It's—too real. Real people have breakfast. I don't wanna be 'real people.' "

Stillness again. The air a little lighter with the breezes of near-dawn.

"Jesse? We've been lying here nekkid for hours and we, uh, ain't *done* nuthin'."

I didn't say anything.

"Don't—don't you want me?" Elaine said.

"Just all the time." Then: "I'm not used to being calm, Elaine. Especially with you. It's been too sweet a feeling to let go of."

"I know. But . . ."

"But . . ."

"Does frank talk embarrass you from a woman? Some men just hate it."

"Don't you know how way past being embarrassed I am?"

"I guess, but—you've come in my mouth, and I don't mean I

266

didn't love it, I *loved* it, but—that's been all. You wouldn't come in my butt and you haven't even *been* in my pussy."

"You've noticed that too, eh?"

"Kind of."

"What I think is—that's your husband's world, that pussy."

"Oh, great. *That's* not even *mine*, hey? 'Husband.' I hate that word. 'Wife.' Vile words."

I felt my prick rise into the air again, just loose in the air, and then it wasn't like it was rising from me but like I was hanging from it.

I took her hand, which was still clasped in mine, and put it around my cock.

"Convinced?" I said.

"I'm wet."

"Hush."

"I'm hushed."

I rolled on her slow, slid on her damp skin, how soft she was, what welcome in her flesh, as I lifted her legs high, her feet above my head, and kneeled with eyes closed before her, and the fumes of her dizzied me, and going into her was so easy, so easeful, and I stayed in the shallows of her, just dipping down, while her wetness pulsed on me, till after hovering at her opening awhile, gently in and out, I *slammed* down in, and down and down, and pressed so hard, and she named my name, as I pulled way out and slammed on back down, and again, and again, over and over. And, pouring sweat, we went on and on while she came in rushes, subsided, and her comes welled up again, with my name bubbling out her mouth, till I couldn't go on and let down her legs and lay myself down on her, a stillness upon her and a stillness inside her, and I hadn't yet come. Soaking wet, we held each other. And she: "Nobody's every gone so deep inside me."

"I love you so much. Elaine."

Lying on her, I felt her heartbeat in her stomach, in her thigh, in her neck where I'd buried my face.

"You can put my eyes out now, Jesse. We can just stick our fingers into each other's eyes *right now*."

I unclasped my arms around her body and slowly drew my hands up to her face and put my thumbs on her eyes. And she put her long-nailed thumbs on mine. And our bodies felt swollen against each other, pulsing like bruises.

"I'm afraid," she said.

"So am I."

"I'm *really* afraid."

"So am I."

I wish we'd done it. Even now, I wish we'd done it.

I lifted my thumbs from her eyes, and she from mine, and slowly I rolled us over so she was on top of me, and she sat up and I held her hips as she pressed down hard, swiveling, rising up, then slamming down, till it was as though she was going inside *me*, and I spread my legs as though I had an opening down there and that would make it easier for her. And as she rose up so only my tip was in her, and hovered there, then bore down to my hilt like she had fallen from ten stories, it was like she was going deeper and deeper in me, but as deep as she went it wasn't deep enough, and she knew it, but didn't want to know it, and finally laid herself down on me. And how wet we were. And the swamp-smell of us. And still I hadn't come. Had wanted to—I think. But it was like I was blocked, I just couldn't. Don't even know if she had. Just that something was cramped hard inside me, deeper than she could or wanted to go, some curdled blockage of old dried sperm that wouldn't dissolve. I couldn't come.

She rolled off me, lay on her back, like we were before, holding my hand. Out there beyond our closed eyes the room was bright with day. My eyes had been shut so tight while we'd made love, my whole head hurt.

"I was moving so hard," Elaine said, "I never felt you come. When did you?"

"The first or second time?"

She laughed softly. Said, "I hate it that it's over. But I just couldn't move anymore."

"Me neither. But feel of this."

I put our hands on my swollen, soaked cock, still sticking up hard. But it made me feel far-off from her, to have lied to her about coming. I was amazed she didn't know. Then not so amazed.

And she: "I feel so crazy. I'm kind of sorry we didn't—do what we almost did. I can't even *say* it!"

" 'Fraid if we say it again we'll have to do it?"

"Let's just shut up about it."

"Let's just."

But a tenderness wafted from one to the other. All the more tender for having somehow, twice now, failed.

"Well, damn," I said. "Guess I missed my chance to be the white Ray Charles."

I feel her smiling.

"That's just what American music needs," she said. "More blind white musicians." Then: "I'm gonna go, Jesse."

"I guess it's time."

"Be careful."

"You, too."

"He won't hurt me. I'll be all right." Then: "I'm going to open my eyes, but I don't want to talk after I do—and I won't look at you. I love that you haven't seen me this whole time."

"Good-bye, Elaine."

" 'Bye, Jesse."

She let go my hand. I heard the rustle of her clothing, the door opening and closing.

I lay there a long time before opening my eyes to this pale, sickly world.

FIVE   *My White Trash to Her White Trash*

With her staying out all night, if it was coming from Johns it would probably come today. I figured I'd wait for it at Dawg's. The good thing about being a little preoccupied with Johns was that it pushed all the strangeness of what had happened the day before from my mind. What was Nade thinking? What was she telling Little Jesse? Where had Danny run off to, why didn't he answer his phone today? It was a lot simpler to think, Would Johns or wouldn't he?

Anyway, there was an odds-on chance Elaine might saunter

into Dawg's. And saunter she did, in a flaming red dress—the girl with the red dress on, if there ever was one.

You don't know anybody until they start to choose. Until they *have to* choose. So maybe I started to know Elaine some that night.

She'd walked in, headed straight for me, we'd held each other, stood right there at the bar with our arms around each other, both of us trembling. It was as though her dress was red with her excitement and nervousness, another of her thin cotton country-girl kind of dresses that felt so hardly there when I held her. And it was so good just to *see* her after those sweet dark hours with closed eyes. Like now our "enclosed space," as she'd said, was dingy Dawg's itself, its low ceiling, cigarette smoke clouding its few lights, the beer-neons behind the bar—ours, though the place was packed hot and loud. We were flaunting it today as much as we'd tried to step around it yesterday.

"Throw it all to the fire wall—" That was the feel of that night, what Elaine said when Stevie Vaughan started riffing, egging him on, as though she could push her whisper at him over the tremendous volume of his music from the bar to the bandstand with just the force of how hard she held my hand.

We couldn't talk, no one could, over Stevie's wail. This was back when he was still a skinny kid, before he'd put the "Ray" between his names and started becoming a star—back when he had no rep out of Austin, no money, nothing to fall back on but a drummer, a bass-man, and those beat-up guitars he'd play. And it was perfect, to look from Elaine's excited eyes to Stevie with his mashed nose and that look that managed to be real innocent and a little mean all at once, his arms like a boxer's and his cocky beret (it was always berets back then, not those flashy hats he wore later), and that big peacock tattoo on his chest that his flashy clothes conceal now. Stevie's was the perfect music for us that night: how he plays like an angel who's run with the devils, seen too many devils and seen through them to a music so fast and clean, so soft and harsh together, and *so* loud, but piercing not because of how loud it was but because of what he played. I mean, one guy hits a note on a guitar and you hardly notice it, you dance on, it's just part of the scene; a guy like Stevie hits the same note and it goes right through you, comes out the other side, it's got blood and memories on it.

"It's a comfort," a girl next to us said to no one, said that of a sound so big, all our ears would buzz all the next day. "Shitfire," Elaine hissed in agreement, and pulled me out onto the dance floor, and though the beat was fast we danced slow, hard together, my white trash to her white trash. When we danced past the speakers their blare was like a wind, you could feel the loudness against your face.

The Snake coiled out of Stevie's guitar, but in Elaine's arms I didn't mind it, it coiled its sounds around us and felt like home. I could maybe learn to live in Snake-time if we were only together.

Stevie geared down to a blues while we all gathered round his music like shivering people around a fire—a man who'd made a secret pact with his guitar. A secret you could dance to. We turned in slow circles and I held Elaine for dear, dear life while someone got killed in a song.

I heard a pistol shoot
It was a forty-four
Somebody killed a crap-shooter 'cause he couldn't
Shake rattle and roll, and when we were right under the bandstand Stevie caught my eye and gestured did I want to sit in? I gestured back yeah, next number or so, and hoped nobody had spilled any beer on that piano, hoped the keys wouldn't stick, because you can't hang back with Stevie. Then I was amazed at myself that I'd want to get up there at all after yesterday, but hesitation hadn't occurred to me, as though my hands were telling me to try again.

Elaine pressed harder against me, said, "I'm so happy, Jesse."

"I know. I am too."

Yet it shot through me right then that maybe we'd never be happier than we were at that moment, whether we lived or not, our happiness protected by the thick cloak of Stevie's music and the boundaries of the dance floor. God help us when the music stopped.

She pulled back and looked hard into me, her happiness like heat coming off her.

My happiness danced with my unhappiness just the way I was dancing with her.

"Gotta pee before I play," I said.

"Well, then, I'll pee before I listen."

We walked off the dance floor, past the bar, into the little hallway of the two smelly little rooms, two adjacent doors.

The men's room at Dawg's isn't there for anyone's health. Wood boards are lousy for men's rooms, they hold the smells and show a stain of just about everything anybody's ever gotten rid of. Every juice a man had in his body, from piss to blood to spit to puke to come, had left its trace in that room. It had a pretty good mirror, though, and I looked into it.

Hey, Jesse Wales—how you doin'?

I was shaking it off when she came in. Just came in and shut the door behind her before I could say anything.

"Hi!" she beamed, very proud of herself.

She looked down at me giving it the last shake and for just a moment the impulse that had gotten her in there left her and her face got trembly, then snapped back to that smile and dared me to show any disapproval at all.

"I came to see the graffiti. I always wanted to, and with you in here it seemed like a good time."

"Perfectly reasonable," I said.

And she held me suddenly, hard, and I held her back, and through her thin dress I felt her pulse beat where my hands were. Since last night it was like she had a hundred hearts in her, and I could feel one wherever I touched her.

Of course the door opened right then and a very big, very blowsy guy blinked at us two or three times, and then with mature deliberation said, "You might as well fuck 'er since you're in there. I'll just pee here in the hall."

And closed the door.

And she laughed.

The door opened and he was back. "Women ortent t'laugh when they're gettin' laid." And he closed the door again.

"I don't agree with that man," Elaine said, "do you agree with that man?"

"Not me."

She pulled down her panties and hitched up her dress with one move.

"Elaine! I *don't* wanna fuck in here."

"You think I'd want to fuck in here? I still gotta pee."

She started to sit down on the toilet and I grabbed her.

"You're gonna catch something on that thing. This ain't the ladies' room."

She saw the stains all over the wood toilet seat and I could see that something made her want to sit down on it anyway, but she didn't. She pulled her panties back up slowly, said, "If I caught something it would be a souvenir of our first night together in public."

"We haven't made it through the night yet."

"The guy who wrote that one knew something." She pointed at a scrawl that said: THE THING ABOUT WOMEN IS—THEY GOT ALL THE PUSSY.

"True enough, but I like this guy's attitude: WE MAY NOT GO DOWN IN HISTORY BUT WE'LL GO DOWN ON YOUR LITTLE SISTER."

The booming of the bass and drums thudded through the walls and planking, but you couldn't quite make out the words Stevie was singing if you didn't know them already. We'd had a few drinks, of course, and the stuffy heat of the little room made us drunker. Then Elaine for no reason started spinning, her red dress brushing the toilet and the urinal both as she spun, and I stood against the wall and let her spin, with her eyes tightly closed, spinning as though if she spun fast enough we would disappear together. The door opened and then slammed while she spun, I didn't see whose face, and she started to stumble with dizziness and I grabbed her and held her tight to me, me dizzy too with the closeness of the room and the fumes and the smell of her hair and my booze coming up in my throat and I started to fall, and she slammed her hand against a wall to brace us. She was crying all of a sudden, naming my name again. We might have been in the bowels of the earth locked in some prison cell, and there might have been no one and nothing anywhere around, and the thudding of the electric bass might have been some huge generator booming far above us.

The door opened.

"This ain't no place to cry, Elaine," said Dawg.

"The fuck it ain't," I told him.

"Hey, Jesse."

"Hey, Dawg."

"I was thinking of putting a TV in here," Dawg said.

"What are you betting on the Cowboys tomorrow?" I said.

"I'm betting they'll break my heart."

"Are we hurting your heart?" Elaine said.

"Just what's left of my reputation. I got three puddles of piss out in the hall. I'm gonna have those cleaned up but I'm gonna let the vomit lie there till I figure out what that guy had for dinner so I don't ever have to eat it, it looks really terrible. I'm ashamed at having such a low class of vomit in the joint."

"We were just leaving," I told him.

"That's considerate of you."

"I love you, Dawg," Elaine said.

"So my troubles are just beginning?"

We were taking the first step arm in arm toward the door and Dawg was stepping back to let us pass and there was Johns. Even Dawg, who was hard to sneak up on for the same reason Johns was, hadn't felt him coming up.

Johns didn't have a gun.

"I need you to come home with me now."

He said it very quietly to Elaine, as though nobody else was there. His black hair hung to his shoulders. He just had a T-shirt on with his jeans and boots, and you could see how strong his arms were, and the muscles on his neck pulled tight. His face was just a face, there were lots of faces like it, but he had eyes that saw everything they looked at as though noting it for some future purpose. His bare arms were straight down at his sides, with all their small shrapnel scars, and the big ugly one where the shrapnel had torn a piece out of his left forearm. There were no scars on his face because he'd thrown his arms over his face when he'd seen the grenade roll toward him and known it was too late. As it turned out, it wasn't too late.

"I need you to come home with me now," he said again in that same quiet way.

Then he looked at me.

If we had faced off as strangers in an argument in some bar, we'd have been about equally nervous of each other. He had some height on me and probably more strength, but I had—presence? Something like that. It counts for a lot in those moments just before men may or may not fight. He was a man who doubted himself more than I doubted myself, which is something two men can just

274

smell out about each other right away, so all things being normal, I could probably take him.

But not now. I was more scared than I'd thought I'd be, because it was clear that he had the right to kill me and that both he and I recognized his right. It might be stupid of him, he couldn't kill me without killing his own whole life, but that didn't change his right. It might be a horrible right, but that was part of its power. We all stood there in the shadow of his right.

And what went through me in flashes was: So this is who she shares her life with. Who she cooks for. Who she watches TV with. Who she visits family with. This tightly wrapped, nervous, shy dude. I *don't* know her at all.

"I need you to come home with me now," he said once more.

And in some dazed way it didn't surprise me that she eased her arm from around my waist, stepped to him, walked past him; him turning without looking at me again and walking after her.

S I X *Just a Blues*

In the South there's this word "trash." Sometimes trash is where you're going and sometimes it's where you come from, and sometimes it's just something you stepped in, but anybody who's made rhythm 'n' blues stick has been trash or has had trash. And you never really lose it once you have it. That's the nature of trash. Nigger trash, honky trash, the blues is the sweet smell of trash as it dreams of being something else.

"Let's just play the blues," Stevie said to me as I sat at the piano and the folks, all worked up by his music, howled and applauded. Stevie and I had pretty different styles, but we felt our trash the same way.

Stevie started a quiet ripply run, my right hand did something high and light, the drums and bass kicked in, and we bore down. Okay, Snake, what can you show me now?

That Snake didn't just moan, it howled out of Stevie's guitar, twisting and rippling and flying into the air, swooping down among the dancers and curling round their ankles, bursting into smoke, molting with shreds of dead Snake-skin in the smoke, then bursting out again stronger—while me, my hands were out for themselves, lighter, like they were *glad* she was gone, like they wanted none of my daze or shock or numbness, like they *loved* that Snake, petting it and squeezing it and digging their nails into its scales and sticking themselves down its endless gullet, daring me to catch up to them. And I did, moved them toward a woman, a woman I'd never held who seemed to live in my music, and as she rose from my hands Stevie's Snake wrapped around her, she loved it, she danced with it, and just when it seemed like you could reach out and touch them, one of us would crash a chord—me going at the keyboard with my elbows and my head, piano-screaming, making everybody crazy— and woman and Snake burst into a thousand shiny pieces that flashed and glittered on their own as they spun wildly around us, then faded to nothing as our last notes disappeared.

My hands were all tingly as I stepped off the bandstand: People hollered and cheered, guys slapped me on the back, women looked at me sweetly, very sweetly, but all their faces blurred into each other as I made my way through them and out the side door. I knew all most of them had heard was music, they's seen no Snake-wrapped woman; all they'd seen was a couple of guys going crazy; all most had done was suck up on our craziness (and thank God they had, because I felt lighter and more myself than I had in a long time). But the beings in our music had been among them, gotten inside them, and they'd take them home, and that was what they really came for, whether they knew it or not.

SEVEN *Hi Yourself*

Standing in that parking lot, under the heavy, sweet Austin air, I just flat didn't get it. How could I want her so much and be so relieved she'd chosen to go back to him? I felt free of her, free of them all. I knew it wasn't true, and might never be—I knew they'd catch up to me, and I knew I'd miss them if they failed to. But anyway I felt—different, is all. I'd made music again.

It was about one-thirty in the morning. My shirt stuck to me with sweat. An oh-so-slight breeze cooled me like the gentlest touch.

"Hi."

It was a light breath of a "hi," I had trouble placing it because my ears still roared with the blast of our music.

"Hi, yourself," I said, looking around.

Then I saw a woman sitting in the driver's seat of a car right by me. It was one of those worthless little things, a Maverick or Pinto or something, with the left front fender smashed in above the wheel. She had a small, sharp-featured face that had never decided for itself if it was pretty or plain, and it would take that kind of decision to make it finally go one way or the other. Smart dark eyes. Shortish brown hair that hung off her head as though it had died. She wore a white uniform.

"Nice of them to keep a nurse in the parking lot," I said. "Just in case."

She liked that.

"Waitress," she said.

She took out a joint, lit it, inhaled hard and passed it to me. I would lots rather have had a whiskey, but I took a hit.

"They gonna play again?" she asked me.

"Any minute now."

"You can't hear a piano too good from out here," she said. So she knew who I was. I always like that.

"You've gotta have a good system to really hear a piano at all these days, with how loud it's all gotten," I said.

"That why you ain't a star?"

"I doubt it."

We passed the joint back and forth.

"I'm sorry," she said, "I know who you are—obviously—and you don't know me. Kathy," she said, sticking a small pale hand out the window for me to shake. She had a strong grip and her palm and fingers were hard.

"Hi," I said.

"I really like that song of yours about the woman who drew the Devil."

"That was a true thing. Somebody did draw one like that, I saw it."

"Nobody you knew *well*, I hope." Kathy laughed. "Billy Joe Shaver's got a good one with the Devil in it. *Devil made me do it the first time—*"

"*Second time I done it on my own.*"

"That's the one."

We were silent a moment.

"I wish they'd start playing," Kathy said.

"Their break won't be too long. They have to start soon, it'll be closing in no time. You might just get in there before last call. Cover charge's only a dollar after midnight, and Stevie'll give you your dollar's worth."

"Oh, I don't go in. I mean, I do, but not when I look like shit. After working, I mean. When I get off, though, I like to stop on my way home, just sit in the parking lot and listen. 'Specially to Stevie. He makes the whole building sound like one big jukebox with the bass turned up too high. I just sit and listen and smoke a joint awhile, and go on home feeling *lots* better. Otherwise I just go home and wanna puke. I *hate* my job." She looked up suddenly, with a flare of alarm. "I don't know *why* I'm tellin' *you* all this! 'Scuse me."

"It's okay, it's not exactly the story of your life."

"That's what you think."

She tried to make a joke of that with her eyes as it came out, but it hadn't been a joke. I was hoping I'd remember to tell Stevie about her, next time I saw him, he'd really like to know about this girl and what he'd done for her.

"Now you think I'm an asshole," she said.

"Nothing of the kind."

"Well, what *do* you think?"

"I don't *think* shit! I'm glad you're in this parking lot, all right? Lighten up."

"I'm sorry," she said. Which made my skin crawl. I hoped she wasn't one of those women who always says "I'm sorry." That's one good kind to stay far from.

Stevie started to play just then, and it was like she'd said, he amplified that building into a brick jukebox, slightly muffled, but the guitar lines strong and clear, and it made the parking lot, the whole deserted street come darkly alive.

We finished the joint without speaking, just listening. The marijuana smelled like the sweetened roots of the trees that hung over the parking lot, it blended so well with the scent of the leaves. We'd look into each other's eyes as we passed the joint—not romantically, just frankly. It seemed that she felt like I did, that when two strangers step into a moment like this together, they suddenly have something important in common: that they've both just left the rest of their lives—even for a little while. It's a fine, weightless feeling, and so welcome. Sometimes they almost love each other for that.

It was me who broke the silence, and it just came out, the question, "What's the worst thing about being a waitress?"

"I always think my hair smells. Even when I *know* there's no burger grease left in my hair, even then sometimes I'm sure I can smell it."

I bent down quickly and lifted her pale brown lifeless hair to my face and smelled it. It was enough to make you a vegetarian.

With our faces close together I said to her, "I need you to come home with me now."

"*What?* Are you kidding?"

What a strange way for Johns to put it.

But no, I told her, I wasn't kidding.

She gave a little desperate laugh and said, "You're crazy!"

"That's been long established."

Kathy just shook her head and laughed that laugh again and stared down at the steering wheel. When she looked up at me her face was so plain and sad.

She whispered, "Yeah. Okay. All right."

My turn to be surprised. But I didn't feel I could back off now. And didn't really want to. Didn't want to go back to my room.

I went around to the other side of the car and got in. She turned the key in the ignition. I put my hand on her hand on the wheel.

"I'm crazy, but I'm not a hustler. This ain't love at first sight or anything. I—really—I just—don't want—I mean I'd awfully like to be with somebody right now."

"Any old port in a storm?" she said.

"That's not what I meant."

She gave a small smile with that frank, up-front way she had. I smiled weakly back. She put the car in reverse and backed into the street.

E I G H T *We Both Stink*

We feld oddly comfortable driving to her place, as though we'd done this before. And of course we had, with other people, taken virtually the same ride how many times? I liked her, how she concentrated on her driving, glancing over toward me now and again but not trying to make conversation, not afraid of the silence.

She was petite, olive-skinned, about twenty-four. Thick eyebrows, wide dark eyes, high cheekbones. A straight nose, a small round mouth. Small hands, with pretty fingers, close-clipped nails. She drove barefoot, her waitress-nurse shoes on the seat next to her. I got the beginnings of a hard-on looking at her feet work the pedals. She had the prettiest, most perfect feet I think I ever saw. Sweet feet. You could write a song about them.

We drove down Lamar, across the Colorado River, to a quiet street in South Austin, a dead-end called Thornton Road. She rented a little wood-frame, not much more than a shack. A saggy plank porch, just a step off the ground, and no insulation—hot in summer, cold in winter, and always fungus-smelling, a slow-rot smell all those little places have in the warm weather. As we walked up to it I felt a weird exhilaration, like I'd slipped away from them all—Elaine, Johns, Danny, Nade—nobody I'd ever known had any idea who I was with or where. I got the crazy idea in my head that maybe I'd marry this girl. And I let the idea float around like a bubble in my head.

Her place stank of a sickly sweet, vanillalike incense that I guess she burned to drown out the fungus smell. Her little living room had a poster of Stevie on one wall, a Butch Hancock poster on another, and a couple of dull prints of paintings that looked like they'd be brightly colored in real life. I knew what her bedroom would look like, it would be like just about everybody's I knew: a mattress on the floor; a stereo next to that with a pile of records; a little TV, probably black and white, at the foot of the mattress; and maybe some photos on the wall. The gals were usually neater than the guys, but it was the same, city to city. I was right at home.

But the incense reminded me I had another smell between my legs—I hadn't washed there since I'd been inside Elaine last night; I don't like to, I like to feel the grease of it when I pee later. But what would this girl think when we took off our clothes? There was only one place the bathroom could be, but I asked her where it was.

She was just standing in the middle of her living room not knowing what to do. She ran a hand through her hair. Straightened her uniform, then started to unbutton it, then stopped. Started to raise her hand to her hair again, stopped herself. Her eyes were just a hint watery with held-back tears.

When she saw I'd noticed, she said, "I'm sorry."

"Hey . . ." But I didn't know what to say.

"Look . . ." She didn't know either.

"You want me to go? It's okay." I tried to say it very business-like without any spin to it. It really *was* okay.

"It's not either. We came in my car." Then: "Anyhow, that's not what I want. *Shit*," she said, and stamped a bare foot down, and turned from me. Her effort not to cry was worse than crying.

I went to her and took her by the shoulders and turned her around—there was nothing else to do, it was this or leave—and kissed her smelly hair and kissed her sweaty forehead and lifted her small round face and kissed her small mouth gently. And she kissed back, a sweet, far-off kiss, and then a closer kiss, and then closer still. The supple life in her lips surprised me. Quick, short, hungry kisses. And both of us smelling of our different trades, hers thin-sweated and greasy, mine the thick dried drench-sweat of performing. We just stood there in our fumes and held each other.

Her hair was in my face. She pulled back after a bit and said, "My hair stinks."

"We both stink."

"We do, don't we? You wanna take a shower?"

I found myself liking her, suddenly and a lot.

"Sure," I said.

She smiled slightly, took my hand, and led me to the bathroom.

N I N E   *Clean Crazy*

We took off our clothes in her cramped bathroom as though we'd been living together for months. I couldn't figure it, because now I was feeling bewildered, and whatever Kathy was feeling it wasn't easy, but we were easy as you please, physically, stepping out of our clothes and looking at each other. Her body was like her feet and hands, touchingly small and well-formed—skin as pale as olive can get, jailhouse-pale. Me, I didn't want to think what I looked like. Thick in the chest, thick in the belly, thin arms, the circles under my eyes gone from purple to almost black. I was conscious of all this in front of her the way I'd never been in front of Elaine—I guess because Kathy was so much younger. She maybe had never seen the body of a man who hadn't taken care of himself. I got self-conscious about her seeing my ass. It probably just hung.

She hung our clothes on two hooks on the door, and I saw how fine *her* ass was, round and firm and how it stuck right up in the air with a life of its own. Naked, it was the liveliest part of her.

She looked over her shoulder suddenly, had felt my eyes on her. Then turned back to hanging the clothes, letting herself be looked at.

Then she turned again and swiftly, suddenly, we were in each other's arms, clinging to each other like two scared kids. Her skin felt cool under my hands, and so smooth. Elaine's skin had kind of sucked to mine, as though it touched back wherever I touched it, and Nade was pillowy, not fat but big, and wonderfully heavy in the hand, while this Kathy's skin was still tense with youth, and gave the way a trampoline gives, ready to spring back. We kissed and—surprise, surprise—her tongue pushed into my mouth, it didn't share her shyness, but lay heavy on top of my tongue, and her heartbeat pulsed in my mouth. Then she gently flicked its roof, here and there, and it was as though her licking inside my head drew a bolt up from the rise of my butt, the small of my back, up my spine, into my tongue, which came alive and curled with hers and went into her mouth, then back into mine, and I sucked on her tongue like it was part nipple and part cock. I was big now and pressed against her belly, and she let me go and stepped back from me, and my cock just hung there bobbing.

She didn't know where to look and neither did I. So she reached into the shower and blasted the hot water. Steam fogged the room. Our skins became slick with it, our smells stronger. She adjusted hot and cold in the shower. As she was about to step in, I grabbed her shoulders from behind and spun her around to kiss her again; I'd had this flush of desperateness that needed to be kissed. But as my face went close to hers I saw that her eyes were wide and wary—I'd spun her pretty suddenly, I guess.

"You happy you startled me?"

"I wasn't trying to."

"Well, don't."

"What are you frightened of, Kathy?"

"A little of everything."

She held the shower curtain aside, took my hand, stepped straight under the hot stream, and pulled me in after her. We stood holding each other under the water, my cock like something *other* pressed up between our bellies, as though if we suddenly stepped apart it would fall off and wriggle of itself in the water at our feet.

She reached up to the soap dish, took a bar of white soap, and rubbed it on herself and on me as we stood pressed together, and I thought of how strange Elaine looked with water flattening down that thick bushy hair to her skull, how bulbous her head looked that way, while Nade's long straight hair clung like shiny cloth. Kathy's short pale brown hair, wet, was like a skullcap.

She stepped back from me. And it *was* like the hard-on had fallen off—my cock had subsided and just hung small. Kathy took a tube of shampoo and lathered her hair furiously, her eyes tight shut—which made me feel queerly alone. Nade said in my ear, "She has repeating dreams, and guess who's about to go around and around in them?" Elaine said, in my other ear, "If you make love to somebody, you carry that energy for six months. So if you wanna make love to someone, you oughta be sure you want to carry them around for six months."

"What are you thinking?" Kathy said with her eyes shut. Smart kid.

"I don't think, lady. It all just kind of runs through me."

She opened her eyes.

"Don't call me 'lady,' okay, Jesse?"

"Got it," I said.

She stepped a small step through the downpour to me and clung, and I clung back.

"I'm so crazy," I said.

"I am *too*," Kathy said into my chest.

All the waitresses were crazy. All the piano players were crazy. All the gas-station mechanics were crazy. All the low-rent beauty-parlor people were crazy. All the people who came out into the night to hear people like me play. And the world is run by people who stay home nights. The future is theirs and the night is ours.

I reached behind Kathy and turned off the shower. We stood there in the sudden quiet.

"I'm glad you're here," she said.

We rubbed each other down with towels, roughly, thoroughly. I couldn't get over how this strange familiarity between us faded in and out. Now, with the towels, we were like brother and sister. Then, standing fresh and dry, cleaner than I felt in I don't know how long—strangers again, about to fuck.

"We ain't got no more excuses, Kathy," I said.

"We'll think of *some*thing," she laughed.

"We *could* have a drink, if you got a drink."

"That's a *good* excuse. I have some wine."

I knew it would be wine. Whiskey in the day, tequila in the bar, and now wine. I could feel my liver sweat.

Her bedroom looked like I'd known it would, and we sat cross-legged on her mattress on the floor in the light of a candle and drank wine out of coffee cups. A sweet wine, too, horrible stuff.

"You know," I said, "we don't have to—I don't know why it should be so hard to say this—we . . . don't have to *fuck* at all. We could—it would be just as good to . . . we could—hold each other and fall asleep."

And then I wouldn't come too fast. Or not at all.

"Why'd you say that?"

She lay on her stomach. I had the weird flash that her ass was staring up at the ceiling. To me it looked like it was glowing in the half-dark. She wasn't looking at me, so she didn't see me getting hard again. And I felt like my hard-on was kind of an intrusion, pulling me toward something I wasn't sure I wanted or could handle.

"So why'd you say that?"

She sounded really hurt. In answer I bent over and kissed her on the spine.

Six months, I thought.

I kissed Kathy's shoulder. My hard-on wanted me to. She started to roll over on her back, but I didn't want that, or my hard-on didn't. I lightly pressed her, she accepted the signal, stayed on her belly. I half-bit, half-kissed her—between her shoulders, at the small of her back, on her soft sides—and she relaxed to it, and I knew she liked it. I didn't want her to touch me, not yet.

"I know why," Nadine said close to my ear, Nadine half-biting, half-kissing my back where I'd kissed Kathy, with Nade's wide mouth and strong teeth, but harder than I was doing it to Kathy, until Kathy turned herself over, resisting my resistance, pulling me down to kiss her mouth, a sharp clean taste to her, not musty like Elaine's mouth. Elaine's taste was in *my* mouth, my Elaine-mouth kissed Kathy, and the Elaine in my mouth sparked Kathy and Kathy kissed back with more passion. Elaine's smell. I felt it come off me for a moment. Too much. Come back.

I couldn't. I was a tuner tuning in on Elaine's body, and my balls, swollen and painful now—no, it was Elaine's tits hanging from under my cock; no, it was Nade's hair hanging down my back; no, it was that I had not come since I'd spurted that dream into Elaine's mouth, it seemed so long ago. Had not come in Mexico, hips trembling with pent-up Snake-knowing. I'm a tuner. Nade's tits on my buttocks hanging heavy, as I clung to Kathy, and she—I couldn't say, "Don't do that," and it scared me so, *six months*—she licked at my nipples, she sucked at my nipples, her mouth all over *my* flat breasts, as I lay back now, woozy with a pleasure I'd never had; nobody'd done that. She bit my man-tits, bit sharp, it hurt deep and good, while my Elaine-tits pulsed beneath my cock and my Nade-tits flattened against my ass as I lay back under Kathy. And I shook, shaking now, *me* molting, Kathy going crazy on my tits, biting harder. And I pulled her by the hair up to my face and mashed my mouth into hers, blood on her teeth, my tits' blood; hair between her teeth, my chest hair. And while our mouths are mashed together I'm shaking her by the shoulders, and she's shaking me, my face wet with pain-tears, and our shaking eases down to shivers, and we don't understand, we don't understand. "I'm sorry," she's saying, "I'm sorry and sorry." But I'm a tuner and words start buzzing in my body:

That the world is all of flesh, every wall and road, and some go around dealing and some go around wheeling, inventing and preventing—

I'm trying to shut this off, it won't shut off.

—politicking and shit-bricking, Commie-fighting and UFO-sighting, breathing a blood called the air, beware, beware, of their repetition of definitions, folks who know just what they *used to* know, while you know where bone meets soul, meets *what*, what's Papa Adam doin' *here*? Jesus, sweet Jesus, Jesus hanging like a hard-on about to spout into what it's fucking all a-bout, I don't fuck to get in, I fuck to get *out*, not love at first sight, love at *last* sight, pass on by or make your pass, I'm gonna pour these words into Kathy's ass.

For as the words buzzed, I'd turned her on her belly and she knew what I was after now, and she didn't want it but she wouldn't say so; had she'd said "no," I guess I'd've stopped, I guess that's a rule, I guess I still believe in *some;* but she just sort of squirmed her "no" and that ain't enough. She shook, I shook, and I wasn't about to get up and look for some Vaseline. I spit into her asshole to grease it up, as globulous a gob as I could fetch.

Oh, I had to coax you, Nadine, for so long, for weeks, touching it now and again, lightly, till that night, Nade, I was feeding on your pussy and I turned you around and stuck my tongue in your butthole till your ass woke up and did its wanting all on its own. And for nights then that great big ass became like our baby, we goo-gooed over it and were proud of it and liked to see how it was doing, learning how ass-life is different from cunt-life. Inside cunt it's like talking or dancing, inside ass it's like falling. You can never get enough of cunt, cunt defies and defines all laws, two creatures occupying the same space together, matter/antimatter, you could explode. But with ass, you fall, fall together, falling through shit, connected but *not* in the same place, clasped but from separate worlds, falling end over end toward where, the black hole, you don't know, end over end, squeeze of pain going in and then that lushness that does not end, not like the cunt that you can plumb the bottom of—"Nobody's ever been so deep inside me"—'cause ass doesn't stop till mouth and then there's just air, that's not stopping. and the never-ending hole of it makes for movement not like cunt's, a rhythm that's a falling till, when you come, it's like a parachute suddenly opening, it jerks both of you up hard, and in the aftermath of come you just kind of float dazed awhile. You don't know where you've been. You do with cunt. You both went through cunt once, you lived it, you wanted to scream into its walls, you pushed against its side with your shoulders, with your feet, you clawed it from the inside, you breathed it, you know it. So no matter how many times you go there, you can't know ass like you know cunt. Would I come now? After you come in ass, both of you smell of her musty shit, smears of it on your dick, with the memory of how falling through the endlessness of ass it's both of you who fall: for clasped at the ass you're both enveloped by it, both like one Prick pushing through something huger that is Ass—*And Elaine's asshole had been so open, she was so used to it, she went back to Johns so easily, she walked everywhere, I knew now, with Johns impaled in her ass. Was why I wouldn't come there, no, she had secrets up her ass I didn't want to know, was why . . .*

I came like I was puking through my cock.

Puking Elaine, puking Mexico, Nadine, Danny, Johns, blues, the end of the world. Till after there was no jism left, my cock kept on jerking like it had the dry heaves.

And Kathy whimpered as I did, whimpering a coming that echoed somewhere in the membrane between cunt and asshole.

With my cock, through the walls of her ass, I could feel her fingers stuck deep into her cunt, touching herself into coming.

Finished, breathless, we lay joined awhile. Stunned with all that had come into us from one another.

I pulled out of her slowly, trying not to hurt her, but feeling her tense against the pain.

We lay on our backs in a kind of shock. Equally amazed. Equally afraid. Wasn't she just a pickup? And, while I could be good with pickups, could lick and squeeze and suck a good long while like we were out of time, I got plopped smack back *in* time when I got inside them and, zap, as I'd made the mistake of telling Nadine once, I was gone in ten seconds or less. "The groupie come," we called it. Anyway, wasn't I just a pickup for them too? It might be a good tune, but it's only the flip side. But here we were, two pickups, and look where the hell we'd gone.

I lay there trying to think. For a change. Instead of just react, like it seems I'd always done. But all I could think was the obvious: This dark small girl had had as much pent up as me. She'd been drawn to the music, as though the music itself had introduced us, she on one side of it and me on the other—like she'd stepped out of the music at me, and I at her. Like we'd been waiting in the music for each other.

But hadn't that been how we'd all gotten together? Coming toward each other through loud dark passageways of music? Weren't we nothing but its faces, its bodies, its hands? And didn't Snake live in it, and spirits we couldn't guess, so much *of* it that we took them for granted? Had we become their agents in the world? More—were *we* the spirits?

Papa Adam smiled, from his deep place of hiding.

T E N *Ablutions*

I lay beside Kathy, afraid, but not panicky-afraid. Thoroughly, quietly afraid. Afraid we were no longer quite human.

Maybe never have been. What the hell is 'human'? Papa Adam chuckled. *Nine to five? Apple pie? Concentration camps? What, you silly dude?*

I was tired, tired beyond telling, of hearing voices.

You've only just opened THAT door. Papa Adam laughed some more.

Wouldn't I be locked up by now if I didn't have the music for an excuse?

"Could you"—the words came out of Kathy like they made her gag—"wash . . . yourself . . . please."

The smell of her shit was strong from my cock. I got up and washed myself. Went back and lay down near her. Too near, because she edged away. We were both lying on our backs, looking at the ceiling, wide awake and far away from one another. What could she be thinking? I looked at her. Her face was averted from me. I leaned over, gently cupped her cheek and turned her head toward me. She looked so forlorn. When I let her face go her head just fell back away from me, the way it had been, like I'd moved the face of a doll.

And I heard myself tell her, "I'm sorry."

INTERLUDE:

Quartzsite

ONE
Welcome to the Land of the Zombies

Ever talk to yourself past tense about something you ain't done yet?

YOU MIGHT SAY IT'S BECOME A WAY OF LIFE.

I wasn't talking to you.

WANNA BET?

You used to be such a nice guy.

NAW, JUST SCARED.

Of anything in particular? Not telling, hey?

Even with the air conditioner blasting, the Mojave's heat pulsed through the walls. In arm's reach on the bureau, the tequila bottle was empty. Didn't matter. I couldn't move anyway. The TV screen had frozen into a kind of jellyish white. I'd slowed down so much, the dots didn't fuzz anymore. One dot pattern had just meshed and hovered, and it was taking an awfully long time for the next burst of dots to shift that jellylike swirl even a little. The word "instantaneous" was taking on whole realms of new meaning for me. What could be slower than a human instant?

But I wished I hadn't been too spaced out, when I checked into this motel, to take the shower I'd promised myself after those bouts of jalapeño diarrhea. Wet shit, caked sweat, soiled clothing, and tequila molecules slowly grated on each other in the vast expanse of my nose. It was like I could smell my stench with my ears, too, and with my hair, and with the gelatin of my long-unblinking eyes.

Welcome to the land of the zombies.

YOU SURE ARE TAKING YOUR SWEET TIME.

Dying's a big deal.

NOT FOR ME. IT WAS LIKE LIFE JUST SPIT ME OUT.

Yeah, well, you were never hardly here anyway.

WHO IS?

Dig it. The dots are shifting. And an incredible thunder, crashing. Where do they get thunder in this sun-stained desert town?

JUST SOMEBODY STARTING THEIR CAR. TO YOU, IT'LL ONLY SEEM ABOUT SIX YEARS TILL THEY BACK UP AND PULL OUT.

Six years *our* time? I'll be dead by then.

LET'S HOPE SO.

PART EIGHT

Didn't He Ramble

Deep inside your body
There's someone you don't know—
I'm gonna introduce you—
Test your very soul—
I'm gonna strike like lightning
Somewhere down the road—
I'm gonna be a story
Mama never told—
                    —Lonnie Mack &
        Stevie Ray Vaughan

O N E   *The Morning After*

Under my closed eyes I heard little scratches. Couldn't make them out. But, for a change, I had a good reason not to open my eyes: I felt comfortable lying there. The smell of our sex, the fresh scent of Kathy's clean sheets, her incense and the mossy smell of the house—it was homey. Yes, I might marry this girl. I accepted that she'd been sent, or I'd been sent, or both, and I didn't feel that morning-after urge to get the hell out. Far from it. I felt my room, two or three miles north, was a cramped, almost evil place I didn't want to go back to. But, I'd move in here in a New York minute.

"I know you're awake," Kathy said.

I opened my eyes. The night before was fresh in me—where'd we'd gone in the bed, and the fears after. But the daylight felt soft and safe. No wonder so many people get up early in the morning.

"How can you stand to sleep so late?" Kathy said.

She sat Indian-style on the end of the mattress, in blue shorts and a red sleeveless T-shirt that fit tight, her small breasts outlined smoothly, the nipples hard. Well, well. Her smile was—frank, like the rest of her. That was the word for her. No ulterior motive whatever—either that, or I was more wrong about her than I'd ever been about any woman. A shudderingly awful possibility.

"What are you thinking?"

"You keep asking me that, Kathy."

"Well—what?"

"Just that I like you."

"You better."

The scratching I'd heard was the sound of a pencil on good thick paper. She was sitting there with a big artist's pad on her lap, drawing me.

"You an artist?"

"No. I just like to sketch."

"Let's see."

297

There's something damn *real* about a pencil sketch, I decided as I looked at the several she'd made of me sleeping.

My face asleep.

"Do I really look that calm when I sleep?"

"I lie when I have to, but the pencil doesn't."

"When do you have to?"

"For survival. You know about survival."

"I used to."

It was a dark face, with lots of shadow—shadow under the eyes, shadow around the mouth—but the nose looked strong instead of broken, and the scars on the chin just looked like experience, not like . . . well, it was the only time I'd seen myself when I didn't look like poor white trash. I looked . . . sensitive, or something. And the creases around the mouth made it strong, not just tough. I like that face.

"I'd like to really look like that."

"When you're awake you have this tenseness, suspicious-like, that makes you look different."

My head from the side, the bald spot bigger than I'd like to think it is, the hair hanging over one cheek, some more of it spread out on the pillow. Lots of gray in the temples.

"That guy's older than me."

"I can't help it, you look older in daylight. You look younger when you play 'cause of how you move, bouncing, shimmying, shaking—all that energy."

"You seen me play much?"

"Lots. But I'm always off in a corner, in the dark—not where you'd notice."

I didn't say anything.

"You waiting for a compliment?" Kathy said.

"Not . . . desperately. Just sort of patiently."

"I wouldn't know what to say. *I* like it. It draws me out. That's all I know."

My body, without the head. *That* was strange to see. The folds of my belly as I lay curled up. The thickness of my thighs. One foot covering the other, curled over it—very boyish, that detail, strange with the chunky heaviness of the rest.

"You used to be skinny, didn't you?" she said.

298

"Fairly."

"That drawing's booze and bad food on a skinny man. You oughta watch that."

"I *watch* it. Doesn't stop me from doin' it."

"Are you a drunk?"

"I never put it that way, but—some. I drink. You got a questionnaire, I'll fill it out."

"I'm sorry. I just want to know what I'm gettin' into. I *am* gettin' into something, aren't I?"

"Feels that way, doesn't it?"

"Want some breakfast?"

"Eat? In a house? I haven't done that in—I don't know how long. Months, at least. Last time I visited my—wife."

"I know all about that."

"How?"

"You're a living legend, remember?"

"I'm *never* gonna live that down, am I?"

"I doubt it. Anyway—you kind of deserve it. Musically, at any rate."

"It's not exactly the story of my life."

"You gonna tell me the story of your life? Hey, before you say yes or no: I haven't slept with a man in a long, long time. I didn't like myself very much as we drove here. I felt like I was playing a bit part in somebody else's movie. But—we went crazy, I guess. An important kind of crazy. I've gotta trust that. I don't know how else to react to it, 'cept to leave, and—this is *my* house; that happened in *my* house. You know? So—I'm real curious about you. I didn't know how the drawings would come out. It was kind of a test. I liked you in the drawings. I like you now. A lot. Those are all the cards I got. Right here on the table, or the mattress, or whatever. If I start to feel differently, you'll be the first to know."

"You're really something."

"Is that good?"

"Kathy—do you think the world's about to end?"

"That's what they say."

TWO *The Last Sketch*

My chest didn't hurt till I stood up.

Dried blood around my nipples. Moving tore the cuts again. Kathy stood, wouldn't meet my eyes, went to the bathroom and came back with a wet cloth and a vial.

"All—all I've got is iodine."

I didn't let her put it on, but I didn't tell her why. It wasn't the pain, it was that I wanted her mouth there again.

She flipped the sketch pad open to the last page.

"I didn't know if I'd show you this."

One bruised nipple filled the large sheet. It looked like the drawing of a small gnarly hill rising out of a desert, with strange vines and several deep, evenly spaced ditches.

THREE *The Story of My Life*

We sat at her little kitchen table all afternoon, having breakfast, then coffee after coffee after coffee, and I told her everything. I'd had no idea how much I'd needed to tell someone. Nadine and the flies. Henry, Missy, Danny. Elaine and Mexico. The movie day —just two–three days ago!—and my hands. What had happened with Elaine and Johns just before I walked out into that parking lot. She listened. Asked questions. Laughed sometimes. Just looked serious mostly. I didn't feel judged or not judged. Never got a flash of jealousy off her. After a night like last night, jealously is a waste of time. Late in the afternoon she called in sick at the diner where she worked. I poured it all out, and it was a great relief, to be off in this little shack, away from all that, with this straight-ahead Kathy, who seemed to *get* it, though she didn't say how and didn't volunteer any story of her own.

Now and then there'd be long silences. And during them I'd try to get *this*, what was going on, why I'd so suddenly cleaved to this young woman. It was as I was wondering that, that right on cue she said,

"You just can't live without women, can you?"

Papa Adam chuckled from far off.

"I never thought of it that way. Am I supposed to?"

"I just don't want to feel like a sweet substitute."

"Only time will tell, right? Know something weird, Kathy? Telling it to you makes it feel like it all happened a long time ago, not like it's still out there happening. I feel like I've been in your house for a week, or weeks, not a day."

"I didn't mean that I was worried about the speed of—whatever's happening to us. That's just how things are now. I mean—they can blow up a whole city in an instant."

FOUR *The Moment "Used to" Starts*

Danny died that night, while Elaine and I argued in Dawg's parking lot.

He was singing when or as he died, his keening voice clear and piercing as always, lifting easily out of the thick air of the club into the sweeter thickness of the humid Austin night. His song's words blurred as they passed through the walls. Only his melody and the throbbing bass-line reached us out at the parking lot's edge.

Elaine stood with her feet apart in a thin green dress, her hair dark in the shadow and dull red where it caught the light. After staring at Kathy's smooth face all the day, I noticed, as I never had before, the little-old-lady creases like insect feelers encircling her mouth.

"I can't apologize for the way I'm made," Elaine was saying. "I can apologize for some of the ways I've handled it, but I'm not about to apologize for what I have *in* me to *handle*. And I think that's what you really want. And that's the *real* difference 'tween you and Johns." Then: "I need you so much. I never said that to any man."

"Who'd believe it if you had?"

"I've never lied to you."

"No, you never *lie*, you just say whatever shit comes into your head and then you convince yourself of it and then you change your mind."

"I'm not laying any claims to being consistent. I just say what's true. Anyway, look who's talkin'? Who's got him a new little honey, young and sweet and dark, and who made a point of dancing real good and slow right in front of our table?"

I'd wanted to see Danny bad, and I'd wanted Kathy to meet him and Dawg. I half-expected Elaine to be there too, but not with Johns—she just about never went clubbing with Johns. I was real grateful to be with Kathy when they walked in together. But Kathy got annoyed, said she'd rather I take Elaine out to the parking lot and talked with her, than have me sitting with her, Kathy, and carrying on a conversation with Elaine in my head. So I went straight up to her table and said, "We ought to talk." Johns looked at me hard and unblinking. Elaine squeezed his hand as she told me okay, got up and walked out with me. I felt both Johns's and Kathy's eyes on our backs as we headed out the side door.

Elaine broke off her argument suddenly, said, "It's just fair to tell you. Johns has got a gun this time."

"I thought that was settled."

"The more he thinks about it, the angrier he gets."

"Why ain't he angry at you?"

"You're the one who's preying on his mind."

"I don't want nothin' to do with his mind."

"Don't bad-mouth him to me or *I'll* get a gun."

I guess it's a waste of time to be with a woman who's not willing to kill you if she has to. With those bites last night, Kathy had proved she was in that league, too.

"Well, while we're all still alive—*isn't* it settled?"

"You know anything that's ever been *settled*?"

302

"Not really, no. But there ought to be a moment when 'used to' starts. I'd sure welcome it."

"I wouldn't. I love you, Jesse."

And the hushed way she said it brought it all back in a rush, made me know that even when she was a gnarly old lady I might want to do what I wanted to do right now, which was to kiss her softly, which I did. The sweetness of her musty cigarette-tasting mouth shot through me, and we held each other so tight.

Shoot me *now*, motherfucker.

And it flashed on me why she'd brought Johns with her; she'd feel she owed him the setup, owed him the chance to go out the front door of the club, work his way around behind us in the shadows, make his decision to shoot one or both of us, yes or no. That's easily what "marriage" might mean to her—and it wasn't a bad definition, as definitions of marriage go.

We held each other and held each other, and I tried to remember what Kathy looked like sitting across her kitchen table that day —and I *did* remember, which was even more confusing.

Weakly I said, "This is silly."

"It may be silly but it ain't easy."

She was grinning. With victory. A victory, I suddenly knew, that had precious little to do with me, a victory over all of us, the stakes she'd been playing for, to be the only one we ultimately couldn't deal with.

I hated Elaine's victory grin the moment I understood it, yet it made holding her that much more exciting. My pants swelled and I pressed against her. I'd've thrown her on the ground right there, and she'd have let me.

FIVE *Knowing*

And sometime during our words or our kiss or her victory, the music stopped in Dawg's. But the quiet seemed to be coming out of us, we didn't even notice how the tune hadn't finished, how there wasn't any clapping or hollering like there always is that time of night for somebody as good as Danny. Didn't really hear the siren, either, till it was right on top of us. What broke our spell was Kathy yelling "Jesse! Jesse!" as she ran toward us, and I thought the expression on her face was because of how I was holding Elaine.

Kathy almost tripped, caught her balance, stopped a few yards from us, tried to say something. Her mouth opened, closed, quivered, then she bit her lower lip.

Johns came right behind her. He looked wild and scared, and I thought, "This is it," and with a rush of adrenaline I let her go and turned to him, ready to fight.

Just then the ambulance wheeled into the parking lot, the siren slicing through our ears, its whirling red light making us all look even crazier. And even then I didn't know.

Later it would seem impossible to me that when that thing burst in Danny's brain *I* didn't fall down, clutch my head, bleed through my ears. But all I'd been feeling, when it had happened, was that there was no difference at all between Elaine's thin cotton dress—green, with yellow-reddish flowers on it, something her grandmother or some Okie prostitute might have worn—no difference between that dress and her skin, as though she stood there naked, a lovely paled frayed green skin, tattooed lightly with her granny's roses.

Two guys in white coats burst out of the ambulance with a stretcher and ran into the club.

Kathy managed to move, reached and grabbed me on the arm so hard her nails dug in, said, "Danny—it's your friend Danny."

She looked so little beside Elaine, so thin, in tight jeans and another sleeveless T-shirt, yellow, her deep dark eyes so scared, but scared for me.

Oh, it hit then. Somewhere my body must have gotten the message and the message had backed up, glitched out somehow, but it let loose now—a cramp from my gut up my gullet to my brain. Your body *knows*, in all its parts, when "used to" starts, when nothing will ever be the way it's been. Your body knows first. Takes your "you" weeks to catch up.

I felt a wave hit me off Elaine. She jerked her hands out of mine and buried them in her hair, clutching knuckles white.

Folks were pouring out of the club now and getting into their cars. Engines revving all around us, headlights flashing on, the ambulance's red bubble-light flashing on the car windows, reflecting on the car doors, as they slowly moved all at once, jockeying to get to the street, the ambulance driver yelling at people to keep a passage open for him.

They brought Danny out strapped to the stretcher and rushed him into the ambulance. People gawked. I didn't once think to run to him. I couldn't move. The ambulance started up, its blaring traffic-horn pulsing so the other cars would get out of its way. It pulled out and its siren faded slowly.

The first of us to move was Johns. He tried to take Elaine's hands out of her hair but she shook her head furiously and clutched her hair tighter.

Kathy took my hand. Led me back into the club. The lights were up, and the joint looked crummy, like one big faded stain. Two waitresses were collecting the half-filled glasses and bottles left on the tables. Danny's band was crowded around the pay phone at the far end of the bar, except for the drummer, who was packing his kit.

Dawg sat at a table by himself looking hard at the wall.

"Hey, Dawg."

"Hey, Jesse."

"Can I use your office phone?"

"Sure. But no point calling the hospital. I got to him first. He was deader than shit."

I squeezed his shoulder as I passed him, he patted my hand. Old Dawg.

Kathy went with me to his office, through the narrow door behind the bar. Like every club's backoffice, Dawg's was plastered with pictures of everybody who'd ever played there and all their heroes. In special frames were Hank Williams and Muddy Waters side by side. Underneath Hank's was a plaque that read "The White Muddy Waters." Muddy's plaque read "The Black Hank Williams." And there were Hubert Sumlin, Clifton, Irma Thomas, Dylan, everybody; and all the locals, Joe Ely, Marcia Ball, Angela Strehli, Paul Ray, Stevie. And us, among others—me, Danny, and Nade, separate and together, recent and as kids, but all the faces swam together in my eyes except his. You'd think I'd have put my fist through that plasterboard wall, but all I did was let Kathy's hand go and pick up the old black dial phone and dial Baton Rouge.

"Do you want me to leave?" Kathy said.

The word "want" seemed stranger than anything. I vaguely nodded no, as the phone rang awhile. Nade would be asleep, she'd joined up with the day people, but she'd know the call was either me or Danny; who else would call so late?

Finally the phone got picked up but nothing got said.

"Nadine?" I said.

My image was that it was a guy, *tonight*, shit, and I said, "Well, who the FUCK is there, is somebody gonna fucking TALK to me?"

"Daddy?" a little voice said.

My stomach turned over. "Little Jesse?" I managed to say. But there really was nobody on the phone now.

Then Nade's white-hot hiss: *"Jesse?"*

"Nadine?"

"What did you say to this boy? WHAT? I want to know, goddammit. He's sitting on the floor with some of the tablecloth in his mouth so you won't hear him cry. You think you can call up drunk at any friggin' hour and . . ."

Like that, till she ran out of breath.

Then nothing, just both of us breathing.

Then Nade: "Talk, or I hang up and take the phone off the hook. I'm gonna get an unlisted number, I think. I've been thinking about that, that's the truth. You want to contact us, you'll have to write, and if a check doesn't fall out of the envelope I'll tear the letter up unread. Well—are you gonna say anything?"

"Nadine?"

"WHAT?"

"It's Danny, Nade. Danny died. Danny's dead."

I waited. Nothing.

"I'm at Dawg's, he was singing here, and he just—dropped, I guess. Nobody knows why yet. But—we know he's dead." Then: "I'm sorry about the kid. I never thought he'd pick up the phone, he's scared of them, isn't he? Put him on before we hang up so I can—"

Dial tone.

S I X   *Up Down Down Up*

JESSE-O. HEY, JESSE-O.

I froze. It was Danny's voice, bell-clear. I was looking right at Kathy when I heard it, and could see she hadn't. Then Danny did Jimmy Reed in my ear:

I'M GOIN' UP

I'M GOIN' DOWN

I'M GOIN' UP DOWN DOWN UP

And then he was gone.

"Jesse?" Kathy said.

My cheeks and my lips twitched and moved on their own.

"Sit down," she said.

I nodded furiously no.

"Then come back with me to my place."

"Can't. Got to be near my phone. Danny's ma. Nade."

"I'll go with you, then. Come on."

I couldn't move.

"It's just like walking at any other time. You just walk," Kathy said.

"Okay. Okay."

Dawg was in the same chair, facing the same wall.

"I'm closing the club for a while," he said to no one in particular.

Then Elaine and Johns came in. Or rather, he led her in, holding her around the waist and walking her slowly. She still hadn't taken her hands out of her hair. Johns took her over to Dawg's table and sat her down like she was an old woman.

Dawg, who never seemed surprised at anything, got up. "I'll get her something."

"Not alcohol," Johns said.

"No. Coffee."

There was a pot simmering behind the bar. Kathy followed him back there and wrung out one of those dirty bar-rags and ran it under cold water. She went to Elaine and dabbed her face with the rag. Even from across the table, what with weeks of sopping beer-spills and whiskey, the rag smelled like a urinal. When Kathy dabbed near Elaine's nose, Elaine gagged. I thought she was going to heave right there, but it got her hands out of her hair. She clutched her mouth now, as though to stop something from gushing out. When she stopped gagging, she let her hands drop to the table.

Then Kathy sat down and I pulled up a chair and sat next to her. Dawg sat down again too. Johns reached behind, pulled a .32 from under the back of his shirt, put it on the table. As though for no reason than that he'd been leaning back against it and it made him uncomfortable. Just as casually, Dawg reached out and un-loaded the .32, but like he was fidgeting with anything handy, not like it mattered whether the piece was loaded.

"That for me?" I asked.

"Sure," Johns said. "You been worried about that?"

"Some."

"Good." Then: "See, I woke up this morning and just didn't care about what would happen after. Why *not* kill your ass? I told Elaine. My *wife*, man. She didn't even look like she was *listening*. Just kept washing last night's dishes. I was fixin' to come for you—maybe you, too, Elaine, I don't know—and that guy Danny drops. Dead meat. I forgot just how *dead* dead meat is. You walk around for twelve years thinking every day you can't forget it, you'll never forget it, and even *that* is just another way of forgetting it. Ain't that a bitch, Dawg?"

"One of many," Dawg said.

"There it is."

They smiled grimly at each other.

"The war, Jesse Wales. You have been pardoned 'cause I don't wanna be back with the war. You're gonna live a long stupid life, and I'm not gonna give a shit."

It had been somebody's job to die tonight.

Good job, Danny.

And *some* door.

S O M E   D O O R   I S   R I G H T .

I swallowed a moan that rose from my gut. Oh, Danny-O, would you *not* have died if this poor bastard hadn't decided to kill me? Is that how it works? Is this fucked world *really* not at all like it seems, not at all like they tell us? A hot sick sweat, with an ill smell, seeped out all over me, my forehead wet with it, my crotch sticky with it. I looked across to Kathy, whose eyes were glued to me, who felt the door open at this table at this moment, felt it but didn't dig it, didn't understand, this girl who'd walked *out* of a door straight to me, like the same rules that made Danny die like this had made us meet; rules Elaine played by and didn't have a clue about, but who did? The smell was like I'd done this horrid fart.

Elaine said, as though we weren't there and she was giving some kind of testimony: "I fucked Johns 'cause I needed him. I fucked Danny because we were after the same thing. I fucked Jesse 'cause of what Danny told me about him."

Dawg didn't mean to laugh but he laughed. One short bark. At which Kathy let go, tried to catch her laugh back as it came out but she couldn't. And *Johns* was smiling, shaking his head, the way you do when someone makes a terrible pun. And there was another laughter too, that none of the rest heard.

S E V E N *A Call*

Kathy was asleep. It was going to be light soon, and I'd be able to see the photos and posters on my walls again. I didn't want to. Wanted to tear them all down, or maybe ask Kathy to do it as a favor, all except the print she'd given me, which she'd put on the door when we'd come in, *The Starry Night*. At her place I'd said, "That's like Hendrix." "You should have it," she said.

The phone was right near my hand. I knew Nade would call and I knew it would be when the sun came up in Louisiana. She did. No hellos, nothing, just silence a beat. Then I said, "I'm really sorry about little Jesse. You think things can't get worse and that's just when they do. I should know that by now, I should have been on guard watching for what could get worse. I'm—really—"

"It's okay, Jesse. It's not, but it is."

It was like somebody had been beating her voice all night with a meat tenderizer.

Kathy's eyes were open now. I had to say it anyway: "I love you, Nadine."

"I know. You don't know how much easier everything would be for me if you didn't. I could write it all off if you didn't. At least, that's what I tell myself." Then: "Is anybody there with you?"

"No."

"Good."

"Yes."

"Yes what?"

"Somebody—Kathy—you don't know her—is here."

"You really can't do *anything* alone, can you?"

"You show Jesus the door and then tell me about 'alone.' "

Quiet a moment.

"Not that tonight," Nade said.

"I'm sorry."

"Me, too. Oh—Jesse, Jesse, Jesse."

"Nadine."

Then, she: "Danny."

And me: "Danny."

Kathy stared at the ceiling while Nadine and I listened to each other breathe.

E I G H T *For Starters*

Kathy had gone to get her things. She was going up to Lubbock with me, to the funeral. I hadn't asked, she'd volunteered. "It doesn't feel right to let you go alone" was all her explanation. And added: "Which is weird, 'cause after last night I'm not even sure if I still like you. I was kind of on Johns's side."

I hadn't said anything to that, and she'd said she'd be back in a couple of hours.

I also hadn't said anything about Danny's voice in my head. Which felt like I'd broken a rule that had grown, silently, between us: not to lie, not to leave out anything important. But I was afraid it might scare her off, and she sure seemed to be right about one thing: Apparently I couldn't live without women.

IT'S AMAZING, WHAT YOU CAN LIVE WITHOUT. LOOK WHAT *I'M* LIVING WITHOUT!

I put my hands over my ears.

THAT'S VERY FUNNY.

What do you want of me, Danny?

FOR STARTERS? GO KILL MY CATS.

That's crazy.

WHAT AIN'T?

NINE *Who Knows?*

On the way over to Danny's I didn't really think I'd do it. I felt like I was being tested, but by the time I got there I didn't know whether it would take killing them or not killing them to pass the test. And by the time I'd killed them—filling the tub and holding them under—I still didn't know.

Waterlogged, dripping, the cats were heavier than you would have thought. I picked them out of the tub and put them in a garbage bag. Got sick into the tub. Couldn't bring myself to put my hand in the water again and pull out the drain stopper. The puke broke up as it floated—greens, yellows, red strands, whites; in chunks and oily juices.

I couldn't remember the colors of the cats.

Flashed on Elaine and Danny taking a bath together, not minding the puke at all.

PART NINE

Lubbock Time

It rained all night the day I left,
The weather it was dry—
The sun so hot I froze myself—
Susannah, don't you cry—
                    —Stephen Foster

If I had possession
Over Judgment Day
Then the woman I'm lovin'
Wouldn't have no right to pray—
                    —Robert Johnson

ONE *A Seven-Hour Drive*

ʮ

Danny's body, they should have driven it to Lubbock. It wasn't right to send it through the air. That was the drive he'd taken twenty years ago toward the rest of his life, and he should have been able to drive it back. Back up to Lampasas, through Brownwood, north out of this lush Austin hill country up to where the land dries out around Santa Anna and flattens around Abilene, where they still have Prohibition; north and west through the other arid and "dry" towns like Sweetwater, and up to Snyder, and over the caprock, across those High Plains, the land as flat as the palm of God's hard hand, where the wind blows all the time, brings snow in winter, dust in spring, rain hardly at all, and tornadoes whenever it feels like. Where there isn't a hill, there's hardly a rise for hundreds of miles, so even the smallest thing seems thrust up to the sky—a windmill or a farmhouse can lord it over a landscape. So you can see Lubbock for miles and miles before you get there, its half dozen office buildings and its fearsome lot of churches. The Hub of the Panhandle, Lubbock calls itself, and gets away with it. There's nothing but wind to argue the claim.

What was it, about four hundred miles Austin to Lubbock? A last drive. It should have been allowed him. But his family just had him crated up and popped back.

TWO *Henry's Caravan Camp*

ʮ

"I don't really know what I'm doing here," Kathy said.

We were in a not-quite-double bed in one of Henry's smaller RVs. All we could see through the window in the night was an RV just like the one we were in. In front and behind and all around us were empty RVs, a maze of RVs, Henry's gigantic lot on the edge of Lubbock—like being in an empty city. For years now, whenever Danny or me gigged in Lubbock, we'd crash free at "Henry's Caravan Camp," his dealership, instead of staying at a motel or with Danny's ma. "They call these 'caravans' in England," Henry once said. "Captures the spirit of the thing, don't it?" When Henry was still fat he'd get on TV in a bright-colored turban and push the slogan that "an RV's a caravan all on its own." Ever since his weight started to melt off he didn't do that anymore, but he was still the main RV dealer in the Panhandle.

So we lay in the RV bunk, she naked on her stomach, me naked on my side, looking out the window at nothing.

"I guess I've quit my job," she said.

"You didn't tell them you were going away?"

"Wouldn't have done any good. Disappear for days after calling in sick, they wouldn't have believed it was a funeral."

"What're you gonna do for money?"

"Pan for gold."

"No, really."

"I've got girlfriends in other restaurants. I'll get something or other. Let's don't talk about it."

I ran my hand down her spine and let it rest lightly on her butt. It seemed so bright to me, so perfect.

A green snake, very small, also perfect, slithered out her asshole and stretched its length—the length of my forefinger—up her crack. Curled in the small of her back. Shiny green.

Something hot and burning made its way up my throat, washed into my mouth, but I got it back down. The green snake vanished. My shakes started again.

The shakes had started after the cats and, off and on, had got worse and worse. I felt god-awful about those cats, guilty like I'd never felt about anything. Shake-guilty. Just past Abilene had been the worst so far. One of those B-52s—*huge* fucking thing—was coming in low to land at the base there, and I thought of Danny in a box way up in the air, and feared he'd speak to me again, and feared what he'd demand, and shook so much we pulled off the road so I could shake. Kathy took and held my hand as I was shaking. I hadn't been able to tell her about the cats—afraid I'd scare her off for sure.

As we started up again, she said, "Was that a B-52 *bomber?*"

"They got a big base around here."

"You mean that thing that just flew in so low over us was carrying *atom bombs?*"

"I guess."

She practically yanked my right hand off the wheel and held it real tight, staring out the window, saying nothing for about forty miles.

THREE *Goin' Down Slow*

Well I've had my fun, if I don't get well no more.
—Howlin' Wolf

Henry was dying. Except, like Henry *would*, he was taking his time about it. Digging it, almost. Savoring it, certainly. It had been going on for a couple of years but it never really hit us because it didn't seem any stranger than any of the other shit Henry was into. Seemed, in fact, like part of what he was into, one more weird project. Or maybe that was just for our benefit, I never could read Henry very well.

What was hard to get used to was that huge moonlike man wasting from round to angular. Not only his clothes but his skin just hung off him now. Flapped from his arms, hung from his high cheekbones. His forehead almost seemed to hang in his eyes. And the eyes—he could still *fix* you with them, but there was something else in there now, something going on all the time that had nothing to do with you. If he touched you, you still felt the charge of that old strength—a charge that never had much to do with muscles anyway. But he used a cane to get around now, and there were new lines around his eyes where he'd made his stands against the pain.

These days he rarely left the big mobile home at the entrance of his RV lot, except to go to the one next door that was his office. The door was open when we got to it. It had been our game, mine and Danny's, never to let Henry know we were coming, to see if he'd psyche it out and be ready for us, and he almost always did. Kathy and I walked in and there were sweet rolls freshly warmed and three cups of coffee laid out, ours fixed how we liked it— Kathy's, whom of course he'd never even heard of, with milk and sugar, mine with just milk. Real Henry-brewed coffee—you wanted to take deep breaths of it. He enjoyed our amazement, looked real self-satisfied in his new gaunt way.

I said, "Henry, this is Kathy," and he said nothing, didn't get up from his chair, just took both her small hands in his huge, now spidery ones. Held them a long time, then just let them drop, nodding all the while like she was confirming something he'd long suspected. And Kathy, for her part, went and got the coffee and sweet rolls for us, as at home as though she'd been there often.

"The walls are thin, aren't they, Jesse? And getting thinner all the time." That was the first thing he said, a typical Henry opener.

"The walls?"

" 'Tween here and—*there*."

He smiled. I smiled back. I knew I was *way* over the edge because Henry seemed to be making perfect sense. Yet I was calm in his presence.

H E   K N O W S .

Figured he would, Danny-O.

H E ' S   N O T   G O I N G   T O   B E   A B L E
T O   H E L P   Y O U   M U C H .

But Henry was sure helping some. The voice, which I hadn't heard since "Go kill the cats," didn't make me want to crawl out of my skin. But the thing I'd done—the panic of those poor creatures once they knew they were going to die—made me feel so heavy-limbed.

"Have some more coffee," Henry said. I started to say no, but Henry said, "Have some. My dear," he said to Kathy, "would you mind?"

Kathy got up and poured me another cup. Then looked to Henry, he nodded at her, and she poured herself one, then him, too.

We sat quiet with the coffee. The wind kind of hummed along the edges of the mobile home, gusted up a little, eased down. The gusts ever so slightly nudged the place, sang quietly in the wires. I liked how Kathy was comfortable in the silence—sometimes Henry's silences lasted a long while. She didn't fidget or look like she thought something needed to be said.

"You enjoy the coffee?" he finally said to her.

"It's unbelievable. Best I've ever had."

"I'm glad." Then: "I oughta bed y'all down."

He got up. The pain lines on his face got tight, but I wasn't supposed to notice, so I let him get his cane for himself. I took our bags and Kathy held Henry's huge flashlight, and we walked slowly, Henry digging his cane into the dusty ground with each step. He liked to bed his friends down in the very center of his RV maze— and you know he had intentionally laid it out like a maze, so he *had* to show you himself, you could never find it just with directions, even if you'd been there many times, because Henry was always shifting his maze around. How did you get out? Henry figured if he led you in you should be able to find your own way out, it was just a matter of "right attention."

It took us a few minutes, with how slow he had to go.

"Here you be," he said finally.

He came in with us, showed us what was what, and sat down in the small dinerlike booth that was the RV's eating nook to catch his breath. I must have been looking at him with some concern, because he gave me a weary smile and said gently, "We are dying of imperfect spells. Not killing spells, but spells of blessing imperfectly known."

He got up slowly.

"It's good to see you, son. And good to meet you, Jesse's lady."

She half frowned, half looked pleased, and said, "Kathy."

"Thank you," he said to her, and left.

For a few steps we could hear his cane dig into the gravel like it was keeping time to something in the wind.

F O U R *Whole Lotta Shakin' Goin' On*

I was in the john when the shakes hit again. Had my pecker in my hand, aiming into the center of the bowl, enjoying the gurgle noise, like you do, and my hand started quivering and the stream went all over. I laughed, on top of it, I shook and laughed with my dick hanging out and messing up the bathroom. Not a laugh anyone would want to hear. Then I wiped up the mess with wet toilet paper, threw the glob of it into the toilet, like you're not supposed to do in an RV, and by this time Kathy had asked was I all right a couple of times and I hadn't said anything.

"*Answer* me, Mr. Jesse Wales! You can scare me, but don't worry me."

"Giuseppe Andriozzi."

"What?"

"My real name."

This through the slatted bathroom door.

"Why'd you change it?"

"Giuseppe Andriozzi sings the blues?" I came out of the bathroom. "I was following in the footsteps of those great Americans, Ellas McDaniels and McKinley Morganfield. Bo Diddley and Muddy Waters to you."

"You don't sing the blues. Blues are black."

"What the hell is it then?"

"Psych-out, shit-out, Night-Time Losing-Time *stuff*."

"In other words, the blues."

"I don't think it's right, giving yourself another name."

"That's what America's all *about*, man, if it's about anything. You can choose your own name."

"Call me Roy, then. I've always liked Roy."

"You're pretty tough, ain't you, Roy?"

"I'm tough like you—scared-tough." Then: "Here we are going to funerals together and you don't even know my last name. How could you not ask that?"

"I haven't asked you a lot of things. You haven't told me your life story yet."

"I will. If we live through this." A beat: "Why'd I say *that?*"

I thought of the cats and got cold all over. She went to the window to stare into the dark. Mesquite was a perfume on the wind. It made everything soft, even the plastic smells of the RV. And the voice came gentler this time:

W E H A V E N O I D E A W H A T W E A R E . N O N E .

Danny-O, Danny-O, what the fuck does that mean?

I ' M F I N D I N G O U T , T H I S S I D E .

Keeping secrets again?

B E I N G K E P T B Y O N E .

I turned on the TV to shut him up. Carson. I turned down the sound. Can't stand the man. Nobody who smiles that much can be right. I keep waiting for Carson to dip into his jacket pocket, pull out a little pistola, stick it in his eye, smile, and *zap.* I turned it off. I turned it on. I turned it off. I turned it on. I commenced shaking.

C O M E O N O V E R , B A B Y , W H O L E L O T T A S H A K I N ' G O I N ' O N .

She came up behind me, lightly put her hands on the back of my neck. Her touch was cool. My shakes eased off.

"You know what you're doing?" she said. "You're trying not to cry."

"I'm not."

"You are. You don't even know it, but you are."

She sat me down. My shakes started in just lightly, shivers, quivers. She took off one boot.

"What are you doing?" I said.

She took off the other.

"The only thing I know to do," Kathy said with tears in her eyes.

"It doesn't make sense," I said, unbuttoning my shirt. My hands quivered a little still.

"I know," she said, unbuttoning her shirt. "But isn't that why I'm here?"

"I thought you were here because you wanted to be."

"I *am,* I *do,* I need this too."

And we went at it. And again I couldn't come. She was on top of me, sitting on my cock, had been now for I don't know how long, and I couldn't, and why should that scare me so? She clenched and unclenched her cunt on me, little movings, subtle twistings, like she had lots of small fingers in there, baby hands, a real mechanic, a control I'd never met. It should have been the kind of pleasure you dream of, but while I felt all the sensations, there was a wall between me and the pleasure, like it was happening to somebody else. My cock felt huge inside her, like it wasn't flesh but a bulging vegetable, like growing out of me was this thick asparagus. It *felt* green. As I thought that, I laughed, a hoarse cough of a laugh, and again, and again, as Kathy sweated over me. And it hit me hard that she'd learned what she knew the hard way, had done this for money somewhere down the road. The effort of our screwing peeled expression after expression off her face, Kathy after Kathy fell from it; little-girl Kathys and crone-Kathys; Kathys-in-hiding; psychotic-shy, ugly Kathys; and Kathys of dark cruel glamour. They passed before me, carnal knowledge indeed, and one paused to come, a furtive thirteen-year-old Kathy coming in fear and against her will, resisting the pleasure of it because her own pleasure was betraying her. And then *she* was gone, and I said to *my* Kathy, "Make me cry," and she said, "Please, no," and I said, "Make me, you know how." She said "I don't, I don't wanna," I slapped her hard on her thigh and said, "That's how," and, before I could blink, her hard waitress's hand came down flat against my face, then her other hand, then again, hard and fast and no holding back, and *she* was crying. And finally, after she was too tired to hit me anymore, finally I did cry. And that was like coming, but with my eyes.

She rolled off me, limp. My asparagus-thing, which hadn't come, shrank back into me. I lay there, finally feeling pleasure: the tears drying on my stinging face. She lay on her stomach with her face away from me. I propped myself up on my side and stroked her back and her bright butt. And that's when she said, "I don't *really* know what I'm doing here," and that green snake came out her asshole, from which this fuck had freed it. It curled on the small of her back and disappeared.

S H E ' S H E R E F O R M E .
Shit. What's *that* supposed to mean?

I'M CALLING HER. SHE CAN
ALMOST HEAR.

"I don't *have* to know why, though," Kathy said. "I know about not having to know."

Why her?

SHE'S STRONGER THAN ANY OF
YOU, AND SHE DOESN'T KNOW IT,
WHICH MAKES HER WEAKER THAN
ANYBODY, LIKE I WAS.

FIVE *That Lubbock Feel*

I woke to "I'm sorry"—Kathy's whisper, damp words hardly said. Her fingers hovering over the bruises on my face. "I'm sorry—"

"Hi," I said.

"Hi."

"What are you sorry about?"

"You know."

"I made you do that."

"Nobody makes anybody do shit."

"I asked you to, then. I needed you to."

"And I did it. Jeeeeeees-us," she laughed. "I think maybe I'd do anything for you. And I'm *sure* sorry about *that*."

She scruffed my hair like I was a little kid.

"Why would you? I don't get it."

"I just sort of decided to do anything for you. It's like . . . if something enters your life in a certain way, you gotta be loyal, not to the person but to the—entrance. Or maybe I was just waiting at that old station so long, I'd decided ages ago to get on the first train that rolled in and stopped. It happened to be yours."

SHE'S HERE FOR ME, FOR ME.

"—Anyway, that old station, they were fixin' to close it down.

And *then* what would I have done? Smith, by the way. My stupid last name is just Smith."

WE'RE INFECTING HER. SHE'S CATCHING US. THINK SHE CAN HANDLE IT?

Yeah. Yeah.

IF SHE CAN'T, GUESS WHO SHE FALLS APART ALL OVER? AND NONE TOO SWEETLY? AND THEN, GUESS WHO GETS HER?

And Kathy: "It hurts me to see those bruises I made on you, Jesse. I know it doesn't *seem* like it from our carrying on, but—I'm not S and M, I've never been into it. Just wanted you to know." Then, to herself almost: "It's necessary sometimes though."

"What time is it?"

It was only about two. But there wasn't any way to go back to sleep. I got up, got dressed again—the same sweat-smelling white T-shirt and jeans. I hate just walking around naked. Even hate walking around barefoot. Kathy laughed when I put on my boots.

'You're either naked or you *ain't*, aren't you? No in-betweens for *this* cowboy.'

She just put on the white long-sleeved shirt I'd been wearing —and looked pretty damned fetching in it too, how her butt held up the shirttail, and her well-formed legs and feet.

"You sure have the prettiest feet."

"Thank you."

I needed a drink. Henry never stocked our RVs with anything but rosé wine. Awful shit. Kool Aid mixed with cough syrup. But better than nothing. And canned goods. Kathy cooked up some Campbell's Pork & Beans. Very homey. The place smelled of plastic rugs, beans, sex, cheap wine, and the mesquite that floated in on that low wind.

"Something feels different here," Kathy said.

"No shit."

"No, I mean—*all* around here."

"It's Lubbock."

"Yeah, so?"

"I've always thought," I said, "I could be somewhere, like,

say, Mobile, and get knocked unconscious, and if I came to in an absolutely dark closet in Lubbock, I'd *know* I was in Lubbock as soon as I opened my eyes and took a breath. Nobody can tell you what it is, but everybody feels it. That's why Henry likes it here. He and Danny'd . . ." And my voice dropped when his name came through it; then I went on, ". . . they'd go on and on about how here the density of existence is thinner or thicker or some shit, or cosmic points, *that* shit."

"Don't act stupid with me. Or with yourself, I can't tell which. You *get* all that stuff. You're as smart as they are."

"Maybe. But maybe I don't want to be."

"Too bad."

"Anyway: I *know* it feels like there's more time in an hour here. Like, an hour in Lubbock is about an hour and fifteen minutes anywhere else. Helluva place to be buried."

"For some reason I thought they'd cremate him."

"Cremate somebody in Lubbock and they'll be down to Waco before the ceremony is over. This is wind country, can't you hear it? I'm glad they're not cremating him. And could we talk about something else?"

S I X   *Visitation 11*

A knock at the door. But I didn't know if it was the kind of knock Kathy could hear. If Danny could talk to me, maybe he could knock at me, too. The knock knocked again.

Kathy said, "You waiting for me to get it?"

"No. I got it." Then called out: "Who is it?"

No answer. So I went and opened the door slow. It was pitch-black outside. But then that dark glared, one burst of flashing light blinded me, my hands went up in fists, I tried to brace for the blow I wouldn't see. But it was Elaine, laughing.

By the time I could see again she was holding a Polaroid in my face. Kathy's slaps had blackened one eye, my face was all swollen and bruised, my mouth bent out of shape with a fat lip. That girl can hit. In the Polaroid every swell caught the light and shone.

"You look like shit," Elaine said, stepping in, *cheery*. "You been in a fight?"

"More like a collision," I said. "Why don't you make yourself to fucking home?"

"Hi!" Elaine chirped at Kathy, and the Polaroid flashed again. Kathy practically fell down, as though the flash had hurled her back, then pushed past Elaine into the bedroom, a hand over her eyes.

"I'm the official funeral photographer," Elaine said. Then called out into the bed compartment, "Kathy? Thanks for the other night."

"What are you doing here?" I said.

"Panning for gold," Elaine said.

Kathy stalked back out in her jeans and a black bra, went straight to Elaine and said into her face, *"Don't ever do that again."*

"Tough cookie?" Elaine said, trying to make it a joke.

Kathy smirked. An expression I hadn't seen yet.

Then I got it: She'd done time!

My, my.

I smirked.

"You know," Kathy said in Elaine's face, "how they say, 'You've seen too many movies'? Well—you haven't seen enough."

Whatever *that* meant.

And Kathy went back to the bed compartment.

I had a real clear picture all of a sudden of Danny sucking on Elaine's flabby little tit.

"You and Danny, eh?"

"Me and Danny. Two years."

"Two years?"

"I said why."

"You did, but you lie a lot."

"Danny—told me that was one of my jobs. 'What *happens* isn't the truth just 'cause it happens.' I think that's a direct quote. This one is: 'Facts sometimes aren't honest.' "

" 'Facts are like playing only the white keys,' " I quoted back. "Just because Danny's dead don't mean he wasn't full of shit about most things."

THAT'S NOT NICE.

Fuck you, Danny-O.

"Did you do . . ." I said. "Did you . . . do like Mexico?"

"Danny . . . couldn't handle that. Not really. We . . . tried, okay? But I had to do all the work, sort of, and it got like a . . . performance, and . . . we both just ended up laughing. With him it was like dressing up for Halloween, just silly. He talked about you all the time. And gradually I saw that, though maybe he wasn't aware of it, he was pushing me toward you. 'Cause he sensed where we could go. But it sure shook him up when it happpened. I think I'm maybe the only full-grown woman Danny ever loved."

"That's great news. That makes me feel just great."

"He never hit on me, like he did the chippies." Then, nodding toward the bedroom: "Speaking of whom?"

"You know better."

Why did I feel like I'd betrayed him, when I hadn't known? Of course. Because I could have known, surely that day of the interview, if I had opened my eyes. How long had it been, how very long, since I'd really *seen* Danny? Talk about betrayals.

I STARTED TO DIE THAT DAY.

I know. You even said so.

I EVEN SAID SO.

No wonder you're pissed.

I WON'T BE PISSED LONG. YOU WILL SATISFY ME.

"How'd you find the trailer?"

"Henry gave me his flashlight. Said to follow the cane marks."

"Nice of him. Ever meet him with Danny?"

"No. Danny didn't think he'd appprove of me. He was right, Henry doesn't like me. I could tell."

"Good."

"But he said, 'It's good you're here. You'll remind him.' "

"Wonderful."

"Knew I was coming, though. Had a great cup of coffee waiting for me. All prepared, black, one sugar. Impressive."

"You're different."

"I killed Danny, didn't I?"

Her eyes clouded.

"I did, too. Danny did. He was always—in danger. Henry warned him. Nade did. He knew what he was doin', I guess—more than most."

"That's why *you* don't feel guilty."

"I feel—responsible. Isn't that different?"

And I know something you don't know.

Don't I, Danny-O?

I TRIED TO TALK TO HER, BUT SHE'S CLOSED IN LOTS OF FUNNY PLACES.

Open in some funny ones, too.

DON'T I KNOW IT.

So it was Danny who knew her ass so well, not Johns. And she'd invited me into it *at* Danny's.

Almost-puking was getting to be a way of life.

Kathy came back out. She looked great in that black bra. I wondered if she knew it, and saw in her walk she did.

She was, what? Fifteen years younger than Elaine? Her body held up by itself every place Elaine's didn't—or mine either, for that matter. But, until tonight, put them near each other in life or in my head and I had to strain to see Kathy. For me, anybody near Elaine shone in her glow. But tonight—Kathy still reflected Elaine's light some, but held her own, like a shadow that somehow stays a shadow even if you shine a light on it.

Kathy sat on the floor and leaned her back against the wall— or whatever you call a "wall" and "floor" in an RV. A rug inside a truck, is how they feel. I was sitting on the floor by then, against the opposite wall from Kathy. Elaine sat on the floor between us with her back to the "living-room" sofa.

But Kathy changed her mind, got up real slow, and seemed to step through the quiet like a person stepping through a puddle so as not to get her shoes wet. She stepped to Elaine and sat down right next to her. So close, their thighs nearly touched. Elaine looked at her nervously, but didn't inch away.

"I just came here to be somewhere," Elaine said softly. "I couldn't stay with my folks tonight." I'd forgotten she was from here. "Could I stay here?"

And it was Kathy who said, "Sure."

"What blood you got in you?" Elaine asked Kathy.

"A little Indian, a little Mexican, maybe a little Cajun. Poor white trash, the rest."

"Where'd you grow up?"

"I ain't a living legend, and this ain't an interview."

"I—just wanted to know, is all."

"Here and there in the trashier parts of Houston. End of questions."

So we all sat quiet a bit, the women leg to leg.

What would I think if I dreamed this?

Elaine's face twitched a little, like she might sob. I got up, got her Polaroid, aimed it at them. Kathy's eyes turned into two black stones.

"Can I take your picture?"

"What do you think?" Kathy said.

She got up and out of the shot.

"This is for your collection," I said, and shot Elaine. The flash seemed to hang in the room a few beats. A flash in which I knew Nadine and my kid were in town by now, probably staying at the Rodeway on Fourth, wondering where I was. "Can't you do anything alone?" she'd said. Fuck, I don't even know if there *is* such a thing as "alone" anymore. Lock me up by myself and it's still a crowded room.

T H A T ' S   W H A T   T H E Y   T H I N K
T H E Y ' R E   D O I N G   T O   M E .

Leave Kathy alone.

I   H A T E   T H A T   Y O U   H A V E
S O M E B O D Y   W H O   D O E S N ' T   L O V E
M E .

You a fag, Danny?

D I D N ' T   L I V E   L O N G   E N O U G H   T O
F I N D   O U T ,   D I D   I ?   W H O   D O   Y O U
L O V E   M O R E ,   M E   O R   K A T H Y ?

That's a good question for a change.

"You been able to sleep since Danny died?" Elaine said.

"Some. I've had help," I said, looking straight into Kathy's eyes.

"I want to help you some more," Kathy said.

"I can't get over it," I said to Elaine. "You'd been sleeping with Danny *two years* before you met me?"

"Don't mind me, guys," Kathy said, "go right ahead."

"Sure," Elaine said to me.

Kathy said to Elaine, "Well—how was it?"

I sort of laughed and Kathy smiled for real. Elaine rolled her eyes, like a high school girl when you ask about her boyfriend. But then she actually told us.

"It was like sleeping with a little boy. I mean, like a ten-year-old boy. Like he was real sweet and didn't remember ever fucking anybody before and you had to show him everything. That was his game, that you had to show him. I hear he never tired of that game —and I *checked*. A ten-year-old with an enormous prick. Did you know that he had an enormous prick?"

Maybe cremation isn't such a bad idea, Danny-O.

This stuff was hard to take on rosé wine.

Kathy laughed like when you don't want to wake anybody up, but stopped suddenly.

"*Don't* mind me, guys," Kathy said again, got up, went to the "kitchen" counter, chug-a-lugged some of the rosé. Then, to me: "I think we should rape her. Really. It would be kind of like a spanking, you know? Stick a broomstick up her ass and a corncob up her twat. I don't know what, for her mouth. The wrong end of a Coke bottle. Just kidding. You bet."

She stalked back to where the bed was and slammed the narrow door behind her.

Elaine looked at me, panicky.

"Don't worry," I said. "You know that's not my style." But as I said it I remembered the cats. And *I* got panicky. "It's really not," I added fast, "and it's not Kathy's either."

I went in after Kathy.

"Boy," she said, "a week ago I didn't have anything to lose. But I lost *that*."

Which is a lot to lose. And it came over me, for the first time, from off her, how so much of love means losing, a losing that's like dying, a losing and a dying that makes room for something new. And that you couldn't love unless you were willing, in that way, to die. Even *really* to die. And she'd be willing to die, was willing to, and, say it again, it's not love unless you are. The rest is hang-ups and marking time. I'm tired of looking into so many eyes that don't know this.

Mine in the mirror most of all.

Kathy's eyes had it deep. Now they changed from stones to pools to stones to pools. The green snake, which had crawled out of her ass, swam now in her eye-pond. It lived under her eye-stone. It had been curled in her always. And it had come out to watch me. And she thought that was love. And it was.

For, though she hadn't seen it, and couldn't yet say it, I felt that she cherished that shiny green snake. The snake Elaine called up—she could conjure it, and when she did it *stayed* conjured, but it wasn't hers, it was the Snake of all. But Kathy's—that snake was her very own, strong way beyond its size.

"I'm sorry," Kathy said into the pillow. "I think."

"Kathy—I'm not going to be with that woman anymore. It's not competition. It's over with her. I don't even all the way know why, I'm not even sure I really want it to be, but I *know* it *is*. She may not know it yet, and she may never really believe it, but it's *so* over. Still—she's part of my family and there's nothing I can do about that. That means she's in whatever I do, somehow, for keeps. But there's nothing wrong with that, is there?"

Kathy smiled, weary. "Watch it, your brains are showing."

"You sure change some around the ladies. Lots tougher."

"Prison. A year. Which we are *not* talking about, not just yet." It didn't seem brainy to say I'd guessed.

She sat up, took a deep breath, said, "Okay. Okay. Look. You're the first man I've slept with in two, three years. Okay? And that wasn't the joint, that started before. Okay?"

"I can't help this, I have to: You turned on by Elaine?"

"I probably would have been. Okay? But—I haven't *really* been turned on by a woman in a long time. 'She's just going through a phase!' But it seems like I was. But I *know* 'em, you know?"

A long silence, and then she said,

"Are you still gonna want me, Jesse?"

I nodded yes, but I couldn't quite say it.

"That's what I was afraid of," she said, and lay down again, with her head turned from me. Into the pillow she said, "Boy, you sure were right about one thing. There's a lot more *time* in Lubbock. And this is just the place where you wish there wasn't." She turned toward me again. "Fuck me, Jesse. It's the only time I know you're real."

SHE MUST BE A SCORPIO.

Shut the hell up.

"I'm not going to help you, I'm not going to do anything. Just fuck me."

I heard Elaine turn the TV on. Heard her turn the channels from static to static, loud static on one channel, softer on another. Then something tuned in. Loud music and gunshots. Ricochets. A Western.

I pulled off Kathy's jeans. Her legs were just floppy dead weight, her eyes were blank. I touched her cunt. It was wiry-dry, like she was saying: I just died, bring me back to life, come to the dead place after me and take me back. Be a hero for once in your life.

Sex has so little to do with sex.

A funny thing to finally learn in Lubbock, Texas.

I took off my clothes while, I suppose, she watched me, if she could see anything out of those stones. Under the circumstances there seemed no way my dick could get hard.

IN THAT CASE, YOU ARE NOT A GREAT MAN.

I stood in her line of sight and spit into my hands till I'd got them wet with spit and phlegm. And her cunt moved. Flexed, like. Then I rubbed all that mouth-goo all over my cock and started rubbing on it. Her eyes moved, softer now, watching. *That* got me hard. I kept rubbing on myself, slow, watching her pussy flex. And, with the flexing, it started to shine. When I finally went into her she shut her eyes. We moved like kids, stiffly, haltingly, as though hesitant to go where we were headed, where we went, to the place where the dead don't know they're dead. We didn't see them. We could feel them. With what was dead in each of us, and with what was dead in both of us together, we could feel them, like when you know where the furniture is in a dark room. Kathy'd spent a lot of time there. A lot of time. It was home. Or had become home. For parts of her. If Danny got her, he wouldn't be taking her anywhere, he'd be keeping her in that home she hated. But she was leaving it, to come with me. To come. With me. And my coming was like shining this bright liquid light into that colorless space. And her coming was like a drinking, an absorbing, of that light.

We breathed together a little while. Then she said, "It's hard to believe it's not morning yet."

"Yeah, well—"

"—Lubbock," we said together, and squeezed each other.

I pulled out of her slowly. Stood up. She stood up.

"You're coming out of me," she said. "Guy! There's so *much*."

She tiptoed to the bathroom to wash herself.

Then, naked, we both looked into the kitchen, living room of the RV. Elaine was asleep on the floor in front of the TV. An exercise show. I wondered was she faking; but no, there's an air of deep sleep you can't fake. Like we'd gone so far away that her body had forgotten we were in the next room.

Elaine, Elaine, my amazing Elaine, my guide who doesn't know where she's going, my initiator who doesn't know what mysteries she passes on, what *would* you think if you dreamed this little domestic scene, Kathy and I standing naked over you in this time-warp-delayed not-quite-dawn?

The lamp was still on. As I went to turn it off Elaine coughed in her sleep, and as she coughed, the lamp dimmed, dimmed just for the moment of her cough, then came up again. Kathy and I looked at each other, grateful and sorry both that the other had seen it too. Elaine coughed again and the lamp dimmed again.

Oh, I do swear, to even God.

And I wondered if there was even one bridge left from the way we are to the way most people live.

SEVEN *Let It Burn*

The light was now blue velvet. Soon it would rip up the middle and be dawn. We'd wakened to the smell of burning. No, the smell of something burned and dowsed. And then fresh burning.

LET IT BURN.

"What's that?" Kathy said.

There was movement in the john, which was just past the bunk. Its slatted door was shut.

I swung my legs over the bunk's edge and got dressed slowly, listening to matches being struck in the john.

"I dreamed about Danny," Kathy said.

"Sh-boom sh-boom."

"What?"

"That old song, *Life could be a dream, sh-boom sh-boom.*"

A thick damp smell of shit wafted through the slats. The match-smell couldn't cover it.

"Good fucking *morning*," Kathy said, and covered her nose with the sheet.

"So what about Danny?"

"How can you even talk?"

"I like shit."

A giggle from Elaine in the john.

"Danny," Kathy said through the sheet, "was singing a song backward. It sounded so awful weird. I asked how could he do that, but he answered backward too and I couldn't understand."

"Elaine?" I said through the slats. "You okay?"

Another match. I jiggled the door some. It was latched.

The stench wasn't going away. It hung on the air, thickening.

"I don't *believe* that woman!" Kathy said, and scooped up her clothes to go dress at the other end of the RV.

"Elaine," I said through the slats, "flush the damn toilet."

"It ain't *in* the toilet."

The crackle of burning paper, and some smoke through the slats.

From the front of the RV, Kathy said, "It has *got* to be morning, why isn't it light?"

From the bathroom Elaine called to her, "You're stuck inside of Lubbock, girl!"

More burning paper and the smoke a little thicker. But the smoke didn't cut the stench. Just kind of carried it. You could feel the shit-smell stick to the walls.

"What are you talking about, it ain't in the toilet?"

"Man, I can't even think of it as *shit*."

"Where *is* it?"

Somehow knowing it wasn't in the toilet made the stink lots worse.

Kathy said, "I'll bet it's in the sink."

Elaine laughed her yes.

"*Jeeeeeeeees*-us"—me and Kathy both.

Then I saw the flames through the slats. Or their glow.

"Don't worry!" Elaine called out. "I'm just burning me some names."

I started hitting the door.

"I thought you *liked* shit." Elaine laughed through the door. "You sure like asses."

We were sucked in. She was raping *us*. Where had she gone in her sleep, that sleep that had soaked up the light from the bulbs? So many worlds to go to, and what you see, and what you come back with.

I wasn't hitting to break the door, I was just hitting to rattle Elaine.

Something made me look back in time to see Kathy fall to her knees, her expression frozen in absolute surprise. She clutched her stomach. Fell forward on her face.

I practically dived to the floor where she was.

"Hold me," she said, and I held.

The slat door unlatched and Elaine stood there, looking at us down the narrow hall. Not like I expected to see her. I expected to see some triumph. But she'd taken off her clothes and was wrapped in a long white beach towel that had Mickey Mouse on it. The skin of her face was slack and the whites of her eyes were almost completely pink. She stood in her own smells like an old, old child. Looked scared. Then laughed. Or something *in* her laughed, used her laugh. Then she went back in and latched the john door behind her again.

I was cradling Kathy on my knees like a baby. She smiled through her sweat.

"Are we having fun yet?" she said.

"Don't we always? What's wrong?"

"You ever hear voices, Jesse?"

"Not in the last five minutes or so."

"So we *are* having fun."

"Oh yeah."

"I heard—what I heard," she said, "then there was this pain like a rip through my stomach. It's mostly gone now. I think I can get up."

She got up and opened the RV door. It had gotten pretty smoky inside. Stench-smoke. Outside, it still looked velvety blue.

Fresh burning. And now it smelled of plastic. And I knew what *that* was.

This was old hat to me by now, right? Especially this part. Because years ago, when Nadine and I still gigged together, we did a week up in Santa Fe, and we were going over great, and there was this waitress, and this waitress and I had *lots* of eye contact. Eye contact and wisecracks. Nothing more, to speak of, but lots to think of. The girl was in my head. I'd had a Polaroid then, had taken pictures of all of us one night, the waitress too. Well, one night this waitress and me had a conversation. Just a conversation. After closing. But Nade got good and pissed. I came back to the hotel and all she did was glare. I went to bed and she stayed up. When I got up and went to breakfast, and went down to the club, it was weird, the waitress wasn't in my head anymore. I'd been thinking of her so much, had been almost ready to go over the line with her, that now I felt the *absence* of her in my head. I kind of missed the thoughts, but they just weren't there. When I got to the club that night, that waitress and I did the same wisecracks, the same eye contact, but it was out of habit, there was no juice in them on my end, and, for my part, it tapered off into nothing. When we were packing to leave Santa Fe, I looked for the Polaroids. Nade had them. I went through them, and that girl's picture—I couldn't be sure now of her name if my life depended on it, but maybe it was Anne—her picture wasn't there. I wasn't going to ask about it, but Nadine, kind of embarrassed, told me she'd been pissed and had burned the picture that night I'd got back to the hotel late. Burned it after I went to sleep. Hoodoo was the last thing in her head. She'd just been pissed, had had no idea what she'd really accomplished.

Don't blame me, it's not my fault it's true.

I hit that slatted door running and crashed through it. Elaine put her arms up to shield herself but I ran into her, her arms went around me, her nails digging into my back, my hands were in her hair, clutching that harsh red stuff, shaking her head as we spun. Broken slats between us, one sticking into us both as we spun, slipping, my elbow smashing the mirror over the sink. I lurched from the pain, we fell into the shower stall, bringing down the curtain, her nails still ripping my back, me still pulling her hair, she fell on me into the stall, my head hit something, the world went in and out, in and out. We lay in some all but bone-breaking position, Elaine on top of me, somehow the Mickey Mouse towel still around her, stained with blood from one or both of us. Then Elaine and I were holding each other, just holding. She said my name and I said hers.

And said into her ear, "What the fuck are you doing?"

Smelling the smell again.

And she into my ear: "Burning the picture you took of *me*, baby. I'm so tired, baby."

A broken slat was still between us, that's how tight we'd clutched as we struggled; it was sticking in my ribs.

And she: "That's Danny in the sink."

And me: "What did you do, eat him?"

And she: "He's sort of been eating me. From the inside. And he grew and grew and then came out. And I've been burning names on him. All our names over and over."

An old whorehouse song sang itself in my head:

I got nipples on my titties
Big as the end of my thumb
I got something 'tween my legs
Could make a dead man come—

And me: "Why burning names?"

And she: "I don't know."

And me, almost laughing: "How can you not know!"

She almost laughed too. I never wanted to open my eyes, never wanted to move. All she could do was breathe deep and not know. And then, in my ear, the slightest snore. Bless her heart.

I lifted her off me, rolled her gently on her back so I could get up. The woman was *out*.

Stood up. There was blood on my T-shirt where the broken

slat had stuck me. Kathy stood by the bunk outside the john. She had her hand over her mouth and nose.

The flush toilet is a great invention. Human stuff seems just to get worse the longer it's out.

"She all right?" Kathy said through her hand.

"That some kind of joke?"

I looked into the mirror, or what was left of it. My reflection jagged, broken, with gaping holes.

I looked down into the sink. A perfect specimen. A thick dark turd about a foot long. Ashes all around and on it. Shards of mirror beside and stuck into it. In the slivers, in the shit, little flashes of me.

T H I S   I S   *M E*.

I wanted to look anywhere else and couldn't. My eyes teared like they were gagging.

S M E A R   M E   O N   Y O U R   N E W   W I F E.

Do *what* on my *what?*

Y O U   H A V E N ' T   G U E S S E D ?
E L A I N E   A N D   I   A R E   H E R E   T O
M A R R Y   Y O U   T W O.

I thought you came to take her.

S A M E   D I F F E R E N C E.

No—it—is—not.

Y O U   W E N T   T O   W H E R E   T H E   D E A D
D O N ' T   K N O W   T H E Y ' R E   D E A D.

Didn't see *you* around.

I   S A W   Y O U.   I   W A S   S I N G I N G.
L O O K   A T   Y O U.   Y O U   C A N ' T   T A K E
Y O U R   E Y E S   O F F   M E.   N O W   D O
W H A T   I   T O L D   Y O U   T O.

You don't even talk like Danny.

I T ' S   J U S T   T H A T   I ' M   S O   M U C H
S T R O N G E R   H E R E.

The refrigerator door opened. Kathy was chug-a-lugging pink wine.

"What are you doing?" I said. "Can you hear this?"

"Not the words. But the sound. This wine is *awful*." And she gulped some more.

In the sink the turd did not throb. But it was like I was hearing it stink.

LISTEN UP—THE SOUL—IS NOT—
HUMAN—DOES NOT WANT—WHAT A
HUMAN WANTS —BUT NEEDS—THE
HUMAN JOURNEY—FOR—ENDS—OF—ITS
OWN—IT HONORS—THE HUMAN—
JOURNEY—BUT NOT—BY
PROTECTING—WHAT IS HUMAN—
THAT'S WHY THE HUMANS—ARE SO
AFRAID—OF THEIR SOULS—THE
RECORD OF THEIR FEAR—IS
CALLED—HISTORY—THEY ARE
SCARED MOST OF ALL—BECAUSE
EVERY HUMAN—KNOWS ITSELF A
PART—OF A RACE POSSESSED—
PRECISELY—BY THEIR VERY—SOULS
—IF ONLY—A HUMAN—CAN BECOME—
UNAFRAID—OF THE SOUL'S
NECESSITY—TO JOURNEY—THEN
ANYTHING—IS POSSIBLE —THE SOUL
—IS—HONORED—AND SHARES—ITS—
BEAUTY—

Then . . .

Sometimes shit laughs.

EIGHT *Nothing Hustles Better Than the Truth*

But I wasn't going to be smearing anything on Kathy.

"Get your stuff," I said to her.

And said silently down into the sink: I'll try to keep all that in mind, Danny-O.

Then turned the shower water on Elaine to wake her.

"You missed it," I told her.

She stood up, let the wet towel drop, showing all the wrinkles on her reddened neck down to her cleavage. Eyes green, but the whites pink.

"Where are the Polaroids?" I said.

"My purse."

I went into the living room, got them out of her purse. She followed but didn't protest. Kathy got our funeral clothes out of the closet. Elaine put on her things.

"Where's Kathy's picture?"

"It's in there."

"No, it's not."

"Then I don't know where."

Kathy said, "I don't give a fuck. Let's go, if we're going."

I said, "You give a fuck, believe me."

It was hard to go back into the bathroom, but I went. Tried not to look directly at the sink. It's hard to believe how much stink can come out of one thing. It felt like we were all going to have to wash it out of our hair.

Was all that soul-talk just a hustle, Danny-O?

NOTHING HUSTLES BETTER THAN THE TRUTH.

Elaine stood in the broken doorway. Pieces of the door hung from the hinges. She had on a gray dress that you button up the front, but it wasn't buttoned.

"I know what you're going to do," she said.

"Good for you."

I kept looking. It was in a box of tissues, hidden about halfway down, the Polaroid of Kathy, with a ragged hole burned in its middle.

"I'm sorry," Elaine said.

"Good for you."

I turned to her and she was weeping soundlessly. She *was* sorry. But her smile broke into a girlish laugh. "It *got* 'er, though, didn't it?"

Kathy's charge was too sudden for me, I didn't see anything but that wine bottle going upside Elaine's head. The blow knocked

340

Elaine into my arms, rag-doll limp, but Kathy wouldn't stop, kept at her from behind. I turned, trying to shield Elaine, figured Kathy wouldn't be hitting on me, figured wrong, 'cause that bottle, which would not break, hit down on my shoulders while Danny squished a laugh from the turd, O H I H A V E H E R , then the bottle smashed against my head, the pain a white light hot as God bursting my brain, and a small voice in me said, Now? Like this? as I went down, stuck my elbow out to break the fall. It hit—*splat!*—in the shit. I let Elaine drop, let myself fall into the shower stall, vomiting, vomiting all over my hands, which had reached out to break the fall, and with each heave my brain tore with pain.

Kathy didn't give a damn; Kathy went to smash Elaine, kill her, but tripped over me, fell, broke *her* fall in the sink, and it would have been the fucking Marx Brothers except that Kathy let rip the lowest, harshest sound I'd ever hear from a human throat.

I N O W P R O N O U N C E Y O U M A N A N D W I F E .

Kathy's rasp gurgled up to something very like a laugh as she sank to her knees and brought the wine bottle down with all her strength onto the toilet-bowl rim, where it finally shattered and splattered glass and pink stuff over everything.

N I N E *Ablutions II*

Kathy stood slowly. Got into the shower, turned it on, me crumpled at the bottom, she half-kneeling over me. The water was cold, cold. She ripped my shirt off and scrubbed Danny off me, then off her. So cold, it hurt.

A B L U T I O N S , A B L U T I O N S , T O S O I L S U C H T H A T Y E M A Y A B L U T E , A B S O L U T E A B L U T I O N S , G A T H E R Y E F A I T H F U L , O A B L U T .

We are the faithful. *That's* sure.

Without a word we picked Elaine up, stuck her in the shower. She revived, woozy, but making no sound. I thanked the stars she wasn't dead. Mostly for her, partly for us. I could just see me and Kathy trying to explain this to The Great World. Some headlines that would've been.

And washing her, the three of us in the freezing shower, me and Kathy washing Elaine, I felt so sorry for the woman in her. So sorry. Flashed on how hard it was, and how little she could help it, to have all this raw magic rip through her. She'd invited it, but without any understanding, and as it bolted through her to us it had no regard for her, it was wiping the woman out of her, and she would be lonely one day for the woman she could have been.

Lurching, we half-dragged, half-carried Elaine into the living room and fell in a heap on the floor, soaking the rug beneath her.

For once I knew what I was going to do, and that felt good.

Elaine lay on her back, staring up; Kathy face-down, eyes lightly closed. Then her eyes snapped open, not alarmed, just mildly surprised: "He's singing that song again, the wrong way around, but farther off."

It seemed time.

I got up, put all our stuff right at the door. Elaine and Kathy dressed and went out, taking our stuff as they went. I had some trouble torching the RV. It's practically all plastic. But it finally took. I felt something like a perfect calm as the fire started to lick across the rug. Panels snapped. Wires sizzled. Plastic oozed. I got kind of enthralled with it, in spite of the fumes, stayed a beat too long, got dizzy. Jumped out.

The women were sitting a few yards away, on the ground, beside Henry.

I went and sat by him. The fire was really blazing now, thick smoke rising, the RV kind of melting in on itself.

"The wind is light," Henry said, "and that unit seems just far enough away from the RVs around it. If it ain't, we won't get out of here. We'll see, won't we."

But we were all so calm, I couldn't imagine it going wrong, as though our mood together was enough and more than enough to make a fire behave.

The sky took that pale pale yellow that happens sometimes

before full dawn. As the smoke rose up to it, a funeral fit for him, I felt great. I thought it was over. You'd think I'd've learned by then that nothing's ever over.

Henry put his big spider of a hand on my knee, squeezed it with some echo of the old strength, said, "You characters with direct access—*messy* bastards."

Then he added, "I was just hanging out. Picking up what I could. But I couldn't've helped. And wouldn't've."

There was only one explosion, when the methane went, a thick puff of black smoke that shot into the air and thinned away fast. Once the flames licked at the side of the next RV, but just smoked it a little. Finally ours collapsed on itself in a heap.

Henry leaned on me as we took what seemed a longer way out of his RV city. One empty wheeled building after another.

"By the way," he said, "y'all owe me about fifteen thousand dollars."

T E N   *Out There*

Elaine got into her Jap pickup and drove off. Kathy put our stuff in the car while I helped Henry into his mobile home.

"You know," he said when we were alone, "you can't tell anybody about this stuff. I don't mean that you shouldn't. I mean that you *can't*. 'Cause it ain't magic, or whatever you wanna call it. It's how intense you're pointed *Out There* every hour. That's what does the work. You ain't got that, you ain't got anything. When you *do* have it, then you just do the little dance or spell or whatever to focus it, at the last minute. And if you're *really* living, you don't even need that. Just happens." Then: "Wish you'd grow up, man. I'd sure like to see *one* of the children grow up." Then, nodding toward outside: "I'd hang on to that little girl if I were you. She's got something better than direct access."

"What's that?"

343

"*Sense,* shithead!"

And he scruffed my hair.

"And she's very old," he said. "Always thought you needed an older woman. But she's tired, that girl. Been tired two, three lifetimes. That's why she's so drawn to you. Needed wakin' up. Which is kind of your specialty. I know you're wasted, but you ain't tired." Then: "We'll see each other one, maybe two more times. Unless you make a mistake. You got it in you to make a monster of a mistake, boy. And I wish you'd decide to make it or *not.* Stop this hanging on the edge of it. 'Cause the suspense is killin' me. Uh, figure of speech, you understand. I'll be thinkin' of ya."

ELEVEN *Welcome to Lubbock—For All Reasons*

WELCOME TO LUBBOCK—FOR ALL REASONS!

I love that billboard. They had one catty-corner from the Rodeway, at University and Fourth, where I knew Nadine would be. Her old blue '73 Chevy, a hulk of an old boat, was in the parking lot, with its Louisiana plate and its bumper sticker: JESUS IS COMING —AND BOY IS HE PISSED! I parked my battered Chevy Malibu in the space next to Nade's. It was about seven-thirty in the morning.

Up in the room I thought of telling Kathy what Henry had said, but she went straight for the phone and dialed long distance.

"Suzanne? It's me. Well, I didn't mean to, but I'm not sorry. I thought you had the early shift. I'm up in Lubbock. Yes, with Jesse Wales, lucky me. Yeah, I figured they'd bounce me." She laughed like a conspirator. "Look, I'll be back in time to cut your hair— don't let anybody else do it—and I'll tell you about this then. You'll think I'm making it up anyway. I can't, he's here. Yes"—looking at me—"I love him. Well, how smart do you have to be? Suzanne, really, not now. I know I woke you up. I just called 'cause I wanted to hear a voice that nobody up here's heard. Say my name. Just say it. That's my name all right. I don't know, but I'll call as soon as I get in. I'll *be* back in time. Promise. I'm hanging up, okay? Bye."

Then: "Jesse?"

"What?"

"Say my name."

"Kathy."

"You almost never say it."

"Sorry. I guess."

"Jesse?"

"What? Kathy."

"I'm asking you for the first thing I've ever asked you for: Don't strand me here. Leaving me is one thing. But I won't be stranded."

I said, "If . . . anything happens, get a ride to Henry's. He won't be at the funeral. Just show up, he'll get you on a plane home. You won't have to explain anything to him—"

"I know I won't—"

"—just show up. Is that good enough?"

"Not really," she said. "But it'll do for now."

T W E L V E *A Family*

Kathy bathed. Slept. I showered, but couldn't sleep more than an hour or so. Kept jerking awake, as though my body feared to lose itself. Got dressed, left without a word or a note, found out Nade's room number. It was about ten-thirty in the morning by now.

The kid opened the door. He flinched ever so little as I reached for him and held him. First he didn't hug me back, then he did.

Then I held him out in front of me, kneeling to his size, and looked into his very dry, tired, dark eyes.

"I'm real glad to see you," I said. "When I called the other night, I was real stupid not to know it was you. I was just yelling, you know, but not at *you*. That was a bad mistake I made 'cause I didn't know it was you—you understand? I'm sorry. I know 'sorry' doesn't help much, but when a person does something stupid, 'sorry' is all they can say."

He just looked at me, tense.

I said, "I love you."

He mumbled, "Love you, too," but it was like he *had* to say it, like I'd made him.

Only then did I look past him and meet Nadine's eyes. They seemed sunk deep into her head, the circles around them were that dark. She had the same skin-pulled-out-of-shape look Henry had, but his was cancer and hers was—I got a fear deep in me. For the boy. He'd been with this vibe for two–three days now.

"Danny's in Hell," Nadine said.

"I don't think so."

"You don't know SHIT." The boy flinched. "You and that CUNT you're with. Oh, I saw your car. When we got up. I called the desk. 'They are in room what's-it.' *They* sure are. They're in room what's-it and Danny's in Hell."

"Nadine—"

"Worshiped any good DEVILS lately? I forgot to tell you, boy, your Daddy's a Devil worshiper. Your Uncle Danny, who's dead now and in Hell, he was too."

And she started to make sounds I'd never heard. Like she'd swallowed a sick rodent and it was crying in her.

I said straight into Little Jesse's eyes, "I'm not a Devil worshiper. I'm not any kind of worshiper—"

"LIAR!" Nadine screamed.

"—and there ain't no Devil and there's no Hell either."

"LIARRRRRRRR!"

"I don't know how to tell you what I know," I said to the boy, "but I *promise* you, I'm not what she says."

"LIARRRRRRRR!"

The boy broke from me and ran into the bathroom.

Nadine said, suddenly soft, "I thought—I thought what would happen was—Danny would go to Jesus, he *would* find my Jesus down the line, 'cause he was, you know, angelic, Danny; he was hardly *in* this world ever, hardly here—and he would finally, on his long road, find our Redeemer. And if he did, you would. He'd *make* you, you couldn't resist, you never could, him. And we'd be family, again and finally. We're a *family*, Jesse. Don't you remember?"

I wanted to go to her and hold her and wipe out somehow the fact that I'd ever held anyone else. But I was afraid to touch her.

And she: "Danny's—being twisted—by the minions—in the fires—of Hell—even as I—take this breath—to speak. Danny is screaming right this eternal moment in Hell."

"Can you hear him?"

"No, I can't hear him, I'm not crazy; I just *know*."

There was no point trying to tell her. There was no way. And maybe it *was* all in our heads. Whatever *that* means.

"Jesse, Jesse . . ." She was weeping now, and I went and held her and I'd never felt those big bones so close to the surface of such thin skin. "Jesse, I can't stand it, knowing he's in Hell. He's in *eternal Hell,* Jesse, *damnation,* and there's nothing I can *do.* Nothing, nothing, nothing. Our *Danny,* Jesse." Then: "And you too, one day. Jesse, I just can't *bear* it."

"Nade, Nade. What did he ever do that was so bad that he has to be in Hell? He'll sing his way out."

She threw me off her, yelling, "There are *no exceptions!* It's *Jesus* or *Hell.* My Danny is in Hell. *My Jesus put my Danny into Hell.*"

I held her again. She eased up some.

"You stop at Henry's?" she asked, rubbing her eyes.

"Yeah."

"How is he?"

"He's all right."

"I thought he was sick."

"He's dying. But he's all right."

"*That* man'll slide down to Hell on his own private chute. I *know* my Danny would have found my Jesus but for that man." But she had no hate in her voice for him. She said, "What's Henry think? 'Bout me, these days? Us. Christian go-getters, I mean."

"You a go-getter?"

"I've done a lot of going. A little getting. Henry ever say anything?"

"He asks about you. 'Tell 'er to visit,' he says, 'now that I'm invalid-ated. I miss that wild woman,' he says. One time a year or so ago we had the TV on, just on, you know, and it was PTL or 700 Club or something, and Henry said, 'Those crazy Christers, I love 'em. *Stir* up the pot! *Stir* up the pot!' "

"Danny's in Hell, Jesse. We're talkin' and goin' about our business in our way and Danny is screaming with his lips on fire and his tongue on fire and his lungs on fire in Hell."

"Isn't there something about how you're not supposed to feel like this about anybody down there, and all?"

"I know. I'm sinning." She actually laughed. "That devious bastard is finally making me *sin* again."

Little Jesse just sort of appeared.

"Over here, kid," I said, and he came over and sat on the bed with us. The family. But if felt like we were in a hospital room. Nadine reached out and took Little Jesse's hand. She said, "*This* guy, I didn't tell you, is doin' pretty good in school. He can read better than the teacher, practically. Better'n *you*, for sure."

"You learn any new piano?"

He said, very softly, " 'Closer Walk with Thee.' "

"Good tune."

He smiled ever so slightly.

Nadine's face kind of clenched. It was her Danny-in-Hell face, but she didn't say anything this time. She probably hadn't till I'd walked in.

"We'd better get our funeral things on," Nadine said. "The—person you're with—she's coming?"

"Yeah."

"I wish she wasn't."

"I could ask her not to."

"You bargain with your own pride, Jesse Wales. Don't you *ever* compromise mine."

"Just a suggestion."

"Any woman you got, I can stare down."

"Sure."

But nobody's sure this time around.

"See you later," I said.

Gave my son a hug and left.

THIRTEEN ‿ Turnout of the Tribes

It wasn't the graveyard Buddy Holly's buried in, but we had to drive past that statue of Buddy Holly on Avenue Q: a huge nice guy in a suit and glasses playing an electric guitar. So far as I know, it's the only statue of a rocker in this country—and Lubbock's a town where they still don't allow liquor stores inside the city limits. I drove around the statue once to show Kathy, but she wasn't very impressed.

We drove out to the parking lot of the First Baptist, where the cortege was going to start. You could tell a lot of musicians had come because half those cars looked more fit for a demolition derby than a funeral. Just about every good club musician more or less our age—too old to be a star and too deep in to quit—had made the funeral, those who'd got the word within a two days' ride. And a few who'd been farther off and had the money for plane tickets. Ely, Hancock, Marcia Ball, Stevie, the whole Supernatural Family Band, Jimmy Gilmore, Angela Strehli, Terry Allen, Paul Ray, David Halley, lots more. Even some club owners. Dawg, of course. Keeping to himself, unable to speak. Anyway, there wasn't much milling. People just helloed and nodded. Quiet smiles, serious, gentle.

I felt good for Danny at the turnout. Nobody much outside of Texas ever had or ever would hear of him, and *that* was all right, but the way he sang was going to echo with a lot of people for a long time. And that had little to do with how nuts he was or wasn't, whom he loved or failed, who loved or failed him. His singing was something that just was, and had an importance of its own, which had nothing to do with anything but how beautifully something can be done now and again. It didn't even depend on the fucking twentieth century. A hundred years ago, a thousand, there had to have been a voice like Danny's singing whatever there was to sing, because a voice like Danny's could sing anything, like an angel, to anyone, no matter *who* didn't deserve it.

The people here didn't have to know that there was nothing in that coffin. Nothing but dead-indeed dead meat. That he'd buried himself somehow in Elaine's body. Been reborn as shit. Burned. Got fired-and-ashed to no one knows where.

It might be he was dead for real now. I hadn't heard him since the fire. Or maybe the fire had burned a voice that was only in our heads and that we'd kind of caught off each other. I'd seen, among the Sanctifieds and the Rollers, folks catch the talking-in-tongues from each other, passing God spastically from one to the other like something too hot for any one person to keep and hold.

In the First Baptist parking lot, the night people were all in their own form of dress-up. The men in fine black leather jackets and black Maverick-kind-of gambling suits, or just black shirts and white ties, black slacks, black denim, like I had, looking all together like some kind of gang or tribe. The women in every which way of black; black prom-dress kind of things, black lace, black heels, black eye shadow and fingernail and toenail polish, even black hairspray on blond hair. All blown by a stiff West Texas breeze that almost was a wind.

The other tribe, Danny's family and their relatives and neighbors, were all dressed like for Sunday, but black, and his relatives were real nervous that we'd shown up. Hard to hide the truth from the neighbors *now*. ("If he had those kinda friends, he must have drug-OD'd himself, *I* say.") It was like different families at a wedding, low trash and high trash, and each side seeing the other was reminded of something they tried every day to forget: what they were made of.

Each side made out of denying the other.

But they would still come to each other's funerals. They had to. Because really they were all formed of the same sticky stuff, more the same than different, however they might howl each other down.

When Nadine finally got there, she looked normal and Sunday

except for her walk, that long-legged, swing-hipped walk that she could never pray away. She hugged all the rock 'n' roll women, Marcia and Angela and all, and a lot of the men, and everybody oohed and aahed over Little Jesse. Kathy and I were her last stop. In heels she had about eight inches on Kathy. She just stuck her right hand out to Kathy, said, "Hello, I'm Nadine Wales."

Kathy met her eyes pretty well.

"I'm Kathy."

Little Jesse said to me, "Is she your wife, Daddy?"

"She's my friend," I said.

"Daddy's got lots of friends, hon, but he ain't got but one wife."

Kathy got red, but stuck her hand out to the boy.

"Hi," she said.

Nadine must have wanted to whip his hand away, but she didn't. Kathy and Little Jesse shook hands and she smiled at him, a frank, brief smile. He liked it, caught it, gave it back. It was almost like they'd passed a note between them agreeing that among these dangerous people they would give each other nothing to fear. And they were like that from then on.

"There's Danny's ma," Nadine said. "I'm goin' to her. Comin'?"

And the four of us walked across the invisible line separating the tribes, and people made way for us, and we went to the limo where Danny's ma was about to get in. She had Danny's high cheekbones, and his straight, once crow-shiny hair, but white now. She'd hardly any lips left, they'd been sliced by a thousand tiny lines and shriveled in. She was around forty when she'd had Danny, her one baby. Now she was pushing eighty. She stood, tiny, with her arms half raised and her hands just hanging limp from her wrists. All that was alive on her were her eyes. Blue-ink eyes, like two little holes drilled in her head.

Nadine stooped to kiss her—Danny's ma wasn't but five feet tall—and said something soft in her ear about the Lord. But the old woman was looking at me the whole time.

"You must be feelin' bad," she said to me.

'I am, Ettie. About as bad as I ever felt."

"Yeah. Well."

As a reflex she tried to pat my arm, but all that happened was one of her little useless hands brushed back and forth on it, as though sweeping it.

She said, "I was always—too old—to *do* that boy. Now—he's older'n me."

"Yes, ma'am."

"Yeah. Well."

And she got into the limo.

F O U R T E E N *The Coming of the Bride*

The graveyard was out on U.S. 84, past the city limit. Land so flat, the sky seems to come right down to your feet. Wherever you're standing looks like the highest place around. Just two—three miles out of town, and the skyline of Lubbock seemed only another low row of tombstones a little west and north. If the other graves hadn't been there, it would have seemed one desolate place to dig a hole.

A preacher stood at one end of the hole, and Danny's two tribes mingled in a crescent around it. His father's stone was nearby. Half a dozen cousins carried the casket. I thought I'd be offended, thinking it should have been us and there should have been music; but, actually being there, I didn't feel that. We'd had him for most of his life, and it was their right, now, to take him back. They claimed that right without much love but with an impressive solemnity. They didn't shirk him. They took him. Whatever they had thought and had said, whatever they would think and would say, the boy of secretive Ettie and long-dead Pete, their flesh, was being offered by his family to a Judgment that they feared for themselves as much as for him. The shadow of that Judgment made them feel close to him. They hadn't any of them felt so close to him since he'd lit out for Austin at the age of fifteen, where he'd met me on a street corner. And we'd known each other by our guitars, and we'd sung "San Antonio Rose" for spare change, and that song would later be the first song played on the Moon.

Knowing how empty of Danny that coffin was, I thought it cruel, how they were being fooled.

Kathy knew. Standing on my right, she looked so prim and proper if you didn't notice her exhausted eyes and her one black-painted, gold-trimmed pinky nail. Little Jesse was on my left, stiffly serious, like a little preacher. Then Nadine, who was privy to, party to, the Judgment. The muscles around her right eye had taken to having little spasms for themselves. For Nade, that hole went straight down. And down and down. And down some more. "He's got time to feel the Fire in every littlest nerve," she'd said. And Nadine, always loyal, was feeling with him. Trying to feel it *for* him, if I knew her. Sinning, then, to boot.

And over Danny's hole: the biggest sky there is, just some high thin cirrus to the west, bright white in a washed-blue sky.

His cousins brought the coffin up, six serious men in their forties and fifties, gone to heavy. They laid it on that machine, or frame, or what-you-call-it, that lowers the coffin down. The preacher took a breath.

And held it.

His eyes bugged a little. We all looked to where he was looking. And walking on the grass, past the stones, with Lubbock low behind her and white cirrus over her, came Elaine—in the whitest, frothiest, most billowing wedding dress you ever saw. With the veil blowing back. And a bouquet in her hand. A little wobbly on high heels in the dirt, but not breaking her stride. And her burning bush of red hair so red under that white bridal canopy.

The veil blew up when the breeze gusted and her face was older than I'd yet seen it, cheeks slack with exhaustion, a bruise up one side of her face where Kathy had connected with the bottle, the whites of her eyes so pink they were almost red. But her wide mouth was set fierce.

She walked the path the pallbearers had walked, leaning in against our shocked, surprised silence as though it was a barrier that weighed against her. And some people, mostly our tribe, rolled their eyes, sort of smiled, shook their heads. And some, mostly the other tribe, quivered in their faces and clenched their fists and their eyes got narrow.

And the Bride walked to the foot of the grave and stopped, planted her feet wide apart, not like a bride at all. And she held the bright purple-yellow-white wildflower bouquet out in front of her like it would protect her. Elaine in white and the preacher in black faced each other across Danny's grave. She smiled slow and her eyes shone glory.

If you do the image pure enough.

The preacher let his breath out. He didn't sputter, I'll give him that. Everybody was waiting to take their cue from him. Drag the woman off or go on with this thing. And he just didn't know what to signal.

Kathy squeezed my hand hard. Our eyes met a moment, and it was the gayest look I'd yet seen on her. She was loving this. Little Jesse, he'd never been to a funeral before, and for all he knew this was how it's done. But Nadine—Nadine stared at Elaine in a kind of rapt horror, with unblinking hate.

The preacher's face went through kind of a sickly what-would-Jimmy-Swaggart-do-in-a-fix-like-this, and, whatever it was, he knew he wasn't going to do it. He had a piece of notepaper taped to his Bible, and he took that breath again and read from it.

"Your source is not on this earth," he read. "It is from another world."

The Bride smiled her approval of *that*. The wind spread her many-layered white dress out behind her, held it gently in the air with small invisible hands.

Ettie was standing across the hole from us. She took one small step forward, looked at the Bride, sort of half-smiled. It was like the old woman thought she was seeing something nobody else could see.

The preacher missed a beat, but when it didn't appear that Ettie was going to make a fuss he went on with, "Jesus said, 'He that findeth his life shall lose it, and he that loseth his life for my sake'—and He said 'for *my* sake'—"

Nadine sank to her knees in the soft dirt. The preacher looked at her, hesitated. She glared at him. He went on.

"—'shall find it.' The question must be asked: How—"

Nadine crawled on her knees to the edge of the hole, sinking inches into the fresh-dug grave-dirt piled there. She and the Bride looked at each other like they were alone there. The Bride smiled holy. Nadine looked down into the hole.

The preacher, who had lost his place, found it again: "How . . . important *is* the soul of man?"

My knees weakened at the question.

"I think the question was answered when He said, 'If you gain the whole world and give up your soul, you gain nothing.' "

And I thought of Papa Adam's laughter, and what Danny had "said" from the sink in the RV, that the soul isn't human, doesn't need what a human needs, but needs the human journey, for ends of its own; that if we honor that, it shares its beauty; if we don't, we live in fear—not fear for our souls, like this preacher wanted us to think, but fear *of* our souls.

Papa Adam turned toward me, from far far away, smiling slightly.

The preacher was going on with some scripture or other—when they intone the Bible, it all sounds the same to me—while I couldn't take my eyes off Elaine. She was going in and out of being the Bride as she stood there. Moments with her face all pride and glory, moments when she'd falter, look around, look down, down at Nade, who was now looking straight up, at the high fast clouds, absolutely still, as though being still would keep Nade pure of this tainted ceremony. Then Elaine would *get* it again, be the Bride. But I knew Elaine, knew standing there *as* the Bride was as far as she'd thought . . . I knew that she was stranded out there on the far end of yet another image, not knowing what came next.

She jerked suddenly stiff, as though someone had popped a stone off her back. I felt it too, almost saw it, something coming in from behind her, attaching to her, something immensely strong. Like an invisible tornado had dipped from nowhere and fastened on the small of her back. She clenched her face against its power.

Had it come from Nadine's prayer? No, for when the Bride jerked stiff, Nade's head snapped toward her, startled, frightened, sensing the Power had arrived. And that was when the preacher pressed the button that started the motor that eased Danny's slow coffin into its hole. Elaine and Nadine hardly noticed. Something from somewhere was trying to push its way through the Bride, maybe it was the *real* Bride that Elaine had just taken on the image of, the *real* Bride all brides dress like, begging for and fearing her Power. They don't know what they're asking. Elaine was finding out, her face asweat with the effort to hold the Power back, trying somehow to keep it off her, but it had got *to* her. Her whole body clenched, from her bowels on out. I felt it. Like this thing or image had gone into the small of her back, down through that rounded hole, into her intestines and was trying to force its way out, like she was struggling not to let it out her mouth, for would it come out like fire or like smoke, consuming her as it did, or, worse, would it come out like words more blazing than fire, murkier than smoke, words she couldn't guess at and couldn't swallow back? Unspeakable words that she would not be able to stop speaking even if they jumped her and held her down till the men came, who would surely come, and take her away to the places where we lock up such words.

I feared for her. I feared for us all. Who knew what worlds she was attempting, shaking now, to hold back? Who knew what would happen if she didn't? For I knew, my bones knew, that Power could pop from one person to another, suck us all in, make Holy Rollers out of the whole crowd, we'd writhe all over the ground among the tombstones. Might not be a bad idea, maybe we needed writhing, but there were people here, Nadine surely among them, who'd be torn to pieces, who'd never leave this place. Elaine's eyes were near to bursting with the effort to contain that Power, not to let it pass through her. Surely if it did, there wouldn't be much of *her* left. Elaine would rip to shreds as it came at us.

Nadine was staring into the hole now, her face averted from Elaine, her two hands clenched in one fist of prayer, begging, begging, begging for deliverance.

Kathy stepped behind Little Jesse, put her hands on his shoulders, held tight. I could see her throwing herself on the boy to protect him if the Power broke loose.

People looked to Elaine as she trembled, dropped her wildflower bouquet. They were nervous just this side of fear. The preacher droned, his eyes closed, the motor hummed, Danny's coffin lowered, a wind came up. Elaine stood as one world tried to press into another, and with all her strength she held it back. She'd been inviting it for so long, so many times, and it had come to her, she knew now, lightly and playfully before this, however bad it may have seemed. But now—now she was in both Worlds at the same time in the wrong place. Standing stock-still, she was fighting harder than she'd ever fought. While all I could do was watch and know.

Her jaw was set. Muscles twitched in her neck. Her forehead shone sweaty through the veil. Spasms shimmied her shoulders. Twitched her legs. Her spike heels twisted into the ground. The Power was trying to marry us all. Maybe she was struggling for herself, maybe she was aware of having to protect us all, maybe you can't make those distinctions where she was. But I knew if she went, I'd go, I felt the Power nearing me, reach me through her. She couldn't help it, she slowed it down, dragged on it, but it neared me. And I felt my—*soul*—stir toward it.

Never, never (even back in Mexico), never did it *really* occur to me till that instant that *I* had one of those things too! Like that thing that spoke from the sink. Made me want to jump into Danny's hole. Oh, it's not the fear of death, it's *called* the fear of death, but it's not. It's the fear of taking the soul's ride instead of the soul's taking yours. And you don't know whether you'll die, you just know all the rules will change for you all the way and for keeps, in this world and likely the next, 'cause you *know* there's a next now. And you didn't *really* want to know that, no matter what you said, 'cause it changes *everything*. A tendril of what Elaine was fighting reached through to me and my soul reached toward it and now I struggled too, not ready, not ready.

But then . . . it receded . . . from me. Back . . . back. I could see again—vision had blacked out without me being aware—and I saw Elaine and she was taking deep breaths, and though her eyes were open her face was like asleep, all tension gone. She'd held it. And it had stopped. Gone. And now, the Power suddenly absent, I missed it, and knew she did. Had this been a victory or a defeat? And would she ever be the same?

Nadine rose from her knees. Soft dirt stuck to her dress.

"Got permission f'my mission," she said, dazed.

People were moving around. I hadn't even noticed them

throwing dirt into the grave. Hadn't heard a word of benediction. And I hadn't—hadn't had one thought of Danny, for whom we'd gathered, and who seemed, now, like no more than an excuse.

I turned, slowly, to see Kathy staring at me with big frightened eyes. I thought: Does she know, yet, that she has a soul?

Nadine was already a few steps away, Little Jesse in hand, walking with her head down toward her car. People were saying things to Elaine that she didn't seem to hear, some admiring, some pissed. She ignored them, took a step toward me, stumbled, re-covered. We looked deep into each other. And were done with each other. Perhaps the Bride had come to join us. But it hadn't come off. Elaine had let it go as far as she could, had gone as far as she could stand—and that's what she'd always wanted to know, wasn't it, just how far she could go before everything in her pulled back? She couldn't be around me and *not* go again, we both knew that, and the next time it might be far too much; she might not be able to return, might be, we both might be, torn to bloody pieces, so . . .

Good-bye, good -bye, we said with our eyes.

She turned and walked, feet dragging, to her little pickup, dropping the white veil as she went, lace that was moved along the ground by the breeze until it wrapped itself around a tombstone.

And I felt alone and alone and alone. Because you're never quite as alone as the first time you feel the Other in you that is you and not-you and more-than-you. The soul. And I watched the people dispersing, the Sunday people and the night people, and felt a silent, secret terror that each of them had what I had. What Danny had spoken of from the shit. What Jesus had promised to relieve them of, take care of for them. No wonder they could love Jesus so. Oh, oh, Nadine.

What I had used women to protect me from, I knew now. *I'll* say I hadn't been able to live without women. I'd loved them, yes, my women, but I'd loved more how my soul had stirred when near these women, and how I'd needed them to feel it and distract me from it both, put their loving bodies between me and this more-than-me that was also me. Using their very bodies like a glove, touching my own soul with and through them. So, sure, I sang to them. God help the people you sing to.

Gotta go.

Kathy touched my face. It startled me. I stepped back. She looked hurt.

I wanted her to hold me, and to hold her to me in turn, keep her by me, but my arms couldn't lift themselves. I was finally going to have to do something all by my lonesome.

We drove back to the Rodeway. She got out and I didn't. I gave her the room key. She asked when I would be back. I couldn't even get my mouth to tell her to go to Henry. She asked again when I'd be back. I wanted to tell her how tenderly, how thankfully, I felt for her. But I couldn't speak.

I pulled out of the parking lot slowly as she watched.

And I didn't stop till Quartzsite.

PART TEN

Knockin' on Heaven's Door

I wanna jump but I'm afraid I'll fall
I wanna holler but the joint's too small
                    —Huey "Piano" Smith

And those poor lost souls in your
shadows—
You forget, they're friends of mine.
                    —Joe Ely

O N E   *Home-Made Apocalypse*

Hey. If we admitted that the dead needed anything, we'd have to change the way we run the whole world.

H O L D T H A T T H O U G H T .

I don't *miss* blinking, exactly. It's kind of educational, to find out *why* the human blinks. One thing is, if you don't blink, your eyeballs dry. They feel in their sockets like a couple of peeled nuts gathering dust. The dust burns. Not bad pain, just slow burn. You can feel little fissures cracking the membranes. They're going to turn to crumbs in your head, your eyes. They go first. Why they close the eyes of the dead. Now you know.

The other thing, if you can't blink, is that you stop seeing shapes and distances. Everything's all line and color, everything's flat and dirty-shiny, like faded patterns on old linoleum. The TV, the bed, the wall, the door fuzz into each other on the same flat plane. Or sometimes one in particular stands out, for no reason, as though a few optic nerves are trying to struggle against the death of the rest, and the bureau, say, becomes perfectly clear, but flat, like a cutout from an advertisement pasted on thick white paper, surrounded with vague designs. And the whole flat papery sight can flare up, bright, as though a spotlight were shining through it into your eyes. Or go gray. Or get soaked, slowly, by a violet wash.

In the far right corner of my field of vision there's the window, I know, its curtains pulled back some. If I could see regular, I could say what goes on in that motel courtyard in Quartzsite, but all I see are sky-glare and ground-glare pulsing at each other in the heat. Shapes on the other side of the glares. Mountains? RVs? And shadows passing through the glares. People, probably. Except that we don't know. Do we? Anymore? I mean, I've gotten a little suspicious lately about what may or may not be a "person."

For instance: If you don't blink or move for some immeasurable wad of time, you get to feeling things the way maybe a rock or wall would. The way maybe a TV sees the room it's broadcasting into. You get to feeling you have more in common, maybe, with a bright bare lightbulb than with people.

A person's just a bare lightbulb packed in meat.
A person's just a storm with skin around it.

And that old Gideon in the drawer by the bed. A greedy white thing with a dark shell, mossy-wet, like a turtle that feeds near a sewer pipe. I hate the thought of dying in a room with such a thing.

Rock 'n' roll is here to stay
It will never die
It was meant to be that way
Though I don't know why
Danny and the Juniors, nineteen fifty . . . eight? Easy to play. Freeze your hands into two claws and bang on three chords.
Careful. Missy catches you, you'll get it with the stirring spoon.

Ma? Missy? I'm sick. You gonna rub me down with alcohol again? Read around me? It would take a lot of rubbing to get this sickness off. Got the fevers.
Got the rockin' pneumonia and the boogie woogie flu!
And the runs. I'm all dirty down there. Gonna take a hot washcloth and scrub me down there? Make it real hot, then. So hot. I'm willin'. To burn. Always have been. My only virtue, I guess.
Hot shit, right?
All my bad words. Gonna scrub my mouth out with soap? That brown soap they used to have? I haven't seen that stuff in years. Thick cake of brown soap that you'd stuff deep into my small mouth, me choking and crying, gagging, and my spit'd dissolve the soap and it'd burn down my gullet and give me the shits. Bad words.

Daddy?

Daddy?

"That's one tough little bugger," Daddy said. Then he drove off to Heaven. Was how Missy put it.

I almost just did that, Daddy. You were drunk, though, right?

Daddy?

"That's not Daddy."
Missy said, "Hush."
Auntie Laura said, "Sugar, they sure didn't do a good job with Joe's *face*."
"That's not Daddy."
Sharp deep sting against my face. Fever rising in my cheek. Feverwater rising into my eyes.
Don't cry, don't cry, don't cry.
Didn't.
Those trousers itched so bad. Black wool. In summer. Crotch all wet with sweat. Dripping down the inside of my pants.
Not sweat.
Feverwater pouring now out my eyes. And in a puddle at my feet.
And they dragged me off, Auntie Laura on one arm, Missy on the other, to the ladies' room, ripped the pants off me, so good to have them off, ripped my jockey shorts, dried me rough with paper towels, with toilet paper. Somebody came in with a blanket. Wrapped me in it. Itchy Army blanket. Now everything itched, arms, legs, butt, dick. Even the smells itched. Auntie Laura's perfume like gardenias, Missy's like magnolias, but like the flowers had been sprayed with gasoline.
"You can't take him to the graveyard like this," Auntie Laura said.
"He can stay in the car," Missy said.
"Daddy died in a car."
"Hush."

It's not like there's anything wrong with my body. But it's like I'm getting lots littler inside it. Just—littler. Like I'm about two squiggles high inside this sticky quivery tower. I'm way down in there. My eyes are far away now, a lot higher, and just *huge*, so if I could actually see out of them would it swamp me? I can't even *think* about my nose. I mean, all those bristles and snots and everything—I'd get stuck in it. It must be smelling something—I have a memory of stinking—but that's got nothing to do with me anymore. And there's a kind of tugging, a blunt pressure somewhere; if I concentrate real hard I can know—but just know, not really feel—that my cock is hard again. But what can that have to do with *me?* That big pale arched thing with veins bulging out, and a blue splotch here, a red splotch there, and that bulb on its end, a squirting bulb, full of stuff nobody knows about, nobody. Me, I'm huddled, a couple of squiggles high, next to the small of my spine, trying to stay as far from *that* thing as I can.

It goes up and down. It shrinks and swells. It seeks and squirts. What huge immense mouths those women must have had, to hold it. What monster hands, with their pointed cracked colored nails. What holes, to take this in, to want it, to be able stand that. No, I'm huddled far away.

Right snug to the spine. But bones inside aren't like bones on skeletons. Not white, not smooth. They're greasy, hot, and I'm sticking to this one like I'm a little chunk of meat the size of a finger joint.

But my spine-bone starts in throbbing. *This* ain't no bone. And a hiss now sizzling out its insides. *Bone* don't hiss. Bone don't ripple like this, bone's hiss don't thicken, swell to Moan—no, not again, no, not Moan here, oh, I'm so, so small and the Snake—is *everywhere.*

Snake inside me all along, straight up my back, no wonder we found it so easy, *that* gets my body moving. *I'm* stuck in entrails now like a bug in a drain, but my heart speeds up with fear way above me, booming its bass-drum thuds that shudder downward while the Moan surges upward in a wave that makes even these enormous heartbeats small. Beat and Moan washing one another through, heartbeat's faster, faster, faster, bulb of my cock throbbing with my heart, oh, I'm coming, coming on, riding a come-Moan, oh . . .

I'm wrenched up, up from the mess of the stickiness in my tininess, going *up*, colliding with organs as I go *up*, getting bigger again, bigger, as the heart beats faster, squiggle-me in mad collision with my parts, *it's like I'm a balloon inflating inside myself*, arms and legs jerk up and down—can feel them again—thighs bounce on the chair like I'm being electrocuted. And the pain in my chest out of this *world* as balloon-me bulges so fast through rib cage and lungs, squeezes *hurts* through the throat, neck bulging in rippling bubbles as balloon-me forces a way through, up the gullet into the head, my head, oh, ain't nowhere else to go but *out*, it's *time*, blow through the top of my skull . . . but instead—

Everything gets real still. I'm back. In my body again. Can sort of see out my eyes.

Feel sticky all in my crotch.

I *came?*

What is *that* about!

And then—and then—like this huge gate slowly coming down, like this thick massive gate being slowly lowered: I blinked.

The gate lifted and lowered again.

Two actual blinks.

What the hell time is it?

C H E C K - O U T   T I M E ?

In more ways that one, Danny-O. My chest's still killing me. Like my balloon-me inflated too much. My balloon-me—my WHAT —got way too small for my body, and now it's a mite too large, swelled out against the skin, pressing the underside of the pores, pushing out sweat. I'm in a sweat all over, and *Christ*, the stink, and —oops!

O O P S ?

Fuckin'-a oops. I've slipped out.

There I am down there.

Well, whadaya know!

That was easy. My balloon-me—my *soul*, Papa Adam? Where the fuck have *you* got to, you old wild man?—my soul, I guess it is, just kind of . . . squeezed through all the pores at once. That last leap didn't hurt at all. Hardly felt it.

But where's the light at the end of the tunnel, or the bright white clouds, or Jesus waiting, or Daddy, or Danny, or whatever's left of Nade's long-gone abortion? Don't *I* deserve some ballyhoo, like everybody else, some welcome on the other side?

No sound. Not even Danny. *That's* weird. For me, that's really weird. I'm up here, kind of floating around the light fixture, looking straight down onto my bald spot, if it's still "my" bald spot—identification right now is kind of a problem. Let's say "my" at least till we know different. My bald spot. Hair still thick on the sides, okay in front, long behind, but right at the crown, where I never see, it's shiny there; its sheen reflects the light, and its few little hairs look so—old. Nadine's tall enough to see that all the time! That's embarrassing. And, baby, it's *strange* to be embarrassed up here on the ceiling.

Holy shit—I'm happy!

Which is something I've said about four times in my whole life.

Kind of airy and happy, not scared at all.

They ain't got no *time* up here on the ceiling, no absence of time either, like . . . everything is very, very, very light. So light, I'm trying to keep my mind on the room because it's like if I thought, say, "China," very hard, I'd *be* there. But no sound. No sound at all. I wonder how long I can stand that. I'm a *musician.* Shit. And . . . what do you do, up by the light fixture, with no "you" to you, if you can't—stand—something?

Danny used to say that spiritual questions—"quest-y-owns," he'd emphasize—always boil down to something real practical. Never knew what he meant before, but it's obvious up here by the light fixture. What *do* you *do?*

But I'm happy. I ain't carrying around that sack of shit anymore. Jesus Christ, the thing's getting a hard-on again. I don't *believe* this. Its pants are unbuckled, unbuttoned, unzipped, and its hard-on's lifting up those boxer shorts like a tent. Shorts all gooey with the last mess. Who'd want any part of that goddamn stinking pus-stuck blob? Hair in its nose and hair on its ass. Who *needs* one a those messy things?

But it can hear. That's one good thing. I'm gonna miss music. Maybe that was the one good thing about me. That, and that I loved some so-called people. And them critters are hard to love.

And yet this *happy* thing. Everything you think up by the light fixture has got this kind of giddy feel to it, like at the dentist when you're on the gas and you feel the pain, some pain, but it just ain't *important* to you anymore.

Being dead is the best high I've ever seen.

. . .

Except that thing down there ain't dead yet. Not quite. That's why I'm up here by the light fixture and ain't getting any farther up. Its head is still straight, its eyes look straight ahead, its boxer shorts are still propped up like a tent. *Something's* going on down there.

Me, I'm up here.

I'll bet I'm shining. I'll bet if somebody walked in, and looked up, even if they couldn't see anything, there'd be some weird shining feel.

God, the things I've seen and the places I've done. I mean: the places I've seen and the things I've done. It's all getting kind of mixed up.

Shit, I've lost up and down. Which is a little scary. 'Cause there's nothing else *here* but up and down. Like, now I'm not *sure* if that sack of shit is down there, or if it's above me and the fixture is on the floor, or if it's on the wall, or what. I—don't fucking remember.

Okay. Okay. I'm not happy anymore.

I really don't remember.
Right at this moment I don't remember *a goddamn thing*.
And I can't scream.

Feels like all my memories are there propping up a pair of boxer shorts. Like my memories are shining from my bald spot. I ain't nothing. A giddy blob by the light fixture.

Danny, how do you stand it?

I'M SOMEWHERE ELSE. YOU GOT TO DECIDE.

Decide? What is 'decide'? I feel like I never decided a thing in my life. In *its* life. What the fuck ever. How can that piece of meat *decide* shit?

SPIRITUAL QUEST-Y-OWNS ARE ALWAYS REAL PRACTICAL.

Very funny.

. . .

Okay. Hold not to what you remember but what you know. That maybe could work. So what do I *know?* I know how to rock a piano. And: I'm a helluva long-distance driver.

Not a very long list.

And: I learned beside a grave that I've been using women ... religiously—don't know how else to put it. And: If you do the image pure enough, shit happens. And: There's such a thing as the Moan. There sure is. And: There's this crystal, might be a snake-eye, sometimes it hovers in Mexican hotel rooms. And: I sure do know I'm up here by the light fixture—I can feel "up" again, I guess that's good. And: That meat down there, which used to be me, *my memories are inside it.*

So what you know and what you remember live in different places?

There's nothing to *do* with this stuff. There's nothing in our world to *do* with it. That's why it makes you so crazy, not because the stuff itself is crazy. It's a *part* of something, but we only got the parts these days and not the something.

Spiritual questions are always real practical:
How do I get off the ceiling?
I'm lonely for my meat.

Am I really going to die?
YEAH, IF IT'S YOUR TIME. NO, IF IT'S NOT—'LESS YOU MAKE A BAD MISTAKE, OR A BAD MISTAKE IS MADE FOR YOU. WITH ME, IT WAS A BIT OF BOTH.
I don't want to.
WE'RE TALKING "COSMIC-BAD" WHEN WE'RE TALKING MISTAKES.
Whatever *that* means.

. . .

Look at my meat down there. That hard-on's still holding up those boxer shorts. They ought to put that thing in a museum when I'm done with it. What a fearsome goddamn thing. It's like it ought to be on somebody else.

How come it was never this active with a flesh-and-blood critter around?

Wonder how long I've been up here? This is no shit to do unless you know what you're doing, and I wonder if there's anyone who does. Anyway, I didn't *do* anything. "Do" is a very funny word up here by the light fixture.

Do-do.

I'm a little lower. I don't know why or how but I'm a little lower. If I had anything to reach with, I could almost reach and touch my head.

And I feel kind of sizzly. Like static.

And I feel—like I'm failing somehow.

Jesus, shit, what's *happening?!* Danny?! I'm getting sucked down and off to the side and away from my body, pulled toward the *what?*

Black. But I know just where I am. I'm in the drawer. The drawer of the nightstand by the bed. I'm in the drawer with the fucking Gideon. Un-be-fucking-*liev*-able. The Gideon's sitting there in the dark with me, kind of buzzing. Like when you turn on a sound system and it's not quite right and one of your speakers buzzes? That little black box of a book dragged me down here. I swear it. Sucked me right in.

I feel like the guy in *The Incredible Shrinking Man.* Except he had that spider and I've got this Gideon. And he had a body and something to *do.* But here in this moldy drawer there's just this kind of—pulling. A sense of pulling. The Gideon's pulling me and I'm pulling back. And it seems like we're both sweating. Can a book sweat? Can a blob, or cloud, or static, whatever I am? But I've got some memory back—maybe because I'm closer to my body?

Except that most of what I remember is the Gideon's. Deserts more naked than the deserts here. Seas aching to part. Moses with the Snake in his hand—the Gideon hates that, needs it but hates it, imprisons the Snake in his staff. While men in robes kill children, wave after wave of them, age upon age of them; the Gideon's just one wave after another of men in robes killing children, with babbles of prophecy between each wave. Take away all the stuff about men in robes killing children, and the threats of it, and the rememberings of it, and you'd have a book about the size of the Idalou, Texas, telephone directory.

Suddenly . . . Kathy's voice, gentle, serious, a voice that has never tried to listen in on itself, fresh. Kathy's voice the day I told my life story, when I got to Nadine's Bible fix, how Kathy said quietly, "You know in the Bible it says, 'And then it came to pass.' It doesn't say, 'And then it came to stay.' "

And the drawer stopped being a drawer. And the Gideon stopped being a Bible. It sat there in the dark like a big black building. Darker than the darkness around me. I was like this small stone about a block away from this high black rectangle. In a world where darkness *is* light.

For the dark itself was bright. Like dark hair shining. And the building—black, towering, blank-walled—slowly parted at its walls, the roof lifted off, the four great walls floated easily, separately, the many many floors hovered. Till each great slab drifted silently, each in its own direction, away.

Then many came. Slowly they came. In scattered clumps, some. Some, alone. They came across rough, wind-rippled ground. In a light made of dark. On a land that sloped toward me from some far place.

They came toward me, perhaps inevitably, but not because I was there, for they are always coming, reaching this place, going on.

And me—no longer rock, nor static, nor meat—no longer me. A rag, a scarf, many-colored, on the ground. Frayed. Stained. Soaked how many times, *in* how many times, with how many bloods, sweats? Wiped how many beards of what foods? Daubed how many cracks of what greasy juices? Wrapped around how many colors of hair? This, that is aware, this shred of "I," worn careless, like a hanky, through what ages, for what reasons, by my, no, by this—soul?

They came, the many, toward and past this sometimes rag, sometimes scarf, sometimes hanky, sometimes bandage, spread on what is sometimes ground. It is me, this rag.

They had been like me. I had been like them. Would be, once again, walking past rags, cups, buttons, the bits of this and that which littered this high plain and were me; bits to be picked up casually, by whomever, in a place that sometimes failed, or didn't need, to exist at all—being a drawer, in a room, by a road, in a desert, near a river, on a globe, in me. They came, and I knew them.

Elaine the Bride before them all. But it was as though the Garment, the Bridal Gown, walked of itself, serenely, while Elaine, within it, kept up with effort, missing steps, then focusing, remembering perfectly, and, for a few paces, wearing the Gown easily, gracefully.

And behind Elaine-as-Bride—Elaine again, but in rough fabrics, double-chinned, with huge breasts resting on the largeness of her belly, yet still Elaine in the eyes, so green, and the wide mouth of a fat victorious laugh. Danny beside her, with long blond hair, delicate sandals, small shapely breasts pointing up, nipples pressed against white silk; but Danny in her eyes, in her high cheekbones, Danny in her careless walk.

Then, farther back, a clump of dirty, tired brown-skinned men, clothes torn, some holding machetes, some old rifles. Bitter eyes, blood fresh on their clothes. Two dragged a litter. As it passed I saw Kathy, roped to it; but it was his muscles straining against the ropes; his head twisting from side to side, pouring fever sweat; his foot that had been blasted off at the ankle, the stump roughly cauterized, his small strong hands that clutched the bloody greenish foot to his chest. But it was Kathy in the sensuous small mouth, supple lips babbling pain.

Then dancers, drummers, wigged men in black robes. Workmen with tools in their belts. Women barefoot, vessels balanced atop their heads. Each one, like Elaine in the Bridal Gown, somewhat ahead or behind being a drummer, a rabbi, a servant, an Egyptian, a Pilgrim, Zulu, Aztec in overalls fresh from work in an LA garage. Walking some in clusters, some alone, some defeated, some determined, some distracted, yet all calm here in their shared need to walk this high plain strewn with small things, bits of cloth, bracelets, scraps of paper, beads. How, with no seeming thought, one would bend, pick from the ground one small thing, walk on, adjusting the new part upon their person.

Missy, a wisp of a thing, elevenish, dress burned, hair singed, staring vacantly, walking slowly, idly chewing on a strand of her long black hair. Nadine beside Nadine beside Nadine—sisters, Arabs, veiled, crying their high tongue-trilling serrated cry. Elaine again, tall, thin, ebony, but Elaine in the walk, the walk that could balance the great headpiece, its crescent, its horn. Beside her, Danny, a small boy, running after, calling to the tall one for attention, his boy's grief that his mother could not (so her ceremony demanded) look back. Johns running brilliantly, bright knees pumping high, skin red-bronze. Henry barefoot, ragged, tangled hair, wisps of beard, eyes big with fear, fluttering his huge hands at something unseen. Kathy black, thin-wristed, eyes wide with grief, seeing nothing, her walking a waiting, her waiting a prayer. Daddy's severed head rolling along the plain, dried blood caked on the gap-toothed mouth. Danny hand in hand with Nadine, hollow-eyed the two of them, two pale-skinned boys, secretive, gleeful, stopping to kiss. Elaine shriveled, hobbling, with stringy white hair, clutching his begging bowl with those big-knuckled fingers. Nadine again, walking freely, hips floating on long strides, robes swirling, proud Virgin of the town, feared for her prophecies. Danny standing absolutely still, yet moving toward me, great knowledge alive in his thick-browed slanted eyes; he's wearing a skullcap.

Then the dancing statues, those of the many arms, the many legs, their faces unutterably serene, the dancing Shiva with its great leg raised in that astounding arc, statues hauled by thousands of small leathery men whose bloody hands soaked the ropes. Henry's hands, Nadine's, Kathy's, Danny's, Elaine's, Missy's, Daddy's.

The same bloodied hands hauling the Jesus-statue.

And hauling the huge stone blocks of the temples.

And from the exhaustion of the rope-pullers rose a penetrating stench. Many followed. Legions of rope-pullers. And behind them, after a great space, Kathy, walking calmly, a young woman remembering a sunken city, as her now-yellow hair grows, grows, grows with each step, till her hair is like a bridal train behind her, she who walks as though her hair were weightless, suddenly saddened as the memory of the sunken city leaves her, perhaps forever, because that also happens, until, even, we cannot remember forgetting, though that which is forgotten lives on in our eyes, looks through us from where it has gone to where it will be once more in yet another form; we who vaguely feel ourselves carriers of what has been forgotten. Something makes this Kathy smile. She opens her hand. In her palm lies curled the iridescent green snake. She gently stoops, her many-layered hair rippling as she does, she picks up this rag, bandage, scarf, me, from where it rests on the throbbing plain, ties it around her neck, saucy, something forgotten clothed in something remembered, which is what "human" means.

In midstep, then, the animals appeared. Danny's three cats first. Dripping wet, as they would always be dripping wet, now. Cat-eyes glowing as though in the dark. Absolutely unforgiving, as it should be. And after them a multitude. Giraffes, galloping, a great graceful herd. An airborne floating whale! A crawling black horizon of spiders. Tiger. Bear. Bird-flights, every color of wing, their myriad shadows rippling across the plain, across the backs of the thousand elephants, great walking pianos! And the people walked among them, neither repulsed by the insects nor awed by the airborne fish. But where, where—my longing, now, for the great Snake. Oh! The plain itself! The long, undulating plain, bright shining Snake-skin, many colors glinting, so huge that all had passed upon it without knowing its beginning or ending. The Moan here gentle as soft wind.

In the wind, voices. One, to me—me who'd searched these passing faces for signs of those I love, a voice saying even to one so hardly there as me: "A face is old, old, old, a face is a great traveler, each face walking through the eras. There is no history. There is this Walk. To here. From here. Past here. For here is where we pass from dream to dream." I did not understand this or the other voices, other words, words I could not use, statements that have said themselves here always, often contradictory, here where everything agrees, sentences not meant for me, passing through me as though I was not there. Then, then . . . the music . . .

. . . which left a silence, the only true silence I've known. Nothing on the whole shining expanse of slowly undulating Snake.

Then: Mama Eve, enormous, deeply black, somber, naked, her

thick flesh in folds as though it wound around her in coils, flesh that moved upon her as though with a life of its own, fold rubbing upon fold, as though she made love to herself with every step, every gesture. Mother of Dance, from whom all songs rise. Her boundless generosity, enticing, overwhelming. Her tenderness the source of all rejoicing.

Bare expanse again.

Then: Papa Adam, Father of Words, muscles shiny-hard, black skin that gives off light, the hard forgiveness of his smile, the exacting gentleness of his knowledge. The Trickster, how easily he leaps, how high he hovers before deciding to touch down once more on his high-arched, bright white soles. He knows the Way. He leaves signs. He goads us on, and tests us as we go. He has no pity, but great mercy. His infinite concern he puts simply: "Only the truth is kind."

Their passage leaves me aching. But from somewhere, farther than I can know, their merging laughter echoed: "The world cannot be ruled!" He yelled, and to this Her flesh danced of itself by the mere effort of her breathing.

Nothing once more.

Then His voice and Her dance merged again with: "No revelation is complete. There is great cause for joy in this secret."

Papa Adam, my Father, hasn't the Bride a Groom?

His laughter! Then: "Whadaya think *you* are? Ain't nothin' around here but Brides and Grooms, son. Haven't you gotten *that* yet?"

And far, far off, across the wide plain, those Garments, by themselves, the bright Gown of the Bride, the dark Robe of the Groom, drifted above the ground, hem brushing hem, marrying everything in their path.

I am looking into a face. I do not know it.

Oh. Mine.

My thick lips. My dark, dark eyes. My misshapen nose. My face. I feel such sweetness toward it. How it very slightly smiles back. It has the calm of stone. A breathing stone. Stone that is not harder than flesh, merely slower, more deliberate. I love this face's manliness, its tenderness, so far beyond me. This is what I have worn so casually, failing to live up to it, this serious beauty.

So a soul, now I understand, sees the face with which it will be clothed, for a time.

"God *is* Time."

I am no longer on the plain. The passing of the Garments took the plain. I am nowhere, looking into a face, an impossible face; tender mouth of Kathy, high cheekbones of Danny, green eye of Elaine, gray eye of Nadine, harsh nose of Jesse. Naked of expression. Fearsome in its utter acceptance of the possibilities.

Another face. Immensely strong. There is great evil. Its voice masterly, contemptuous, matter-of-fact: "How have you escaped me?"

"This is all you were interested in, all you chose?" A close voice, angry, this. "There is so much more there! You're squandering yourself on human love!"

I want to weep.

Nadine, Danny, my son, Elaine, Kathy, Henry, Missy, Daddy —for moments I see their faces, the faces of their faces, as I had seen my own. I am filled with unbearable tenderness.

It takes forever to say good-bye.

Maybe that's what forever's for.

And every time we were, we were not.

It is time to go.

D O N ' T   G O .

It is time.

W H A T   A B O U T   M E ?

I can't stay here.

I   C A N ' T   L E A V E .

I love you so much, Danny. I thank you so much.

J E S S E ?

Good-bye.

J E S S E ?

TWO *Something Just Happened*

Something just happened. A procession of some sort?

Sometimes, where there can't be memory, there is longing, and it serves.

I am heavier, wetter, soaking in the dark of the drawer. The Gideon is empty, parched.
Poor old book.

"Jesse?"
Kathy's voice.
"Jesse? Jesse, Jesse, Jehhhhhhhhhhh-sssssssss-eeeeeee . . . *Jesse!*" And I remembered that as a child I had heard such voices, between waking and sleep, calling my name, over and over, in many ways, and I wondered when they'd stopped calling; or had they ever stopped, had I stopped hearing? "Jessejessejesse. Jesse. *Jesse.*"

I am going home.

THREE *One More Time*

The knee is a strange place. Bent, there's not much room in there for anything. I am a sliver of meat on the inside of the back of my knee. A strange place to wake up in.
Above me, the slumped weight of the sticky tower, still staring, breathing in irregular wheezes. I feel the webbed nerves like an electrified net with the power almost gone. Living is such a *job*. How can anything this huge, this disconnected, manage to live?

I oozed, a slug, up the underside of the skin of my inner thigh. And felt all the muscles of the groin pulled taut toward the hard-on. Tough to go against that pull. And what if I got trapped inside that risen thing? There'd be only one way out of it, a spurt out the tip as the rest of me died.

The rest of me just might. Something quivering in the grainy muscle fiber, something panicky that soon might be twitches, then spasms. Then, instead of wanting me back, my body would cast me out. And there would be no way then to return, I knew.

That what happened to you, Danny-O?

But Danny would never answer me again. I could feel him trying, but it was like a station on the car radio as you're driving out of range. The music fades to a static that's *almost* the music and then—just static.

I do hope you're *really* gone, man. Gone on. Or have you only melded with the walls of this motel room in Quartzsite, Arizona, your final resting place, eternal, yes, but only by-the-night? Is that the hell for those who go too far without going far enough?

Me, I crawled, oozed, sucked my way, pulling against the hard-on's pull, in a burst of panic that skidded me and slid me through the passages of this sticky membrane-tower that behaved sometimes like a man—till I stopped my skittering slide embedded in hot greasy shit.

How could it even be here? When was the last time I'd eaten? The burn of the jalapeño answered me, the peppers I'd gulped to stay awake on the drive. Loose, slushy, fiery swamp-mud, this shit, shiny, dark, phosphorescent. Now the walls of the gut began to twitch, a spasm; it was like with the prick; knowing if my bowels flushed now I would die, would disperse into oblivion, even if maybe my body would go on, this thing wouldn't be me anymore, would be spiritless; old friends would look into my eyes and think, What in hell ever happened to this guy? How many—drug-burned, booze-burned, electro-shocked, Libriumed, work-beat—how many had I looked at that way, not guessing in which tossing sleep they had given up what I knew now was rightly called the ghost?

Stench itself was sweetness now.

Shit is the smell of the soul.

That's why nobody minds their own smell.

Gut-spasms sloshed me in true shit rock 'n' roll, an intestinal shake, a belly-quake, and I knew if I somehow didn't *become* my body now, I would be spewed; so, as a slug, a cell-width thick, I sucked to the wall of the gut with all I had as shit flushed in a torrent over me and down into the seat of my pants.

My bowels hadn't squished the last shit out when my cock, aching, swollen to the point of ripping, gushed its charge so painfully, every nerve in every fiber of my flesh flashed white, glare-white, all membranes within glowed, muscles flapping like they were trying to break loose, till the last stinging drop of jism wrenched itself out. What a grief, that *that* had not gone into a woman I loved. For I knew my charge would never reach that pitch again.

But, in the aftermath, I found that I and my body were the same once more.

And my joy, for one bounded moment, knew no bounds.

F O U R *The Good People of Quartzsite*

I was in my body. I was the same size as my body. I was, give or take a few eternities, my body.

I heard—*that* was a strange sensation, made me want to cry and laugh; you're there in your own self minding your own business when something just *zap! enters* you whether you like it or not, and they call that "hearing," which I then take and bend out of shape into something called "music"—well, I heard the slowest, deepest thunderclaps I'd ever heard. Then two more. Then this awful clacking and creaking, like the building was fixing to fall down. Then huger thunders, which shook the floor. And this big white thing slowly moved into my field of vision. I could not get my body to do anything yet, could not get my eyes to focus, could just see this huge white glob and feel, not see, its she-ness.

I mean, this she-thing was huge. And moved soooooooo slooooooooooooooow.

When the next sound hit, it almost killed me. Really. Like that metal-torturing-metal sound when your very own car, with you at the wheel, is smashing into somebody else's car, and how long it seems to take for your head to hit the windshield while your ears get torn to pieces by that sound.

It was this she-thing, screaming.

Then more great thuds, and she was gone.

I knew two things: First, that if this cleaning lady had stepped in even one minute sooner, the shock would have disrupted what-all was going on and cut me off from any return and Jesse Wales would have been DOA. Second, that I'd better get some semblance of my act together or I was in big trouble. What's almost as bad as DOA is having the local badge diagnose you as CAS: Crazy As Shit.

The only thing I could trust now was the television. I couldn't remember what the rest of the room was like anymore, still couldn't see it, it was all flat-dimensioned and blurry, but a television is a television is a television and it's *supposed* to be flat and a little blurry.

That cleaning lady had let sound back in full force, so I could hear the box again, even as low as I had the volume. But now there was *the same fucking guy* in a cowboy hat pulling that lion by the leash, telling me he was personally going to stand on his head to make me a deal. I love this man. I mean, he's standing there telling me about Fords and sticker prices while the lion is looking kind of grouchy, and I am *weeping* with *love* for this man. And I want to tell him about everything that's been happening—which is when it hits me, and I mean hits, that Danny would have loved this guy, too, and that Danny was really and finally gone.

I missed him so. The tears ran down my face. I had so much to tell him.

The guy with the lion had split. It was a quiz show now.

I missed *him*, too.

But it was the cleaning lady who came back just then, with a few friends. I couldn't manage to turn my head to face them, but I could sort of see out of the corner of my eye. Her, an old guy with a beer belly, and two women behind them I could make out. They looked mostly at me, but also they kept glancing over at the quiz show.

"Inez, *he* ain't dead," the old guy said, "he's cryin'. Christ, what a stink in here!"

"He looks like a goddamned *zombie* to me." This was Inez.

"There's no such a thing," said one of the others.

"I can't take this smell," the old guy said, backing out.

"*You* can't take it!" This was Inez. "*I* gotta *clean* it."

That Bible needs watering, I wanted to tell her. But I couldn't get it out. Guess it's just as well.

"I think he's had some kinda attack." One of the others said that.

"OD, I'll bet," said a new voice.

"ODs die, don't they?" said the old guy.

"Not necessarily, I don't think," said the new voice.

"Oh, to hell with you people," said Inez. "Only drug you know a thing about is Maalox."

"Woman of the world!" the new voice said.

"She sure is," another said, "she was down to Blythe just last week."

And they all laughed. But they were *real* nervous.

"Where the hell is Evans?" Inez said.

"Here the hell is Evans. You got a scare, hey?" Evans, I guess, said.

"I did wee-wee in my pants, I got so scared."

"Jesus, Mary, and Joseph! What a specimen!" This was Evans.

He had a good smoky whiskey voice, upwards of fifty. Very, very slightly I moved my head toward him. The motion somehow snapped my eyes back into focus. Evans didn't look like a doctor, but he was standing there with an old-timey doctor's black bag. Almost bald, with the taut leather skin of the desert man. It must have been Inez right behind him, a woman about my age with a triple chin. I couldn't see the others, they were outside, blurred by the strong light.

"He's movin'!" Inez said, and the people behind her pushed to see.

"Shit," said Evans.

"Isn't that a good sign?" Inez said.

"Good for who? We don't know what we have here."

"Oh, yeah, I see what you mean."

Evans came cautiously closer now. I just stared at him. Inez followed a couple of steps behind.

"What-all's that all over him?" Inez said.

"Little of everything, looks like."

"Not hard to figure what's on his underwear," Inez said.

"Or how it got there," Evans said, and they laughed.

I said, "Fuck you."

My voice sounded like a needle scraping across a record in slow motion. But it stopped them.

The older guy was in the door. "We oughta just back out of this until we get some help."

"Can you move?" Evans said to me.

"I'm—always—moving," I said.

Inez said, "Charlie's right, Evans. Who should I call?"

"Jerry Lee Lewis," I said.

My voice wasn't any better but the words came out easier.

"Parameds down in Blythe, I guess," Evans said. "He might have had a cardiac arrest or something—"

"—'arrest' is the magic word—" Charlie said.

"—and all I got here's first-aid stuff from the quarry. I guess they better bring a straitjacket too."

That got me going a little. The blood speeded up. The snake they call my spine opened its eye somewhere at the back of my head.

"*God*, this man stinks!" Evans said.

I said, "You ever smell your own mind?"

Inez said, "I think we oughta call Steve."

"I haven't seen the sheriff's car all day, I think Steve's down to Phoenix," Charlie said.

"I don't want that on my head," Evans said, a little panicky. And if he was scared, *I* was scared. "Steve'll just walk in here, take one look and shoot him. I really don't want to have any part of that."

Evans was backing out now.

"I'll go call," Inez said, "I'll call the parameds."

"*I'll* try to get ahold of Steve," Charlie said.

"Charlie . . . " Evans said.

"Sometimes I don't understand you, Evans," Charlie said.

I said, "Isn't that wonderful, Evans? Sometimes that dippy motherfucker doesn't understand us."

And I started to cry again. Big greasy tears. Felt my face get red with them, heard the hoarse harsh sobs scrape themselves out of my throat. Ached to be held in somebody's arms. Started to slip off the chair, but first Evans and then Charlie grabbed me before I hit the floor.

"I think I'm gonna puke," Charlie said.

"Well, puke on him, not on me," said Evans, as they lifted me up, each clutching an arm, and dragged me two steps toward the bed.

It was the way they clutched my arms. And that they were dragging me backward. I feel bad about it now, because Evans, now that my eyes were better focused, looked in his sixties, and Charlie was even older; on the other hand, they weren't weaklings, and I know I didn't hurt them, couldn't, in my condition. But this surge of juice shot up my back, I stood up straight and turned as I stood, jerked one arm free of Charlie and used it to slug Evans—hit him somewhere in the chest, I think. He let go and backed up, I think more surprised than hurt, and Charlie backed up too. I was between them and the door now, and they were scared. I stood there kind of weaving and waiting for the first one to move on me, but they weren't moving on anybody. Then I—laughed! And held out my hands, palms up.

"No trouble," I said. "No trouble."

But something broke all over me from behind, something glass, too thin for the tequila bottle, must have been the vase, and it was another old man—who wasn't sixtyish, who was *old*—but he hit me between my shoulder blades, not on my head. Over-eager, I guess. So I hit Charlie. He was closest. And there I was with three old men all over me and I didn't want to hit *any* of them and I was still crying and we all did more crashing into furniture than anything else.

I don't know how it stopped. It just suddenly did. Probably everybody needed to take a deep breath at the same time. Every muscle in my legs jerked spastically. I was laughing and crying at the same time. I *loved* these guys. I really did.

They didn't love me much.

I held my hands up high, as though they were holding guns on me.

"I—don't want to—hurt—*anybody*. I swear."

Charlie was nearest the door and he ran out. Calling Steve, no doubt.

"Then steady down, mister," Evans said.

"You okay?" I said to the oldest man.

He just glared.

In their prime any one of them could have kicked my ass, that was clear.

I did the wrong thing and laughed again. I wasn't making fun, I just suddenly had the image of these grizzly dudes lynching me to the highest tree, if there even *is* a lynchably high tree anywhere near Quartzsite.

"Not at you," I said to the oldest guy, "not laughing at you."

And I felt my soul slip again. Like something was tuning in and out of my body. And I clenched my fists, my mouth, my butt, to hold myself together. I held.

The older guy made his way around me slowly and left.

Evans kept staring at me. He had lots of curly white hair at the top of his chest to the neck, and on his arms. A thin face. Stern dark eyes, but good-stern.

"Which way you headed?" Then: "No, don't tell me. Just head that way."

"I—can't. Been awake—days."

Then Evans started to gag. My smell, I know. But he swallowed it down.

"I gotta get away from you," he said, and started moving cautiously around me.

"Hey, Evans. I'm not—a criminal—or anything."

From behind me he said, "If you don't get your ass out of here, you will be."

He split.

I staggered over to the bureau, leaned on it, looked into the mirror. Oh, fuck me. No wonder these good people freaked. I'd lost maybe fifteen pounds, maybe more. My skin was the color of wax paper. My face all bruises and gauntness and black-gray whiskers. There was *lots* of muck stuck in the corners of my eyes, even on the lashes, caked, pasty. Everything trembled oh, so slightly and visibly. My hair was matted with all those sweats. Somehow, seeing myself made my smell much, much harder to take.

I pushed off from the mirror, ordered my legs to walk, left that room forever.

F I V E   *Things I Should Do*

Stepping into that desert sun was like stepping into a microwave. Every cell on the surface of my skin felt pressed down by the heat. Nobody was in front of the motel cabins. Good sign? Bad sign? The light made every surface everywhere unbearably bright. RVs, trailers, passing cars, store signs. Heatwaves rose off the sharp-edged desert hills.

My Chevy Malibu was parked in front of the cabin. It seemed such a long time since I'd seen it, but it was probably only twelve–fourteen hours. I'd pulled in sometime around four; judging by the light, it must be around six. There were two–three hours of light left.

Things I should do. Should check the radiator and oil—I'd run twenty-odd hours the day before, not stopping but for gas. There was a slow transmission leak, I should check that. The old '69, dented all over, paint scratched and chipped, looked like I'd look if I suddenly turned into a car. But I'd better get out of this lot before I checked anything.

Without thinking, I quickly opened the car door, got in, closed it. The Mojave had baked that car all day. It must have been one hundred fifty degrees inside. The closest, hottest heat I'd ever known. I was, literally, cooking. My heart fluttered, skipped, my chest hurt like hell. But I was too shocked with the heat to open the door. Yet not too shocked to decide that Something was overdoing it a little.

Which pissed me off. I addressed the Whatever: "I've learned —all—I can—for right now. Whoever, Whatever—You're pushing it. I ain't asking mercy. But You kill me like this, you ain't proving —a fucking—thing."

I guess it was the anger, or maybe It heard me, but I got the strength to open the car door and roll off the seat. The parking lot's heat, which had seemed so brutal when I'd stepped out of the motel, seemed just about room temperature now.

My heart settled down. I picked myself up. *Now* I could worry about whether those people had called the cops, and whether ol' Steve was down to Phoenix or not. I opened the doors, rolled down the windows, got in, started the engine. It sounded good. I didn't owe any money—knew when I'd checked in at the night window that I'd sleep past check-out time, had paid for two days. Pulled slowly out of the parking lot, onto the access road that used to be the old highway and that went through what there was, all there was, of Quartzsite.

Turned back the way I'd come.

There was lots of traffic on the access road, going real slow. Seems Quartzsite has, or is, kind of a permanent crafts fair. There's every roadside booth you can imagine—jewelry, fossils, hats, leather, baskets, tamales, pop—and behind each one an RV or a mobile home. Everybody, on the mile or so of road that is Quartzsite, seems to live in those. I didn't see one actual house. A little sign said LIBRARY and pointed down a gravel driveway to a tin-roof building the size of a two-car garage. You got to respect a bunch of people who end up on top of a range in the high desert to watch the world go by till it figures out what to do with itself. They were Apocalypse People too, in their own way. Fact, if there's anything left of New York or LA after the shit hits the fan, they'll probably look something like Quartzsite. Maybe I could settle in a place like this, open me a fossil stand.

My fingers were doing little twitches separate of each other— like a player piano, how weird it is to watch the jerky keys move without you. I was one big ache. Had to *think* about every move. "Okay, turn the wheel now, right, now brake a little, okay, give it some gas, no, not too much." That bad. Figured I had an hour, two at the outside, till sleep hit me. No way I could drive the drive I had to drive.

I figured they'd call the state cops if ol' Steve wasn't around, and maybe even if he was. No all-points or anything drastic. But they'd get my plate number from the motel register, determine I wasn't wanted, except for the misdemeanor complaint ol' Charlie would surely file. The late-day/early-evening shift would get the complaint on the misdemeanor sheet, which half the guys wouldn't bother to read. (I know some state cops in Texas, and it's probably the same routine here.) All they'd see in the dark is headlights anyway, though sometimes, when they got nothing else to do, they check out plates with infrareds from their speed-trap nooks. But my chances were good, especially if I got about two car-lengths in front of a semi and cruised there. I don't have a front plate.

So if I could get clear of Quartzsite and ol' Steve, pull off a back road and sleep four–five hours, then I could drive till dawn, cool out in a motel till dark, and get out of the state the next night.

At the south end of town there was a do-it-yourself car wash with berths for two cars. A blessing: It was at an angle from the access road, so passers-by couldn't see into it. I pulled in, turned on that hose with its hot jet of soap water, got under it, then the clear cold water. Twice. The water burned, even the soap burned, and the jet hurt, but it woke me some and cleaned me good when I'd taken off my clothes and gave myself another round. Then got a change out of the trunk—faded jeans and a soft white cotton shirt —changed in the car.

There was a donut shop across the lot from the car wash, The Camel's Hump or something like that—a cartoon on its wall showed how around the turn of the century they'd experimented around here with how camels would take to the Mojave. (The camels hadn't.) Inside it was little-old-lady heaven. I mean, run by, and full of, little old ladies. Some desert mamas with those scary-clear eyes, faces all leathery. One real fat old broad, face-flesh hanging off her skull like it was a big tit with a face painted on it, and a few of your church-type old women.

"Can I help you, young man?" Tinted-blue permed hair. No color left in her eyes. Thin as a rail.

"That ain't a young man, that's a 'sir,' " the fat one said.

"Why, Carol!" the first one said. "Don't be flirtin'.'"

And everybody laughed.

"Ma'am," I said, "three black coffees, please, large, and, I guess, six of those glazed donuts there."

"You a'right, son?" the blue-haired one said. I felt this rush of gratitude toward her, wanted to tell her everything, make her understand.

"Yes, ma'am."

Fat Carol said, "Well, you're shakin' like a dog tryin' t'shit a peach pit."

"Carol! Stop showin' off!" A church-type sitting with her laughed.

"Y'a'a'right? Y'sure?"

"Slight case of white-line heebie-jeebies, ma'am. Be fine once I get some a that coffee."

"Trucker, right?" the blue-haired one said. "Oughta get out of that profession while you're more or less young. Bad for the kidneys. Prostate, too."

"Thank you, ma'am," I said when she gave me the take-out bag. "I'll consider your advice."

"Not if you're a trucker you won't," she said kindly.

I winked at Fat Carol as I left. She winked back.

Yeah, I like it here, except for ol' Steve. Not a bad place to end up.

The first bite of that first glazed donut was like biting into a sweet white cloud—the sweetest, best bite of anything I think I've ever had. So rich it almost came up on me right then, but I kept it down and gulped another. They don't have these in Russia, a trucker told me once.

S I X *Long-Distance Call*

My car still out of sight, parked behind the car wash, I walked down the access road about a hundred yards to a phone booth. My leg muscles wriggled all over their bones. Called Kathy's number collect. No answer. Then, on a hunch, I called my own.

It got picked up on the first ring.

"Jesse?" It was Kathy. My eyes teared up.

"Yeah."

"Thank God."

"Good idea."

"What?" I said nothing. She: "Nadine's—"

"I'm very, very glad you're there, Kathy. Kathy Smith."

"—Nadine's lost it."

"Lost what?"

"Her fucking *mind.*"

Should have known, should have known, should have known. That I wouldn't be cracking up alone.

Nobody does, in the long run.

Kathy said, "Did you hear me? She's lost it, she's crazy, *very* crazy. And the boy's scared to death. He'll be crazy soon, if he isn't already. Me and Dawg have been calling everywhere for you. Where are you?"

"Arizona. Near to California."

Silence a moment. Then, very tired: "How far is that?"

"Twelve hundred miles, more or less."

"Too far," she said so soft. Then: "Fly back."

"No."

"How can you say *no?*"

The suddenness of my clarity amazed me. I knew, but sure didn't know how, that it had something to do with being up there with the light fixture.

Said, "I get off the plane in—where is she, Austin, Lubbock, Baton Rouge?"

"She was right here in your room till last night. Now they're gone, Baton Rouge or Shreveport, I think. She said both and it could be either or elsewhere. I just called Baton Rouge, she's not there, not yet, anyway."

"Right. So I get off a plane in Austin or Baton Rouge and *then* what? I ain't got cards. What if I gotta chase her from Baton Rouge to Shreveport and back? What if she's been popped and I gotta steal my kid from a institution? Your car won't *make* Austin to Baton

Rouge and back, I heard its engine. I take a plane, I'm helpless. This is rich, man. There's even some question about me getting clear of Arizona. The *po*-lice may object, you dig?"

"Oh, Jesse."

Evans passed in a pickup, slow, staring right at me. My heart beat like crazy. He didn't have any expression for me to read. Just stared as he passed.

I told Kathy there was no way I could drive from Quartzsite to Baton Rouge in the condition I was in. Not alone. Needed sleep soon, real sleep. I was a couple of hours out of Phoenix. Asked her to fly there, the next plane she could get. From Phoenix it's about a twenty-hour drive straight through to Baton Rouge; we could take shifts and be there the morning after tomorrow. Better getting there late than getting there powerless.

"Except—get a round-trip plane ticket. Case *I* get popped before I can pick you up. Hang around a reasonable time. If I don't show you'll know I'm in jail. If you can't make my bail you'll need that return ticket."

"If I do this, I have *no* money left."

"So?"

"I don't *believe* you!"

"You want me to beg?"

"You already are." Then: "I don't mean this as any kind of blackmail. I'll come regardless. For the kid, if nothing else. But I gotta know. 'Cause it's *stupid* to do this for somebody who isn't—well—my man."

"Then do it." I heard her inhale that. "I mean, I am. Do I even have to say that?"

"Oh, yeah."

And she hung up.

I could just see her, sitting on my piano bench, the phone in her lap, looking from photo to photo on my wall, seeing my life pass before her eyes, clutching the phone with white knuckles, not knowing herself if she was being weak or strong.

Evans passed again in his weathered white Ford pickup, going the other way. Our eyes locked as he passed. Still couldn't read him. He was keeping an eye on me, maybe to protect me, maybe to turn me in, maybe just to try to figure me out.

The heat beat. The first guy who used that expression knew what he was talking about. It really has a beat, a pulse, heat this bad. I wondered, as I walked back to my car, was there a way to get that into my music. The first thought like that I'd had since Mexico. Then wondered should I quit music. I'd *be* a pretty good trucker. Then was amazed at myself—never crossed my mind before, to quit music. And felt for the first time a deep shadowy sadness that I knew we'd all feel more and more as the years went on and we got farther and farther from that first irresistible sound that had changed us all. Had brought us—me, at least—down such a strange road.

Got lost in that thought, couldn't keep my mind on my emergency, I was that tired. Stopped at one of the fossil stands, looking for something to bring Little Jesse. Bought him a rock he could hold in one hand, a rock with the indent of a small fish. There are thousands in this desert.

Evans's white Ford pickup followed my Chevy out of town. Made me dizzy to keep glancing at it in my rearview, that's how tired I was. I saw my hands on the wheel but didn't feel them. hardly felt my leg on the pedal, had to keep looking at the speedometer to stop from going too fast or too slow, had no sense of the speed. And the highway seemed hundred-laned, wide as the world. My mouth was all I felt for sure. Teeth sticky with sweet glaze.

P A R T
E L E V E N

Some Disease of
the Dream

I walk for miles
On the highway
But that's just my way
Of saying I love you
          —Patsy Cline

O N E   *Sore Finger Road*

Sore Finger Road's about forty-five minutes southeast of Quartzsite on I-10. Somewhere along there, Evans turned his pickup around and went back. I didn't notice just when. I do think he was trying to make sure ol' Steve wouldn't do whatever it is he was famous for without a witness around. There were some stories worth knowing back there, and, willy-nilly, I'd become one. It'll no doubt go the rounds of Quartzsite's two bars, and a few of the bars in Blythe and Phoenix; some people'll like Evans for his attitude and some'll turn on him. I admired that good man, and hoped, sleepily, that I 'd be worthy of his care.

Turned off on Sore Finger Road, drove a few miles down that two-lane, pulled off on a dirt road, then off that, parked behind some boulders for shade, and slept. Woke shivering under a million-starred desert sky, fearful, having no idea of the time. Headed for Phoenix.

T W O   *Too Pure*

Elaine, if you do the image *too* pure—it'll kill you. You've really got to do it . . . just . . . pure . . . enough. Because it's stronger than you are. Even though you're who it came through.

But sometimes too pure *is* all that's pure enough, and then you take the heat or the heat takes you.

THREE *Loving Him*

I used to think that I didn't ask to know any of this. Now I know that I let Danny ask for me. He asked for all of us. He called that loving us. And the letting him ask, we called that loving him. And it was.

FOUR *A Home*

Those thoughts were just vague nudges on the drive to Phoenix. Took lots more drives to get them clear.

It was still barely dark when I got there. Parked on a side street, called a cab for the airport, just in case of cops. No sense blowing it now. The cabdriver offered me a swig of wine, but I declined.

In the airport I found Kathy asleep on a molded plastic chair, her head pillowed on her purse, an overnight bag on her lap. White sneakers, jeans, a dark blue blouse, a bright yellow scarf tied around her neck. (Got flashes off that, but couldn't quite remember yet.) Her short dark hair shiny clean. I sat across from her and just watched her sleep awhile, loving the oval of her finely featured face, lovely small mouth, lips pressed in sleep. So fresh and sad.

Went and got her coffee from a machine, sat in the chair next to her and nudged gently.

"Oh," she said. Her smile was as weary as it could be and still be a smile. "That for me? Thanks." Then: "Jesse! You look—dead."

"I maybe was."

She sipped her coffee, looking around us carefully without seeming to. I remembered then that she knew what it was to have

396

reason to fear cops, and realized, as I'd been too tired to in Quartz-site, the courage it took for her even to get close to the possibility of a bust.

"Are we in trouble?" she said.

"Could be. Could be not. Hard to tell." Then: "Were you worried I wouldn't show up?"

"Actually, on the plane I tried to spend some time worrying about myself. We better go, hey?"

"Kathy. Thanks for coming."

"Isn't that what you say to an audience at the end of a set? 'I wanna thank y'all for comin' out t'night'? I'm not an audience, Jesse. If you don't know that, I'm making an—impressive mistake —even by my standards."

I didn't know what to say.

"This is my twenty-five-thousand-feet-in-the-sky speech. I know you need somebody, but I don't know if you need me. And if you don't need *me*, in particular, you have to be straight with me about that. I'll help you through this drive, but then that's it." Then: "Listen to *me*, the girl who came to Phoenix—without the bread for a return ticket! But, Jesse—I don't believe in return tickets."

"Neither do I. I don't know what to say to you, except—I've never been so deep-down glad to see anybody. *Anybody*."

"I haven't either."

"I may have to take my kid."

"You think I don't know that? I like your kid."

The hems of the Bride's Gown and the Groom's Robe brushed us lightly as they floated past.

The first real memory I had of what I'd seen.

"You're trembling," she said.

"It's getting so I hardly notice. We'd better go."

We didn't touch till I'd told the cabdriver where to drive and he pulled out. And then we held each other, gently, lightly, with immense relief. This was home. This holding. We both knew it, and that we'd neither of us been there before. Been a lot of places, but not home. For those moments it was a spacious, welcoming, nervously new place—like when you've just signed the lease on an apartment, and it's still empty but it's yours, and you're standing in it for the first time alone.

FIVE *Even the Border Has a Border*

I knew the land I was sleeping through. Tucson, then passing the exit to Tombstone, the climb and descent of the last part of the Rocky Mountains spine, called by other names down here but one with that ridge of mountains that surfaces here and there like a long snake, from Canada to Mexico and on south. Passing the Route 666 exit. All those backward question marks for The Thing, one of those weird places where the rocks do some weird stuff with magnetism, like gravity going backward, as though the planet were winking at you. The New Mexico border, and that sign somewhere in Cochise country, "We Haul Water Ten Miles—Please Don't Waste Any." Into New Mexico. What's left of Lordsburg, the town in that John Wayne movie that they're trying to get to in the stagecoach. Over the Great Divide. On to the Texas border. Eight–nine hours of rolling sixty-mile-an-hour sleep. Kathy didn't wake me till El Paso.

"Did like you said, waited for two convoying semis, planted us a couple of car-lengths between them, and Arizona was a breeze."

"I heard singing," I said.

"You heard singing, you heard talking, you heard lots. Kind of experimenting with how it would be to lay my life out for you. It was sweet, being alone and not alone at the same time. Isn't that what everybody wants?"

"I just want whatever comes after Baton Rouge. I want what comes next."

"I hope you do," she said softly. Then: "You been thinking about Elaine?"

I didn't have any words yet for what had happened to me in Quartzsite—I hadn't even begun to remember most of it, as though my mind was numb from all that had happened, so I said the simplest true thing, which was not even half true, and answered: "Yes."

She let that ride. We were where El Paso's outskirts become

city sprawl. Could see across the Rio Grande to the Mexican shanties. I had her pull off and take this street I know south. It crosses the Rio Grande—which is just a muddy stream here—but the border checkpoint isn't till about a half-mile farther, so you can be on the other side of the river yet not technically in Mexico. But the other side *is* Mexico. You feel it as you cross. You're in both countries and not really in either. I like to pull off the side of the road there just past the bridge. There's houses around, if you want to call them that; a convenience store down the way; kids, mostly Mexican, some black, at the river; and dogs. Anybody you see older than a kid is *really* older. Most everybody here over the age of fifteen has the eyes of old people.

I'd just wanted to be with Kathy a moment in Mexico. See if I missed anyone.

I didn't.

We watched a few Mexican kids playing in the knee-deep river. The way they called each other's names sounded like bird-cries.

"About Elaine," I said. "Stuff—happened to me—up in Quartzsite."

"Besides losing about twenty pounds?"

"Yeah. I—don't know what to say about it, yet, or how, or even if I *remember*. I . . ."

"What, Jesse?"

"When it got over—I called you. Didn't occur to me to call anyone else. That's the way it is. That's the way it's gonna be. I'm as sure of that as I've ever been of anything."

"Which means not much?"

But she said that smiling.

"That's the *really* weird part. I *am* sure."

We reached for each other's hands. Clasped hard. Watched the kids play in the river. It felt so quiet and calm between us. A sentence rose up in me, and I said it:

"Even the border has a border."

"I don't know what that means."

"I don't know either. It's the kind of thing Danny would have said. Then he'd give half a laugh and forget all about it, but you wouldn't."

"Where is he?"

"Back in Quartzsite, as far as I know. There's a motel room back there—I shoulda burned it down. Probably would have, if I'd thought of it. Free him, if he'd got stuck in those walls. Good idea in any case. People are gonna stop there and, because of me, or because of *something*, some of those people are going to have dreams that weren't meant for them, and there'll be those who aren't strong enough for those dreams."

"You can't mosey around the Southwest burning down RVs and motels whenever you feel like it."

"I guess not." And then: "I'm—probably never going to know. About Danny. That's what's hard to take. I heard the voice, *you* heard stuff, and . . ."

And nothing I could think of. But there on the border of the border I started actually to remember what had happened to me, in some detail and sequence instead of just high points and flashes. I can't say for sure, but I strongly suspect that if I hadn't had Kathy to tell it to, I would have lost it or it would have faded. Or—I wouldn't, mightn't, have had to live up to it, like I've felt since.

Though I couldn't tell her for some time. Still, I lived with knowing I had to.

"You okay to drive?" she said.

"Nobody ever used to have to ask me that. But—yeah, I'm okay. And I'm really, really hungry. I think it's the first time I've been hungry since we met."

"Let's get some Mexican food."

S I X *Across the Pecos*

She woke a ways into West Texas, as we crossed the Pecos. For miles there'd been no house, no light at all but an oil rig a few miles off-road lit bright as a bare light bulb. And here and there a burn-off: a hole in the ground, raw oil flaming out of it about the size of a big campfire, a greasy smell on the air for so many miles you almost get used to it.

Cloud cover. No light but my brights, and sometimes the shining eyes of deer by the road. The saying is that when you can see the deer ahead, it's already too late.

"Were you scared, I mean bad scared, up in Lubbock?"

"Plenty," Kathy said, "but I've been scared so long that getting a little more scared, about something I'd always sort of suspected anyhow, didn't seem like such a big deal—after it was over, anyway."

"How do you mean, suspected?"

"Just suspected. From life. And from—before I got stupid and busted, I was an anthropology major and—"

"I don't even know what that is—"

"Just one more thing that invents itself as it goes along, like everything else. Anyway—that stuff sort of reaches out to you all the time in little ways. Like in traffic, when you suddenly turn your head and look at someone looking at you. How do you know to do that? Happens every day. Nobody gives it a second thought. We just got smack-dab in the middle of that stuff, I guess."

Jackrabbits frozen in our lights by the side of the road. Deer-eyes shining. A crushed something, bloody, with a tiretrack through it.

A few dark miles later she said, "Something I gotta tell you. Elaine and I were on the same plane back to Austin. We sat together. Yeah, I thought that'd grab ya. She cried the whole time. She cried and I held her. She'd been so shook, when all was said and done, she couldn't even drive her car back. I almost told her about that light dimming when she coughed in her sleep, then didn't think that would do her much good. I'm gonna tell you that while I was holding her and stroking her hair I even wanted her a little. *Just* a little, don't panic. *That* made me feel close to you, you know? Understand something about you. She said she was sorry she tried to hurt me, and I believed her. Told her I didn't much blame her—I mean, when I suggested maybe shoving a broomstick up her ass, I wasn't quite kidding, was I? She told me about doing the image pure enough—and it surprised me she did. I doubt she'd ever told a woman that stuff before. Said how she'd never been careful, that now she'd have to be, she'd just have to. And she didn't know if she could be who she was and be careful at the same time, and *that* scared her more than anything. She seemed so alone, I felt sorry about her. But why I'm telling you, I thought of something as I held her and she cried, her plight taught me it, and I think we're gonna need it. How it came was: You can't build a house *on* the river, you gotta build it *by* the river. We gonna try to do that, Jesse Wales? Build a house by the river? I am."

"Johns meet her at the airport?"

"He did, yeah. She ran to him like a little girl. And he took her in his arms like she was one, too."

When you see the deer, Johns, it's *really* too late. But I guess you've known that lots longer than me.

SEVEN *Like a Saturday Night*

I thought of Nadine—feared for her and the boy; feared, more, that I'd be no use to them again. Thought of Danny in that Great King Bee Diner in the Sky. Of Henry, cancer gnawing on him like a dog on a bone. Of Elaine, wondering if she'd ever get to her own personal Quartzsite, where she was headed just as surely as I'd been. All my teachers were silent, now that I knew for sure that teachers were what they'd been. And I had little to teach in return except maybe that the parts of us that are most alive are the parts that touch the dead. That dead isn't dead at all but is of a vaster world, that *this* world is like a small island sticking up out of the vast ocean of that world. And that to be wet with that water, shaking like a cold, dripping dog, is one of the few ways to find out a damn thing. But I guess my teachers had always known that, one way or another. I was just catching up. A late bloomer. On Interstate 10. In the middle of nowhere, as usual. The fragrant night air swirling through the windows at sixty, wheel firm in my hand, every muscle still aching, but softly now, and with hardly a twitch.

But not quite as usual. Not at all. Not with this Kathy here, curled half-asleep on the seat, so easy yet alert, like a cat. And that's when the first image came, quietly, insistently. Do me pure enough, it said.

My voice started doing a slow two-step Danny had loved to sing, *I'm goin' out where the lights don't shine so bright*
I'm goin' out where the lights don't shine so bright
When I get back
You can treat me like a Saturday night

It was good to have a song in my mouth, it washed out some acidy tastes still left from Quartzsite; it woke Kathy and she joined in on that chorus, though she couldn't carry a tune on her back. The image was having its way with us, me beating time soft on the wheel, as I pulled over easy on the shoulder, cut the engine, cut the lights, and our voices wavered in the wide long dark.

I got out of the car. Kathy followed, humming now over the crickets and the wind and the chinks and rustlings of the engine as it cooled. A revving engine, something with a lot of power and still far off, was coming from the east. I held her and we started moving in half-time, slow four-four, *Treat me like a Saturday night*, and we danced pressed together on the eastbound lane of the Interstate as something sped toward us on the westbound side, something the image (not me) had somehow known was coming to complete it, something low and dark and fast that caught us in its brights and held us there, but too briefly, at such speed, for that driver to be sure anything had been seen.

E I G H T *Over the Great River*

Kathy woke me over the great river, on the Mississippi bridge to Baton Rouge. The air was just this side of being water. The windshield caked with splattered bugs. I'd resisted waking for miles, because I could feel that granddaddy swamp all around, could hear in the tire-sound how high the road was raised off what passes for ground in these parts.

The air held its light differently here, was saturated with it, the way a sponge is with water. A thick, hazy light. We drove slow through Baton Rouge, Kathy at the wheel, me giving directions. The faces on the street were different from Texas, different from Arizona, not more relaxed but more distracted. Nobody moves quickly in Louisiana.

We stopped at a Woolworth's to get what I needed for the new image that had come to me as I lay with my eyes closed through the swamps. It's like how the music comes through you as you play. You don't feel it's yours. You just try to be clear about what it wants you to do. You don't know what it means, you don't know why it's there, or how it's going to hit anybody. Like, maybe the image on the Interstate had come as much for whoever was in that passing car as for us. You don't know what the connections are. You don't know whether images speak to images Out There. You just take the weight, and do it.

Danny had done them without knowing he'd done them, or without letting himself know. That was probably—was certainly, as it turned out—pretty dangerous. Not knowing, he hadn't taken the weight. You *got* to take the weight. Elaine, she'd forced them. That was *real* dangerous. She'd gone out of her way and called them down to her, not let them just come of their own. So she always got more than she'd asked for, more than she'd known what to do with, stuff coming through that damn near killed her and everyone around her. Henry worked on another level altogether, and I wasn't close to being able to think about it, and might never be. That level likely would never be my job, and that was just fine. You take the weight that's measured to you. The images know better than you do.

And if they're coming at you and you *don't* take them, I suspect that the Lord spews you out of his mouth.

NINE *It Most Certainly Seems*

It most certainly seems
Some disease of the dream
Has been goin' round
                    —Terry Allen

When we got to Nadine's, her big blue '73 Chevy was in the driveway. The right side had been crushed in from the passenger's door on back.

No. No, no, no, no, no.

A clean fear stripped me of everything but: No.

But Kathy went straight to Nadine's car and looked in the front seat.

"There's no blood, Jesse."

We walked up to the porch. I started to use my key, but the door was open. Nadine was sprawled across the couch as though she'd fallen on it, out cold. Little Jesse sat on the floor in front of her, hugging his knees, staring at the TV, with the sound just barely on.

Calmly as you please he said, "Are you growing a beard, Daddy?"

"When you forget to cut it, it kind of grows of itself." I sounded calm, but I was only imitating him. "How you doin', son?"

"You look like Jesus."

I took him in my arms.

"I just look like a guy who needs a shave real bad."

I hugged him hard, but it was like hugging a rag doll. His body had simply turned off.

"Hiya," Kathy said to him.

"Hello," he said.

"You hungry?" she said.

He nodded yes.

"Show me where the things are in the kitchen, okay? I'll bet your ma's hungry too."

He looked down at the floor when she said that.

Kathy said, "Come on, show me. You can help me."

I shut the TV. Sat on the piano stool. Ran my fingers lightly over the keys. Played a couple of high notes, soft. One low note, softer. Tried to think of the price my kid was paying for all our wanderings. A far bigger price than mine, for sure. And Nade—all I could do for her was the image, give her one more memory of us all, step into the dream with her. And let her know, if I could get through, that the kid was coming with me, and I'd try to be good for him.

For sitting on the piano stool, looking at her unconscious slump, I knew she was gone, and I knew where. Why shouldn't I know? Weren't we all the same person? Hadn't I at least learned that? And the world we drove through, we were either way ahead of it or way behind; it didn't matter which, but for us that world was just something by the side of the road.

So I went to the car, got the crate of candles I'd bought at the Woolworth's, and settled in to wait for twilight.

Soon Kathy'd cooked up some bacon and eggs, refried beans, country potatoes.

"It's weird," Kathy said, "this house is full of food. But can you imagine her shopping this week? The potatoes were seasoned and everything."

We ate. I told the kid that his ma was real sick. He said that she'd said she'd have to go away soon, and he was to "sit tight." And he'd been doing just that when we'd walked in, sitting *real* tight.

"She say anything about me?"

He looked down at his plate. Not about to rat on his ma.

Kathy said, "Want to come back with us? Back to Texas?"

His eyes got full of tears but he just kept shoveling in the food.

When he was done he looked up at Kathy.

"What should I call you?"

"How about Katherine? I really like that name, and hardly anybody calls me that."

"Does he call you that?"

"Not yet, but if you do, maybe he'll start."

"Okay."

"Why don't you pack his stuff," I said, taking her aside. "I mean—I'm not trying to order you around or anything, but he can hardly look at me. Better, probably, you take him upstairs and pack with him."

"We don't know yet if we have to, do we?"

"Second thoughts?"

"No. I just don't have the right to say anything about that boy," Kathy said.

"Well. I got to. And you do if I say you do."

"You can't take that back and forth, you know."

"I know."

"Your life isn't going to be the same. At all."

" 'Bout time, don't you think?"

"That's up to you."

"Yeah. *Yeah.* I guess it is." Then: "What about you?"

"I signed up. I'm gonna spend the rest of the next part of my life finding out why. No way for me to find out but by living it out. I don't think about everything like you guys do. I mull a lot, but that's different. Do you know you're an intellectual? Well, you are. Who'da thunk it? I *love* you, Jesse. That's why I'm here. Do you love me?"

"I can't say—those things—in this house."

"No. I guess you can't."

"I'm sorry."

"You don't have to be."

We held each other. And how, in our holding, we accepted each other's need—felt very good. Then she and Little Jesse went upstairs. She came down a little later.

"What's he doing?" I said.

"Trying to decide what to take—the toys."

"Did he say what happened to the car?"

"He said he doesn't remember. Jesse, I think he's glad—just that somebody's taking charge, sort of."

We sat around. For the first time since Quartzsite I wanted a drink. I let it pass.

It passed, but slowly.

407

Twilight came. The boy was asleep. It was time. And now that it *was*, it didn't seem like such a great big deal; why, lots of people were probably doing this very thing all across America at this moment. I felt silly, and driven, and trembly, but I tried to put all that behind me and do it pure. Lit candles all over: living room, kitchen, bathroom, dining room, the whole downstairs, with Kathy—Katherine—going behind me putting plates and things under them and making sure they were away from curtains and such. I hadn't asked her, she just thought of it. Kathy didn't question; not that she was just following, but she was taking it as it came at her, quietly judging each moment before she went on to the next. So far, it was all right with her, this image.

The house flickered wonderfully with candlelight.

I went up to the kid's room and carried him down. He didn't stir. Laid him on the floor in the living room, put a pillow under him. Kathy and I sat on the floor, me by the piano, she by the door. And we simply watched Nadine. A watching like a prayer, though I don't think either of us knew the first thing about prayer. And, watching, I realized this image had reached out to me from Nadine's dream back in New Orleans all that time ago, the castle lit with candles that were eyes of flame. When she'd seen that the eyes were donated by living people, she had run. And I'd heard her dream from mine.

The eyes in the flames weren't hard to see.

I'd gone over again—but never so gently, never so calmly, as this. The image tuned in and out of how it looked and how it *really* looked. As though the image itself were flickering in the room.

I told Kathy about Nadine's dream.

"You two could really listen in on each other's dreams?"

"It just happened, every now and again. Like one night I had a dream about Ricky Nelson, of all people. But that night he was singing 'Traveling Man' in my dream and 'Lonesome Town' in hers. That kind of thing."

"I'm really sorry you two didn't make it. I really am."

T E N   *Sweet Fires*

It was a long time before Nadine stirred. Straightened herself out, sat up, eyes still closed. Sat that way a bit, turned her head this way and that, but you felt she was as aware as a blind person that people were near her and that the room had changed.

I said her name as softly as I could.

She opened her eyes.

"Oooooooooooooooo," she sort of sang, as she looked around. Even soft, her voice was sandpaper, scratchy and rough, its smoothness ripped, its roundness shattered. She must have spent days screaming to get her voice into that shape. What had they been through?

"These are . . . sweet . . . fires. Not like . . . you-know-where."

"Nadine, Nadine."

"And lookee there!"

She peered very hard at the candles.

"Oooooooooooooooo."

Then looked over at Kathy. "I never . . . met your sister . . . before. I always . . . resented . . . that. 'Cause . . . I never had one. A sister-in-*law* . . . is nice to have. You gonna . . . give me a kiss?"

Kathy got up and kissed Nadine on the cheek, then on the hair. Nadine took Kathy's hand, looked into her palm, and kissed it.

"You should . . . visit more. Everybody . . . waits . . . too long." Then: "So! Danny's-in-Hell. My-Jesus-sent-my-Danny-down-to-Hell."

She said it singsong like a jingle.

"And-I-can-go-there-when-I-want. Permission's-been-granted. Per-MISSION. P'mission f'm'mission. But . . . takes time. Takes . . . so much . . . eternity . . . to fill up . . . just a little bit . . . of time. This old earth . . . soaks up eternity . . . like a sponge." Then, to me, just as conversationally as you please: "And God is NOT time, Jesse. The idea!"

"I just heard it," I said. "Don't mean I agreed with it. Don't even *get* it."

"Is that so?"

Kathy looked at me, questioning, but I just squeezed her hand.

Nadine jingled "My-Jesus-sent-my-Danny-down-to-Hell" a few more times. Then, clear as a bell, straight at me in her old way: "We'll leave when the candles are all down, right? Good. And anything you wanna do is okay. Just see Little Jesse don't forget his mama. And—don't scream at him. Don't. Your sister will know what to do, won'tchya, hon?"

"Sure, Nadine. I'll try real hard."

"These are . . . *sweet* . . . fires. I'll remember. I'll . . . try to, Jesse. That's what you want, right? I can't promise, but . . ."

"You just try."

"I *said* so, didn't I?"

"Yeah."

"That's all, then."

She sank off the sofa, sat next to her sleeping son. She stroked his hair and hummed her jingle some.

C O D A

Slowly
Slowly

Gonna take my life
Right outta my mind
Gonna lay it down
On the border line
      —Terry Allen

ONE A Formality
Six Months Later

It was strange to wake in so white a place, as white as that room was; white walls, white linoleum, white bedding, white hospital smock, the shade drawn on the window glowing white with the bright day outside.

All kind of wires and tubes attached to me. My heart making squiggly lines across a TV screen. Katherine in a chair by the bed whenever I opened my eyes—usually with the sketch pad in her lap, drawing me. "I had it set in my head," she told me later, "that you *couldn't* die while I was drawing you. So I sat there and drew you and drew you."

Many pages of a kind of haunted calm. Just my face. Sleeping, mostly. The face of my face. The face she saw deepest in me, that she loved. A face I wanted to have but still only half recognized. And to open my eyes to *her* face—fierce, apprehensive, softly dark. Eyes so bright when she'd look into mine.

Haunted calm was how we all looked, I guess—me, Katherine, Jes. We shared the vibe so much, it was that more than anything that made us a family.

When Jes saw me in the hospital he was real curious about all the paraphernalia and only cried the first time. I knew I would live awhile yet, so Jes believed me when I told him. It had only been about six months since we'd gotten him from Baton Rouge, but it seemed lots longer. I was a little short of forty. When Dawg visited he gave me the cheery news that the average life span of a jazz musician was forty-two. Said, "They don't think it's worth their time to figure it out for you honky-tonk heroes."

"Club owners live forever, right?"

"Jack Ruby was a club owner."

But mostly, that week, I just felt like I was floating in the whiteness of that room, knowing my heart hadn't so much attacked as shifted gears—that, after Quartzsite, this was just kind of a formality.

T W O   *Dream Time*

Elaine followed me in my dreams. Every few weeks—sometimes every few nights—she'd be there. Once she came with her hair on fire, head-hair and cunt-hair—the Burning Bush, indeed. Sometimes she'd squeeze up out of things—bathtub drains, toilet bowls, air-nozzles on tires, like she was a cartoon. Sometimes it'd be almost normal. Once we took a very long walk in the rain, talking, talking, and only after we'd walked a long time did she start to dissolve in the rain down to her shiny bones. I looked down at my hands and they were bones too. But not like it was morbid, more like we'd become two of those jaunty Day of the Dead skeleton-dolls come to life. And our bones had musical qualities, made chimelike sounds when our hands touched.

In the dreams she always looked as she did when we first met. In life, she got fat—almost with a vengeance, willfully, it seemed like, as though if she could conceal that weird beauty of hers she'd have some real control over her life. The marvelous redness of her hair went metallic because she was dying it to keep out the gray. So in real life she seemed dreamlike too, unreal, as though the added flesh was just a veil she could whip off anytime she really wanted to.

The dreams she starred in tended to get less weird over time. We'd talk in them, or meet up with each other on city streets strangely deserted at high noon, and it was like all we had to do was look at each other and secrets would be exchanged. While in more or less real life we seemed to make a point of not running into each other—I didn't go out much but to play my own gigs, and she'd rarely come to them, and when she did she'd stand way back, at the bar, her eyes gleaming as ever out of that thickened face. And I'd wonder how I looked to her, my hair still long, but much thinner, with lots of gray now—it came on fast after Quartzsite—but skinnier, because of Katherine's health-food cooking and having had to cut way down on the booze. So it was like Elaine and I were seeing each other in carnival mirrors.

My favorite dream of her is the one where I go into that old church up in Chimayo, New Mexico. It's a small church that the

Spanish built hundreds of years ago, and it has "healing dirt," which cures the sick. Folks make pilgrimages to it from all over; there are lots of crutches and braces left by people who've been healed there. Off in a side room there's a Jesus in a long blue dress—*that's* no dream, that's really there, your regular Jesus with a beard on the cross but in the kind of dress a little girl would put on a doll. Near the gowned Jesus, in this dream now, there's a little niche, and it's an Elaine-altar. Not a statue of her or anything, but holy candles like you can buy in those Latino *botánicas,* tall cylinders of glass filled with colored wax—bright green wax, and red and blue—but the candles smell of Elaine's smell, that's how I know it's her altar. I light the candles and feel very calm and right about who we are for each other, knowing she's doing the same in her dream, but in hers it's a Jesse-shrine, and that's what we've become, kind of secret shrines for each other, dream-visited.

And I woke from that, a clear wakefulness with no residue of fatigue, and watched Katherine sleep, thinking that's what we all were, really, shrines for one another.

THREE   *Just Eyes*

Missy, after her stroke, was just eyes. Eyes in a bony little body in a smelly but not-too-bad home in a suburb of New Orleans. Not that the place was dirty, just that no one could scrub out the thin whiff of excrement that laced the scent of sweat from bodies that are mostly dead. I wondered if she could smell. Her eyes looked like they could smell, talk, walk, if they felt like it. I put *that* thought away. Didn't need to dream about Missy's walking eyes. When I'd visit, there was nothing I could do but stare into those eyes and talk. So for the first time she heard what was *really* on my mind, if she could hear at all.

Once I got an image: I brought some candles, Catholic candles, and had them placed where she could stare at them. Made them promise to keep them lit for her all the time, told them it was a religious thing—which it kind of was, really—and they bought that.

NIGHT TIME LOSING TIME

I felt like her eyes were grateful, being able to stare at those flames. Candles are the simplest things, but I've gained tremendous respect for them, and for whoever thought them up. *Powerful,* in the quietest of ways, and so much can hover around them. I'd come to love candlelight as much as I love anything. There's no end to looking at a candle, once you've shifted gears, and Missy's body had done that for her. I felt those candles were the only real thing I'd ever done for my mother my whole life.

F O U R   *Molting*

I dwelled on the physical changes a lot, they were so drastic. Missy's so sudden and final; Jes's body just about molting all the time; Elaine, Nadine, me, becoming each a different kind of middle-aged. Which made it kind of dreamlike that Katherine—who was just twenty-four when we met—went for the longest time without changing physically at all. Her hair would be long or short, but her face and body seemed so constant it was spooky. So in my eyes, when we made love, it was like she glowed in the dark, and like I'd be touching her and going inside her to enter the glow.

Not that I wanted her to stay young—I don't think I cared about "young," truly. But like one time when I came in from a gig about four, on one of those Austin nights in June when the air's so fragrant, almost creamy, so fresh and wet you feel like you can rub it all over you—she was sitting naked in candlelight in front of a mirror, sketching herself. She didn't look up at me when I came in. I sat on the floor in the corner and watched her. Her expression was earnest, concentrated on the technique of what she was doing—not rapt, not self-loving. Her skin glistened in that Austin humidity. The musk of the candles, the sharp edge of my gig-sweat, the perfume of Katherine's bath soap thickened the air even more. And I thought I saw the slightest, barely perceptible lag-time between Katherine's movement and the movement of her body in the mirror —that body that had given itself for money at one time, knowing so many men and women, till it had settled on the life we had. I

416

knew she was doing an image. And thought it had to do with what I'd seen (but never talked about) in her body right from the first, when I'd looked at her ass in the bathroom of that moldy shack she'd lived in. As if here she was exploring, for herself, the strange aliveness of it that was such as part of her so private power. Had she done this often when I wasn't around, before I'd gotten home from a gig or when I was out on the road, but timed it now so I'd see? As if she was claiming her flesh back for herself, painstakingly. And once she had, she could finally let it change. Not that I thought this all in my head right then—I just felt it so deep as I stared at her in wonder.

Finally she took a deep breath, let it out slow.

"Jesse? Could you snuff out the candles now? With your fingers."

When I had, she stretched like a cat and lay on the floor.

"I'm gonna want our baby sometime, Jesse. Think you can handle that?"

I said that I thought I could.

FIVE *The Family Motto*

About three years after my heart thing, Nadine sent me a note from her hospital. The envelope wasn't addressed in her hand but the note was, in pencil on a napkin. Just:

"SLOWLY—SLOWLY—WALK BETWEEN—YOUR DYNAMITE—AND THE THING IT KNOWS."

Sooner or later, every family has to have *some* motto. Katherine framed the napkin and put it up in the kitchen. She said, "Someday Nadine'll walk through that door and when she sees that, she'll know she hasn't been absent."

"And then?"

"We'll all have coffee."

"And then?"

"It'll be hard to talk."

"And then?"

"We'll talk too much!"

"And then?" I felt like a back-up singer with the Coasters.

"Whatever happens won't be stupid. I have *that* much faith, don't you?"

S I X *By the River*

So, like Katherine had once said, we tried to build our house by the river, not on the river. Not that the river didn't rise sometimes, for whole seasons sometimes, damn near drowning us. But you got to expect that with houses by rivers. What Henry had called "direct access" got real quiet, real private with us—proceed slowly, slowly, just like Nade'd said. It wasn't all flashy and crazy like Danny and Elaine had done it, though they're how I'd learned it, and I was grateful to them every day. But no matter what went down, we had left for keeps the world that liked to think things would settle, that tried to behave like it was okay just to be by the side of the road—had left it except for little things, like paying the rent and all. We weren't in that world, and we weren't quite in any other. The river was the border, and that seemed our territory, and it seemed apt to us.

By the time Nade had psyched the family motto, I'd put a new band together. Called it Smoke—for the smoky, kind of spooky sound we had. Not that we didn't rock hard and crazy—but it had another quality to it, like a smoke that steamed slowly off our instruments, a smoke not at all like that phony colored stuff of the stadium bands. We usually made the bills with our music, even made a couple of records on small, local, temporary labels. They were young, my new guys—and a hot, nineteen-year-old girl drummer skinny as a rail—and on the road I felt like a den mother. Kind of liked that, actually. Katherine and Jes came with us on the road whenever they could—she only had to work part-time, usually, and she could sketch, read, and "mull around" otherwise. Mulling was her favorite thing. "Right attention," I think Henry would have called it.

But why I'm tagging all this on is to give a little background feel to the thing that happened that more or less ends this story, insofar as stories end, which they never do. (For instance, about a year later, Katherine did get pregnant.)

It was a year or so after Nadine's note. Jes was, oh, tenish. Just as quiet as ever, maybe quieter, but always really *there,* so I always liked having him along or just hanging out at the house with him. I don't mean he wasn't a pain in the ass half the time—he was a *kid* —but that good quiet thing in him was always there, looking out, intent as a small wolf. And it was my job to look back at it. Not at the kid but at the wolf-thing in the kid. That's how he'd know it was real and keep it alive. I didn't give a shit how he did at school. He played piano pretty good already, and was starting on guitar. He read everything he could get his hands on. I had all Danny's books in boxes in the cellar—couldn't make myself throw them out or put them in the house—and every now and then I'd get nervous about Jes finding them too young. Yet all the while I knew I was keeping them for him. I wasn't going to push it and I wasn't going to stop it. It was as much Jes's right to get them, if he wanted, as it was Danny's to pass them on, like I know he'd have wanted.

Nadine was doing a bit better now, but still clung to the hospital—"for proper privacy for you-know," she put it on one visit. Every few weeks Jes and I, and sometimes Katherine, too, would drive to Shreveport to visit her. Deep down it felt like the right thing to do, even though for a few days after, Jes would get moody, sometimes throw tantrums, get sarcastic with Katherine, testing us. We'd roll our eyes at each other and meet the test the best we could. But if we didn't go for a long while, Jes would ask to go.

Well, Jes and I were driving back from Shreveport in the rain. We were a little east of Houston. Jes was pissed that I wasn't letting him work the gas pedal, like I often did, but I wouldn't do it in weather. The rain started coming down so hard, the windshield wipers just sort of smudged it around, the glass never really cleared. It was a two-lane and the oncoming cars were just big double blobs of smeared light. If you turned hard, you'd skid. If you hit the brake, you'd skid. You couldn't tell where the white line was, or the shoulder. I was bent to the wheel. Jes was *still* pissed. I got pissed back and didn't even realize I was going too fast. I felt him get scared, but instead of understanding it I just took it to mean that I'd won the argument. Just as dumb as any father, "direct access" or not. We hit a turn too fast, the old car held the road, but it was so fucking scary that both of us were shaken.

I said, "I'm sorry, Jes." Something ran in front of us, a cat or a cat-size dog, as near as I could tell, and we hit it with an ugly clunk. An instant later a back wheel ran over it. I got a little sick. Just the thought of that twisted blood-thing in the rain. Jes looked at me with those wolf-eyes, as angry as I'd ever seen him. I met his eyes. That was my job. I'd look down the road and then over at him. It was the strangest struggle. Neither of us said a word, each of us wanted comfort from the other. And the rain beat down. And the spray sound of our tires on the road. And every car that passed the other way raised a wash of water on us.

And suddenly I felt a weird elation. We were completely cut off from the world. We were Out There. Together. Hurtling through something that was and wasn't a storm. I mean, of course it was a storm, but it was also an intoxication, something meant, I mean *meant,* to induce that state of mind, or out-of-mind, that for a few months now I'd only gone in and out of rarely while playing, or sometimes in bed with Katherine. Hadn't felt to do an image in a while, and hadn't wanted to force that, but now—I felt the storm through the vibrating steering wheel, loved the pounding drops on the hood, the watery hiss of the wheels, and felt approval in the storm, knew it pleased the storm to be driven through like this, and must have had some crazy grin on my face because when I looked over at Jes again he was surprised, said, *"What?"*

"Isn't this a great STORM!"

And I reached over and grabbed his hand and squeezed it hard. And he didn't say anything but he laughed. We both did, and the storm laughed back at us, and I said, "hear that storm laughing, man!"

And I prayed he'd remember this one day, he and his strange old man hurtling through the rain, laughing after a bad time. And that maybe he'd psych someday, sooner than I had, that the storm is there for our elation as much as for the crops.

We drove out of it soon, into a light drizzle. Everything calmed down. He fell asleep. I don't think there's anything I like better than driving at night while somebody I love is asleep in the car. Especially when the windows are closed, and the heater is on, when the scent of their sleep is so lovely.

I heard voices in the drizzle. Couldn't quite make them out. His dream, perhaps.

There was a Burger King and I pulled into it. Jes didn't wake when the car stopped. He was sleeping deep down into where he had to go to take in the visit and the storm. It was somewhere around midnight. I didn't wake Jes. Went in for some burgers and coffee. Burgers were way off my diet, Katherine would have had a fit, but every now and again, on the road, I'd give in to the yen.

I got a Whopper, fries, and coffee, and picked a booth where I could keep an eye on the car, where Jes slept. Dipped in ketchup, the fries were perfect—the kids at this place understood the art of just enough grease. The Whopper-with-cheese was so packed with stuff it barely held together, and when I'd bit into it the juice dripped on the tray. The dead hot taste of a past life, of drives longer and harder than I drove anymore—not that the Shreveport-to-Austin run isn't the real thing, maybe 450 miles, but that's less than half, say, from Lubbock to Quartszite. Steaming, battery-acid coffee, black. It scalded my tongue. A bunch of white high school kids came in, very scrubbed, boys and girls loud with trying to impress each other. I had no idea what music they listened to. The kind of AM rock they call Pop now, I guessed, where the drummers sound synthesized even when they aren't, not rock at all. But I guess that's old-man talk. None of my business, anyway. They were welcome to their music and it didn't have anything to do with mine, or with the kind of joints we played it in, and there were still enough of those left for me to make a working stiff's living—though who knew for how long? Well, as far as the rent was concerned, I could always be a trucker.

I went up for more coffee. I turned back to the booth, with the cup hot in my hand—and *he* walked in. I didn't realize, at first, why he startled me. But I couldn't take my eyes off him. He caused this strange hollowness inside, like there was an enormous space in my chest. Then it hit: He looked *just* like me. More like me than Jes ever would. I mean: exactly. Like a twin, but younger. That's why I hadn't realized, consciously, at first, though my chest had known —I hadn't seen *him* in the mirror since I was a kid. He was about sixteen. Even give or take two years, he would have been born sometime during that period when Nadine and I were inseparable, so I knew he wasn't mine. I was an only child, I only had three cousins, they were a lot younger than me; he couldn't be some side-fling of theirs. Anyway, he was Mexican—from Mexico, not a Tex-Mex, you could see by how he carried himself. I sat there, forgetting to breathe, trying sort of to stare at him out of the corner of my eye and figure all the possibilities, and there weren't any. The spooky thing was, he didn't only *look* precisely like me, he wore the same cut of shirt and wore it like I wear mine, open down the front, a T-shirt underneath. And the way he used his hands—how he put his fingers to his lips or his forehead, I didn't even know I did that stuff till I watched him do it and realized I was looking in a mirror. His hands, his walk, the way he slouched in the booth—he was me. All that was different was that his eyebrows were thicker.

I was strangely frightened; I wished Katherine were with me, not only so I wouldn't think I was imagining this, but because with her I could have gone up to him, learned his name, told him that if he wanted to know what he'd look like in thirty years, he just had to look at me.

I was sure he knew I was staring at him, but he was cool about it. If I went up to him alone, God knows what he'd think. Better this way, just to watch, not spoil it.

I wanted to tell him everything that had ever happened to me. That's probably why I'm telling you.

He—me—at his burger in a booth near the Anglos, eyed the girls, who eyed him back. The guys avoided his looks—he could plainly take any one of them. When he finished eating he walked with just my slouchy swagger out into the parking lot. Then spun, like a gunfighter in a Western, to stare straight into my eyes through the window. He had known every instant that I was watching him, sure. He was deciding what to do about it. I knew that his body recognized me, like mine had him, but he hadn't realized. His look wavered, seemed confused, his eyes questioned. He turned uncertainly, walked away, out of my line of vision. I wondered if he'd remember me. I called after him, in my head: Remember, remember! Maybe, just maybe, in thirty years he'd look in a mirror and all of a sudden *really* remember. I wanted to call him back, I wanted to tell him to . . . I wanted to get down on my knees in Burger King and pray to God. And I wanted him to pray with me.

Seeing him had seemed a kind of proof. Of something more intricate, immense, and unnameable than I would ever understand. It seemed a mark, a seal, upon my life.

As I drove on, I felt a great tenderness. For that boy. For my own son. For the very rain.

It was three, maybe four, when we got to Austin. The rain had stopped. I carried Jes to his bed. He opened his eyes without waking, mumbled, "Night, Dad," as I laid him down. In the morning he'd tell Katherine, with great excitement, about the storm. But not while I was around.

I wanted to run into the street. To *do* something. Stop all the cars. Drag people out from their beds and tell them—everything. That the highway ran through each and every one of their living rooms. All the time. Sixty-, ninety-mile-an-hour traffic. East, west, north, south. *There was no side of the road.*

But not only couldn't I tell those people—I knew that this would recede from me, too, and return just as suddenly. I was dizzy with knowing.

I sat, woozy, on the piano bench. I ran my hands over the keys. They always feel so delicate. My right hand—of itself, almost—floated up to the keyboard and began, hesitantly, lightly, playing a few high notes. The notes gathered into a melody, a high, lilting, slowly moving bit of loveliness. A folk song I'd heard once? Some fragment of some forgotten lesson? Or was it mine—whatever that means—coming out of the piano toward me? With my left hand I laid down a chord far beneath it, carefully, a heavy bluesy dissonance, and the melody drifted above that chord like a shred of cloud above the earth. The music drifted from my home into the damp acoustics of the street, went its way, as it came to life effortlessly under my hands, which seemed so far off from me now and very old. Everybody was asleep. Jes, on his small lumpy bed, and Katherine whose sleep was always so warm, on our mattress on the floor, as ever. Danny and Henry in the open-eyed sleep of the dead. Elaine, breathing close to Johns's scars. Missy, in candlelight. And Nadine, not asleep but tranquilized, as though wrapped in dark gauze. And me, asleep now too but for my hands, which were far far off, in the other world.

ACKNOWLEDGMENTS

Jan Ventura midwived this book. Bob LaBrasca and Jeff Nightbyrd helped mightily. The book and I also owe: Bill Bentley, Helen Knode, Deborah Milosevich, Robert Bly, Albert Kreinheder, Mayer Vishner, John Powers, John Densmore, Jane Bauemler, Andy and Debby Krikun, Dave Johnson, Paul and Diana Ray, Michael Berger, Sherry Oliver, Bob Asahina, Melanie Jackson, Sam Joseph, Rosetta Brooks, and Steve Erickson.

The New Orleans club described here, Tipitina's, no longer exists—though there's now a club on the same corner with the same name. The other clubs, donut shops, RV camps, graveyards and motels are either fictional or long-defunct or both. And (with the exception of a brief description of the young Stevie Vaughan) there are no more-or-less realistic portraits of anyone more or less living or dead.

Michael Ventura
Los Angeles—29 Palms
1985–1988

ABOUT THE AUTHOR

Michael Ventura was born in the Bronx in 1945. He first appeared in print in *The Austin Sun* in 1974. The Venturas now live about 270 miles west of Quartzsite, Arizona.